Influencers

Influencers

Ray Lancaster

This book is a work of fiction. All names, characters, organisations, places and events are either fictitious or used fictitiously.

Copyright © 2021 Ray Lancaster

All rights reserved.

ISBN-13: **9798729645626**

Dedication

To my mother, Annabelle Lancaster.

Table of contents

Dedication v
Table of contents vii
1937 1
Chapter 1 3
Chapter 2 7
Chapter 3 13
Chapter 4 17
1941 21
Chapter 5 23
Chapter 6 27
Chapter 7 31
Chapter 8 39
Chapter 9 43
Chapter 10 47
Chapter 11 51
Chapter 12 55
Chapter 13 57
Chapter 14 65
Chapter 15 69

Chapter 16	73
Chapter 17	75
Chapter 18	79
Chapter 19	83
Chapter 20	85
Chapter 21	89
Chapter 22	95
Chapter 23	103
Chapter 24	105
Chapter 25	111
Chapter 26	115
Chapter 27	117
Chapter 28	123
Chapter 29	125
Chapter 30	127
Chapter 31	133
Chapter 32	135
Chapter 33	139
Chapter 34	141
Chapter 35	145
Chapter 36	149
Chapter 37	153
Chapter 38	163
Chapter 39	165
Chapter 40	169
Chapter 41	173
Chapter 42	175
Chapter 43	181
Chapter 44	183

Chapter 45	185
Chapter 46	189
Chapter 47	191
Chapter 48	193
1937	197
Chapter 49	199
1941	201
Chapter 50	203
Chapter 51	205
Chapter 52	211
Chapter 53	213
Chapter 54	217
Chapter 55	219
Chapter 56	221
Chapter 57	223
Chapter 58	225
Chapter 59	227
Chapter 60	231
Chapter 61	235
Chapter 62	237
Chapter 63	239
Chapter 64	241
Chapter 65	243
Chapter 66	245
Chapter 67	247
Chapter 68	253
Chapter 69	255
Chapter 70	257
Chapter 71	259

Chapter 72	261
Chapter 73	263
Chapter 74	269
Chapter 75	273
Chapter 76	277
Chapter 77	279
Chapter 78	281
Chapter 79	287
Chapter 80	289
Chapter 81	293
Chapter 82	299
Chapter 83	303
Chapter 84	307
Chapter 85	309
Chapter 86	311
Chapter 87	315
Chapter 88	317
Chapter 89	319
Chapter 90	321
Chapter 91	325
Chapter 92	327
Chapter 93	331
Chapter 94	333
Chapter 95	335
Chapter 96	343
Chapter 97	345
Chapter 98	347
Chapter 99	351
Chapter 100	355

Chapter 101 363
Chapter 102 365
Chapter 103 367
Chapter 104 369
Chapter 105 371
Chapter 106 373
Chapter 107 375
Chapter 108 377
Chapter 109 379
Chapter 110 381
Chapter 111 383
Chapter 112 385
Chapter 113 387
Chapter 114 389
Chapter 115 393
Chapter 116 395
Chapter 117 397
Chapter 118 399
Chapter 119 401
Chapter 120 403
Chapter 121 413
Chapter 122 415
Chapter 123 417
Chapter 124 421
Chapter 125 425
Chapter 126 429
Chapter 127 433
Chapter 128 435
Chapter 129 441

Chapter 130	443
Chapter 131	445
Chapter 132	447
Chapter 133	451
Chapter 134	453
Chapter 135	455
1937	457
Chapter 136	459
1941	463
Chapter 137	465
Chapter 138	471
Chapter 139	473
Chapter 140	475
Chapter 141	479
Chapter 142	483
Chapter 143	485
Chapter 144	489
Epilogue	493
Author's notes and acknowledgements	495
The author	497

1937

Two years before World War Two

Chapter 1

Friday 6 August 1937
New York - USA

As Anna Vogel walked out of Curtin's, her favourite clothes shop in Manhattan, the August heat reached up from the sidewalk and slapped her face. Seconds later, stray droplets of water had an opposite, refreshing effect on her forehead and cheeks as a little girl ran by in the opposite direction with a squirt gun, chasing two boys.

Water of the drinkable sort, gallons of it, was just a three-minute walk farther south on Sixth Avenue at Dino's, her favourite café. With his wide Italian smile, the owner proposed to her every ten days on average, nine of which had passed since the last time. "If I moved my café from Sixth to Fifth, would you at least think about it?" he'd once asked. Her mistake had not been to turn him down but to hesitate half a second before doing so, a time lapse Dino had interpreted as a love declaration.

Of all the things the collision could coincide with, a swirl of hot wind was the least helpful. A man reading a newspaper emerged from 48th street and walked straight into Anna, knocking her off her feet. As she fell backwards two things happened: her papers flew in all directions, some carried considerable distances by the swirl, and an answer to her dilemma came to her.

The man with the newspaper looked terrified. Stuttering his apologies he knelt beside her in a manner suggesting, from where Anna lay, imminent last rites. He helped her up and apologised again and she said it was nothing really as a little girl ran up to her with two sheets of paper she'd picked up. Anna thanked her and promptly managed to drop all the papers again, which made her and the little girl laugh but not the man with the newspaper, who was still apologising.

Patting down her blue summer dress, Anna waited for the little girl to be out earshot before fluttering her eyelids at him. "If you apologise again, I'll accuse you loudly of having tried to grope me."

He stood there clutching a dozen of her papers and blinking. But his pale blue eyes were deceptively innocent, she decided, and his build deceptively slight. This was a powerhouse, both intellectually and physically. His ordinary grey suit made him seem deceptively younger than fortyish, too.

"Make yourself useful," she said. "Is there dust on my back? And please check my hair; is it still dark brown, shoulder length, swept back and ostentatiously unpretentious?"

Grinning, he made a show of walking round her. "Your dress is fine and the fall has improved your hair."

"Thanks. Truth be told, instead of you apologising to me, I should be thanking you. For some reason, being knocked to the ground has helped me choose between two options."

"Not two fiancées, I trust."

"Job interviews, actually. In two different European countries."

"And the winner is?"

"Neither. They're both paying my travel expenses, so why should I pre-select one?"

The man picked up his newspaper. "Glad to be of assistance. Where should I send my bill? I knock women off their feet for a living."

"Send it to Anna Vogel, third table on the left, Dino's, Sixth Avenue. As a matter of fact, you can have two cups of coffee brought to that table in three minutes' time if you like."

He checked his watch. "I'd be honoured. I'm David Cassell."

As they walked in silence towards Dino's, Anna wondered why they hadn't shaken hands.

As they sipped coffee five minutes later, she wondered why their collision had disappeared so fast from the conversation.

As she returned to their table from the ladies' room ten minutes later, she wondered why he hadn't asked which European countries her interviews would take place in. Anyone would have asked that, she thought, but not him.

"Our collision wasn't an accident, was it," she said suddenly.

He said nothing.

"It was carefully planned," she went on. "So carefully that I was first to raise the possibility of coffee."

Still no reaction.

"If I'm wrong, you're taking a long time to object."

"You're right, it wasn't an accident. How did you guess? A hunch or something specific?"

"A hunch."

"In that case, let's not stop at coffee. Have dinner with me this evening."

Chapter 2

Monday 22 November 1937
London – England

"Welcome to London, Miss Vogel, and thanks for travelling all this way."

Unlike her friends, most of whom were unhappily married, Anna had never made a habit of turning any man she met into a list of reasons she would never have married him anyway. She wasn't about to make an exception for Brendan Bracken. She guessed his age to be late thirties and his red hair to have been the target of countless jibes in earlier years. His charm had a self-taught quality to it, stiffened by his badly stained teeth and his three-piece suit yet softened by the round rims of his glasses. This was a man, she suspected, who considered it his duty not to patronise women but ended up doing so for that very reason.

She peered up at the Savoy Hotel's glass cupola. "I'm impressed. My favourite café in New York is a place called Dino's. Their idea of opulence is a light bulb that isn't flickering yet. Is the Savoy your favourite café, Mr Bracken?"

"Only when afternoon tea is my only remaining weapon."

"The next time I fly over, remind me to seduce a millionaire on the aircraft so I can book a room here. I'm staying at Elephant & Castle with distant relatives that I have no intention of getting any closer to. Oops, someone's been found out."

"I beg your—?" Bracken followed her gaze. A photographer was standing over a nearby table where a couple was pretending so hard not to be flattered by his attention that they happened to be smiling when the flash went off. A red-faced waiter materialised and escorted the photographer away.

"Someone famous?" Anna asked.

"Infamous, more likely."

"You don't seem much concerned. Aren't newspaper men supposed to make a fortune out of fame?"

Bracken sipped his tea. "The newspapers I publish are more interested in how fortunes are made or lost. If our work makes people famous, they usually deserve it, which is more than I can say for most of our film and theatre stars. Is this your first time in Europe?"

"No, I grew up in Germany. When the American automobile industry decided to switch its strategy from quantity to quality, it realised German engineers could help them. So they crossed the Atlantic with their cigars and blank checks and recruited people like my father."

Bracken offered her a cigarette, which she turned down. "Are you still German?"

"No, I'm American now. Are you wondering how a woman with playful brown eyes like mine could reach the age of thirty-five without marrying anyone?"

"Yes, I'm curious."

"I'll tell you if you tell me first how come you've reached your age without being married either." She waited as he scratched his head. "Then let's talk about why I'm here."

"In my line of business I have close ties with the powers-that-be in this country but even closer ones, or so I believe, with the powers-soon-to-be. The powers that be mostly believe Adolf Hitler and his gang are a flash in the German pan. The powers-soon-to-be believe Hitler is now the pan itself. Another major war with Germany is imminent."

Anna eyed a cress sandwich suspiciously before nibbling it. "Could a war with Germany ever be minor?"

"The difference this time is we'll be fighting two wars with them simultaneously. The first will be military and it's just a few months or years away. The second is already being fought now. Call it propaganda, communication, persuasion, influence, information, public relations or whatever you want—it's a war Hitler and his propaganda side-kick Joseph Goebbels are already fighting and winning. So much so that the powers-that-be now believe we'd be better off appeasing Hitler and giving him what he wants rather than confronting him."

"Who are these mysterious powers-soon-to-be?"

"My money's on Winston Churchill, but it's an uphill battle. His problem is that he sided with Edward VIII during the abdication scandal three years ago. Supporting a king who preferred to marry an American divorcee rather than reign without her at his side was a brave thing to do but politically suicidal. Many people in this country still haven't forgiven him. His other problem is his romantic vision of holding on to the British Empire. I see his point and can sympathise with it but the empire's coming apart at the seams and costing us a fortune that we should be investing in this country rather than abroad. Churchill refuses to see that. Money isn't his forte anyway. The man's virtually bankrupt himself."

"Why don't you take his place then?"

Bracken scoffed. "No, I couldn't take that kind of scrutiny."

"Why? What have you got to hide?"

"It's more a question of what I don't care to show."

Anna cocked her head. "Your Irish origins, perhaps? They're not something to brag about in some circles here, I would imagine. But your Irish accent is mixed up with something else. Australian, perhaps? It's unusual."

"Both. I was born in Ireland and lived for a few years in Australia." Bracken forced a half-smile, signalling the end of that line of enquiry.

"So what does all this have to do with me?"

"As I told you in my letter, I'm interested in the fact that you've worked for Mr Public Relations himself, Edward Bernays. I've been watching his work in America for many years now and I think we could use his kind of approach here, too. I like his idea that where most people see reality as something to be revealed, understood and adapted to, he sees it as something to be designed, engineered and actively shaped. Within limits, of course."

Anna shook her head. "No, Mr Bracken, no limits." She poured them both some more tea. "The only limits Edward Bernays understands are the number of dollars currently in circulation in the USA and the number of American votes that can be cast in any election. He will lower any standard and organise any public relations campaign to channel as many dollars or votes towards whoever pays for his services. Mr Bernays and I didn't part on the best of terms."

"Yes, he told me."

Anna froze. "He told you?"

"I was in New York myself a couple of weeks ago and made him the same offer I'm making you today. He refused. American corporations keep him more than busy, apparently."

"You probably can't afford him anyway."

"But he talked about you and what you've been doing since you parted ways. Your work behind the scenes for the Democratic Party and the New Deal, for example."

"That was supposed to be confidential. How did he find out?"

"As a man who keeps his own influence on reality confidential, he probably knows your tricks. Why did you part on bad terms?"

Anna sipped her tea in silence.

"The reason was his attitude to women," she said finally. "I got a job at his New York office in 1926. I was much plumper in those days and Bernays advised me to take up smoking because tobacco made women lose weight. I followed his advice and weeks went by and I was smoking a pack a day, but I didn't lose weight. I mentioned this to Bernays and he asked me at what times I smoked most. I answered that I smoked all the time. Then he said something I'll never forget. 'Miss Vogel, you need to smoke more strategically.'"

Bracken frowned. "And did you?"

"No, I stopped smoking that very same day and took up basketball instead. What he meant was that smoking didn't make women lose weight directly. It was something for women to do whilst they didn't eat. He wanted to engineer an American reality where women would no longer be welcome unless they were thin. And women could achieve that, according to Bernays, by destroying their health in a two-pronged attack: smoking and starving. One year later that reality was everywhere you looked. The American landscape was a giant billboard showing thin women smoking Lucky Strike cigarettes." She took a deep breath. "Two years later, in 1929, he went a step further with his Torches of Freedom campaign."

"My favourite," Bracken said. "Making it acceptable for women to smoke outside the home."

"Or making it acceptable for women to smoke, starve and destroy their health in full view of the neighbourhood." She shook her head sadly. "Then three years ago, in 1934, he went a step too far. He decided that American reality didn't look green enough. So he organised highly publicised events of all kinds where the decorations were green and where women had to dress in green. Suddenly, out of nowhere, green was all the fashion."

Bracken winced. "Green?"

"Green was used by Lucky Strikes cigarettes in their packaging. Just a coincidence, of course. When my ten-year-old niece walked out of her bedroom dressed in green, pretending to be smoking and asking her parents if she could skip dinner, I decided it was time for Bernays and I to part ways. The next day I told him what I thought of him and his attitude to women, handed in my resignation and went to work for the Democratic Party. So if you were hoping to recruit me so I could bring Bernays's tactics into this country, think again."

"I see."

Anna cocked her head. "What do you see, exactly?"

"Bernays's tactics are like weapons. You can use them to attack people or defend them. But I'm sure they'll come here sooner or later anyway. What have you been doing for the Democratic Party?"

"Didn't Bernays tell you? He seems to know more about my activities than I do."

"He said you were being, er, disruptive."

"Coming from him, I'm flattered. It's now been four years since our Democratic President, Franklin Roosevelt, launched his New Deal. As you're well aware, it was presented as the biggest economic relaunch program in the history of this corner of the Universe. Did you ever read the New Deal document itself, Mr Bracken? Or at least the first version of it?"

"I'm a journalist specialising in business. So yes."

Anna jutted out her chin. "What was missing in it? What has now been included in it that dozens of economists, writers and contributors left out of it at the time?"

Bracken rolled his eyes. "Countless things, I imagine. I'm sure many mistakes were made."

"Not countless things, Mr Bracken. Just seventy million of them. Women. The document almost completely ignored them."

Bracken stared at her.

"So what have I been doing at the Democratic Party? I've been using my research methods, experiments and measurements to help them apologise to those 70 million women without actually using the word 'sorry'. Yes, dear female voters, the New Deal depends as much on you to rebuild this country as it does on men."

Bracken stiffened and adjusted his glasses. "Miss Vogel, why don't you shift your research methods, experiments and measurements from the USA to the 47 million multi-class, multicultural, blood-and-guts inhabitants of this one? We want you to study them. We want you to uncover truths about them that are staring us in the face but that we can't see, least of all Churchill. We want you to find out what really drives them, what they really care about, what they really want."

Anna eyed the plate of biscuits. "What sort of reality do you want to engineer in those British minds, Mr Bracken? One where they can't help smiling, dancing and singing at the prospect of another war with Germany?"

"We want a reality where they see things actually move. Take Hitler and Goebbels. What's their secret? Movement. Ceaseless, relentless, highly visible movement. Germany on the move. Movement makes Hitler irresistible. The day the Nazis stop moving and annexing places, they'll fall apart, but that's not going to happen anytime soon. What's our secret here in the United Kingdom? Lack of movement. Ceaseless, relentless, highly visible immobility.

Our politicians, including Churchill and myself, are stuck. We're frozen. We're dusty. We believe in the virtues of free enterprise but ignore the fact that those virtues feel like chains to ever-growing numbers of voters."

"And what would ceaseless movement look like in this country?"

"That's what we want you to find out, Miss Vogel. All we ask is that you come up with something different from conquering neighbouring countries and throwing minorities and opponents into concentration camps. Needless to say, my friends and I will fund your research generously, very generously, and for eighteen months at least. We'd expect a first set of recommendations after twelve months."

Anna smiled and patted her hair. "It looks as if Europe's going to be my home for a while."

Bracken's mouth opened, revealing a half-eaten scone. "Really? That's wonderful news. If you need to have equipment and personal belongings sent over or even flown over, we'll pay for that too, of course."

"No need, Mr Bracken. Berlin will pay for that."

"Berlin? I don't under—"

"I'm grateful for your offer but I'm turning it down. I'm flying to Germany tomorrow." She waited for him to put the rest of the scone down. "Your letter arrived eight days after another one, from the Third Reich's Ministry of Public Enlightenment and Propaganda. From Goebbels himself. Like you, he was interested in using what I learnt from Bernays."

Bracken blanched. "Do you realise what kind of people those Nazis are? I'm not even sure 'people' is the right word to describe them. You'll be working for a system run by Jew-baiting thugs. You'll be helping them."

"Tell me something," she said dryly. "If you wanted to undermine a system run by Jew-baiting thugs, would you criticise it loudly from hundreds of miles away or would you infiltrate it and weaken it from the inside?"

Bracken blinked several times as he fingered the handle of his teacup. "If that was your plan, why did you bother to come and see me?"

"Because I was hoping to hear you say the magic word. The word that would have shown me that you, Mr Churchill and all your powers-soon-to-be truly have your priorities in the right order and truly want to get this country moving. You haven't said that magic word once since I got here. Oh and you don't need expensive research carried out by people like me to identify it. It's right there under your nose. Here's the deal: if you say the word right now, I'll tell Goebbels to get lost. You've got five seconds."

Bracken stared blankly at her for twice that long.

Anna nodded at the cups and plates on the table. "Was I your guest?"

"Of course." Bracken fumbled for his wallet.

She stood up. "If you arrange for a taxi, I'll show you something that'll give you a clue to that word. The next round's on me."

Chapter 3

Monday 22 November 1937
Berlin - Germany

Frank and Tina Winter followed the crowd out of the Adlon Hotel's plush conference hall and up one floor to a reception room. Frank was one of nine attendees, all male, holding a framed certificate recognising their respective contributions to professional excellence, medical excellence in Frank's case, in Berlin. That they'd all been members of the National Socialist Party for at least three years as well was a coincidence noticed by all and discussed by none.

"Don't tell me you're completely pissed off," Tina murmured. "We're at the Adlon on Unter den Linden no less and your achingly attractive first wrinkles and grey hairs will be in the newspapers tomorrow."

Frank shrugged. "I don't want to sound petulant, but I deserved to receive this kind of award from the hands of a party official worthy of his title, not from a basement-level stand-in who couldn't spell his title to save his life."

"I can confirm you sound petulant, my dear. Where are you going to lodge your complaint?"

A waiter approached with glasses of Sekt.

Tina took two and held them back playfully from her husband. "Just one of these each, agreed?"

As Frank nodded, he noticed a man admiring Tina's figure from behind her. Two other men had done likewise from the front an hour earlier, on the way in to the event. At thirty-nine—to his thirty-eight—Tina worked hard to keep her body slender, partly for her own satisfaction but mostly, as always, for his. Her hips, the shape of which she allowed no clothes to hide or distort, could still cause him to rush back to her to give her one more kiss whenever they parted and she loved that, especially when their friends' wives noticed him doing it. To keep him happy she also styled her long light-brown hair as he wanted and made up her grey-green eyes and lips as he prescribed and wore the ridiculously uncomfortable shoes he found so irresistible, but they both knew he was anything but happy and hadn't been for years. Their private joke was that if he were to lose control of his body, at least he could find consolation in controlling hers and enjoying the envy other men made no effort to hide when they looked at her.

Now though and for the very first time, Frank experienced that envy differently. As this third man scanned Tina's body, Frank realised the look in his eyes had nothing to do with envy. It was lust. Which got him thinking: had any of those other men's stares over the years ever been about envy? Or had they always been about lust and he'd been too naïve, self-centred or arrogant to think otherwise? If so, what about Tina? Had she secretly drawn the same conclusion? If so, why did she always put those stares down to envy herself? Was this her way of downplaying the fact that she enjoyed their true nature?

"What shall we drink to?" Tina was asking. "Us or you? Your little speech made my support sound more peripheral than crucial."

"You deserve this thing as much as I do and we both know it."

"But does the National Socialist Party know it? What evidence can you give me that at least one person in this room thinks I do more for your career than keep your stomach full and your balls empty?"

"That person is drinking Sekt with you right now." He kissed her on the cheek.

"Why didn't Rudolf Hess turn up to present the awards, by the way? Better things to do in Munich? What about Goebbels?"

"I don't know about Goebbels but I know for a fact that Hess is in town. But rumour has it he wants to be more than just the Führer's designated successor. Apparently he's studying hard to become our self-appointed astrologer-in-chief. Maybe the planets told him to avoid us."

Tina giggled. "Someone said he might join us for dinner. Even astrologers have been known to eat."

"I'd be surprised. Apparently Hess has gone all vegetarian too and only eats stuff he brings himself. Not the sort of behaviour expected at the Adlon. If he turns up at all, it'll be now, but only for a glass of mineral water."

Rudolf Hess strode into the room five minutes later with two soldiers in tow. Wearing a beige suite and an expression better suited to a funeral, he let the master of ceremonies guide him briskly around the room to be presented to the award winners.

"You should ask him what time we should have sex to get me pregnant," Tina murmured as the master of ceremonies drew closer. "It must be written in the stars somewhere."

"And this is Doctor Fritz Winter, Herr Reichsminister," said the master of ceremonies. "His award is for distinguished services to medicine."

"You mean Doctor Frank Winter," Hess said as he kissed Tina's hand.

The master of ceremonies blushed. "My apologies to you both. I didn't know you were acquainted."

"We aren't," Hess said as he shook hands with Frank. "Or shall we say I'm acquainted with the files I received on today's winners and that I actually read, as you can now testify. I'm not sure all my colleagues would have done likewise. Your file is refreshingly thin, by the way, Herr Winter. Unlike Herr Arnold's here."

The master of ceremonies forced an appreciative smile.

Hess touched Arnold's arm. "Do you mind if I have a moment alone with Herr and Frau Winter?"

"Of course not. I'll return in a minute."

Hess edged closer to Tina. "Your husband's file isn't so thin that it fails to mention your nationality. You're British, correct?"

"She is," Frank said.

Hess's deep-set eyes didn't leave Tina. "Herr Winter, I'm sure your wife has learnt to speak better German than both of us by now and can answer for herself. Am I right or am I right, Frau Winter?"

"I survive, Herr Reichsminister."

"As today's award recipients will never forgive me my absence at the ceremony, I'm trying to make it up to their wives. Tell me, how is life in Germany treating you?"

Tina glanced nervously at Frank. "Fine, Herr Reichsminister. Absolutely fine."

"Happy here?"

"Yes."

"Then why not add a little administrative and social comfort to your happiness by applying for German citizenship? A word of advice: the way things are going, and I can assure our beloved Führer is taking those things to places of interest, I would apply sooner than later if I were you."

She gave Frank another glance. "Well noted, thank you."

Hess looked around to catch Arnold's eye. "And when our stellar bureaucracy gets around to asking you for character references, which it will, please feel free to mention my name. Obstacles should vanish, interviews

15

should be fewer and your religious ancestry should receive only cursory attention. I wish you both well."

Chapter 4

Monday 22 November 1937
London – England

The air in the White Hart pub, just west of the Elephant & Castle junction in south-east London, was thick with the smell of erratic personal hygiene and thicker still with tobacco smoke. As she stood inside the door waiting for Bracken to fight his way back from the bar, Anna smiled confidently at any of the seventy or eighty customers who looked at her, which quite a few did.

Bracken returned and handed her a half-pint of beer, followed by her change. "I don't know about New York bars, but chairs aren't a standard fixture in London pubs, especially in areas like this. Cheers. I hope you weren't expecting any."

She raised her glass. "Cheers. I wasn't."

"So what's this mysterious magic word?"

Her voice cut effortlessly through the smoke and din. "It's what's missing in here."

Bracken made a show of frowning as he surveyed the crowd. "What, women again?"

"Sorry to bore you."

"No, that's not what I mean, but—"

"Goebbels wrote the word three times in his letter to me. Quite effortlessly, too."

"Forgive me, but isn't the role of women to be beautiful and bring children into the world?"

She cocked her head. "You don't sound as if you're joking."

"I'm not. I'm just quoting Joseph Goebbels, the killer who'll be calling himself your boss tomorrow. He said it in 1934 or '5. Or would you prefer me to quote his boss, Adolf Hitler? Küche, Kinder, Kirche. Kitchen, children, church. The three official Ks that define flourishing womanhood in Nazi paradise. The Weimar Republic may have been imperfect but it did more for women's rights in a decade than any other government I can think of. Then the Third Reich came along and cancelled the lot. Women are secondary citizens again."

"Well, at least the Third Reich has an official policy on women. I happen to think it's the wrong one personally, but at least it's a policy. They've thought it through, passed laws and set lots of money aside to enforce them. German women today know exactly where they stand and what's expected of them."

Bracken grinned dismissively. "How many women helped write that policy? And how many women voted in favour of it, assuming they voted at all? And what do those Jew-baiting thugs have in mind for Jewish women?"

"Good questions indeed, Mr Bracken. Here's a question for you: what's the United Kingdom's policy on women?"

"For a start, we don't throw female doctors and civil servants out of their jobs. Germany's doing that as we speak to give preference to men."

Anna shook her head. "Forget what Germany's doing and answer the question: what's the United Kingdom's policy on women?"

Bracken emptied half his glass in one go. "I would say that women have meaningful voting rights and true freedom of speech in this country, but I'm sure you have a way to make them sound like an elaborate plot."

Anna jutted her chin out in several directions. "I wonder about the role of the women who aren't in this pub right now. If Goebbels thinks the role of German women is to be beautiful, I put it to you that many of the wives of these men use ugliness as a strategy. Ugliness is their only defence against their husbands' drunken advances when they get home from this place. Tomorrow morning they'll still be ugly when they get up and check that their husbands are still snoring. That's their opportunity to quietly search their husbands' clothes for money. Because what these ugly women desperately need to know is how much of it is left, i.e. wasn't spent on alcohol and pissed against the neighbourhood walls the night before. Because they need what's left to pay the rent and buy food for the kids that they've, and I quote, brought into the world, unquote. And once they've done all that and cleaned the house and washed the clothes, they'll make a cup of tea, sit down and light a cigarette in honour of the voting rights and freedom of speech they're so privileged to have in this country. And if they're lucky, they won't be interrupted by their husbands waking up with a screaming hangover and asking why breakfast isn't ready yet. Do you have any idea why I brought you here, Mr Bracken?"

He shook his head.

"The distant relatives I told you about—the ones I'm staying with—live a couple of streets away. There's a man in the family apparently but I haven't seen him yet. I've only heard him. He's my aunt's cousin's new husband. When I asked her where he was, she told me he spends his wages in here every night before staggering home and trying to grab her backside. So I decided to take a look—at him I mean, not her backside. I never found him, so I'll leave for Germany without us ever having met." She looked around. "It doesn't take a genius to work out that this place is no different from thousands of others up and down the country. Countless men making the lives of the mothers of their children utterly miserable; disrespecting them, humiliating them, baiting them. And that's just the non-violent ones. How many women will get beaten up by their drunken British husbands tonight, Mr Bracken? How many British wives will die of their injuries? Somewhere in the United Kingdom, at least one will have passed away before the end of our little conversation. I can hear her last rasping words from here: 'but the good news is that I had voting rights and freedom of speech'."

They both emptied their glasses.

Anna placed a hand on Bracken's forearm. "Would you allow me to offer a big fat patronising suggestion free of charge and make a humble request?"

Bracken nodded.

"The patronising suggestion comes from the researcher in me: you need to be less naïve, Mr Bracken. Every time you point your trembling finger at the Jew-baiting thugs running wild in Germany, remember to point another one at the woman-baiting thugs running wild in this country. Tell Churchill to set up a nationwide policy on women, tell him to give it a full set of financial teeth and tell him to enforce it. All sorts of interesting things, including election victories, will follow, believe me. Don't let him make the same mistake President Roosevelt and his party made with the New Deal."

Bracken stood there blinking.

Anna smiled. "The humble request is could I have another drink, please?"

1941

Chapter 5

Wednesday 30 April 1941
Chartwell – Kent – England

Winston Churchill put his paintbrush down and looked up at the cloudless sky, as if expecting something to drop out of it.

Something bearable for once.

Something other than news of yet another German bombing raid on yet another British city. Now in its thirty-fifth week, the so-called Blitz had spent last night paying destructive attention to the buildings and population of Cardiff. Before leaving London early that morning, Churchill had phoned the Welsh capital's authorities to enquire about damage and a woman had told him, cheerfully, that "only thirty-three people have been killed this time, Prime Minister." This, he mused, was what months of fitful sleep at best, terror at worst, did to people: three dozen deaths became good news.

Something other than yet more worrying reports on British military forces fighting for survival, let alone victory, on distant fields, roads, sands or waves.

Something other than yet more totals of merchant ships sunk in the Atlantic, along with their precious cargos of food, equipment, raw materials and fuel, by U-boats[1] determined to starve the United Kingdom into capitulation.

---

[1] "U-boat" is short for "Unterseeboot" in German and means submarine

Something other than yet more feeble American excuses for staying out of the war, thereby increasing the United Kingdom's chances of turning into a nation of fluent German speakers.

Something other than yet more aerial photographs of German troops and tanks massing with clearly uncharitable intentions along the Soviet Union's western border.

Something more like a solution, he hoped, to a month-old personal crisis he could no longer prevent from appearing as dire to him as anything Nazi Germany's Wehrmacht could muster. Clementine, his wife, was dying.

Twenty-five miles south of Central London, Chartwell was the Prime Minister's country home in the Kentish countryside. It had been mothballed early on in the war because its grounds were too easily identifiable from the air and thus too tempting a target for German dive-bombers. But Churchill had never accepted his status as persona non grata in his own home, however well-meaning the intention, and made a point of escaping to it on rare occasions for a few hours of landscape painting. His arrangement with his security detail was that if they gave him no reason to spot their presence, he would find no reason to paint them into one of his landscapes and force them to purchase it at an inflated price.

On the east side of the house, a vast lawn sloped down to two lakes side by side. The left-hand, "upper" one was smaller than the "lower" one, the southern end of which was hidden from the house by trees. The previous year soldiers had drained both lakes and camouflaged them with brushwood, leaving just enough water for the fish.

Churchill had set up his easel half way between the house and the upper lake, facing the early morning sun. Dislodging a folded sheet of paper from one of the easel's joints, he re-read the five names typed on it, lingering on the single-word comment beside each. Franklin Roosevelt, to his credit, had taken hours, not days or weeks, to have the names selected and sent via encrypted message across the Atlantic. Sensing the urgency and perhaps the personal nature of his British counterpart's request, the American president hadn't asked for an explanation.

Churchill checked his watch and debated whether to carry on painting or prepare a radio broadcast to the people of Nazi-occupied Poland. He chose the former because the man who could help him parse the list, Neil McCrew, would be joining him within the hour and he needed to think. In their three meetings to date, the younger man had impressed the Prime Minister with his directness, clarity and calm and had given him no reason to doubt his opinions and advice.

This time would be different.

Churchill found himself torn between his trust in McCrew's ability to put professionalism above any personal considerations and concern about a detail he'd spotted in McCrew's eyes within seconds of meeting him. It had neither disappeared nor faded as the two men had got to know each other; the kind of detail Churchill relished and even thrived on in his political rivals but didn't expect in a surgeon, least of all the one looking after his wife. McCrew hated Churchill and, least reassuringly, made no effort to hide it.

Chapter 6

Wednesday 30 April 1941
Hampshire – England

A derailed career in piloting tends to stay that way, especially if the career is military and the pilot makes the same derailing mistake twice. Examples must be set, appearances maintained, rulebooks upheld and wider contexts considered, of course, but arms may also be twisted, strings pulled and quiet words spoken into carefully selected ears. Should the derailed career survive all this, it might resume on a narrower, flatter or more subterranean path, but it will not resurrect.

So when Roddy Danes suddenly had an idea that might resurrect his derailed career, he knew it was so precious that nothing and nobody could be allowed to obstruct it.

The idea came to him seconds after an aircraft caught his attention during his daily early-morning bicycle ride. It was flying in his direction from the west. Not that aircraft were an unfamiliar sight to him—Danes was a flight lieutenant based at nearby Farnborough Airfield, Hampshire—but this one interested him for two reasons that had merged in a flash to generate his idea: the black smoke trailing intermittently from one of its engines and the aircraft's German nationality. A Junkers Ju 88.

Danes stopped his bike in the middle of the country lane to watch. The pilot had obviously spotted Farnborough's runway in the distance and was hoping to land there (the irony that several Junkers Ju 88s had tried to bomb Farnborough off the map ten months earlier, in August 1940, was not lost on

Danes). But the aircraft was already too low and a crash about two miles short was all but inevitable. It was also too low for anyone to parachute.

As the aircraft roared overhead, Danes turned to cycle in the same direction and did some calculations. The explosion would be close enough to Farnborough to act as its own alarm for the emergency crews. These in turn would not be as complete or sharp as they could be at this early hour. The ensuing delay would give Danes a few more minutes to turn the likely deaths of German airmen into an opportunity.

But what was a German bomber doing over southern England at that time of day? After the first few weeks of the Blitz in 1940, daylight bombing had become a rarity. Reconnaissance, he decided. The aircraft had probably been spotted and attacked as it took photographs of damage inflicted by its Luftwaffe[2] colleagues the previous night—possibly on the city of Bristol, judging by its course.

The Ju 88 crashed on to an area of forest that Danes had ridden through only minutes earlier and exploded. A surprisingly narrow column of smoke shot upwards. Danes cycled towards it, staying on the road until he spotted debris on the ground some fifty yards to his left.

The aircraft's body and wings had been no match for the thick oak trees in its path. Smoking or burning debris had been projected in every direction. Many pieces hung from branches. The air wreaked of gasoline.

Listening for human shouts or moans and hoping to hear none, Danes left his bike by the road and hurried through the trees to where he guessed the largest remnants of the aircraft would be. The first dead body he found had no head attached to it and was missing a right arm. Kneeling and patting the German's blue-grey uniform, Danes found a Walther P38 pistol and two wallets, one containing photos and tightly folded letters, the other a wad of Reichsmark banknotes. Danes was about to pocket the cash and throw the wallets away when he realised he'd taken no precautions for fingerprint traces. He pocketed the lot.

Twenty yards farther on, a second body lay face down next to a large piece of fuselage. As Danes approached, he assessed the airman's height and bulk and decided they were close enough to his own. Kneeling again, he shook the airman's right shoulder and got no response. He turned the body over and immediately looked away, forcing back a wave of nausea. Something had punctured the airman's forehead and a mixture of brain matter and blood was seeping out of the hole. Danes forced himself to focus on the uniform, checking for burns, tears and personal effects. He found and pocketed

---

[2] German air force

another wallet and Walther P38 before stripping the uniform off the airman and folding it into a rough bundle. Glancing around to check he was still alone, he spotted a third body on the ground fifteen yards away.

As Danes rounded a tree on his way to inspect it, he came face to face with a fourth airman. He yelped with fright and leapt backwards. Blood covered the German's head and face and his eyes were wide with terror, a sight made all more unsettling by the absence of a body to support them. The head was floating in mid-air.

"Was this what you were looking for?" asked a female voice from behind the tree. Its owner, a woman in her sixties, stepped into view. Her left hand was holding up the German's head by its hair. The other was restraining a black Labrador on a lead. She dropped the head to the ground, where the dog set about inspecting it. "I'm sure our laws against looting apply to the corpses of enemy airmen, too."

However much Danes stiffened to his full height, five foot nine, she remained an inch taller. Her blue eyes stared at him through thick square glasses which amplified her disapproval. "Give me one good reason to believe you're looting cash and clothing from these men for charitable purposes and not your personal benefit, young man. You'd better be convincing if you don't want me to report you to whatever authority turns up here in the next ten minutes."

Danes smiled in a way he hoped would appear more disarming than condescending. "I don't need to answer that but I will. I'm a pilot and I need the cash and the uniform to test a new idea I've had. It's all for King and country, I can assure you."

"Then why steal them instead of making an official request to use them?"

Danes shook his head. "It's more complicated than that."

"Well, as there are no survivors around here to chat to, I suggest you test my intelligence with a full explanation. Then I'll decide whether to report you or not."

Danes sighed. "A few weeks ago I wanted to impress a few girls with some beating up in a Spitfire."

"Beating up?"

"Low-level acrobatics. I got reprimanded and made the mistake of doing the same thing again a few days later. I've been grounded ever since, piloting nothing more glamorous than pencils and sheets of paper at the RAE."

"RAE?"

"Royal Aircraft Establishment. It's that huge complex of buildings attached to Farnborough Airfield just up the road."

"So that's what they call it."

"We do research on new aircraft and how to improve existing ones: range, speed, weight, weaponry, handling, that kind of thing. An engineer's paradise. My job is, or was, to examine and test captured German aircraft or—" He picked up a piece of blackened metal with twisted edges. "—what's left of them. We look for German ideas to steal, mainly. I also train fellow pilots on what to expect from enemy technology."

"Why does the RAE keep you if you're so undisciplined?"

"Because the RAE knows but can't admit that it thrives on indiscipline. It needs rebels. It needs creativity. It needs idiots like me. I wouldn't be good at what I do if I was disciplined. If the RAE kicked me out, they'd be sending a message to Britain's young pilots that their best chance of survival is to follow rules." He gestured towards the surrounding debris. "Following rules is what Luftwaffe airmen do."

The woman pulled her dog away from the head. "So young man, what's this big new idea you need to loot cash and a uniform for?"

"Professional resurrection. But the problem, dear lady, is that I can only explain my idea if you prove you've signed the Official Secrets Act."

"Don't be ridiculous. And I don't expect a twenty-two-year-old to dear-lady me."

"I'm twenty-six and I don't expect an ageing lady to young-man me either."

Danes's comment had an edge to it and the woman must have sensed it because she suddenly bent down to pat the dog's head. "Your not-so-innocent blue eyes have made me realise something," she said softly. "You only mentioned the Official Secrets Act after explaining what went on at the RAE." She stood up again. "Those activities are secret too, I assume."

Something exploded nearby, giving them both a jolt.

"They are. Highly."

"So not only do you know that I know you're a thief who'd do anything to save his career, but you also know that I now know things about your work that I bloody well shouldn't."

"Indeed."

She closed her eyes briefly. "Would you do me a favour?"

"Of course."

"The dog's name is Julius. Please don't harm him."

"I won't." Danes slammed the edge of the piece of metal he was holding into the side of the woman's neck. It struck her below the right ear, rupturing an artery. Blood spurted immediately from the wound. The woman crumpled to the ground. Julius turned away from the German's head to lick her face.

Chapter 7

Wednesday 30 April 1941
Chartwell – Kent – England

Neil McCrew looked up from his document as the black Austin Ten suddenly slowed and turned off the road. "Is this it?"

The driver didn't answer. Twenty yards ahead two men were chatting and smoking beside a Humber Pullman, also black but cleaner, which was parked under a tree. One of them signalled to McCrew's driver to park under a tree, too.

"Reg Parker and Walter Thompson," the driver said.

"Who?"

"Churchill's driver and bodyguard. I can't go any farther, sir. You'll have to do the rest on foot."

"Why stop here?"

"Camouflage. Vehicles parked directly outside the house would tell the Germans the place is occupied. If you follow that wall on the other side of the road, you'll come to a gate guarded by two soldiers you can see and probably at least two others you can't. Have you been given a password of some kind?"

"Yes."

The driver looked over his shoulder and grinned. "Whatever it is you're meeting him about, it must be bloody important."

McCrew slipped the document into his briefcase. "You don't expect me to deny or confirm that, do you?"

"No, but I've never seen him up this early. Unless he didn't go to bed, that is."

"Think painting."

"What about it?"

"Early morning light. That's what's important to him. Will you wait for me here? I shouldn't be more than an hour."

"Fine, sir."

McCrew got out and nodded to Parker and Thompson as he crossed the road. The entrance gate to Chartwell was seventy yards farther on. Two soldiers stepped out of camouflaged sentry boxes on either side of it.

"Good morning, gentlemen," McCrew said softly. "I've been strongly urged to mention chocolate cake if I want to stay out of trouble."

"Thank you, sir," said the soldier on the right as the other opened the gate. "You'll find him on the other side of the house, on the lawn facing the lakes. Go round the right side."

Purchased in the early 1920s, Chartwell's main building was an ochre reddish colour that McCrew found gloomy. As he walked past the main door and around the terrace at its southern end, he found himself comparing his situation to that of the man who had turned up at his family's doorstep a quarter of a century earlier to announce his father's death.

In 1915 Britain's First Lord of the Admiralty had pushed for an attack by British forces and their allies on the Ottoman empire. Poor planning, strategic mistakes and inadequate equipment had turned the campaign into an eight-month disaster costing some 100,000 lives, including 40,000 British ones. To countless critics, including McCrew, everything about it had been senseless, especially the shell—friendly fire, it later emerged—that had blown his father's head off on the Gallipoli peninsula. McCrew was sixteen at the time.

The news he was about to break to that same First Lord of the Admiralty, now Britain's wartime Prime Minister, was not about a loved one's death. If anything, and he based his hunch on three previous meetings with Churchill, this particular piece of news would hit him harder. As a forty-two-year-old surgeon and professional, McCrew felt duty-bound to remain dispassionate about that prospect. As a man, he felt compelled to appear to care about it. As a son still missing a beloved father, however, he struggled not to feel satisfied.

"If the footsteps behind me don't belong to Doctor Neil McCrew," said the famous voice, "please be aware I have no unstabbed areas left in my back."

"Good morning, Prime Minister."

They shook hands. Churchill's white overall was covered in paint stains. McCrew noticed he was wearing a suit and bowtie underneath it, presumably in readiness for a hectic day back in Whitehall later on.

"Unfold that seat on the ground, my dear fellow. I brought it for you. Do you mind if I put some finishing touches to this whilst you wreck my future? It's a present for an acquaintance of mine in deep turmoil and I have to finish it today."

McCrew refrained from commenting on Churchill's rendering—blandly competent, he thought at first glance—of Chartwell's upper lake and the trees beyond it. He stood his briefcase on the grass beside the easel, unfolded a wooden seat and sat next to the Prime Minister.

"I need a second opinion, Doctor. Should I paint the lake with or without the camouflaging stakes and brushwood? Are you an idealist or a pragmatist?"

McCrew adjusted his glasses. "My father used to say that idealism is the art of deciding which parts of reality to ignore."

"I'll camouflage the camouflaging, then. Which is precisely what I *don't* want you to do now. What's the news?"

"Mrs Churchill's tumour has grown again. It won't be long before the dizziness, vision problems and headaches she's already experiencing prevent her from walking." He reached down for his briefcase. "I've brought a couple of X-rays if you want to see it."

Churchill raised his free hand. "No, I'll take your word for it. Can you operate?"

"I could if the tumour were on the outer edge of her brain, but it isn't and my skills aren't up to it. We've got two surgeons in this country who could operate on her but one's ill, critically so, and the other's injured. Car accident. He'll recover but not for several weeks."

"What if we do nothing, Doctor?"

"As I told you before, the tumour will eventually do permanent damage to the surrounding brain tissue. It will cripple her, then kill her. My opinion hasn't changed."

Churchill shut his eyes and slowly shook his head. "I sent President Roosevelt your description of Clemmie's condition and asked him for a list of surgeons able to operate on it. I didn't say it was for Clemmie. He sent back a list of five possibles." Churchill picked up Roosevelt's list from the easel. "Any guesses?"

"Manzoni. Luigi Manzoni. If he's not on it, the list's worthless."

"He's top of it, but Roosevelt writes that he's, and I quote, incapacitated. No details supplied."

"Pity. Ironically I was due to spend time with Manzoni to learn how to do operations like the one your wife needs."

Churchill look at McCrew contemptuously. "If that comment's supposed to console me, Doctor, it isn't succeeding. Why didn't it happen?"

"Germany invaded Poland, sir."

Churchill grunted and looked at the list. "Who else?"

"I would imagine Damian Mercer's on there, too."

"Correct. He's third but unavailable apparently, which is probably Roosevelt's way of saying he's too scared to travel to a warzone."

McCrew scratched his head. "The only other man I can think of with the skills is St. James. Edward St. James."

"He's second but, and I quote, unreachable. It's Edwin St. James, by the way. Why am I beginning to think there's a coordinated plot on both sides of the Atlantic to let people with complex brain tumours die?" Churchill put his paintbrush down and produced a cigar from an inside pocket. Have you taken up smoking since we last met, Doctor? Would you like one of these?"

"No, thank you. Frankly I can't imagine who the two other names might be."

Churchill took his time to light up. "On the contrary, you know at least one of them well."

McCrew held the Prime Minister's gaze.

"It's you, my dear man." Churchill resumed his painting. "It seems you're the only member of your distinguished profession who believes he can't repair my wife's brain."

"With respect, sir, no one in the States has seen the details of her case. Nor have they seen the X-rays. In effect they're making educated guesses about what I can do."

"Still, it's an interesting coincidence."

"What is, sir?"

Two Hurricane fighters suddenly flew low overhead, heading east.

"The one thing my position gives me access to," Churchill said, "is information. Oceans of it. So I asked a couple of our best deep-ocean divers to plumb the depths in your vicinity. They resurfaced with what happened to your father at Gallipoli and your belief I was directly responsible for his death. According to you, and I quote, I murdered him. You've made no secret of that belief over the years and it's now no secret to me either. You hate my guts, Doctor. You've got a score to settle with me."

McCrew stood up. "If you're suggesting I'd harm your wife through inaction, that's an appalling—"

"Not my wife, McCrew. You've got nothing against Mrs Churchill. In fact you probably think greatly of her, as I do. No, this is more subtle. The person you'd be harming is me. Widowhood would be a fate worse than death for a political leader who depends as much on his wife as I do."

"That's grossly insulting, sir."

Puffing on his cigar, Churchill looked up at him. "Then explain something to me. You said a moment ago that you'd planned to do some training with Manzoni to learn how to operate on patients like Clemmie, correct?"

"Yes."

"If so, why would Manzoni personally recommend you for an operation he knows you're unqualified for?"

"That's not possible, sir. I'm only on the list because someone in the States knows I'm a brain surgeon, not because Manzoni personally recommended me."

Churchill cocked his head. "Are you calling the Prime Minister of the United Kingdom a liar?"

"Yes, sir."

Churchill said nothing for a moment as he pretended to be fascinated by a detail on the painting. When he spoke again, his tone was curt. "Consider yourself lucky to be living in a democracy, Doctor. If you'd said that in Germany, a firing squad would already be taking aim at you. What makes you think I'm lying?"

"The fact that I lied to you myself. No training with Manzoni has ever been planned. I made that up. It was no more than wishful thinking and still is. He and I have never met. He might know of me—brains surgeons are a small community—but that's not enough to recommend me for that kind of operation."

"Well someone in the USA thinks you're good enough."

McCrew raised a hand. "Respectfully, Prime Minister, I disagree. Don't forget they positioned me fourth on the list. In our profession, that's the doldrums. The only good news is that I'm not fifth."

Churchill smiled. "I was only taunting you. I wanted to make you feel as insulted as I do whenever someone suggests that good men were killed at Gallipoli because of my political ambition, not by appalling decision making. I wanted you to feel as sick to the core as I do whenever someone suggests that my personal success is more central to my life than the lives and welfare of ordinary British soldiers like your father. Or indeed of ordinary Britons. Are you leaving or staying?"

McCrew sat down. "I've only ever heard one person suggest that."

"Suggest what?"

"That you're selfish in the extreme."

Churchill scoffed. "You should spend an hour in my shoes in Parliament."

"That person was Mrs Churchill, sir."

Churchill stiffened.

"She told me she comes a distant second in your life to you. And the fact she puts up with it day to day is the reason you're so scared of losing her."

"Oh," Churchill muttered, lost in thought. "When did she tell you that?"

"She didn't. I was only taunting you."

Churchill smirked. "Touché. Back to our list: tell me what you know about Frank Winter. He's fifth."

McCrew laughed.

Churchill touched the right side of his painting with the tip of his thumb. "Acquaintance of yours?"

"Barely. I haven't had any contact with him for, er, seven years at least and then only briefly."

"Could he be our man? Could he operate?"

"Yes, absolutely."

"So professionally at least, his fifth position on Roosevelt's list isn't the doldrums."

"No, sir. Professionally, Winter's up there with Manzoni: outspoken, innovative, courageous. The main difference between them is that Winter's more ambitious: new instruments, new anaesthetics, new procedures. We all owe him something. Politically though, I'm afraid he's lower than the doldrums. I don't know if he's actually a member of the Nazi party, but he's—"

"He is. Berlin branch. But that doesn't necessarily mean much. He might have joined to keep the hounds at bay whilst he attracts new customers."

"No, he's a believer, sir. The last time I saw him was in 1934 at a medical congress in Wiesbaden. Hitler had been in power for a year and Winter had nothing but stars in his eyes. He couldn't talk about anything or anyone else. You're not seriously considering him, are you?"

Churchill turned to face him. "To be clear, McCrew, if I could find a way in spite of the war raging between our two countries to put Mrs Churchill and Herr Doktor Winter in the same operating theatre, what would her chances be?"

McCrew adjusted his glasses again. "Her chances are never going to be excellent, but Winter can make them as good as they can be. But how would you bring him here? Kidnap him?"

"Believe it or not, we've already considered that and please don't ask who 'we' is for the moment. Kidnapping would probably be too risky, not least because it would involve several people abducting him under SS and Gestapo noses in central Berlin. And there'd be no guarantee Winter would cooperate once he gets here. So our best bet is to persuade him to come of his own free will, which means sending someone to Berlin that he'd at least listen to, if not trust. Someone able to portray the whole thing as an irresistible, once-in-a-lifetime medical challenge and not some form of ideological betrayal."

McCrew scoffed. "Good luck with that."

"I was about to say the same thing to you."

McCrew froze.

"You're the only person who can pull it off, Doctor. Winter wouldn't listen to anyone else."

"And how do you expect me to get there? I don't speak a word of German. I'd be arrested in under a minute."

"The logistics of it are my problem, not yours. You'd have a German-speaking companion with you at all times, except when you're with Winter himself. He's fluent in English, I gather."

"Yes, he studied at Cambridge. But this is madness, sir."

"No it isn't, McCrew. This is about Clemmie's life and my sanity."

"What about my life, sir? I have a wife too and she depends on me as much as Mrs Churchill depends on you."

"I know, which is why you have every right to refuse. But let's take a look at what would happen if you accepted. First, I'd make sure you're able to resume the research you were doing before the war interrupted it. You'd also get all the funds, staffing and peace and quiet you need. Second, you'd find out what really happened to your father at Gallipolli. As I told you, I have access to oceans of information. What do you think?"

"I—"

"Forget it, McCrew. I can't offer you anything like that. The only thing I can offer is my personal undying gratitude. But as that certainly won't be enough to persuade you, you'll have to find your own reason for risking life and limb on my behalf. If you find one, fine. If you don't, the vehicle that brought you here will drive you back to London and your life will go on. Make no mistake: I'm fully aware of what this looks like. Here I am, telling the British people day after day, bombing raid after bombing raid, what I expect them to sacrifice and assuring them I have nothing to offer but blood, toil, tears and sweat. Meanwhile here I am, pulling every available string, including a Nazi one, to get my wife the kind of medical care everyone else to do without in the name of our fight for democracy and freedom. And here I am, asking you to risk making your wife a widow so that my wife doesn't make me a widower. Oh, before I forget."

Churchill took a small brown envelope from a different inside pocket and handed it to McCrew.

"Here's something that might help your decision making. Don't worry, it's not cash. Read it on your way back to London. I need your answer by tomorrow evening. If you agree to do this, you'll be given a week's training in the German language, a few survival basics and dirty tricks. If you decline, our conversation today will never have happened." Churchill gestured towards the easel. "In fact the only discernible trace of this meeting will be this painting. It's for you."

Chapter 8

Wednesday 30 April 1941
Farnborough – Hampshire – England

"Mike?"

Roddy Danes's voice echoed around Farnborough Airfield's Hangar B, which housed five captured German aircraft. The Heinkel He 111, which he stood under now, was his favourite. He loved the fact that flying it was an uncomfortable, exhausting and deafening experience for Luftwaffe airmen. He loved the pointlessness of its glazed 'greenhouse' nose, which either blinded the pilot when the sun was shining or raised the temperature inside the aircraft to intolerable levels. He loved the fact that it was a slow and easy target for British fighters. He loved the fact that it wasn't big enough, even in large numbers, to make a true difference in the Third Reich's bombing of British cities; if anything, the 111's shortcomings had prolonged the campaign. He loved the aircraft's beautiful inadequacy.

"Workbench," a male voice shot back from somewhere.

Danes skirted a Focke-Wulf Fw 190 fighter and ducked under the wing of a Junkers Ju 88 similar to the aircraft that had crashed that morning.

Mike Paterson was sitting on a workbench behind the tail of a Junkers Ju 87 dive-bomber, better known as a Stuka[3]. At thirty-eight, Paterson was as proud of his Jamaican nationality, culture and dreadlocks as of his legendary ability to squeeze practical mechanical solutions out of the most desperate

---

[3] Stuka is short for "Sturzkampfflugzeug"

engineering problems. Intent on not losing Paterson to other airfields or War Office departments, the RAE's management had calculated that leaving the length and appearance of his dreadlocks unchallenged was as a good a guarantee as any that he'd stay.

Paterson held up a valve as Danes approached. "This thing's useless."

Danes kissed him softly on the lips. "Are you alone?"

"A little late to ask, my friend." Paterson switched on a torch and examined the inside of the valve."

Danes reached up and patted the Stuka's fuselage. "When can I try this thing?"

"Two weeks at least. This is one of three parts I have to repair or replace, or maybe even make myself. Our pilots really must shoot German planes down more carefully."

Danes reached up and patted the Stuka's fuselage. "Two weeks it is, then. I've received a request to include this thing in training sessions for new pilots as soon as possible. Know thine enemy etc. Next session's on May 19th, just over two weeks from now. I'd like them to see me fly it. Hear about the crash?"

"Heard the crash itself. Hell of a din. Higgs said it was a Heinkel."

"Yours truly says it was a Junkers 88 on its way back from recon. It was so close I thought it was taking pictures of me."

Paterson put the valve down and shone the torch in Danes's face. "You've got my attention."

"I now own a whole lot of Reichsmarks, two Walther pistols and a Luftwaffe uniform that actually fits. I was first on the scene."

Paterson's eyes widened as he switched off the torch. "Anyone see you?"

"No. Remember that crazy little plan we had to help me get my career back? I've got all the equipment I need."

Paterson shook his head. "No, Roddy. Leave the crazy little plan at the bar where we came up with it. We were pissed, remember?"

"You came up with the plan, Mike, not me."

Paterson eased himself off the workbench and grabbed Danes's arms. "Forget the plan. You won't be flying again anytime soon, so live with it. Mess around again and you'll end up in prison or dead and where will we be then?"

"We?"

"Yes, we." Paterson returned to the torch and valve.

Danes turned mock conspiratorial. "What if our crazy little plan had a bigger dimension to it? What if it did more than just wipe my slate clean?"

Paterson looked up.

"Something else happened with the 88," Danes said. "Before it crashed, it was trailing smoke from both engines. For some reason one of the trails was intermittent, as if the pilot was controlling it. That gave me an idea."

Paterson said nothing as Danes took the torch and valve from his hands and placed them on the workbench. "Darf ich Sie zum Tanz bitten?"

"English, please."

Danes led Paterson to the space between the Heinkel bomber and the much smaller Focke-Wulf fighter. Turning to face him, he stretched out his arms. "I was only asking you to dance. Now shut up and obey."

They began to waltz between the aircraft.

"You're a German fighter pilot flying over the Fatherland," Danes said. "You suddenly spot a Heinkel 111 bomber, also German obviously, flying east with black smoke trailing from one of its engines. The aircraft's clearly in trouble but it isn't losing height. So it's not in dire trouble. You try to radio the guy but no response. Although your gut tells you the pilot's going to be able to land on one engine, you decide to see how things are and position yourself alongside the 111. You exchange hand signals with the pilot and he gives you a thumbs-up. What would you do?"

"Can a 111 really fly on one engine? If it can't, I'd be aware of that as a Luftwaffe pilot and would have doubts about what I'm seeing."

"What sorts of doubts? Would you seriously imagine that the smoke might be fake?"

Paterson stopped dancing. "No."

"So?"

"I'd warn airfields ahead to get their fire extinguishers ready."

"And then? Would you stay with the 111 or piss off?"

The waltz resumed.

"Probably not," Paterson said. "If I were confident he could land, there'd be nothing more for me to do for him."

Danes smiled. "That's what I'd do. So there's a good chance the 111 would be left alone to fly on to its actual destination."

"Yes."

"In broad daylight. Hiding in plain sight."

"Yes."

The dancing stopped.

Danes stepped back and opened his arms. "Just imagine. The 111 could get close enough to any target in Germany with this thing to slip a bomb up its arse."

Paterson nodded slowly.

"Can you make black smoke, Mike?"

Paterson lost his temper. "Make it? In case you hadn't noticed, Roddy, all my waking hours, passions, dreams, nightmares, strengths, weaknesses and identity are devoted to *eliminating* black smoke. It's the enemy."

"Point taken. You've just earned yourself twenty-four additional hours— that's forty-eight in all—to make black smoke come out of a perfectly healthy aircraft engine."

Danes led Paterson towards the Heinkel. He slapped its fuselage a few inches away from where the port wing emerged. "Even when this thing's loaded with bombs, there's enough room above them to load something else. That's where you'll put the canisters or whatever that generate the black smoke. How the smoke is created is your problem. Chemical reaction, perhaps? I don't know. If you can't think of a way to do it, give the Vatican a call to see how they create black and white smoke during papal elections." He ran a hand along the underside of the wing towards the engine. "The smoke must travel along a tube attached to the wing and emerge somewhere near the engine so that any onlooker will believe the aircraft's in trouble. But all that is theory, my friend. We're practical men. We assume things will go wrong until they don't. Which is why, in forty-eight hours' time, I'll be flying this thing over Germany. With any luck, the black smoke will do two things. First it will prove we can get closer to bombing targets in broad daylight without being challenged. Second it will help me pull off our crazy little plan to wipe my slate clean. Oh, and please add an extra fuel reserve." He slapped the fuselage again. "My destination might stretch this thing's range a bit."

Paterson shook his head. "You're out of your mind. Firth will never authorise this."

"Of course he won't. He's the guy who grounded me. So the first he'll hear about my flight is when I get back from it. Now kiss me again, please."

Chapter 9

Thursday 1 May 1941
Lanke – March Brandenburg– Germany

Joseph Goebbels scanned the eleven faces, five male and six female, around the table at his country house near Lanke, in the countryside north of Berlin. He'd received the house as a birthday gift from the Berlin authorities in 1936 and spent as much time there as possible, whether to write, think or entertain mistresses. The sparsely decorated dining room, where Goebbels and his guests were seated now, doubled as a conference room.

He let the silence last longer than usual, pre-injecting additional drama into whatever he said next.

All in their early twenties, the young adults staring back expectantly at him hadn't been invited because of their ability to quote Mein Kampf or Goebbels himself, although the Minister of Propaganda had no doubts they could. Nor could they be described as conforming, goose-stepping products of what eight years of National Socialist power had done to German society and culture. On the contrary, the Reich Ministry for Public Enlightenment and Propaganda, known as the Promi to its staff, had picked them for their courage in criticising Hitler and other Third Reich leaders, including Goebbels himself, during recruitment interviews. Goebbels considered such a trait to be as vital to the ministry's inner workings as it was unthinkable outside its walls.

"As you know," he began, "our beloved Führer will address the Reichstag directly and therefore the German people indirectly next Sunday. What if he announces or even merely hints that the war will continue beyond the end of

1941? How should our messages to the German people reflect or build on that, if at all? I remind you that the Fuehrer told the nation in his new year's message that the last of our enemies would be crushed this year. If he announces a longer war, he'll be contradicting himself."

Sitting at the back of the room, not quite in the minister's line of sight, Anna Vogel grinned approvingly as she scribbled Goebbels's questions on her notepad. She had been the one to suggest organising such sessions to him when she had arrived herself at the Ministry, four years earlier. His willingness to join in frank and regular discussions with young recruits contrasted with the aloofness he displayed towards other staff at the ministry.

"The new year was four months ago," said a freckly woman called Andrea Bechstein. "Do you really think anyone remembers? I mean surely—"

Her neighbour, Rita Korth, blushed as she interrupted her: "The Führer is much less visible or audible these days than before the war. That makes people pay all the more attention to anything he communicates today. Most would notice any inconsistency in his statements."

"I agree," said Lutz Reinhardt over his rimless glasses, which added ten years to his mere twenty-one, "especially if they have a family member fighting out there who might have to risk his life for longer than expected."

Andrea Bechstein turned to Goebbels. "Excuse me, Herr Reichsminister, but do you know the answer to your question?"

"No, I don't," Goebbels said. "That's why we must prepare for several scenarios. The Führer's probably writing his speech in Bavaria as we speak—well perhaps not right this very minute because it's still morning. The Führer's not the world's earliest riser."

They all laughed.

"I think there will be a problem if he contradicts himself," said a deep-voiced woman called Helga Kerrl. "Short of announcing defeat, I can't imagine a worse thing for the German population's morale than a war lasting into 1942."

"Do you think such a contradiction would make him seem fallible?" Goebbels asked.

The room remained silent. Goebbels lit a cigarette.

"Well," a plump young man called Frank Krost said carefully, "we've been positioning him—or rather he's been positioning himself—as a kind of, er, well—"

Goebbels slapped the table. "Spit it out, Krost."

"The word I was thinking of was 'divinity'."

Goebbels smiled. "Precisely. Adolf Hitler, the divinity. A divinity capable of anything by definition. Of anything except, as it turns out, divining the future, or at least the short-term military aspects of it. Meine Damen und

Herren, the Third Reich proudly presents Adolf Hitler, its fallible divinity. Make no mistake: that's exactly what many Germans will think, which is why we praise the Führer for his powers of divination in peacetime but not in wartime. So how can we correct this?"

Rita Korth raised a hand. "I'd say our role is to turn the Führer's contradictions to Germany's advantage somehow."

"But our enemies at home and abroad will still see them as contradictions, won't they?" This from Lutz Reinhardt.

Goebbels slapped the table again. "Oh, and they won't just see them as contradictions. They'll talk about them, laugh about them, write about them, paint them on the walls of London and Washington and turn them into Hollywood movies. Hallelujah, Adolf Hitler has confessed at last to a mistake!"

"I think that kind of admission would make the Fuehrer seem honest," a male voice said softly.

Goebbels stiffened. "Who said that?"

A blond man called Joseph Himer raised his hand.

"Explain yourself."

Himer swallowed hard. "Well, Herr Reichsminister, if we imagine ourselves one year into the future, in 1942, and the war isn't over yet, anybody looking back could conclude the Führer did one of two things. Either he made a mistake in his predictions about the length of the war or knew the war would last longer than expected but kept that crucial, life-and-death information away from the people. As a result, he would appear either fallible or dishonest. But if the Führer admits right now that the war is probably going to drag on until 1942, he'll appear to want to be frank with his people, to hold no information back, to be as honest as possible. We could use that."

Goebbels glanced towards the window and frowned. A car was drawing up outside. His gaze met Anna's, who had seen the vehicle, too.

"It looks as if I have an unexpected visitor," he said. "I'll let you carry on the discussion with Fräulein Vogel." He stood up and turned to Himer. "You've got a point, but the Ministry of Propaganda would be shut down in an instant if we went down that path. Think about it: if we suddenly praised the Führer for his honesty with the German people we'd be suggesting he was less than honest in the past. Can you remember any lies he might have told? I can't." He winked.

Chapter 10

Thursday 1 May 1941
London – England

"Why don't you just do it, for God's sake?" Violet McCrew snapped. "We've been talking for two hours now and getting nowhere. This whole thing probably has a silver lining, you never know."

Adjusting his glasses, Neil McCrew observed his wife calmly from across the breakfast table. He put his knife and fork down, most of his weekly ration of bacon and his entire weekly ration of one egg now too cold to be edible.

"The only lining I can see is at best a silk one for my coffin. But don't waste the money. Wood is just as good."

She put a hand over her mouth. "I'm sorry, I had no right to say that."

"But you said it anyway." Neil took a deep breath. "Violet, leaving aside Churchill's role in my father's death, if I do what that man wants and go to Berlin, I'll be accepting that his wife's life is more important than any life-threatening risk I might take, that her survival is more important than all the desperately injured people I save every day in my job and that 'till death do us part' will describe the Churchills' marriage for much longer than ours. I know Mrs Churchill does a lot of great work to help bombing victims, but so do countless other people, including you in your volunteering work and me at the hospital."

Violet grinned.

"What's so funny?"

"No, I was just thinking about the longer-term prospects of our marriage. As it's sixteen years old, we're in the middle of its longer-term prospects right now."

"And?"

The grin vanished. "When did our marriage begin to fail, Neil?"

"I beg your pardon?" He folded his arms.

"I can tell you," she said. "It began to fail on May 23rd 1924, five seconds before you and I turned our backs on the vicar and began to walk back down the aisle with these things—" she pointed to her wedding ring "—freshly on our fingers and dozens of familiar faces smiling at us."

He waited.

"Five seconds earlier, you'd kissed the bride. This was your big chance to show me and our respective families what kind of marriage I could expect. I'd shut my eyes and prepared my lips for action, my life for meaning, my identity for completeness, my body for pleasure and my belly for kids and all I got was a miserable peck on the cheek. A courteous, dutiful, humble, almost endearingly apologetic brush of your lips against my face. I realised there and then—I felt it—that you didn't love me. Never had. Never would. You married me because you were too polite and decent not to."

Neil sighed. "Well, thanks for not waiting sixteen more years to share that thought with me."

"Why are we still married?"

"Because about thirty seconds before my peck on your cheek, we both vowed to stay that way till death do us part."

"No, Neil, I'll rephrase. If you were to describe to a complete stranger how we met and got married, what would you say?"

Neil rolled his eyes. "Do we need to talk about this now, Violet? The Prime Minister's expecting an answer today."

"Indulge me." She lit a cigarette and crossed her legs.

Neil took a deep breath. "Violet and I met in Cambridge, where I was studying medicine and she was working in a popular restaurant owned by her parents. The first time she saw me, she hated my demeanour, especially my shoes, which she managed to pour coffee on. It was supposedly an accident but I didn't believe a word of it. She did however find my personality attractive: courteous, dutiful, humble, almost endearingly apologetic. She didn't tell me so until just after our first kiss, the tongue-down-each-other's-throat variety, and God it was clumsy, whereupon I reminded her there was a local law in Cambridge punishing any attempt by a non-student to distract a student from his books with the shape of her bosom. That first kiss happened exactly eleven days after the coffee incident. We were on a bus on the way back from some boring student play that neither of us had paid attention to anyway. She realised that if she didn't ask me to sneak through the side-door of her parents' house to have sex with her that same night, I would be too courteous, dutiful, humble and almost endearing apologetic to bring up the subject. Besides, such an outrageous request so early in a relationship between two unmarried Brits would have shocked me. So we had sex that same night anyway. By the way, the joke about the local law forbidden distractions had a serious edge to it. Violet was disrupting my concentration and my studies and I had to impose severe limits on the time we could spend together. She hated this.

"Anyway we pulled through and got married eighteen months later. We lived at Violet's parents' house in Cambridge until I finished my studies, at which point we moved to London, where I could specialise in brain surgery and we could both work to make ends meet. I was an intern and Violet worked in restaurants. By this time it was obvious there was a problem with one of us because Violet never became pregnant. We had tests but no problem could be found. Luck of the draw. As neither of us fancied adopting a child, the subject fell by the wayside. A few years later I was earning enough for us to buy a house in Bethnal Green, where I come from and where I could be close to my mother. It's not the prettiest part of London and my young wife was uneasy at first, but I asked her to give it a chance and she did. Today, despite the terrible damage inflicted by the Blitz, we wouldn't live anywhere else unless a German bomb forced us to."

Violet fiddled with her cigarette. "Care to hear my version?"

"Not really."

She ignored him. "I agree with everything except two details. The first is that we came to live here in Bethnal Green so that you could be close to your mother. Hogwash. She treated you like a dog and still does. The only true parent you ever had was your father and the only reason we came to live here was so you could be close to the Great War remembrance plaque with his name on it at the cemetery. You go there every day to talk to him—every single bloody day. Fine, you loved him and he loved you, but he died twenty-six years ago, Neil. Get over it."

"The second detail is all this business about me distracting you back in Cambridge. Hogwash again." She lit a second cigarette off the first. "My body was fine for your physical needs, but nothing I could say, write or express in any way could satisfy your emotional ones. No, that kind of satisfaction came from elsewhere, or rather from someone else. I called her the slag back then. The irony is that I was the one who pushed you into her arms. I dropped your watch one day and she happened to run a local jewellery and watch repair shop with her parents. No less a slag, though."

McCrew shifted imperceptibly in his seat.

"You're shifting imperceptibly in your seat, Neil. Surprised I knew that? So all the limits you placed on the time we spent together so you could concentrate on your books were actually designed to give you time with the person you truly loved. The slag. It went on for a few months like that and you were getting ready to ditch me and everything was perfect and your future with the slag looked set until boom, she ditched you. She'd met someone else. That almost destroyed you. I could feel something was adrift at the time but I assumed you were torn between me and your studies. How naïve of me. And how naïve of you too: you moped for weeks hoping the slag would change her mind. Then she disappeared. She ran off with her new boyfriend to live with him in his homeland, Germany. You even knew the chap, Frank Winter. Like you, he wanted to become a top-flight surgeon. You both succeeded."

"I only discovered the slag's existence and name after we got married. I was putting away some things one day when I came across a photograph of you and her in one of your drawers." She pointed upwards. "It's still there now. 'I love you. Tina,' it says on the back. Not a day goes by without you looking at it. Her name's Tina Winter now, Neil. She's probably a fat, beer-swilling mother of six Hitler Youth members now, but that's not how you think of her."

They drank tea in silence.

She reached across the table to stroke his hand. "You're the most courteous, dutiful, humble and almost endearingly apologetic man I know, Neil. But you're still carrying the same two crosses on your back today that were already there the day we got married: abandoned by a father who forgot to duck at Gallipoli and abandoned by a girl who forgot to choose you in Cambridge." She took her hand back. "Last year, after fifteen years of waiting for you to emerge from the shadow of those two crosses, I finally decided to leave you. I actually packed my bags and bought a train ticket back to my parents' home in Cambridge. Then something lit up my life. Rays of hope suddenly descended from the sky."

Neil drummed the table. "You realised I loved you after all."

"No, Neil, sorry." She flicked ash into her teacup and rummaged briefly in a handbag behind her. "That's the train ticket to Cambridge I never used," she said, throwing a small piece of cardboard at him. "Check the date. Saturday 7 September 1940. The rays of hope lighting up my life were German bombs exploding out of the sky. That's the day the Blitz began."

Chapter 11

Thursday 1 May 1941
Lanke – March Brandenburg – Germany

Joseph Goebbels had recognised the unexpected vehicle immediately. It belonged to Norbert Gerscher, a childhood friend who had quietly worked his way up the ranks of the Abwehr, Germany's military intelligence organisation. The two men had lost sight of each other in the late 1920s and only met again when Gerscher came across information about one of Goebbels's numerous mistresses in the mid-1930s.

The mistress in question, a Prussian actress, had arranged for photographs to be discreetly taken of their lovemaking, including angles showing Goebbels's misshapen right foot, a congenital deformity. Their publication would have been disastrous. Unfortunately for the actress, her chosen photographer, a man called Erich Schönmann, had a standing arrangement with the Abwehr, who guaranteed him a higher price than any other bidder for duplicates of sensitive material concerning foreign military officials.

In charge of setting up and managing such arrangements in the Berlin area, Gerscher sometimes came across compromising material concerning non-military officials as well. Some of these were German and, in April 1935, Goebbels had turned out to be one of them. Three days after a phone call from Gerscher to warn him about the photographs and what the actress was likely to do with them, she had died in a car accident.

The incident had opened up an unofficial, permanent and indispensable channel of communication between the two old friends. As both worked in environments where withholding information from colleagues for career purposes was standard practice, the rumours and gossip they exchanged often filled critical gaps in their grasp of events, enabling both to prepare for developments that would otherwise have taken them by surprise.

"Norbert, so good to see you," Goebbels exclaimed as they shook hands in the hallway. Gerscher towered over the diminutive Minister but could not compete with his taste in beautifully tailored suits and general neatness. Goebbels poked Gerscher's enormous belly as he led him into a lounge and shut the door. "If you promise to keep on getting fatter, I'll promise to keep on limping. Coffee?"

"No, I'll only stay a minute. It's a good thing my parents live just up the road. Stopping here looks like the most natural thing in the world."

"Which is precisely why it looks suspicious."

They laughed and sat down.

Gerscher took a sheet of paper out of his briefcase and handed it to Goebbels. "This came up at a meeting I attended three hours ago. It's a weekly inter-departmental get-together where we try to decide what to do with intercepted messages that aren't of a military nature or don't seem important at first blush. Usually the only thing we agree on is not to share anything with the SS. I volunteered to look into this one but it's more of interest to you, I hope, than me."

Goebbels read it.

"That list was sent by Roosevelt to Churchill yesterday evening," Gerscher explained. "Our people decrypted the message five hours later. As there's no context or other explanation, we can assume it's an answer to a request of some kind from Churchill."

"And you haven't found the original request, I take it."

"No, nothing that seems to ask for a list of some kind. But there was a problem with a series of messages on Tuesday that were either lost or garbled. Heads are set to roll. Now Tuesday was two days ago. If Churchill's original request was among the lost messages and Roosevelt answered it yesterday, that suggests urgency."

Goebbels kept his eyes on the list. "Who are these people?"

"Our people in the States have already identified two of them as surgeons: Manzoni and St. James. Brain surgeons, actually. Our people are obviously using that as a clue for the other three. As you can see, each name has a comment beside it, apparently about the person's availability. Three of the five, including Manzoni and St. James, are unavailable for whatever Churchill requested and Roosevelt has put a question mark beside the other two."

Goebbels handed the list back. "Why would Churchill need a list of American brain surgeons? Don't they have that kind of thing on his little island?"

"Assuming all five are brain surgeons, and that's still only an assumption, I can only think of two scenarios. One: a British surgeon needs urgent advice or a second opinion on something and needs high-level help to get the information quickly. Two: the British don't have the right surgical skills for an operation and are asking the Americans for help. Either way the patient must be an important one if both Churchill and Roosevelt are involved."

"Churchill himself, perhaps?"

"Now you see why I came here."

"Yes, thanks." Goebbels scratched his head. "Well unless Churchill has better acting skills than we thought, he hasn't seemed impaired recently, unless the Brits are passing off old newsreel as new."

"Brain tumours don't necessarily impair you. My sister had one for months before it impaired her in any serious way."

"Somebody in his Cabinet, perhaps? One of his generals?"

"I can get my people to check for any unexplained, prolonged absences in their high-level military circles recently. Obviously that's a lot of people, so we'll stick to the top ones for now."

"Good. And I'll get mine to check the royal family and other major personalities—actors, performers, etc.—whose death might affect public morale."

They stood up and headed back to the hallway.

"What about politicians?" Gerscher asked. "What about Churchill's family and friends?"

"I doubt that Churchill would go to those extremes to help a fellow politician, even somebody from his own party. He won't want to risk the British public finding out he's pulling strings to help an elected official jump a medical queue. If however the patient is a family member or a close friend, we'd have to assume Churchill would be self-centred and hypocritical enough to use British state resources for private purposes."

They looked at each other and grinned.

"I'll get my people to check his family and friends first," Goebbels said.

Chapter 12

Thursday 1 May 1941
London – England

Violet McCrew lit another cigarette as her husband opened the kitchen window to let in some fresh air. "Those bombs changed everything, even the ones exploding around here. I pretended to be terrified when you were around, but I actually found the whole thing exciting. All the volunteering I did and still do gave a whole new meaning to my life. The dead bodies, the awful injuries, the burning houses, the grieving survivors, the wrecked lives, the screaming children, the looters, the black marketeers, the prostitutes selling sex in the ruins and spreading disease in the rubble, the selfishness, the lack of medical equipment, none of it got through to me. All I felt was boundless energy and an unlimited ability to help and be useful. I loved it. The only thing I worried about was a bomb hitting a hospital where you might be working or our house. Otherwise I hate to say it but whilst the Blitz was killing thousands of people, it was saving me."

"At what point did you meet Sebastian?" Neil's tone was neutral, matter of fact.

She blanched.

"Don't worry," he continued, "I haven't been following you through the ruins and rubble. In fact I didn't know Sebastian existed until yesterday. Churchill's people have been doing background research on me, which means they've been doing research on you as well. The old bastard handed me a half-page of information about your relationship and I must say Sebastian sounds like an interesting sort of chap. Quite your type."

Violet stared at the table. "I met him in September last year. He was a volunteer like me. Nothing happened, but something was there. A spark. I saw him three or four times and then not at all until the attack on December 29th last year. He cut himself whilst carrying an old lady out of a burning house and I looked after him. We talked all night and that's when he told me his wife had been killed during a raid back in October. They'd had no children. After that we managed to see each other a few times for a cup of tea, as friends. But the Blitz doesn't allow men and women to be just friends. All it does is kill off people today and remind everyone else that tomorrow might not come."

"When's the baby due?"

Violet's eyes opened wide. Her chin began to tremble. "How did they find out about that?"

"They didn't. I asked on the off-chance. When's it due?"

"Neil, I wish I could—"

"Answer me. How many periods have you missed?"

"Two."

"Does Sebastian know?"

"No."

Neil absorbed this for a moment. "How would he react if he did?"

In tears now, Violet looked up at the ceiling. "He'd be over the moon. Having his children's his big dream."

"But is it his big dream with you?"

She looked at Neil and slowly began to nod. He smiled, reached across the table, grabbed her pack of cigarettes and crumpled it.

"In that case, you can tell Sebastian you smoked your last cigarette for a long while in my presence. Some of my colleagues are noticing birth defects in children whose mother smoked heavily during their pregnancy. Don't risk it. Let's keep this simple, Violet. We'll arrange for a divorce so you can be with the father of your child."

"Neil, please."

He raised a hand to interrupt her and stood up. "Salvaging sixteen years of marriage will never be as important as giving your child a mother and a father who love each other." He walked round the table and kissed her on the forehead. "I wish you well."

She grabbed his hand. "And what are you going to do?"

"As you rightly reminded me, I've got two crosses on my back. I'm not getting any younger and they're not getting any lighter."

Chapter 13

Thursday 1 May 1941
London – England

Brendan Bracken stood smoking on the pavement outside 10 Downing Street, his home since May 1940. Churchill had asked him to move in when he had become Prime Minister. The telephone call from a secretary at the Houses of Parliament had been brief, demanding that he make himself available for an urgent chat with the Prime Minister during a car ride from Downing Street to Paddington Station. Churchill was due to travel overnight to Plymouth to inspect damage caused by intense German bombing.

The last time this kind of chat had been organised was when a mutual friend, a minor lord with a major heart problem, had died whilst lunching alone in a Chelsea restaurant. During dessert he had fallen off his seat and died within seconds of his head hitting the floor.

Or so the official version, the one presented to his widow and politest friends, had claimed somewhat too convincingly. During a short car trip across London, Churchill had prevailed on Bracken to prevail in turn on employees of the newspapers he published or edited to dig up a more truthful account. Churchill had been due to meet the lord in question three hours after his final meal.

An eye-watering bribe, fully reimbursed by Churchill at a later date, had jogged a waiter's memory: the lord had not eaten alone and had retired not during but *for* dessert—of a more physical nature—to a conveniently unused and lockable room at the rear of the premises.

A second bribe, this one eye-drenching, had teased out the fact that the lord's companion had not been female. This version satisfied Churchill's curiosity and Bracken promptly killed the story.

Churchill and Bracken had met in the early 1920s. Just twenty-three at the time, Bracken had enthralled the older man with his self-confidence, knowledge and wit. The two men had soon met again, quickly becoming close friends—too close as far as Churchill's wife Clementine was concerned for Bracken, a bachelor, was ever-present in their lives. As Churchill's political career had tossed and turned in the 1920s and 30s, Bracken had become a successful newspaper publisher, a demanding business manager and himself an elected member of parliament.

Yet never had Bracken been happier than as the devoted, forty-year-old employee in Churchill's service that he was now. As Churchill's parliamentary private secretary, Bracken was at once his slavish henchman, financial fixer, fellow drinker, gossip provider and intellectual sparring partner. They argued constantly, sometimes bitterly, but treasured their relationship too much for their differences to become personal. Twenty-six years Bracken's senior, Churchill repaid his loyalty and friendship with trust, access and quasi-fatherly affection (indeed unfounded rumours that Bracken was Churchill's illegitimate son has swirled around them for years).

As Churchill's bullet-proof Humber Pullman swept into Downing Street, Bracken noticed that Churchill's personal bodyguard, Walter Thompson, was at the wheel and not Reg Parker, his usual driver. But he had no time to dwell on this break with custom for a rear door opened from the inside and the Prime Minister's voice bellowed, "Hurry up, Brendan, my train's threatening to be punctual."

As Bracken settled, the front passenger looked over his shoulder and grinned at him. At twenty-six, John 'Jock' Colville was one of Churchill's assistant private secretaries and, like Bracken, a frequent companion.

"Off to Plymouth as well?" Bracken asked Colville.

"Yes. We're picking up Mrs Churchill on the way and the others will join us at Paddington."

"I'm told the damage in Plymouth is worse than reports suggest," Churchill said. "The Luftwaffe's reduced the place to rubble. It's a miracle anyone's still alive. Looks like Liverpool's in for the same treatment. Did you hear about last night?"

Bracken nodded sadly. "Yes, I've got family there."

"Listen," Churchill said as he removed a magazine from a large envelope on his lap. Bracken recognised the Berliner Illustrierte Zeitung, a popular German illustrated magazine. Churchill flipped through it and showed him a photograph. "Taken six weeks ago at the UFA film studios in Babelsberg, just outside Berlin. Recognise anyone apart from Goebbels?"

The photograph showed the Minister of Propaganda smiling for the camera and surrounded by actors and studio employees. Bracken scanned the smiling faces. "Should I?"

"The woman at Goebbels's right shoulder."

Bracken looked closer and felt his throat go dry. The left side of her face was partly hidden by Goebbels, but it was unmistakably Anna Vogel.

Churchill turned curt. "How come a woman you quietly met in London back in—when was it? 1937?—suddenly pops up at Goebbels's side in 1941?"

"How on Earth—?"

"I'll tell you. I had a meeting with Duff Cooper a fortnight ago to find out why the Ministry of Information he runs, which is already the butt of countless jokes, is now dubbed the Ministry of Insemination in some quarters. His response was to throw that German magazine across the table at me and to point out that he at least, unlike his opposite number in Berlin, refrained from surrounding himself with actresses to satisfy his need for attention. When I looked at the girl beside Goebbels, I couldn't help feeling there was something familiar about her."

"You mean you know her?" Bracken asked.

"No, I'd seen another photograph of her, taken in London. As you know, 1937 was a difficult time for me. I was depressed and needed to know who my real friends were. So I pulled a few strings, took a few risks and did what I considered necessary at the time to check the loyalty of a few individuals, including you. Shameful behaviour, but it coincided with your little encounter with Miss Vogel."

Churchill took a large photograph from the same envelope. It showed Bracken and Anna having afternoon tea at the Savoy four years earlier.

Bracken glanced at it and handed it to Colville. "She was a social psychologist whose research in America, especially for the Democratic Party, had come to my attention. I invited her here to see if she might want to work for us."

"Us?" Churchill asked.

"You, me, the Conservative Party, whoever. Our discussion never got to that point. I was worried about your political future and felt we needed new perspectives on voters and the British public's expectations in general."

"Define worried."

"I wasn't getting through to you, Winston. In 1937 nobody was. You were only listening to yourself. You were living in a parallel universe—years ahead in some things, decades behind in others, out of touch with the here and now.

Adrift. I felt that this young woman's approach and attitude might trigger something and help you see things differently, that's all. When she turned down my offer, I put her out of my mind."

Churchill shifted his position to face Bracken. "Out of touch, was I? So unapproachable and remote that you went behind my back for help?"

Bracken nodded at the photograph. "Looks like going behind people's back was something we had in common."

Churchill grinned, winked at Colville and placed a hand on Bracken's arm. "Touché."

"What's your point, Winston?" Bracken asked.

"Have you had any contact with Anna since 1937?"

"None. Before she left, she did say that Goebbels had contacted her as well, but I thought she was optimistic about her chances of making a mark over there, especially as a woman. I assumed Goebbels would pick her brains for a few days and send her back to the States."

Churchill gathered up the magazine and photograph and put them back in his briefcase. "Well four years later she's still in Berlin and still linked in some way to Goebbels. I've asked for a few discreet enquiries to be made over there but it's still not clear what her activities are. What we know for sure is that she lives alone and that is key to what I want you to help me with. Gentlemen, what I'm about to say is confidential. I want no traces of it in any notes, messages or diaries. I don't want Pug, the Prof or Beaverbrook[4] to know about it either."

Colville and Bracken both noticed his eyes welling up.

Churchill's took a deep breath, his voice quavering. "Clemmie's ill. Brain cancer. If she's not operated on urgently and expertly, I'll lose her."

The car slowed for traffic. Colville and Bracken glanced at each other.

"But I spent all evening with her yesterday," Colville protested. "She seemed fine."

Churchill wiped a tear away. "She wasn't fine. She actually had a headache that would have caused anyone else to cancel the engagement, but she carried on. That's the way she is. Her condition makes her so giddy at times and

---

[4] All three men were close to Churchill and frequently in his company. Major General Hastings 'Pug' Ismay acted as go-between between Churchill and military authorities. Frederick 'the Prof' Lindemann advised Churchill on scientific matters. Max Aitken, better known as Lord Beaverbrook, was a newspaper publisher whom Churchill appointed Minister of Aircraft Production because of his skills as an organiser. After Beaverbrook's resignation on 30 April 1941, he briefly became Minister of State, then Minister of Supply.

affects her vision so badly that she can hardly stand up. Our problem is that her tumour's not easy for a surgeon to get at and we don't have anyone in this country who can operate on her. Nor do the Canadians or Americans, apparently. In fact the only man who can do it is a German who lives and works in Berlin. His name's Frank Winter. He's also a fully paid-up member of the Nazi party."

"And you want to bring him here," Bracken murmured.

"My goodness," Colville said, "how would that work?"

Churchill regained his composure. "Obviously we can't expect him to parachute down from a German bomber. Nor can we send him an envelope full of cash and ask him to swim out to one of our destroyers. Nor can we kidnap him, because that would probably backfire. Honestly, gentlemen, I don't know. What I have done is ask someone from the SOE[5] to come up with some ideas. But our biggest challenge will be to persuade a Nazi to do his country's worst enemy, me, a personal favour. The good news is that brain surgeons are a small community who tend to know each other. We've got one here, a surgeon called McCrew, who has actually met Winter. They both studied at Cambridge and if anyone can persuade Winter to come, he's our best bet. He sent me a message 30 minutes ago to say he'd do it. A brave man."

Bracken scratched his head. "What could he possibly use as an argument to persuade Winter? Money?"

"Probably not. Winter's a highly successful professional. McCrew will have to find something else. Another challenge is that McCrew will need somewhere to hide in Berlin and someone to speak up for him at security checks when he moves around. He doesn't speak a word of German. Brendan, this is where your dear friend at the Ministry of Propaganda, Miss Vogel, comes in. We need her to act as McCrew's innkeeper and chaperone in Berlin."

Bracken scoffed. "Why on Earth would she do that? Don't we have other people in Berlin? Professionals, I mean?"

"Of course we do but I can't let this thing go through normal channels. Think about it: day and night, directly and indirectly, I ask the British people to make sacrifices, to think less of themselves and more of their community and country, and to put up with niceties such as food rationing, dead or injured loved ones, an uncertain future and desperately overworked medical

---

[5] Special Operations Executive (SOE). Formed in 1940 the SOE was a secret British organisation dedicated to spying, reconnaissance and sabotage in regions occupied by Germany and other Axis powers.

facilities. Meanwhile I, their pontificating Prime Minister, happily divert precious government resources to ensure my wife gets world-class surgery. And whom does my wife get that surgery from? From the very same people who drop bombs on the cities, houses and children of our citizens every night. Needless to say, some of those houses and children belong to members of our intelligence services. They might be professionals but they're also human beings and they're making sacrifices, too. Which is why I want to keep this operation off the books as much as possible. If anything leaks, our cover story is that we were trying to recruit Miss Vogel as an agent inside Goebbels's Ministry of Propaganda. In reality we only need her to chaperone McCrew."

"We've arrived, Prime Minister," Thompson interrupted as the car slowed to a halt outside a surprisingly white town house.

Colville spoke to Bracken. "Perhaps Vogel could do both: chaperone first, agent later."

Bracken scoffed. "And what does she get in return?"

"Four years is a long time, Brendan," Churchill said. "She might be more than happy to know there's a job waiting for her in Britain after the war. By then, and assuming we win, she'll be one of many looking for an employer willing to ignore her activities in Germany."

"How do I contact her?"

"You don't—at least not directly. The day after tomorrow you and I have an appointment at Chequers with Colin Gubbins of the SOE. Your message to Vogel will go through him and his contact in Berlin. You've got forty-eight hours to come up with something irresistible."

"Is Mrs Churchill aware of any of this?" Colville asked.

"She knows she's got a tumour and will die if she doesn't get an operation. She's unaware of anything we've just talked about and so are my children."

The three men got out and climbed some steps to the front door of the house. Churchill was about to ring the bell when the door opened and Clementine Churchill appeared in a plain grey dress.

"Good evening, dear," Churchill said.

Clementine didn't give Bracken and Colville time to greet her. She extended her right hand towards Bracken. "You must be Mr Bracken. How do you do. I recognised you because Mr Churchill told me about your red hair."

They shook hands. Bracken frowned, unable to understand why Clementine was talking to him as if she'd never met him before and why her accent had switched from English to broad Scottish.

"And you must be Mr Colville," Clementine said to the younger man, who was frowning for the same reasons as Bracken. "How do you do."

"Mrs Churchill," Colville managed, "we had dinner together last night. Don't you remember?"

Churchill chuckled. "Mission accomplished, I think. Gentlemen, may I introduce you to Jenny Macleod. She fooled you both just like she fooled my daughter Mary a few years ago at an event in Glasgow. Mary ran towards her thinking she was Clemmie. That's how Mrs Macleod and I met. I tracked her down to see if she'd stand in for Clemmie at public events whilst she recovers from the operation."

"With my accent, it'll only events where I'm seen and not heard," Jenny said with a grin. "Mr Churchill's daughter in law, Pam, will do the honours at dinners and receptions."

"Pam already does that anyway, as you both know," Churchill said.

"Do you and Mrs Churchill know each other?" Colville asked Jenny.

"No, dear."

Churchill scoffed. "Clemmie doesn't even know of her existence."

"The resemblance is astonishing," Bracken murmured, slowly shaking his head.

Churchill glanced at his watch. "We've got to go. The real Mrs Churchill's waiting for us at Paddington. Brendan, could you take a cab from here back to Downing Street, please?" He took Jenny's hands in his. "Thanks again for doing this."

Jenny smiled. "I must say I'm looking forward to the first time you'll pat my backside thinking it's your wife's. I've never whacked a prime minister before."

Chapter 14

Friday 2 May 1941
Farnborough – Hampshire – England

Group Captain James Firth was used to hearing all sorts of aircraft engines revving, roaring or spluttering outside his office. The noise could be deafening and distracting at times, but it was also a healthy reflection of the RAE's intense research activities spread over dozens of buildings and hangars. The engines he heard now, however, were different. Their deeper, more guttural quality caused him to look up from a pile of weekly activity reports and glance out the window.

What he saw caused him to grab his telephone and dial the flight controller's office.

"Control. Merton speaking."

"Firth. What's the Heinkel doing?"

"No idea, sir. No activity's been scheduled that I know of. I'll find out and call you back."

On his feet now, Firth hung up and pressed his face against the window as the Heinkel He 111 taxied towards the runway. A loud knock resounded.

"Yes?"

Mike Paterson put his head round the door. "Quick word, sir? I think you know the topic."

"What's going on, Paterson? Don't you dare tell me it's Danes. Don't you bloody dare."

"It's Danes, sir. I tried to dissuade him but you know him as well as I do."

"Where's he going?"

The phone rang.

"Firth."

"Control again, sir. I can confirm it's Danes but Christ knows what he's doing. His radio's off. Paterson might know something but he's not answering."

"Paterson's with me. Keep trying to get Danes on the radio." Firth slammed the phone down and glanced at Paterson. "Come with me." He rushed to the door. "Where's he going?"

"No idea but I know what he's doing," Paterson said as they ran along a corridor.

"I'm all ears."

"He's a testing a way to simulate engine trouble."

"What?"

They charged down a flight of stairs.

"He reckons no German pilot or anti-aircraft battery would challenge a German aircraft with smoke pouring out of one of its engines."

"Why should I care?"

"Missions in broad daylight, sir. Not only can the smoke get us closer to targets but we can see them much better for bombing purposes, too. Danes reckons over 95%."

They reached the ground-floor and ran along another corridor.

"To hell with Danes. And where's he going to test this smoke? Don't you dare say Germany, Paterson. Don't you fucking dare."

"He didn't say, sir, but—"

Firth opened a door and sprinted across a driveway on to a vast expanse of grass. Farnborough's runway ran parallel to the driveway, fifty yards away.

"But what, Paterson?"

"I can't think of a better place to test it, sir."

"Shit," Firth shouted as he looked left.

At the other end of the runway, the Heinkel was turning in preparation for take-off.

Firth ran even faster towards the runway. "You helped him set this whole thing up, right? Don't you dare say 'no', Paterson."

Firth slowed on the runway itself. He positioned himself at the centre of it and began to walk towards the Heinkel. Out of breath, Paterson joined him and walked beside him.

"Yes I did, sir," Paterson said.

In the distance, the Heinkel's engines revved up for take-off and began to move towards them.

"He wouldn't mow down his commanding officer and an engineer for the sake of a trail of smoke, would he?" Firth asked.

"I don't know, sir, but he's determined to prove his idea works."

"Wrong, Paterson. Danes is determined to prove that his cock is bigger than mine and that my decision to ground him was misguided."

The Heinkel kept accelerating. Firth and Paterson stayed in its path.

Paterson stared at the approaching mass of metal, especially its two propellers. "Sir, he needs your help to complete the test."

"It's a little late to worry about that, isn't it?"

"Not if you act now, sir. There's a big chance he'll be shot down by an anti-aircraft battery or a fighter when he returns."

"I don't give a damn, Paterson."

"Respectfully, sir, you do. You wouldn't be trying to block him if you didn't care."

The Heinkel gave no sign of slowing. Danes was now recognisable through the greenhouse nose, slowly shaking his head. Paterson wrapped his arms around Firth and pushed him sideways over several yards before they both fell to the ground. The Heinkel roared past them and took off.

Firth was white with fear and anger.

Paterson helped him to his feet. "As I was saying, sir, he needs your help for the return trip. He asked me to ask you to please contact any anti-aircraft or fighter unit that might try to intercept him between the coast and here. He told me he'll aim to cross the coastline between Worthing and Brighton and then follow the South Downs."

"You're finished, Paterson. I'll have you and Danes court-martialled faster than you can say 'trail of smoke'."

"No objection, sir, but would you please make those calls? He'll be back in a couple of hours at most."

"And how are our people supposed to differentiate between a friendly Heinkel 111 and the sort that drops bombs on British cities every night?"

"Smoke colour, sir. Danes will release black smoke over Germany to simulate engine trouble and red smoke as he approaches England to signal his peaceful intentions."

Chapter 15

Friday 2 May 1941
Wanborough – Surrey – England

The short woman—under five feet, McCrew estimated, including whatever heels she was wearing—reached across the desk to shake hands. "Good morning, Mr McCrew, and welcome to Wanborough Manor. I'm Lieutenant Sylvia Rowe of the Special Operations Executive, or SOE." She settled back in her seat and began to read a single sheet of paper. "By the way, that was the last time you heard me refer to you as Mr McCrew and to myself by my Christian name. You'll be Bruno Radke from now on and I'll simply be Lieutenant. All the papers for your new German identity are being forged right now."

McCrew assumed it was acceptable for him to sit down too and did so. He would have liked to be offered a cup of tea but judging by Rowe's clipped tone, piercing brown eyes and stiff demeanour, that was unlikely to happen. She was in her mid-fifties and her shortness contrasted with the size of her hands, the right one of which had just signalled to McCrew via the power of its squeeze that she could crush him on a whim and would probably enjoy it.

Rowe looked up from her reading. "Most trainees stay with us here in Surrey for three weeks of basic training before moving on, assuming they answer our expectations, to learn more demanding or dangerous skills elsewhere. Feel free to explore the building; it's bigger, uglier and cosier than it looks. But don't feel free to strike up friendships with its inhabitants. The less they know about you, the better. I've been given a measly seven days to train you. I will fail, therefore, and so will you. But however much you make a fool of yourself during the coming week and however often I'm tempted to shoot you for the sake of national security, you have already been selected for the mission. You are, it seems, the only individual alive who can pull it off. But that won't stop me treating you as if you have dozens of competitors I could pick from."

She looked at the sheet of paper again and scribbled something in the left-hand margin.

"Do you know what my mission is?" McCrew asked.

"I've been known to answer questions ending with the word 'Lieutenant'."

"Do you know what the mission is, Lieutenant?"

"No. Even Major de Wesselow, who runs this place, has no idea."

McCrew folded his arms. "Then how will you know what to train me on, Lieutenant?"

Rowe lifted the sheet of paper disdainfully by one of its corners. "All I know is that your mission is urban, specifically Berlin, and that you'll be accompanied at all times in public places by a German-speaking local. So I'll be taking you through the rudiments of persuasion, terminal persuasion, daily life in the Third Reich, Berlin geography, uniform and rank recognition, German language and parachuting. As you've never jumped out of an aircraft before, you'll be jumping every afternoon, starting tomorrow. From Tuesday onwards you'll jump every night by moonlight, too. Due to time constraints, we'll assume against my better judgment that your physical fitness is sufficient as it is and that you can both read a map and use a compass. You'll receive no training on advanced map-reading skills or communication technology such as morse code, encryption and radio equipment. You will however be taught how to liaise with one of our agents in Berlin, who will handle messages to and from England for you. You will not be trained on explosives, sabotage or any weapons other than your bare hands."

"Hence terminal persuasion, I imagine."

"I've been known to answer questions ending with the word 'Lieutenant'."

"Apologies. Is that what you meant by terminal persuasion, Lieutenant?"

"Yes. I will be your sole trainer. You and I will be living in each other's pockets—not each other's underwear, I hasten to add—for the next seven days. Unless I decide otherwise, we will speak, breathe, eat, parachute and swear in German at all times. Any notes you take will also be in German. The only word I expect you to say in English and with an English accent is 'Lieutenant'."

McCrew scoffed. "But I don't speak a word of German, Lieutenant."

"Seven days from now you'll be brilliant at the basics, Radke, and with a decent accent, too. Most of your dreams, including the wet ones, and all of your nightmares will also be in German. Now I suggest you go off and get a good night's sleep. You'll find a tray with sandwiches, biscuits and fruit in your room. That's your supper. Be here at six sharp tomorrow morning. We'll have Frühstück together."

"We'll have what together, Lieutenant?"

She made a knife-and-fork gesture. "And one more thing." She stood up, reached across the desk and slapped him.

"Ow!" he yelled.

"Congratulations, that actually sounded German. 'Ouch' would have betrayed you."

Chapter 16

Friday 2 May 1941
Nottuln – Westphalia-North – Germany

The airfield Roddy Danes was looking for appeared farther to his left than expected, its grass runway stretching out surprisingly close to the northernmost houses of the small German town of Nottuln. As Danes circled once above it to make sure it was still disused yet usable, he saw a few faces looking up at the Heinkel He 111 from the streets and gardens.

The flight had gone smoothly. To save time and fuel, and after a heated debate with Paterson, Danes had decided to fly the most direct route possible from Hampshire to the German state of Westphalia-North. This had meant skirting London by the south and dashing east to cross the coastline at the Isle of Sheppey, staying agonisingly low the whole way. His cheek had paid off; nobody had shot at him or chased him. Only when the North Sea opened up below him did Danes breathe his first sigh of relief. Thereafter he'd spotted several German aircraft in the distance along the way, especially over the Dutch coast, but none had shown enough interest in him or his trail of black smoke to take a closer look.

Danes reached up to the additional control panel that Paterson had installed above his head. It consisted of a wooden bar with a row of twelve levers. Nine of these were black and three red, each wired to its own metal smoke canister in the bomb hold behind Danes. Pipes led from the canisters to a shared ventilator system, which in turn pushed the smoke along a larger pipe towards an exit below the left engine. The control panel could be shifted back and forth on a makeshift rail to give Danes access to the standard Heinkel controls above it.

Of the nine black-smoke canisters, he had used up four over the Netherlands and Westphalia-North. Each had lasted twenty minutes, exactly as Paterson had predicted. Danes now switched the lever of the fifth back to the closed position and watched as the last wisps of black smoke trailing from below the left engine disappeared. It took half a minute, also as predicted by Paterson.

Danes made a low pass over the runway to check for any dangerous holes or bumps. Satisfied, he circled back and landed the Heinkel smoothly, glancing regularly towards a low-rise building on his right for any sign of life.

He parked the aircraft so as to keep the building between it and anyone looking in that direction from Nottuln and shut down the engines. After clambering out of his seat and down through the bomb hatch, he stood on the grass and reached back into the aircraft for a foldable two-wheeled trolley. Elated yet numb—the Heinkel's engines had deafened him for well over an hour—he adjusted his Luftwaffe uniform, felt the reassuring bulge of a Walther P38 against his chest and set off at a brisk pace towards the town centre.

"Und jetzt der verrückte kleine Plan,"[6] he murmured.

The trolley squeaked behind him.

---

[6] "And now the crazy little plan."

Chapter 17

Friday 2 May 1941
Atlantic Ocean

"If you don't want a second hole in your arse, leave that hatch shut and get down here right now."

Erster Wachoffizier[7] Ernst Hedner didn't need to look down to know what was going on beneath him. The U-boat's captain, Kapitänleutnant Erich Seidel, was looking up at an unmissable target and pointing his Walther P38 at it.

Hedner opened the hatch anyway and cold North Atlantic air rushed into the submarine's conning tower. In less than a minute its smell would reach every man on board, an event which under normal circumstances would have lifted their spirits. In this case they barely noticed it. They had a face-off between U-693's[8] two highest ranking officers to worry about.

In the confined space of the conning tower, the noise of the shot sounded, indeed felt like twin hammers hitting Hedner's head. The bullet somehow missed the lower parts of his body and went clean through his right arm, travelling vertically through the open hatch. Deafened but not yet in pain, Hedner climbed down and faced the captain.

---

[7] First Officer
[8] This was Germany's identification system for submarines. The U stood for Unterseebot or U-boat (submarine). In order to hide the number of U-boats in service, the authorities didn't always number them in sequence.

Seidel held the Walther close to his body, its nozzle aimed at his second-in-command's chest. "The second bullet will do much more damage."

An amplified voice resounded through the hatch. It spoke German with an English accent. "Surrender immediately and you will come to no harm. Abandon ship now, all arms above your heads."

Bullshit," Seidel muttered at Hedner. "Those British wankers will extract your fingernails so slowly during questioning that you'll confess you sucked Hitler's dick at art school in Vienna and enjoyed it more than he did. Do I need to remind you what we're fighting for, Eins W.O.[9] Hedner? We're Germans. Our Fatherland is a sacred reason in itself to sacrifice our lives. We have a duty to do so. There isn't a man on this ship who wouldn't prefer to drown rather than surrender."

"You're wrong, Herr Kaleun[10]. The British might be wankers but they're not torturers. Our duty is to destroy the encryption material and sacrifice the boat, not to commit collective suicide. And that's what we'll do. We'll quietly slip the Enigma and codebooks into the water during our surrender. I agree that you have a reason to sacrifice your life, but it has nothing to do with the Fatherland. The rest of us would rather live, thank you very much."

The U-boat lurched.

Hedner pressed a hand on his wound. "Dying here would suit you fine, wouldn't it. You and all the witnesses to what really happened on 7 March 1941 would conveniently disappear."

"What's that supposed to mean?"

"Oh, the reports might still be secret and they might not all give the same explanation, but the facts are clear enough. We were diverted from our course to help Gunther Prien's U-47, Otto Kretschmer's U-99 and other boats in a joint attack on a convoy. During that engagement and over protests from your officers, including myself, you ordered a torpedo to be fired at a converted whaling factory ship, the Tirje Viken, knowing full well Prien's U-47 was on the other side of it. You argued that the Tirje Viken was so big we couldn't miss it, even in bad weather. In reality you wanted Goebbels's propaganda to put your name up there in bright lights as a U-boat saviour of the Third Reich. The inevitable happened: the torpedo either went straight through the whaler's hull and hit Prien on the other side or it just missed the

---

[9] "Eins W.O. (pronounced "Eye-ns Veh Oh") is an abbreviation of "Erster Wachoffizier", meaning First Officer
[10] "Herr Kaleun" is a common abbreviation of the German navy's rank of Kapitänleutnant, equivalent to Lieutenant in the Royal Navy and US Navy.

whaler and hit Prien directly. Either way, Prien's radio signals went dead and U-47 was never seen or heard of again.

"One of Germany's true U-boat heroes was needlessly killed that day along with his entire 45-man complement. And you did the killing. Luckily for you, all the reports suggest other explanations. Some believe a depth charge sank him. Kretschmer thinks Prien might have been sunk himself when one of his own torpedoes circled back on him. You and I know better. For your fatal mistake to remain a secret, however, you needed the loyalty of your crew members. If one of them opened his mouth, you were done for. In return, would it have been too much to expect of a commanding officer in that situation that he take extra special care of his men? That he not be an obstacle to the odd commendation, promotion or favour here and there? Not in your case. Instead you tried to get the youngest and most vulnerable of your crewmen into bed during shore leave – remember a kid called Heinrich Nunst, Herr Kaleun? – and threatened to destroy their careers if they refused."

"I don't know what you're talking about."

"You have one minute to surrender or we'll open fire," shouted the amplified voice.

"Oh yes you do, Herr Kaleun," Hedner continued. "At some point, however, you began to realise that treating your men like shit was a second fatal mistake. You realised that sooner or later that the right information about Prien's sinking would reach the right people and a proper investigation would be launched. You realised that kids like Heinrich Nunst couldn't be kept quiet forever. So what better way to save your reputation than to die with an entire crew of embarrassing witnesses in a blaze of sacrificial glory?"

Seidel lifted the pistol. "You can't prove anything."

"I don't need proof in your case, just three clues. The first is your pistol pointing at me. The second is the fact Heinrich Nunst committed suicide two weeks ago when he heard that his transfer request had been denied and that he'd have to sail with you again. The third is that there are four dozen crew members on this boat and that you don't have that many bullets in your pistol. If you shoot me again, someone else will stop the massacre. You're finished, Seidel.

Seidel stared at Hedner a few seconds longer before raising the pistol to his right temple. He pulled the trigger. As the bullet exited his skull, it smashed a depth gauge.

Chapter 18

Friday 2 May 1941
Nottuln – Westphalia-North – Germany

The pigeons pecking at imaginary crumbs on Nottuln's Kirchplatz took no notice of the Luftwaffe pilot walking briskly past them with a trolley.

The Zur Sonne beer hall was larger on the inside than its outside appearance suggested. Its size was out of proportion with Nottuln's diminished wartime population and amplified even more by the vast leafy beer garden at the back. A century of tobacco smoke had darkened the wooden interior to a shade which, in any other public building, would have seemed more sinister than authentic but which the locals, even the sober ones, somehow found welcoming.

The owner looked up from his newspaper as Roddy Danes entered. His grey beard was carefully trimmed to ensure its tip didn't rest horizontally on his enormous belly. "Tag."

"Guten Tag," Danes said with a broad smile, relieved to note that all the other lunchtime customers, a dozen that he could see through the windows, were sitting outside. "Pils, please. Small."

The owner positioned a glass under a beer tap. "What brings a Bavarian pilot to this area?"

Danes had lived in Munich as a child for a few years in the 1920s. As the deadliness of the post-war pandemic of Spanish Flu had waned, his parents, both English teachers, had moved to the Bavarian capital to co-found a language school. Political and economic instability had soon got the better of them, driving them back to the United Kingdom in 1923. The experience had left their son fluent in a mix of standard German and Bavarian dialect.

"Are you Helmut Ammann?" Danes asked.

"Yes."

"Believe it or not, I've just landed at your little airfield."

Ammann arched an eyebrow. "No one's done that for a while. Is there a problem?"

"I'm taking a Heinkel 111 to Dortmund for urgent maintenance, but I couldn't resist the temptation to stop off. You don't know this, sir, but you're a hero to someone I know."

"Really?"

"He's a pilot like me. His name's Dominik Dissinger but that probably doesn't mean much to you. Before the war he was a salesman who drove through here from time to time on business. He always stopped by because of your beer. You brew it yourself, right?"

"Yes I do, with my wife and two sons. The war restrictions don't make things easy for us but I haven't been forced to stop yet. Here, try it."

Danes did and nodded his approval. "Herr Ammann, I'd like to surprise Dissinger tomorrow by arriving with a barrel of your beer."

Ammann's eyes widened. "So you landed in that field just to buy beer off me?"

"No, Herr Ammann. I landed in that field to put a smile back on my friend's face. Two months ago his older brother was sunk by the Brits near Iceland. U-boat U551. Dominik hasn't been the same man since. He needs a reason to smile, believe me." Danes produced a wad of Reichsmarks from inside his uniform. "Your price will be mine. Don't forget to include the cost of the barrel itself. I can't guarantee you'll see it again. I'll also need a fitting for the tap."

Ammann began to shake his head. "Listen, I'm flattered by what you're doing but I promised my father before he died that I'd never allow our beer to be sold outside Nottuln. Customers must come to our beer, he said. Our beer mustn't go to them."

Danes emptied his glass and put it down. "I respect that. But you said you had two sons. Why did Dissinger tell me you had three?"

"He didn't tell you that. I don't believe you."

Danes smiled. "You're right, he didn't. I simply counted the people on your family photograph by the entrance. But there are three boys on it, not two."

Ammann fidgeted impatiently. "Joerg was killed in the Atlantic as well."

"U-boat?"

"No. Now if you don't mind, I'll—"

"Herr Ammann, you promised your father that you'd always make customers come here to taste your beer. How does that promise work for customers who would have loved to come but can't because the war has either crippled or killed them?"

Ammann stopped fidgeting and waited.

Danes placed both his hands flat on the bar. "It's my turn to promise you something. Tomorrow my friends and I will take Dissinger out for a drink and toast the memory of his brother. But I will ask everyone also to toast the memory of your son Joerg and your late father. And they'll do so unquestioningly because if it's important to me, it's important to them. That's the way our friendship works. Obviously we'll toast those three men with the glasses we're holding, regardless of what's in them. But it would put a lot of smiles on a lot of faces, especially Dissinger's and mine, if our glasses could contain beer made by you."

Chapter 19

Friday 2 May 1941
Berlin – Germany

Tina Winter sat in her living room waiting for the sound of her husband's key in the front door. The time he'd take to find the hole would be a reliable indicator of what she could expect next. The longer he took, the drunker he was and, ironically enough, the safer she would be. He was only violent when he'd had less to drink and was still in control.

The first time Frank's hands had struck her was after an event where, yet another irony, those same hands had been publicly praised for the exquisite precision of their surgical work. In the car on the way home, he'd suddenly turned on her. "Enjoyed that, did you?"

"Enjoyed what? Keep your eye on the road."

"I saw your expression when they talked about my hands."

"Would you have preferred me to laugh?"

The car jolted to a halt. He would have slapped her on the cheek if she hadn't shifted her head to avoid it. His hand swiped her face instead and clipped her nose. Without a sound, she moved to get out but he accelerated.

"Stop the car right now, Frank." She touched her nose and inspected her fingers, checking for blood, finding none.

"We've got some talking to do."

"That didn't feel like words, Frank. Stop the car. I want to get out."

Glancing at her face, he became apologetic. "Sorry, I didn't want to do that. You're not bleeding."

"Oh, wonderful. Should I feel relieved?"

That was two years ago. June 1939.

"If you let the first time go by," a friend with bruised arms had told her three days later, "a seed is sown in a man's mind, a seed telling him he can beat up his wife and get away with it. If the seed isn't destroyed or removed immediately, it grows."

"Destroyed or removed by whom?" Tina had scoffed. "The police? They're too busy beating up Jews and communists to take any notice of a beaten up wife."

For three hours after the first slap, Tina had refused to listen to Frank's apologies. She'd then relented, more out of tiredness than an urge to forgive, let alone forget. Then she'd found it difficult to stop him kissing her nose and then the rest of her face and then her neck and then her shoulders and then pretty much everywhere she liked to be kissed and everything had been fine between them again, heavenly actually, for two weeks, until he spotted her smirking again when someone mentioned his hands.

Now she could hear him fumbling with his keys outside the front door. The tip of one of them tapped the area around the keyhole several times before slotting in. Drunk, she concluded. She'd be safe for a few hours this evening at least, hopefully all night, too.

Chapter 20

Friday 2 May 1941
Farnborough – Hampshire – England

Squadron Leader James Firth cleared his throat and straightened in his chair. "Summing up, sir, I recommend that Flight Lieutenant Roddy Danes be banned immediately from the entire Farnborough campus, including the airfield and the Royal Aircraft Establishment. Despite being grounded, the man has shown yet again that he's a danger to the public and to himself. As you know, though, my group answers to both yourself representing the War Office and myself representing the Royal Air Force. Danes's fate thus depends on both our decisions. I think you should be aware, sir, that whatever you decide from the War Office's perspective, my own report to the Royal Air Force will recommend stiff disciplinary action. Danes will probably be kicked out of the RAF and either locked up for gross negligence or transferred to a menial ground job."

Sitting across the desk from Firth, William Farren, director of the Royal Aircraft Establishment, cleaned his wire-rimmed glasses with an over-sized handkerchief as he listened. Just shy of fifty, he'd taken over at the RAE earlier in the year and devoted much of his considerable energy to ironing out inter-departmental rivalries. He had mostly succeeded but his relations with the RAF in general and Firth in particular remained a challenge.

"Is Danes even back from his flight yet, Major?" Farren asked brusquely. "Can't you wait for him to land before burying him?"

"This case requires immediate action, sir. I've managed to arrange for an air corridor up from the coast, so he shouldn't be shot. But he's still exposed.

If a stray fighter spots him, he'll be in trouble. Heinkel 111s aren't exactly famous for their agility."

"Look, Firth, I can see why Danes pisses everyone off and I can understand why the RAF would want disciplinary action. But I also believe that if you put a man in charge of something, you should give him full power and all means necessary to do the job. With all due respect, I don't think you've ever given Danes that kind of power and that's why we're both sitting in my office right now trying to deal with the consequences."

Firth opened his mouth to speak, but Farren raised a hand to interrupt him.

"When Danes gets back, send him here. I'll make a decision from the War Office's perspective afterwards."

"But sir, we've got hundreds of people working here. We can't let them all do what they want."

"I beg to differ," Farren said tersely. "Your starting position with people is to shut all doors to them and open only the ones they need. Mine is to open all doors, closing only the ones I must. If you start with all doors closed in a research centre like this, you might as well close the place itself. So please send Danes here as soon as he lands. I want to see him alone."

Firth stood up. "Yes, sir. Thank you."

As he closed Farren's door, a voice called out from the end of the corridor.

"Sir?" It was Mike Paterson.

Firth moved towards him. "Is he back yet?"

Paterson's voice was trembling. "I don't know but an urgent meeting's been called about him in room 14. They're waiting for both of us."

"Who called the meeting? Why?"

"I haven't had time to find out. I was asked to find you and take you there. It sounds serious."

They charged down a flight of stairs to the first floor and along another corridor. When they reached room 14, Paterson stood back as Firth knocked and entered without waiting for a response.

"Surprise!" the room roared.

Some thirty of Firth's colleagues and subordinates were standing in a half-circle facing him, all of them holding well-filled glasses. Those standing in the centre parted to reveal Roddy Danes, still wearing a German pilot's uniform. Firth turned with a raised eyebrow to Paterson.

Paterson grinned. "Apologies, sir."

Danes stepped towards Firth. The room went silent. "Six months ago, sir, you put a question to me in this very same building. What would I accept, you asked, as proof that the war had truly ended? If my memory serves me correctly, I answered that the day a complete stranger said 'Guten Tag' to me and I didn't immediately reach for my gun, the war could be considered over."

A few people clapped. Firth remained expressionless.

"Then I turned the question back on you," Danes continued. "What would *you* accept, sir, as proof that the war had truly ended? You thought about it for a second and said this: the day I'll be able to return to the village of Nottuln in Westphalia, Germany, and have a glass of beer made personally by Herr Helmut Ammann, owner of the Zur Sonne beer house, I'll know the war is truly over."

A bald man stepped forwards and handed two glasses of beer to Danes, who in turn handed one to Firth.

Danes raised his glass and looked around the room. "What I saw as I looked down on Germany from a Heinkel 111 today was proof that this war is not over yet. But what I purchased from the boss of the Zur Sonne beer house in Nottuln was proof that we have at least one good reason to end this war as quickly as possible. That reason tastes incredible, it's in the glass you're holding right now and it was made by Herr Helmut Ammann himself. Your very good health, sir, and happy birthday."

"Happy birthday!" yelled the room.

Firth moved closer to Danes as conversations resumed around them. He smiled and lowered his voice. "You've got style, Danes, I'll grant you that. But this isn't over. Drink up because Farren wants to see you right now. Assuming he doesn't ban you indefinitely from this whole complex, I'll see you in my office on Monday at eight. And don't expect congratulations or gratitude."

William Farren stood up and walked round his desk to shake hands with Danes. "How were the smoke-filled skies of Germany?" He gestured towards his own seat. "Please make yourself comfortable. I'll do some nervous pacing."

Danes sat down hesitatingly. "I'm familiar with this, er, trick, sir. Now that I'm in your seat, you're going to ask me what I'd do in your position with a loose cannon like me."

Farren began to pace. "I might be the director of the Royal Aircraft Establishment, but I'm an engineer first and foremost. That means I can be a tricky chap at times but I don't play tricks. I'm practical."

"Apologies, sir."

"I asked you to sit in that chair for a practical reason. Are you comfortable?"

"Yes."

"Then it's yours. I hate the damn thing. I'll have it sent to your office as soon as my new one arrives. Tuesday, I hope."

Danes smiled. "Thank you, sir. I'm not an office man, myself but I'm sure I'll enjoy it for paperwork. Unless of course the chair's your goodbye present to me."

Farren ignored the remark. "You're in office 31."

"No, sir, that's my boss, Major Firth. I'm in 33."

"It wasn't a question, Danes. You're in office 31. Or rather you will be as of Tuesday, if you so wish. Firth is being transferred. Monday's his last day."

Danes blinked.

Farren stopped pacing to face him. "It's no secret to anyone that he and I have never agreed on a practical definition of the word 'teamwork'. That's why I made a formal request to the RAF a month ago for him to be put elsewhere. Although it's none of my business to recommend a replacement, strictly speaking, I did in this case and your name is the one I put forward. I'll break the news to Firth on Monday afternoon. I was going to do so today but it's his birthday apparently."

"So he doesn't know yet?"

"How to put it…" Farren searched for his words as his pacing resumed. "Let's say that the shorter the notice he gets, the less time he'll have to spread even more ill will throughout the organisation. Interestingly, the RAF hasn't objected to my request in any way, shape or form. I rather suspect they only sent Firth here in the first place to get rid of him."

Danes smiled. "If the RAF's okay with it, I'd be honoured to accept the position, sir."

"Glad to hear it."

Danes stood up and they shook hands.

Farren put his left hand on Danes's shoulder. "I want to give you and your team the responsibility and freedom that Firth spent too much of his time taking away from you. What I ask for in return is full information. I want any idea you bounce around, however crazy, to bounce at least once off me before it bounces anywhere else, especially on German-occupied territory. Is that clear?"

"Yes, sir."

"One more thing. Does your smoking-engine idea work?"

"Technically, yes. But I can't confirm the Germans are fooled by it because no one got close enough to me to challenge me."

Farren nodded. "I like that answer. It shows humility. Many pilots I know would have used their safe return from Germany as proof of concept in itself, carefully omitting to point out that no German actually saw the concept. Not you. Do you mind if I talk about it to someone who might be able to use it?"

"Not at all, sir."

Chapter 21

Saturday 3 May 1941
Chequers - Buckinghamshire – England

Forty miles west of Central London, surrounded by 1500 acres of heavily guarded grounds, Chequers was the British Prime Minister's official country residence. Its off-red brickwork housed enough precious works of art for a museum but somehow managed not to feel like one. Its ten bedrooms had welcomed numerous honoured guests of the state and its halls had eavesdropped on their secrets and concessions.

Colin Gubbins stood in the Grand Hall, pretending to be interested in the portraits on display above him whilst congratulating himself on his newfound reserves of patience. Churchill was thirty minutes late and counting. Gubbins would have preferred to invest the time in details of an imminent mission to blow up an electrical transformer station in Pessac, near Bordeaux, France.

"Gubbins!" Churchill exclaimed as he strode into the room with Brendan Bracken.

"Good morning, Prime Minister."

"Somehow you got caught in the crossfire between my wife wasting my favourite honey on some obscure project of hers and a radio broadcast to our Polish friends that I'm still trying to finalise. Have you met Brendan Bracken, my parliamentary private secretary? Brendan, this is Brigadier Colin Gubbins of the Special Operations Executive. Everything this Scotsman does is dubious, deniable, dangerous and behind enemy lines, a description which arguably applies to his visit here this morning as well."

Bracken and Gubbins shook hands. They settled in absurdly uncomfortable armchairs in one corner of the hall.

"But the most dangerous thing he does is in this country and he does it with frightening regularity," Churchill went on cheerfully. "He puts women in positions of power. As a result there isn't a man in our government or armed forces who doesn't think he's a madman or some kind of traitor." He turned to Gubbins. "Who knows you're here?"

"One trusted colleague and my boss, Hugh Dalton."

"What about MI6[11]? Won't you be needing their help in Berlin for messaging?"

Gubbins cleared his throat. "You asked for this to be kept quiet, sir. So I thought it preferable to leave MI6 out of it."

Bracken scoffed. "Are you suggesting MI6 can't keep their mouths shut?"

"Not at all. I don't think you need me to remind you that government departments and entities of all kinds spend as much time fighting each other as they do fighting the Germans. The last thing we want is for a sensitive operation like this one to start a turf war."

"You're right, Gubbins," Churchill said. "The last thing turf wars are is quiet."

"Then how will McCrew communicate with us?"

"What Gubbins is probably trying to say is that the SOE has an agent in Berlin with a radio transmitter that MI6 doesn't know about. Something of that order, Gubbins?"

"Yes, Prime Minister."

Churchill lit a cigar. "And how's our dear Doctor McCrew settling in to his training at Wanborough? Shock of his life, I imagine."

"Too early to say, I'm afraid. I'll hear how he's doing when I get back to London." Gubbins turned to Bracken. "The most urgent matter for now is this person you want as his chaperone in Berlin, Miss Vogel. The way it works is that our agent will briefly make contact with her in a public setting, ideally tomorrow morning. His objective is to set up a second meeting somewhere else, ideally tomorrow afternoon, where he can explain your plan to her. What I need from you right now is a few words the agent can use during the first contact, something he can say to her in passing that she will associate unmistakably with you and will get her attention. It should make her curious enough to attend the second meeting yet keep her self-confident enough to

---

[11] MI6, which stands for "Military Intelligence, Section 6", is an alternative and more widely used name for the United Kingdom's Secret Intelligence Service (SIS). MI6 gathers and analyses overseas intelligence.

turn up without SS bodyguards. We'll be sending the message to Berlin this evening."

Bracken shifted uneasily. "I've given it some thought but I—"

There was a knock and Jock Colville appeared in the doorway. "Sorry to butt in, gentlemen. Prime Minister, the new draft for the broadcast is ready if you'd like to take a look."

"Ah, yes," Churchill said. "Excuse me. I'll be back in a few minutes."

Gubbins waited for him to leave the room. "May I speak openly?"

"Of course," Bracken said.

"My job is to organise some of the most dangerous missions imaginable. Call them dirty tricks, ungentlemanly warfare or whatever you like, their chances of success are rarely better than marginal. Which is why I'm a pragmatist. Which is why my colleagues and I rely on skilled professionals at every turn, the best. We train them for months. And we keep on training them. We train them on details. We train them to understand that the difference between success and failure, between life and death, is one inch, one second, one ounce or one word. Now this little caper of yours in Berlin, which I won't dignify by calling it a mission or an operation, hinges on two individuals who might be experts in their respective fields, one a surgeon and the other a propaganda expert, but who are complete amateurs in mine. They can't even spell the word 'details', let alone apply it. To make matters worse, they've never met but are expected to work together as experienced infiltration operatives. With all the optimism I can muster, Mr Bracken, their chances of success are zero."

Bracken folded his arms. "If we don't try, Mrs Churchill's chances of dying are 100%."

Gubbins was struggling to keep his composure. "What are Mrs Churchill's chances of survival if she's operated on?"

Bracken stroked his chin, deep in thought.

"Well?"

"McCrew reckons her chances of a full recovery are 20%."

"At best or at worst?"

Bracken shrugged.

"Is she aware all this is being planned?"

"No, not yet. Churchill will tell her when everything's organised."

Gubbins crossed his legs. "So we're putting the lives of a British agent in Berlin, a British brain surgeon and the British aircrew flying him to Germany at mortal risk for a medical operation with a higher than 80% chance of failure. Am I seeing things clearly?"

Bracken closed his eyes and turned his face upwards for inspiration. Gubbins waited.

"No you're not seeing things clearly, Brigadier. What no one's saying out loud is that this mission or caper as you call it is about the Prime Minister. It's about protecting one exceptional man's ability to lead this country to victory. I know him well. If his wife dies or ends up a vegetable, he'll lose that ability. Simple as that. Or he'll end up so diminished for so long that someone will need to step in. Would you care to name that replacement, Brigadier? Can you think of a single individual in this country who could step into Churchill's shoes and do the job half as well? I certainly can't. Which is why I'm a pragmatist as well, Brigadier."

Gubbins stared at the floor. "Liverpool was bombed again last night. A childhood friend of mine lives there with his wife and two children. I've had news they were hit and that he and wife were killed. I don't know about the children but I do know they were at home with their parents last night. What I can't help imagining, Mr Bracken, is those two children not getting the top-quality medical attention they deserve. I can't help imagining them being pulled out of the rubble dead or with awful injuries. I can't help imagining them being assessed by an overrun doctor without enough staff or equipment. I can't help imagining him glancing at everybody and having to decide in seconds flat who gets first priority." He held Bracken's gaze. "The Prime Minister doesn't have to imagine such things for his wife, does he."

"Is that you, Mr Gubbins?" a female voice asked from the other end of the room.

They both leapt to their feet.

Tall and pale, Clementine Churchill looked older than fifty-six as she moved towards Gubbins with her right hand outstretched. "Winston told me you'd be dropping by but wouldn't be staying for lunch, is that correct?"

"A prior engagement, unfortunately. But I'm delighted to see you again, Mrs Churchill."

"How's your health? You're awfully pale compared to last time." She hadn't let go of his hand.

"A little strain, perhaps. I'd love to tell you I'm due for a holiday but sadly I'm not."

"I'm sorry about your friends in Liverpool. What a tragedy. Winston and I are still devastated by what we saw in Plymouth."

Gubbins frowned. "Forgive me but how did you know about my friends?"

"Winston knows everything about everyone. I heard him asking about your friend on the phone a few minutes ago." She looked from one man to the other. "Didn't Winston explain why he arrived late?"

Gubbins cleared his throat and glanced at Bracken. "He said something about his favourite honey and a broadcast to Poland."

Clementine rolled her eyes. "Rubbish. The honey incident happened much earlier this morning and Jock's been writing most of the broadcast speech, not Winston. No, he was late because he was on the phone to Liverpool enquiring about your friends. Mr and Mrs Furley, correct?"

"Foley."

"Well whoever he was on the phone to in Liverpool told him that Mr Foley and his wife had passed away but that the girls were alive. Injured but alive."

Gubbins gasped.

Clementine placed a hand on his arm. "Nothing life-threatening, don't worry. Winston told them in no uncertain terms that he expects an update on those children's condition every six hours." She turned imploringly to Bracken. "Didn't he tell you all this?"

Bracken shook his head.

"Back again," Churchill announced as he walked into the room. "I think we've finally nailed my speech. Ah, Clemmie, Brigadier Gubbins won't be staying for lunch."

"You've already told me that, dear." Clementine patted Gubbins's hand. "Will you be all right, Mr Gubbins? Need a stiff drink?"

Gubbins was staring in bewilderment at Churchill. "No thanks, I'll be fine," he managed.

"Then I'll leave you gentlemen to it." She smiled at Bracken and left.

They all sat down again.

"Where were we?" Churchill asked.

Bracken scratched his head. "We were talking about what our agent in Berlin could say to Anna Vogel to get her attention. I'm a little stuck because it was four years ago."

Gubbins leaned towards him. "Don't try to remember what you said. Try to think of something *she* said and that she'd be pleased to note you remembered. An unusual fact, perhaps? A warning? A number?"

Gubbins and Churchill watched in silence as Bracken stood up and began to pace.

"She gave me a piece of advice," he said at last. "She recommended that I be less naïve."

Churchill laughed. "I'll bet that hit a raw nerve. How perceptive of her. You really must introduce me to this Anna Vogel woman, Brendan."

Gubbins ignored the Prime Minister. "So if our agent uses the words 'less naïve' in some way in her presence, she's highly likely to think of you."

"I think so."

"What did she want you to be less naïve about?" Churchill asked cheerfully.

Bracken stared at him. "Have a guess."

Chapter 22

Saturday 3 May 1941
Lanke – March Brandenburg – Germany

"Are you Jewish, Krost? Joseph Goebbels asked.

The eleven young faces around the table, including a blushing Frank Krost, watched him in silence. This was the third and final day of their retreat with the Minister of Propaganda[12] at his country home. Anna Vogel was sitting to one side of the room, just inside the door.

"No, Herr Reichsminister."

"Because if you were, I'd consider using your excellent question as an excuse to send you for a couple of weeks of meditation and fasting at the nearest concentration camp." He held Krost's gaze for a few seconds, then smiled. "No, I don't have an answer. Thank God the Third Reich hasn't made ignorance illegal yet, especially mine."

Everyone laughed.

Goebbels glanced at his watch. "Before we go for breakfast, I'd like to bring up a subject I've deliberately avoided so far because I wanted us to spend three days together first. Based on our discussions, what are the golden rules we always try to follow in our work? I say 'try' because the ministry doesn't decide alone what should be said or not to the German public. Nor does it always decide when, where and how. My own opinion carries enormous weight, of course, but what the government says is discussed much

---

[12] Joseph Goebbels's full title was Minister of Public Enlightenment and Propaganda.

more than people imagine Opinions differ, sometimes extremely so. The Führer sets the direction of what we do but even the clearest direction is open to interpretation. A single word can trigger hours, sometimes days of debate before the message containing it reaches the public, who will in turn interpret it in multiple ways anyway."

Joseph Himer raised a hand. "The golden rule I've noticed so far is consistency."

"Between what and what?"

"Between our messages. We can't say blue's the best option one day and yellow's the best the next."

"That's why we must keep on repeating that blue's the best option until it becomes the truth," Lutz Reinhardt said.

Helga Kerrl raised a hand. "But what if yellow objectively evolves to become a clearly better option? We'd look stupid, obstinate or old-fashioned if we refused to change our mind."

"In that case," Lutz Reinhardt said, "we must simply deny we ever said blue was the best option and shoot anybody who presents evidence to the contrary. Then we keep on repeating that yellow's the best option until it becomes the truth."

More laughter. Goebbels turned to Anna and winked at her.

Anna raised her hand. "May I say something?"

Goebbels smiled. "Of course, Fräulein."

Anna stood up and positioned herself next to Goebbels. "Consistency is a fundamental human need. Indeed we spend most of our lives checking that thoughts, behaviours and events are consistent with each other and that the world is consistent with our expectations. What is National-Socialism? It's a set of expectations. And a lot of people, including us here, spend a lot of time working to ensure Germany and its people are consistent with those expectations."

"Our prisons and concentration camps exist for that same purpose," Goebbels added. "To ensure consistency between National Socialist expectations and National Socialist reality."

"And how do we at the Ministry of Public Enlightenment and Propaganda contribute to that effort?" Anna asked. "By ensuring, for example, that our propaganda messages are consistent with each other, that we don't say blue one day and yellow the next. If we fail to do that, we lose credibility with whoever we're talking to."

"Can anyone tell me what happened to a British ship called the Athenia in September 1939?" Goebbels asked.

The participants looked at each other.

"Is that the one the British sank on purpose so that they could accuse us of doing so?"

"Exactly. There were one thousand women and children on the Athenia. When it exploded and sank the British accused us of being cold-blooded monsters. We denied having anything to do with such an appalling act, of course, but the British stuck by their accusation. So we ran an investigation and ended up proving that the British had, on Churchill's orders, placed a bomb on the ship. They'd sunk it on purpose and killed all those women and children so they could accuse us of doing so. Can you imagine such callousness?"

There were gasps around the table. Goebbels drummed the table-top.

"In reality the Athenia was sunk by one of our U-boats, the U-30," he said quietly. "By the time the captain returned to port and reported what he'd done, we had already denied being the culprits. It was too late to change our story and apologise. We'd have looked like liars and murderers. So I personally invented the story about the British putting a bomb on board themselves and published it all over Germany. That, my young friends, is how important consistency is to us."

There was tense silence.

"Another major challenge to our consistency was the Non-Aggression Pact we suddenly signed with the Soviets two years ago, in 1939. It followed years of virulent anti-Soviet propaganda which had been orchestrated and often written by myself. How could we possibly get the German public to believe in such a reversal? By making it consistent with something else. In this case we explained that Germany and the Soviet Union were simply reverting to traditional cooperation our nations used to enjoy and that this was what many Germans wanted anyway."

"Of course there are less extreme situations," Anna said, "where our messages have to be tweaked or even reversed to reflect a changing reality. From time to time we simply must be inconsistent. So the trick or golden rule is not to offer rigid consistency between our messages, but to offer people consistency between our altered messages *and something else they care about—something they recognise and value* unquestioningly. Public safety in an emergency, for example. Or national security in the face of a foreign threat."

Goebbels raised an index finger and grinned. "Never underestimate our Ministry's ability to produce an emergency or a foreign threat out of thin air, especially to cover an inconsistency in our messages."

A few titters greeted this.

"If our messages can't answer people's fundamental need for consistency," Anna continued, "they must answer other fundamental needs.

If they fail to do that, the German people will not only reject our messages but in the privacy of their own minds they'll reject us, too.

"The question is," Goebbels said, "what are people's other fundamental human needs? Identify those and you'll identify the golden rules of our propaganda."

Four hands shot up.

Goebbels licked his lips. "A word of warning. If one of you says food, sex or beer, I'll throw you in the lake up the road."

The four hands were lowered. The room laughed again.

"We're looking for three fundamental human needs. Consistency's the first. What are the other two? Think about it over breakfast. Back here in one hour, please." He turned to Anna. "Will you join me, Fräulein?"

As the eleven participants headed off to a neighbouring dining room, Anna followed Goebbels to his office, where a small breakfast table for two was laid. One of her two joys in having regular working breakfasts with Goebbels was the quality of his coffee. The other was his black cherry jam, which he refused to reveal the source of.

"This jam could be used as a torture method," she said. "Threaten to deprive me of it and I'd confess to the Reichstag fire[13]."

Goebbels smiled absent-mindedly but she could tell he wasn't really listening. Nor, she noticed, was he eating.

"Joseph, may I make a personal comment?"

The Minister had asked her to call him by his first name three years previously, in 1938, albeit only in private meetings. That he should do so had been a goal of hers for several months. Her opportunity came when she walked into a supposedly empty office at the Ministry to fetch a chair and found Goebbels sitting in a corner, smoking and weeping. He ordered her to leave and she said she'd do so but only if he let take him through back corridors to an office he could lock to weep in peace. By the time they got there and she supplied him with an extra handkerchief, she knew she'd no longer need to leave. She sat with him as he explained in astonishing detail that his heart was broken. Hitler had just forced him to break off an extramarital and badly hidden affair with Lida Baarová, a Czech-Austrian actress. Listening to him, Anna didn't know whether to feel privileged,

---

[13] The Reichstag (German parliament, Berlin) was severely damaged in an arson attack on 27 February 1933, one month after Adolf Hitler became Chancellor. A Dutch communist was found guilty of the attack and executed (his actual guilt is still disputed). The Nazi government used the attack as an excuse to ban political opposition and curtail citizens' rights, installing a dictatorship.

worried or both. Goebbels rarely displayed emotion at the Ministry and might not like the thought of an employee having seen him lose his composure. At the end of their unplanned meeting, however, he simply thanked her, insisting that they have coffee together on a regular basis from that day on. To her surprise this happened and he asked her to call him Joseph on the first such occasion.

"Of course," Goebbels murmured.

"You've changed over the last few weeks. You seem worried. Whatever it is that's on your mind, it's showing."

Goebbels snapped out of his reverie. "Please forgive me. Is it that visible?"

"I even overheard two of our young employees discussing it during a break the day before yesterday. Is there anything I can help you with?"

Goebbels seemed about to answer but the phone rang. "Excuse me."

Anna watched him limp across the room to his desk to pick up the receiver. She poured more coffee.

"Goebbels... Good morning, Norbert... No, not at all... Tell me... Him too?... That's three out of five. What about the other two?... I see... Keep me informed if you find anything else... No, nothing suspicious at my end... Everyone who's anyone in the UK seems to be in fine form... Churchill and his wife were in Plymouth yesterday. That's on the south coast, I think. They were inspecting Goering's bombing damage... Yes, you too... Goodbye." He hung up and returned to his chair. "So I look worried, do I?"

Anna waited.

"We're about to invade the Soviet Union, Anna."

More waiting

"Some of us thought—prayed, actually—that the Führer might pull back but he won't. We're sending in two to three million men."

Anna forced her tone to remain matter of fact. "What about the non-aggression pact with Stalin?"

"Dead. It was already dying as the signatures dried on it in 1939. The Führer needed to keep Stalin out of the way whilst we invaded Poland. He succeeded. Now it's the pact that's in the way. Curiously, Stalin still seems to believe in it even though he can see our massing troops and tanks along his border."

Anna drummed the table. "So what's worrying you in particular? The scale? The ambition? That the Führer's opening a second front even though he hasn't finished off the Brits?"

Goebbels looked away. "It can only fail, Anna. Two to three million men might sound enormous, but it's nothing compared to the size of that country. Supply lines alone will be impossible to sustain."

"Is that all?"

He scoffed. "Isn't that enough? It's the beginning of the end!"

"Perhaps, but that's not the sort of thing that depresses you. If anything, hopeless situations give you energy. It's something else. Something more personal."

He sighed. "Two things. The first is that he wants this Ministry to fool everyone into believing we're going to attack Great Britain. How are we to do that with millions of men and mountains of equipment heading east? The second is that I, the Minister of Propaganda no less, have only just been told about the invasion. It's been on the cards since last year."

"When were you told?"

"Late March. Five weeks ago. Why would the Führer keep such a massive event away from me? Where's the trust? Where's the teamwork? I'm the one he'll expect to present the whole thing as a walk in the park to the German public whilst tens of thousands of dead bodies—dead *German* bodies—pile up. And they will pile up, believe me. If consistency is one of our golden rules, I guarantee there will be very little consistency between the conquering messages we publish and the reality of sons, brothers, cousins and nephews never returning to their homes. Propaganda of that kind and on that scale requires preparation and a strategy. By excluding me until the last minute from all the thinking and discussions that led up to this invasion, the Führer's forcing me to improvise."

"You sound as if you feel betrayed." Anna winced at her own words.

"The Führer used to tell me everything, Anna. Everything. Now I have to assume that at any given moment in any given situation, he's holding back something crucial from me. I have to second-guess him all the time."

"Forgive me, Joseph, but second-guessing is what you and all the other leaders do all the time anyway. The Führer might be building one nation but he's certainly not building one leadership team. Why do you think he's holding crucial information back from you?"

Goebbels leaned back in his chair. "He does it to all of us. Divide and rule. Deliberate ambiguity, that kind of thing. So we all lose sleep analysing the variations in what he withholds from one individual to the next. Take Rudolf Hess, for example. The man went from co-authoring Mein Kampf in prison with the Führer in the early 1920s to being his designated successor in the 1930s to being all but excluded from high-level decision making today."

"But he brought his exclusion on himself, didn't he? You told me he's become a little strange."

"He has. The poor man's all but lost it. And the Führer's attitude towards him hasn't helped."

Anna softened her voice. "But *you* aren't losing it, are you, Joseph?"

Ducks quacked loudly just outside the window.

"No, of course not. But then again, I'm not about to send two to three million fit and healthy young Germans to injury or death, for many of them and almost certain defeat for all of them." He winked at her. "My job is merely to describe them to Germany and the world as bullet-riddled German martyrs with bullet-proof Aryan souls."

Chapter 23

Saturday 3 May 1941
Wanborough – Surrey – England

Neil McCrew stared at the country road ahead.

Fifteen minutes earlier the Humber 'Box' had picked him up in full parachuting attire at Wanborough and he'd sat in the back saying nothing for that same length of time.

"The first time I jumped I was glad I was wearing brown clothes," Sylvia Rowe explained from the front passenger seat. "I also threw up all over the trainer, which didn't ingratiate me to him."

McCrew stared at the country road ahead.

His first morning at the SOE's training centre had been spent on German small talk and Berlin geography, specifically the areas where Anna Vogel and Frank Winter lived and which backstreets to use to get from one to the other if ever he ended up alone. Rowe and he had spoken German during meals and tea breaks and they'd both been pleased—astonished in Rowe's case—to note how good his recall was.

"Haben Sie Angst?" Rowe asked. "That means 'are you scared?' or, word for word, 'do you have fright?' For some reason the Germans are a lot more possessive than us in their language. For instance, 'haben Sie Hunger?' means 'do you have hunger?' Anyway, scared or not you're going to jump at least twice a day all week except today. We've got some theory to get through, so we'll keep it to just one jump. You're a lucky man, by the way, Radke. Sie haben Glück. You have luck."

McCrew stared at the country road ahead.

"We won't be training you on how to pack your chute. That'll save some time. The downside is that you'd better stay on good terms with the packer and leave his girlfriend alone. What we'll show you though is how to gather up your chute once you've landed and how to dispose of it. The biggest risk, assuming your parachute opens and you're not shot at as you dangle in the air, is injury on landing. If you land on a tree, a roof or water, we've got a few survival tips for you. If you sprain or break something, that's a different matter. But you're a doctor, right?"

McCrew stared at the country road ahead.

Rowe glanced over her shoulder at him and spoke to the driver. "Would you pull over for a moment, please?"

The Box turned into a narrow side-road and almost crashed into a tractor. Both vehicles stopped abruptly. McCrew hurriedly opened his door, got out, moved a couple of yards away and vomited.

The drivers shrugged at each other.

McCrew returned to his seat less than a minute later. The Box reversed back on to the main road.

"Which brings me to parachuting in the dark," Rowe said. "What you need to know is—"

"Forget it, Lieutenant," McCrew interrupted. "If Churchill wants this thing to work, parachutes need to be removed from the equation. Please turn back."

Rowe nodded her approval to the driver. There was silence as he turned the vehicle round.

"Did you say Churchill?" Rowe asked as they set off back to Wanborough.

McCrew winced. "No, of course not."

Rowe stared at the country road ahead.

Chapter 24

Saturday 3 May 1941
Farnborough – Hampshire – England

As his Morris Eight sped south from Chequers to Farnborough—a forty-mile drive—Colin Gubbins mused that having lunch at Chequers with the Prime Minister would have been a more pleasant experience than the stodge the Royal Aircraft Establishment's would no doubt have on offer in its canteen. But the thought quickly evaporated. Gubbins was impatient to hear and see details of what William Farren, director of the RAE, had vaguely described on the phone as a "smoky idea' to enable daytime flights over enemy territory. To a man whose business was covering operations behind enemy lines, this was something not to be ignored.

Once through security at the RAE's main entrance gates, it was a short drive to the administration building. Farren was already standing in front of it, gesturing that he wanted to get into the car.

"Good to see you, Colin. Drive across the runway to the hangar on the left. We can take a look at the Heinkel before Danes and Paterson go to lunch. Danes is the pilot and Paterson the engineer. They came up with this together. I thought it would be a good idea for you to meet them."

Gubbins slowed before the runway to check for aircraft in both directions. "I appreciate it. Thank you."

"Forgive me for prying, but did I strike a chord or something last night? One phone call to you and bang, you're here."

Gubbins glanced at him. "I need your help, William. I can either explain my problem with Danes and Paterson present or I can wait till after we've seen the aircraft. Frankly I'd prefer the first scenario. Can these two keep their mouths shut?"

"Yes, of course."

Gubbins stopped the Morris Eight in front of Hangar B and reached behind for a briefcase on the back seat.

Danes and Paterson came out of the hangar to greet them. After introductions, they showed Gubbins the new fittings on the Heinkel 111, providing details on piloting and technical challenges respectively.

"Doesn't the smoke tube running under the port wing affect aerodynamics?" Gubbins asked Danes.

"Mike's fitted an identical dummy tube under the starboard wing to even things out. It's a shitty aircraft to pilot anyway."

Gubbins nodded at all three of them. "I'm impressed, gentlemen." He glanced around the hangar. "Are we alone in here?"

"Yes, sir," Danes said.

From his briefcase he produced a photograph and a large map of Western Europe. He spread the map on Paterson's workbench and held up the photograph. "What I'm about to tell you is highly sensitive. This is a huge forest called Eifel, which straddles the Belgian-German border. On the edge of it is a castle called Schloss Merode." His finger circled the Eifel Forest and pointed to the castle. "Three weeks ago we received intelligence that thirty-five high-ranking SS officials, including Heinrich Himmler, would be meeting here for three days of talks. Their objective was to discuss Germany's invasion of the Soviet Union and to work out the details of how the SS would contribute to it."

Farren folded his arms. "What German invasion of the Soviet Union?"

"Vast numbers of tanks and troops are massing at the Soviet border as we speak. They'll attack in a few weeks. June 22nd is a date we keep on hearing. It's colossal."

Farren, Danes and Paterson flicked glances at each other.

"What we know is that Hitler talked to his generals back in March and used the word annihilation when referring to communist officials. As those officials are more likely to be found in the civilian population than in the Soviet army, we're guessing the SS will be in charge of rounding up those officials and dealing with them after the soldiers have gone through. We're also guessing the SS won't be any friendlier to Jews and other minorities in the Soviet Union than in Germany. It'll be a bloodbath."

Danes took the photograph from Gubbins. "So what's the plan at the castle?"

"What *was* the plan, you mean. Obviously, a gathering of that many top SS officials plus Himmler was too good an opportunity to miss, so we decided to plant a bomb. Three days ago we dropped a team of three SOE agents in the area to do just that but things didn't go to plan. They were ambushed at the castle. It looks as if no SS meeting had been planned there at all."

"Deliberately faulty intelligence, then," Paterson said.

"We're investigating." Gubbins placed a fingertip on the right-hand side of the map. "We've since found out from a different source that the meeting will be much bigger and will take place here in Pletzsche, much farther east, at the end of this month. Either way the mission's been a disaster. But something's popped up. Two of the team were killed but one managed to get away." He moved his fingertip across the map to the green area south-west of Merode. "He's lying low somewhere here. Chap called Ramsay. He sent a message just after the operation and then nothing more for two days. Turns out he was ill and mostly slept, probably in a cabin or cave or something. He's come round now but is hardly fit and able. He says he's got access to water but only enough food for up to four days, assuming he rations it and his luck holds."

"How do you know he didn't spend those two days being tortured by the Germans until he collaborated?" Paterson asked.

Gubbins held his gaze for a few seconds. "Before an operation like that, we agree on a word to include in messages if their content can be trusted. Ramsay's okay." Gubbins rubbed his forehead with two fingers. "Now if you thought that was sensitive information, what I'm about to say now is even more so. As you can imagine, I want to send in a team to rescue Ramsay but I've been turned down so far. I depend for aircraft on what Bomber Command's prepared to lend me and they're arguing that we'd be putting at least two additional lives at serious risk to rescue a man who's probably not fit enough to get to a rendezvous point anyway. I'd just been turned down a third time when you called last night, William."

"What about MI9?" Farren asked. "Aren't they specialised in getting escaping prisoners and Brits in trouble out of Germany? Don't look so startled, Colin. MI9 aren't quite the state secret they think they are."

Rattled, Gubbins shook his head. "No, they think it's too risky as well." He took another photograph out of his briefcase. "But I'm not giving up just yet. This is an aerial photograph of the woodland south-west of the castle. It's one of several we took whilst we were setting up the mission." He looked up at Danes. "As you can see, there's a long and narrow clearing here, about two and a half miles from the castle. Ramsay shouldn't be too far from it. A small aircraft could easily land there but it's way beyond the range of anything we fly. A De Havilland Mosquito could do the job, but no one wants to lend me one. Another problem is that there won't be enough moonlight over the next few days. So this has to be a daylight operation. Which brings me to a question: what's the wingspan of your Heinkel?"

"About seventy feet, sir" Danes said.

"Exactly seventy-four," Gubbins said, "but you'll check that, won't you. Assuming seventy-four feet, there are two places along that clearing where you'd be down to an eight-feet clearance on either side. Assuming no side wind, of course. Do you think you could do it?"

Danes stared at the map.

"Assuming you squeeze through those two narrow stretches," Gubbins continued, "there's only barely enough room at the north-west end to turn the plane round to take off again. As turning round at the other end's impossible, you'd have to approach from the south, which is where you qualify for a bonus." His fingertip touched a square pencilled close to the bottom end of the clearing. "This is a military base about half a mile south. As you'll make a lot of noise flying over them, someone might be tempted to investigate. Tick-tick-tick."

"Any good news?" Danes asked.

"Yes. I've had the ground magnified as much as possible. It looks bumpy but at least it's flat. Either way, if you're up for this, you'll have to practice your arse off landing and turning the 111 on a handkerchief. No, make that a folded handkerchief."

There was silence.

"It's dangerous, Danes," Farren said. "No obligation."

"I need an answer by noon tomorrow," Gubbins said.

"Now if you'll excuse us, gentlemen," Farren said. "The brigadier and I have a few administrative matters to discuss over lunch."

Gubbins was still looking at Danes. "Are you married?"

"No, sir," Danes said.

"Is there someone who matters? A loved one?"

Gubbins and Farren stared at him. Paterson looked away.

Danes's eyes were on the floor. "There is, sir."

"Ramsay has a loved one, too. His wife. He's probably spending most of his time in that German forest thinking about her. But there's one big difference between him and you. In a very real sense he signed up to take that kind of risk and end up alone in a forest thinking of his wife. You didn't. The odds of you squeezing a Heinkel between those trees are low. The odds of you doing it twice in a few minutes—once in, once out—are abysmal. So if you decide not to go, no one will blame you, ever. Least of all me."

"Question, sir," Danes said.

"Yes?"

Danes moved back to leave a space between Gubbins and himself. "We're about eight feet apart now. That's the gap you said I'd have on either side of the plane."

"Yes."

"Is that the distance from the wingtip to the outermost leaves of the trees or to the tree trunks?"

"The eight feet include two feet clipping the outer leaves and twigs."

Chapter 25

Saturday 3 May 1941
London – England

Brendan Bracken sat at his desk at 10 Downing Street, trying in vain to spot a square inch of actual wooden surface amongst his papers. Clearing these up, he reasoned, would be both a Saturday evening well invested and a welcome respite for his liver.

The phone rang.

"Unfortunately for you," Churchill's voice slurred, "there's been a lull in the conversation here. So I thought I'd give you two opportunities to show your brilliance. Shall I talk about them now or do you have better things to be brilliant at in Downing Street on a Saturday evening?"

"Please carry on."

"The first is about my wife. I haven't worked out how to tell her we're planning to fly a German surgeon in to operate on her. She'll refuse, I know. Any ideas?"

"Does she need to know, Winston? McCrew could hold her hand as they administer the anaesthetic and Winter could take over once she's asleep. It wouldn't be the first time you change a plan at the last minute."

"Sorry, Brendan, you're showing your competence, not your brilliance. No, I want her to know what's going on."

"Why do you think she'll refuse?"

"She'll see it as selfishness. In Plymouth on Friday she saw what overrun medical resources look like. She saw injured people waiting too long for attention. She saw the exhaustion of the doctors and nurses. She won't think she deserves special attention."

"For Christ's sake, Winston, she's dying."

"I know, but she wants the same British medical attention as everyone else. If that means being operated on by a British surgeon with little or no experience of her kind of tumour, so be it."

Neither man said anything for a moment.

"Maybe it isn't about whether she deserves special attention or not," Bracken said. "Maybe it's about changing the way your marriage works. You've been the centre of attention your entire married life. Clemmie's been selfless, standing in the wings, devoting everything to you. Maybe she needs someone's permission to step into the light."

"But whose permission should she ask? Mine? Our children's? Yours?"

"Her own. She has to give herself that permission."

Churchill chuckled. "That's not brilliance, Brendan. Nor is it competence. It sounds worryingly like honesty."

"Tell me about the second opportunity."

Churchill cleared his throat. "Yes, I can't stop thinking about something you said on the way to Paddington the day before yesterday. That I'm out of touch with the here and now."

"That was 1937. This is 1941."

"No, I'm thinking of 1942 or '43 or whenever this bloody war ends. Assuming we prevail, and I'm in no mood to assume otherwise, one thing's for certain: the British people won't want to return to the old ways. Several new bombs—social bombs, economic bombs, political bombs—will be ticking loudly by then. Deafeningly in some cases. I need someone to help me decide which bombs to defuse and in what order."

"I thought you wanted Anna Vogel to work for us from the Ministry of Propaganda in Berlin."

"I do, but I'm not talking about her. I'm talking about you. I want to put you in charge of the Ministry of Information. Duff Cooper's not the right man for the job and never has been. In some ways you're not the ideal candidate either. The exposure's ruthless and people know how close you are to me. You'll have to live down accusations of cronyism every day. But if anyone can pull it off, you can. You'd take over at some point this summer."

Bracken spoke slowly. "Wow. Of course the newspaper publisher in me hates the very idea of a ministry of information. Sounds like a ministry of censorship."

"But the journalist in you loves the idea of running the bloody thing, too. I can see cartoons already: you and Goebbels throwing typewriters and microphones at each other from opposite corners of a Europe-shaped boxing ring."

Bracken adjusted his glasses. "Winston, if you're expecting me to put the Ministry of Information at your service to help you win the first post-war election, it won't work. And if I accepted the job, I'd put a halt to all those ridiculous propaganda campaigns telling people how to think and behave. The British people aren't children."

"Hear, hear. What I would expect the Ministry to do under your direction is more, much more research on morale and expectations."

"The Home Intelligence Reports?"

"Yes, they're the Ministry's one shining light. We need more of that kind of thing. But how you gather the information and what questions you ask is up to you. No interference from me." Churchill chuckled. "Having said that, any advance copies of your publications would be most welcome."

Bracken lit a cigarette. "Is this your roundabout way of telling me you'll be standing for election after the war?"

"Do you want the job or not?"

"I'll consider it. But if I accept you'll have to commit to putting up with a lot of discomfort."

"My current job's not exactly comfortable as it is. No change there."

Bracken spoke slowly. "You do realise that people will only vote for you after the war if you show you seriously care about them *during* it."

Churchill turned angry. "I beg your pardon?"

"That's what I mean by discomfort, Winston. True, you visit bombed-out cities and mingle with survivors. True, your speeches are an inspiration to everyone. True, you've proved to be the right man to lead this nation in these wretched times. But you're still a man of privilege. You represent a class of people and a way of thinking far removed from people at the bottom of the scale, whose only certainty as they struggle from day to day is that they'll be able to vote in the next election. You need to show them you know about and care about the kinds of things they know and care about. You'll have to do more, much more than settle back in an armchair to read yet another harrowing report on their living conditions. When those people press an ear against your chest, assuming they could ever get close enough, they want to hear *their* heart beating in there, not yours. Once the war ends and all threats to their freedom have been removed, do you know what they'll do? They certainly won't stand around reminding each other that you improved the comfort of their air-raid shelters. Nor will they drink toasts to the democratic rights and freedom they managed to preserve. They'll move on. They'll concentrate on their individual day-to-day plights: jobs, pay, housing, health care, holidays, pensions, education. Having risked their lives for their country,

British men will expect their country to give them a better life back. And having held the economy together whilst their husbands were away fighting, British women will refuse to fade back into the shadows. Will you be ready for them? How will they know that you and your kind care about something more in their lives than their freedom from tyranny? What good is their freedom if they're poor, unemployed, badly housed, badly fed and in poor health? What can you and your party do right now, whilst Nazi bombs are still exploding around you, to show you're prepared to go an extra step for each and every one of those people—sorry, those voters— once peace arrives?"

Churchill scoffed. "What more can I do for the British people, Brendan? The war keeps me busy twenty-four hours a day."

"Here's the deal, Winston. I've got an idea I want to try as quickly as possible. If you give me free rein with it, I'll look after the Ministry of Information for you."

"As long as your idea shows I care for people, go ahead."

"No, Winston. Caring for people is a socialist thing and you know what I think of socialism. My idea will show you care for individuals. Each and every one of them."

There was silence.

Churchill hesitated. "What do you need?"

"A German submarine. A U-boat."

"I beg your pardon?"

"We captured one yesterday. U693, it's called. I want to talk to its crew on Monday morning before they all get sent off to prison camps. Could you make a few personal calls to the Royal Navy to make sure that happens?"

Chapter 26

Saturday 3 May 1941
London – England

Day or night, Colin Gubbins was a familiar sight both at the headquarters of the Special Operations Executive in Baker Street, London, and in his own fast expanding department in Berkeley Court. A few minutes before 10pm he strode into the SOE's main communications room. The man he was looking for was wearing headphones and sitting hunched over a desk against the far wall.

"Good evening, sir."

"Good evening, Snape." Gubbins slapped a sheet of paper down in front of him. Those are the words to fill that gap in the message I gave you earlier." He glanced up at a clock. "You're sending it at ten, correct?"

"Yes, sir." Snape read the slip. "Less naïve," he murmured.

"Thanks."

In his office a moment later, Gubbins did something he rarely did alone: pour himself a glass of single malt from a bottle he kept in a lower drawer.

There was a knock.

"Good evening, Brigadier," said Jeff Stafford, one of his office staff, who was holding four slips of paper.

"Anything from Ramsay?"

Stafford glanced at one of the slips. "At four pm he wrote quote 'where's my bloody rescue team?' unquote."

"Really?"

"Not quite, sir. Somehow his words came out as 'Standing by.'"

Gubbins grinned. "What else?"

"Colonel Matthews wants to see you yesterday and General Holden wants to see you the day before yesterday. They both said you're fully aware of their, er, urgent requests."

"The only urgent thing about their requests is the full night's sleep I'll have before tending to them. Is that all?"

"Just a call from a Lieutenant Sylvia Rowe at Wanborough. She said to tell you the surgeon refuses to use a parachute."

"What?" Gubbins leapt out of his chair, grabbed the slips from Stafford's hand and glared at Rowe's message. "How does that idiot expect us to get him to Germany then? In a horse-drawn carriage?"

He sat down again, took a sip of whisky, changed his mind, emptied the glass.

Chapter 27

Saturday 3 May 1941
Lanke – March Brandenburg – Germany

As Goebbels and Anna Vogel returned to the meeting-room, the eleven young employees were already seated and waiting.

"So my young friends," Goebbels said, "what two other golden rules of propaganda have you come up with apart from consistency? Telling the truth is one of them, obviously. Would anyone care to explain why?"

There was silence as the employees exchanged awkward glances.

Hilda Neubert, the most ardent note-taker in the group, raised a hand. "I think I speak for us all when I say that telling the truth is important, but possibly not a golden rule."

"Are you suggesting we should lie to the German people?"

Blushing, Neubert shook her head. "No, I didn't mean to—"

"Yes, Herr Reichsminister, we should lie to them," Lutz Reinhardt said calmly. "We already do so anyway. They know it, we know it, they know that we know it and we know that they know that we know that they know it."

A few people tittered.

"Then tell me, Herr Reinhardt," Goebbels said, "does the truth play any role in what we do?"

"I think it plays a role when it helps our overall storyline. Otherwise it's just a nuisance."

Goebbels raised an eyebrow. "You hold the work of my Ministry in high esteem, I see."

"I do, Herr Reichsminister, but not because of its insistence on honesty."

Goebbels looked around the table and smiled. "Young Reinhardt's a brave man to say such things but he's right. We don't tell the truth. We are servants of *a* truth. And the truth we serve is that Germany is the greatest country this planet has ever seen and that Adolf Hitler is the greatest leader the world has ever known. And because that is the truth we serve, every message our Ministry communicates to the German people must be consistent with it. Note my use of the word 'consistency' again. Any message at variance with the truth we serve or that doesn't support it must by definition be a lie. Saying, for example, that the Führer wasted an opportunity to eliminate most of the British army and a great many French soldiers at Dunkirk last year is a lie. And to hell with the fact that 300,000 Brits and Frenchmen actually escaped across the English Channel. Saying that Jews have produced some of the finest music and literature in history is a lie. And to hell with the fact that we've all sat and wept at the beauty and perfection of their work. Saying that the Führer farts uncontrollably on all occasions is a lie. And to hell with the fact that I regularly experience the phenomenon at close quarters myself and almost need to be revived." He surveyed the faces questioningly, as if daring them to laugh. "Propaganda doesn't measure its success by the amount of truth it contains. It measures its success by its ability to make the people believe something. Anything."

Anna raised her hand. "There is an exception, I think: a ministry of propaganda cannot succeed if it lies to itself. Whatever we say to the outside world, we must be honest with each other."

"Good point, Fräulein Vogel," Goebbels said. "And I agree. So what are our two other golden rules?"

"One of them might be that we should always promote control, Herr Reichsminister," said Rita Korth.

"Tell us more."

"As I see it, the Führer has built his entire career around the idea that Germany lost control over its destiny after the Great War. Its present and future were dictated by foreign powers and the Treaty of Versailles. Everything the Führer has done since then, and still does today, is about taking back control."

"How is that a golden rule for us?"

"We always try to portray Germany's actions, especially unpleasant ones, as attempts to take back control or increase it."

Goebbels looked around the table. "Or? There's something missing."

Frank Krost raised a hand. "Or avoid losing control."

"Precisely. If you want people to smile and clap politely, show them what they're in control of. But if you want them to do something for you, to obey you, to vote for you or to go to war for you, show them what they've either lost control of or might lose control of. And how do we do that in practice?"

There was silence.

"We make everything look and sound simple. Make no mistake: simplicity is always an illusion. Always. The simpler something seems to be, the more complexity it hides. Simplicity fools people into thinking they understand something and therefore that in some tiny way they're in control of it, which of course they never are. Simplicity makes control seem possible. Simplicity is the light we shine of everything; pain is its shadow. For example, economic and political problems are incredibly complex. Even the experts struggle to understand them. Solution? Blame someone else: foreign agitators, neighbouring countries, immigrants, Jews, communists, Bolsheviks, gypsies. It's their fault. Simple. Control."

"But what about people's daily lives, Herr Reichsminister?" Rita Korth asked. "How can we expect them to feel in control of their Fatherland's destiny if they're struggling to find food to feed their children and coal to heat their homes?"

"I recommend that you all spend some time in our archives," Goebbels said. "You'll notice that our propaganda isn't just ideology. It also refers to practical things—food, clothing, heating—and does so constantly. People's sense of control over their lives begins at home. If we show an interest in their daily concerns, they'll listen to ours."

Andrea Bechstein raised a hand. "What about community, Herr Reichsminister?"

"What about it?"

"Isn't it a golden rule that the Ministry of Propaganda should always remind people what they have in common and who they depend on?"

Goebbels nodded. "Ein Volk[14]. We're one and the same under the Führer's rule. But answer this: what about free-thinking individuals? Don't we have a need for people who take personal initiatives? What about our heroic U-boat captains, for example? Do they beat the enemy by thinking and acting like the rest as of us?"

Hilda Neubert raised a hand. "No, they don't. But they wouldn't exist without the entire German population working as one to make their heroics possible. Somebody else built the U-boat. Somebody else put food in it. Somebody else provided the clothes. Somebody else supplied the torpedoes and instruments."

---

[14] "Ein Volk" means "one people". This refers to the Nazi slogan "Ein Volk, ein Reich, ein Führer» (one people, one realm, one leader).

"So what's the golden rule, Neubert?" Goebbels asked.

Andrea Bechstein raised her hand again. "Community, as I said."

"Community's a word, not a golden rule. What should we always or never do?"

"We should always remind people that they can't do it alone," Lutz Reinhardt said. "They need to stay connected to their country, community and loved ones."

Goebbels looked around expectantly. "You're right but we're going put an awful lot of people to sleep if we put it like that. What is it that actually binds people together? Handcuffs? Their insatiable hunger for facts and figures?"

"Love?" Hilda Neubert suggested timidly.

"More general than that."

"Emotion," Rita Korth said.

"Emotion," Goebbels repeated. "There's your third golden rule right there, my young friends: speak to people's emotions. Go for their instincts, their passions, their loves, their hates. Don't give them facts and figures. Or if you really must, make sure you bury them in an interesting story." He paused. "So summing up, golden rule one: if our messages can't be consistent with each other, we make them consistent with something else that people value—with security, for example, or with a higher truth such as 'we are superior'. And once we've decided on a message, we repeat the hell out of it. Golden rule two: remind people of the control they've either lost or might lose over their lives and that they must take that control back. Above all give people a feeling of control by making things simple for them. Golden rule three: speak to people's emotions. Remind them of what connects them to each other and of the high cost of being different and therefore isolated or excluded."

"A question if I may, Herr Reichsminister," Anna said. "Do you think the Führer will talk about his plans for the Soviet Union during his speech on Sunday?"

Goebbels stiffened. "Why do you ask that?"

"When you left this room the day before yesterday to greet your unexpected visitor, we had a conversation about our respective personal situations. It turns that five people here have brothers or cousins who've been sent to the Soviet border. This sort of information isn't supposed to spread, of course, but rumours are rumours."

"My best friend's been sent there too," Siegfried Aust added, articulating carefully to compensate for his Bavarian accent.

"We're not in the business of dignifying rumours by discussing them," Goebbels said carefully. "If anything, we're in the business of starting and spreading them."

Nervous smiles greeted this.

"Herr Reichsminister," Anna said, "you agreed earlier on that honesty must be a golden rule among ourselves within the Ministry walls. Could you tell us what's going on with the Soviet Union?"

Goebbels gazed at the centre of the table. "As I mentioned earlier on, Germany and the Soviet Union signed a non-aggression pact two years ago, just before war broke out," he said carefully. "If the Führer launched an attack on the Soviet Union, would that be consistent behaviour? If so, consistent with what?"

"Soviet provocation?" Rita Korth said.

"There hasn't been any. Stalin's as docile as a lamb."

"What about the Führer's Lebensraum[15] policy?" Andrea Bechstein asked.

"Possibly," Goebbels muttered without seeming convinced. "There's a historical precedent, you know, to an unprovoked attack on the Soviet Union, or rather Russia as it was called then. Napoleon Bonaparte tried it and failed over a century ago. He underestimated the size of his ambition, the scale of the country, the need for preparation and supplies and the fighting spirit of the enemy. The whole operation looked less like France trying to extend its control over Europe than its leader losing control of his sanity. How many men do you think our Führer would need to invade the Soviet Union successfully? How much equipment? What kind of equipment? Give me three Berlin winters rather than one Russian one. How many tanks, aircraft and horses? Would we have all that under control? Because if we don't and we launch an attack, an awful lot of our brothers, cousins, neighbours and best friends won't come back."

He stood up, leaned over the table and placed both hands flat on it.

"Most importantly, how united do you think the German people would remain if that happened? Would they still believe in propaganda about the importance of connecting to each other if they had fewer and fewer people to connect to because they're all being killed? So let's wait and see what the Führer says on Sunday." He winked at them. "I'm due to speak to the Führer on the telephone later on. Can I pass on any messages from you to him about golden rules for his speech?"

---

[15] "Lebensraum» means living space. Adolf Hitler believed Nazi Germany had a right to invade neighbouring countries in order to give more living space to its citizens.

Chapter 28

Sunday 4 May 1941
Berlin – Germany

Anna Vogel was now as familiar a figure at the Kaffee Nur Freunde in Berlin as she had been at Dino's in Manhattan four years earlier. She enjoyed drinking tea—the ersatz coffee[16] was atrocious—and reading a book there on her rare days off. There should be a law, she believed, against any Sunday morning decision being more complicated than picking a park to stroll in later on.

"Darf ich?"[17]

The newcomer's voice was soft and his features delicate. In his thirties, he was wearing a black raincoat—possibly dark blue given the Nur Freunde's yellowish lighting—which made his build seem less slender that it was.

"Danke," he murmured.

After signalling to a waiter to bring another black tea, Anna carried on reading. The man ordered apple juice.

"My raincoat has never attracted this much interest," he said casually. "I'm quite jealous."

Anna didn't look up. "I was trying to work out if it's black or dark blue."

"Black, actually. Would you like to know its address and phone number? You two should get along fine."

---

[16] Substitute coffee, often made from acorns.
[17] " May I ? »

Anna grinned. "No, thanks."

"Pity. That's another chat-up strategy I'll have to cross off my list. I must say I've become less naïve about chat-up strategies recently. In fact I've become less naïve about a lot of things."

Anna stopped grinning and looked up. He'd said the word 'less' in English both times. It was harder to tell if he'd said 'naïve' in English too because the word was almost identical in both languages.

The man smiled. "If you want to discuss reduced naivety, take a stroll on Lützowplatz this afternoon at five. Alone."

He took out his wallet, put a banknote on the table and left.

Chapter 29

Sunday 4 May 1941
Farnborough – Hampshire – England

For the fifth time the Heinkel He 111 circled back over the countryside surrounding Farnborough Airfield and positioned itself for landing.

For the fifth time Danes peered down at Farren and Paterson as they repositioned themselves on either side of the runway. They stood exactly ninety feet apart. Earlier on Danes had insisted on measuring the distance himself, equivalent to the Heinkel's wingspan plus eight feet on either side.

For the fifth time Farren and Paterson seemed achingly too close to each other for a medium-sized German bomber to squeeze between them.

For the first time, however, the distance didn't seem impossibly narrow. This change in perception was what Danes had been practising for. One more full day of this, he knew, and ninety feet would feel comfortable. Farren had refused to let him look for, let alone land on, a narrow tree-lined clearing in the area for more realism.

For the fifth time Danes watched Farren and Paterson lie down on their backs, parallel to the runway. By looking straight up both men would see if the wingtips on their respective sides passed over them or stayed clear. On the first two tries Danes had landed too far to his left, clipping the airspace above Paterson's face. On the third he'd landed perfectly. On the fourth he'd clipped Farren's airspace but only just.

"The military base will be useful to you in one respect," Farren had remarked. "You'll know if there's a side wind by looking at their swastika flags."

For the fifth time Danes brought the aircraft down steeply. He could make out Farren and Paterson covering their ears. By now a crowd of RAE employees had assembled to watch their antics from the side of the runway. Paterson had suggested drawing marks on the Heinkel's glazed nose so that Danes could line them up with the clearing's most dangerously protruding trees but Danes had rejected the idea. He wanted to feel the distances rather than measure them.

The Heinkel landed and roared through the gap between the two men on the ground. Paterson raised an arm. The aircraft had clipped his airspace.

Chapter 30

Sunday 4 May 1941
Wanborough – Surrey – England

"Beautiful place, this," Neil McCrew said, breaking the silence.

At Sylvia Rowe's suggestion, they had taken their notepads and turned the session into a stroll around the grounds of Wanborough Manor.

"As you'll be needing persuasion skills in Berlin," Rowe said, "the purpose of this session is to give you ammunition in that area. Did your medical training include any interviewing or conversational skills?"

"Our training teaches us that we're gods, Lieutenant. Rightly or wrongly, what we say is up there with the ten commandments as far as most patients are concerned. No need for psychology. Why, are you a psychologist?"

"No, I'm a trained interrogator. Question: is your target in Berlin a patient?"

"No. I truly need to be persuasive."

"Will you allow me to help you?"

McCrew frowned. "Why shouldn't I?"

"I offered to help you learn how to parachute yesterday but, er—"

McCrew raised a hand to interrupt her. "Lieutenant, I've already apologised for that. There's a difference between parachuting and persuasion."

"You're right, the difference being that persuasion skills are more frightening than parachuting. Do you realise your refusal to cooperate yesterday has all but screwed up the mission?"

McCrew shrugged.

"All right," she went on, "supposing the mission is maintained, how would you go about persuading the target to comply?"

"I haven't given it much thought, I'm afraid. I've been more worried about German grammar and the geography of Berlin so far. I'll play it by ear, I suppose. One god to another."

Rowe glanced at him, cocking an eyebrow.

McCrew chuckled. "Oops. Yes, the target's a doctor. A brain surgeon like me."

"Stop there, Radke. I'm not supposed to know."

McCrew swung on her. "Well I'm going to tell you anyway."

Rowe gestured towards a bench next to a small pond. "Shall we?"

"Churchill's wife has a life-threatening brain tumour," McCrew said as they sat down. "The only surgeon who can operate with a not-too-abysmal chance of success is a German called Frank Winter. Hence Berlin. He's also a passionate Nazi. My task is to persuade him to come to England to operate on Mrs Churchill. I'm not a total unknown to him because we both studied at Cambridge."

Rowe stared at the pond. "What does not a total unknown mean exactly?"

"We knew each other's names, barely more. What I do know is that he turned out to be an exceptional surgeon. He's world-famous in our profession."

"What about his private life?"

"Well if you really want to know, he stole my fiancée in Cambridge and took her back to Germany to marry her. C'est la vie. No children as far as I know."

"How do you know he's a passionate Nazi?"

"We bumped into each other at a medical congress in Wiesbaden in 1934. All he could talk about was Hitler as Germany's saviour or even as the human race's saviour. A medical god in love with a political one."

"That's seven years ago. That's a long time. How do you know his love for the Führer hasn't worn off?"

"I don't. But it's probably safer to assume for our purposes that it hasn't."

Rowe stood up and opened her arms, turning in all directions. "Let's imagine that this garden is Mrs Churchill's brain—full of democratic flowers, freedom-loving trees, tolerant lawns, fair-minded vegetable patches and bushes of multiple classes and religions. Suddenly we discover that something or someone has added this pond. It's poisonous and its contents are slowly seeping out into the rest of the garden. A cancerous tumour. Solution? Get rid of it. Cut it out before it destroys the garden. That's what you want Frank Winter to do to Mrs Churchill's brain in London, correct?"

McCrew nodded whilst adjusting his glasses.

"Now imagine that the garden represents Frank Winter's brain—full of Nazi flowers, antisemitic trees, undemocratic lawns, book-burning vegetable patches and goose-stepping bushes. This pond contains Frank Winter's little secrets. All his addictions are here. All his mistresses are here. All his fantasies are here. All his exceptions to the rules are here. Compared to the garden, the pond is only a tiny part of Frank Winter, but it's also fully functioning and necessary. Frank Winter wouldn't be Frank Winter without his little secrets, would he. The question is, how much seepage is there between the pond and the whole garden? If the pond wants to avoid its contents spilling into the garden, it needs the garden's cooperation. Likewise the garden needs some access to the pond in order to hide Frank's secrets there. So there must be at least a little seepage in both directions. Could you write something down, please?"

McCrew opened his notepad to a fresh sheet.

"Write this: 'surgery on Mrs Churchill's tumour', then tear out the sheet."

McCrew did so.

"Crumple it into a ball."

He did so.

Rowe pointed at the ball. "What are you going to do with that request when you come face to face with Winter?" She gestured in all directions. "Will you simply drop it in his garden somewhere?"

McCrew shrugged. "I suppose not."

"Why not? All this is his brain, isn't it?"

"Yes but it's Frank Winter's brain. He's got a lot of reasons to turn me down."

"Namely?"

"Operating on Mrs Churchill would be a huge personal and professional risk. He might damage his career beyond repair. As a Nazi he'd be considered a traitor for helping the enemy. He could be imprisoned or even shot for it. He'd be going against everything he stands for."

"Then why bother to go to Berlin, Radke? What's the point?"

McCrew stared at the ground, shaking his head. "Good question."

Rowe stood over him. "What do you think of Nazism?"

"It goes against everything I stand for."

"Then start loving it right now."

McCrew scoffed. "I beg your pardon?"

"Are you a Nazi, Radke?"

"No, I'm not."

"I'm asking you to be one. Are you a Nazi, Radke?"

He shook his head.

She slapped him. "Are you a Nazi, Radke?"

He raised his arms to protect himself. "All right, all right, I'm a Nazi."

"You hate Jews, right?"

"Yes, I do."

"My husband's a Jew. Is that a problem, Radke?"

McCrew shrugged. "I, er, suppose—"

She slapped him again. "I asked you a question. Is it a problem?"

"Yes, it is."

"How big a problem?"

"Massive. Huge."

"What do I deserve for sleeping with a Jew?"

"Problems, lots of them."

"And what does he deserve for just being a Jew?"

"Bigger problems, much bigger."

"What sorts of problems, Radke?"

McCrew hesitated. "Loss of rights, exclusion, insults, unemployment, poverty."

She raised her hand to slap him again but he was quicker to raise his arms.

"Okay," he continued, "banishment, imprisonment, concentration camps, hunger, disease."

"What about death, Radke? If you've taken away everything he had, why bother to let him go on living? Why not kill him off?"

He sat there shaking his head.

"You're not much of a Nazi, Radke. Can't you just pretend?"

"Nazism makes me feel sick, Lieutenant."

She sat beside him. "It isn't Nazism that makes you feel sick, Radke."

McCrew blinked a few times. "Then what?"

"It's your identity. Whenever there's a challenge to who you are and what you are—to your identity—your brain perceives it as a mortal danger, as a threat to your survival. It also warns you to do something about it. The warning comes in various forms but one of them is a feeling of uneasiness or sickness. Give me the ball of paper."

He did.

"So if you simply drop this request in the garden—in Frank Winter's brain—you will face the toughest resistance imaginable. Asking Winter to operate in London is more than a challenge to his surgical skills or political beliefs. It's a threat to his identity, to his survival as a person. So whatever you do when you come face to face with Winter, you've got to leave this entire garden—his identity— exactly as it is. He mustn't feel the slightest challenge from you on who he is and what he stands for. If he's a Nazi, let him be a Nazi. If he's wrong about something, let him be wrong. If he wears women's underwear when he does brain surgery, let him wear women's underwear. If you're not a threat to his identity, he'll feel comfortable enough to listen to you."

"So you want me to encourage him to persist as a Nazi. That's perverse."

Rowe was enjoying herself. "The word we use for such tactics at the SOE is ungentlemanly." She threw the ball of paper, which landed in the centre of the pond and floated on the surface. "As I pointed out before, this pond is a tiny part of the garden. If you drop your request there, the rest of the garden won't feel threatened. In practice, face to face with Winter, it might sound something like this: Frank, I wouldn't have risked life and limb travelling to Berlin to start preaching to you." Rowe pointed towards the pond. "I'm here because I believe there's a tiny part of you that can see Mrs Churchill for what she is: a dying patient who, through no fault of her own, has a brain tumour and needs the kind of help only you can provide. Would helping this woman just this once make a difference to who you are and what you stand for?"

McCrew grinned. "I don't remember you saying yesterday that there must be a tiny part of me that wants to throw itself out of plane and parachute to the ground."

"An unforgivable omission."

"And you think Winter will fall for it?"

"If he does, it won't be immediately. Remember what I said about seepage between the pond and the garden?"

"Yes."

Rowe nodded towards the pond. "If Winter rejects your request immediately, you really will have to play it by ear. If he doesn't reject it immediately, he'll to leave it there on the pond. But if he leaves it there, he'll have to find a reason to do so and justify its presence. He'll have to justify to himself a tiny change to his brain. But justifying a tiny change is pretty much the same thing as accepting it. And once he's accepted the tiny change, it's just a question of time before it seeps out of the pond and begins to change the rest of his brain. If you want perversity, it's right there."

"If it's all the same to you, Lieutenant, I'd rather consider myself ungentlemanly than perverse."

Chapter 31

Sunday 4 May 1941
Farnborough – Hampshire – England

At his desk at the SOE headquarters, Brigadier Colin Gubbins read the latest decrypted message from Ramsay for the umpteenth time. It had arrived at six am. 'Lying in bed waiting for breakfast,' it said. The drier the irony, Gubbins knew, the more uncomfortable Ramsay probably was. He looked up at the clock. At least two lives depended on the words he'd hear in the next few minutes. The noon deadline for Roddy Danes's decision on whether to attempt a rescue or not was now. The telephone rang.

"Gubbins speaking."

"Good morning, Brigadier. It's Danes at the RAE. How's your man in the forest?"

"Living up to our expectations. We aren't living up to his yet, though."

"Would he be fit enough to check the clearing for extra obstacles?"

"We'll ask him in our next message. How's the testing going?"

"Nine landings so far, sir. Six failures. And that's without side wind."

"What about turning the aircraft round?"

"No problem with that."

Gubbins lit a cigarette. "I need a decision, Danes."

Danes cleared his throat. "When do you want this rescue to happen?"

"In three days' time, on May 7th."

"Why wait so long? Has your man found food or something?"

"The only thing he won't die of is hunger, believe me. The wait's because you need more time to practise and I'm feeling generous. Will two days be enough?"

Danes sounded relieved. "Yes, sir. In that case I'll do it."

"Excellent. Is Farren okay with that?"

"He left it to me."

"And Paterson?"

"Paterson, sir?"

"Would you do this without his green flag?"

"Er, no I suppose I wouldn't. He can see a million things going wrong, obviously, but he's basically okay with it."

"One more thing: how receptive would you be to a slight change in plan?"

Danes hesitated. "I can't help noticing you secured my approval before mentioning any changes."

Gubbins laughed. "So there's caution in you after all."

"Beware my uncontrollable caution, sir. What sort of change do you have in mind?"

"You'll have an outbound passenger. Two missions for the price of one."

Chapter 32

Sunday 4 May 1941
Berlin – Germany

Anna Vogel hadn't returned to Berlin's Lützowplatz since a daytrip to the capital with her parents as a child. For reasons best known to him, her father had decided the fountain topped by a statue of Hercules at the centre of the square was an unmissable attraction. His wife and little Anna had disagreed but had been bought off with a promise of ice cream. They had devoured it sitting on the fountain steps.

The statue had seemed towering back then and still did now—fifteen metres, she guessed—as she walked towards it. The man with the coat hadn't said where exactly to position herself, so she decided to sit on the fountain steps again, minus ice cream. The square was quiet.

She took a book out of her bag and pretended to read, wondering how long Bracken had taken to come up with 'less naïve' as a clue to his involvement in this, whatever 'this' was.

5.10 pm.

"Don't look at me," a male voice said in English behind her.

She disobeyed. The agent was two metres to her left, pretending to be fascinated by the fountain. The black coat was gone; shirtsleeves now.

"I said don't turn—"

Standing up, she extended her right hand. "I'm Anna Vogel. Pleased to meet you."

The agent shook her hand weakly. "Deutsch, bitte."[18]

Anna switched to German. "Now we've done away with the cloaks and daggers, let's sit down. Do you have a name we can both pretend is not a false one?"

"No."

"Then tell me what Bracken wants."

"It's in two parts," the agent said as they settled. He scanned the surroundings them without moving his head. "The first part is short term and is based on the fact that you live alone on Fasanenstrasse. Your apartment belongs to the Ministry of Propaganda, your employer since 1937. An acquaintance of Bracken's will be arriving in Berlin in the next few days. He's English, he doesn't speak German, he doesn't know the city and he urgently needs to meet a contact who lives in Charlottenburg. Two or three meetings may be necessary for the man to achieve his objective. Bracken asks if the man could stay at your apartment for a few days and if you could accompany him two or three times from Fasanenstrasse to Charlottenburg and back. You will not be told the man's name, profession and mission. Nor will you be told the name of the contact he's meeting in Berlin. The second part is longer term. Bracken wants to recruit you as an agent inside the Ministry of Propaganda. You'd supply intelligence on a list of topics supplied in due course by Bracken and on anything you think useful to the British."

"And what do I get out of all that?"

"Assuming Germany loses the war, Bracken can guarantee you British citizenship, a ten-year career in your area of expertise as well as a clean slate regarding your propaganda work for the Nazis. If you believe Germany's going to win this war, this conversation's over and you'll never hear from Bracken or me again."

They sat in silence.

"Why me for the first part?" Anna asked at last. "Why don't you do it?"

"Their choice. It's not my job to speculate on their reasons."

"Might there be something so sensitive about his mission here that Bracken can't afford to go through the usual channels?"

"It's not my job to speculate."

They stopped talking as two laughing soldiers walked by.

"Are you an unusual channel yourself?" Anna asked.

"I'm not at liberty to say."

Anna stood up. "You can tell Bracken there's not a single thing of interest to me in his offer. Nothing. So he can shove both parts of it up his arse as far as I'm concerned, unless..."

---

[18] " German, please."

"Unless?"

"Unless he and I can have a face-to-face discussion about what he means by 'less naïve'".

The agent scoffed. "There's a war on, Miss Vogel. How are you going to get to London?"

"Simple. If Bracken can fly his acquaintance from England to Germany to meet a contact in the middle of a war, he can fly me in the opposite direction to meet him in London. Take it or leave it. You know where to find me."

Chapter 33

Sunday 4 May 1941
Chequers – Buckinghamshire – England

Clementine Churchill stirred in her sleep as her husband entered her darkened bedroom at Chequers. He nodded to a woman who was quietly rearranging flowers in a vase and she left. As Churchill leaned over Clemmie to kiss her on the forehead, she opened her eyes. He rubbed his nose against hers.

"Headache?" he asked.

"Only when I try to remember where I've seen you before."

He grinned. "Would you like to join us outside?"

"No, I'll stay here. Has McCrew found a surgeon yet?"

"Possibly." Churchill sat on the edge of the bed.

"You're taking too long to elaborate, Winston. What's the matter?"

"His name's Frank Winter. McCrew speaks highly of his skills as do, er, other people we've asked. In fact his peers in the German medical corps would speak highly of him too if only they'd come to the phone."

Clementine scrutinised her husband's features long enough to eliminate any suspicion of a joke. She closed her eyes again.

"We want to bring him here, Clemmie."

"Will you ask for Hitler's permission in English or German?"

"I'm not joking."

"I can just imagine one of those Luftwaffe pilots over London. Should we drop the surgeon before or after the bombs, mein Führer?"

Churchill took her hand. "Stop it, Clemmie. I'm serious."

Clemmie took her hand away. "I know you are. And I'm just as serious when I say it's out of the question. How can you possibly reconcile one German saving my life with hundreds of others bombing and ending British lives up and down the country? With any luck I might even be able to hear the explosions from the operating theatre. No, Winston."

"Clemmie, listen. You're the most unselfish person I know. You've been tireless in caring for me and others day after day, year after year. This is a time to let me care for you. But I need your permission to do that. Above all you need to give yourself permission to be cared for."

Clementine sighed. "Who's been feeding you such claptrap, Winston? Bracken by any chance? If an operation's to be attempted, I want McCrew to do it."

"He can't. Or rather he won't. He doesn't have the skills."

"Nor do three quarters of the volunteers giving first aid to bombing victims, Winston. I've seen them myself. Their lack of experience kills off additional people needlessly. But they still take a risk and rightly so. Why shouldn't McCrew do the same?"

Churchill reached for her hand again. She kept it away from him.

Chapter 34

Monday 5 May 1941
Berlin – Germany

Adolf Hitler's voice echoed around Joseph Goebbels's unpretentious office at the Ministry of Propaganda.

"...An unassailable, unprecedented spirit has arisen in our nation. A dedicated sense of community has gripped our people. No world power can take away from us what we have gained from the mistakes and inner struggles of our journey and which, compared to other nations, make us so proud. In an era of Jewish, capitalistic, gold- and class-ridden madness, the National Socialist people's state stands like a monument to social justice and clear reason. It will not only survive this war, but also the coming millennium!"

Joseph Goebbels reached across to press a button on the tape recorder, cutting off the approving roar of the Reichstag deputies the day before.

Anna Vogel poured them both some more coffee. "What do you think?" she murmured, silently awarding herself a medal of valour for resisting a third slice of bread with black cherry jam.

Goebbels shook his head angrily. "Fifteen to twenty minutes too long. He's taken to rambling and listening to himself. He does it at the Berghof, too. It was a fine summary of our military activities in the south-east, but did he really need to list all those details about operations in countries most Germans, let alone their deputies, couldn't find on a map to save their lives? And all those numbers, for God's sake. Why put everyone to sleep with how many divisions, rifles, guns, ships, troops, prisoners or victims are involved in everything we do? Where's the emotion? Where's the passion? Where's the simplicity? Details like that should come out of other mouths, not his. I've told him a hundred times."

"Why doesn't he listen to you?"

Goebbels sipped his coffee, calming himself. "I think he's desperate to reassure them. The longer the list of victories and numbers he can reel off, the more he sounds as if he's in control of the situation, or so he thinks. But there comes a point where long lists are self-defeating. They make him sound as if he's reassuring himself."

Anna cancelled her medal of valour and took a third slice. "Do you really think that?"

"He's beginning to sound defensive. Another problem is his constant references to Churchill."

"Eighteen. I counted. The Jews only got eight."

"I believe in repeating messages over and over, but eighteen stabs at Churchill in a single speech is fourteen too many. He's right to be tough on the old fool, but soon he'll be blaming him for the cold weather we're having, too. It's childish."

"To his credit, he did mention our own mistakes at the end."

"True, but that's much too late. If he's going to mention our mistakes, he should do so early on in his speech. It establishes sincerity. Whatever he claims afterwards automatically becomes more credible. By leaving our mistakes to the end, he sounded as if he was burying them."

Anna raised an eyebrow provocatively. "What do you think our young employees will make of it?"

Goebbels grinned and raised one finger. "Consistency. They'll notice that the Führer makes all our military actions and political positions sound justified by and therefore consistent with foreign provocations." He raised a second finger. "Control. They'll notice that the Führer portrays everything we do as a struggle for control over our lives and destiny." He raised a third finger. "Emotion. Despite all the boring statistics, they'll notice that the Führer insists, especially at the end of the speech, on the community that binds all true Germans to their country and to each other. Will the Führer ever have the guts to break one of our golden rules?"

Anna laughed.

"It's not funny really." Goebbels's face lost all expression as he nodded towards the tape recorder. "Eighteen references to Churchill in the west. Not a single reference to the Soviet Union in the east. The only signal that something loud and violent is about to happen in the Soviet Union is the Führer's silence on the topic. It's misdirection, of course. He's lying by omission to his own assembled deputies to make them look elsewhere." He shook his head. "Courtesy of Russian winter conditions and temperatures, between four and six million testicles are about to be frozen off the bodies of their German owners. Once that happens, there will only be one golden rule left for our beloved nation."

Anna looked at him expectantly.

"Survival."

Chapter 35

Monday 5 May 1941
London – England

The Cabinet War Rooms were an underground complex built in Whitehall to ensure that essential government operations could be maintained during a conflict. Colin Gubbins had been waiting outside the highly sensitive Map Room for less than a minute when the door opened and Churchill appeared. He turned and took one step back into the room. "Do you need a parting shot from me or will you come up with one yourselves?" He closed the door and winked at Gubbins. "Good to see you. Follow me."

He led the way along two corridors to a tiny meeting room. "Bracken can't join us this morning," he said as they settled on either side of a desk. "He's off to Bognor Regis of all places. Anyway talk to me. I'll brief him later."

Out of his briefcase Gubbins took three small squares of paper, a miniature airplane and four lead figurines, three male and one female. He set the squares out in a row facing Churchill, each with a location written on it: 'England' on the left, 'German-Belgian border' in the centre, 'Berlin' on the right. He placed the miniature airplane on 'England', the female figurine on 'Berlin' and a male figurine on each of the three squares.

"We're killing two birds with one stone, Prime Minister, and hopefully only metaphorically. The idea is to combine a rescue operation with a transport one. This is the starting position."

"Rescue operation?" Churchill asked.

Gubbins touched the square in the centre. "Here on the German-Belgian border there's a huge forest."

"Yes, the Eifel. I know it."

Gubbins touched the male figurine. "This is a stranded and very weak SOE agent. He's the sole survivor of a failed operation three days ago. He's hiding and awaiting instructions. We've spotted a clearing in the forest not far from him and we think we can land the Heinkel there." Gubbins touched the 'England' square, to Churchill's left. "Here we have Doctor McCrew and the Heinkel 111 bomber and here..." He touched the 'Berlin' square, to Churchill's right. "... we have Anna Vogel, who'll be looking after McCrew in Berlin, and Frank Winter, the German surgeon that McCrew will hopefully persuade to come here."

Churchill gazed at the desk, fascinated.

"Something new has popped up, Prime Minister." He pointed at the female figurine on 'Berlin'. "Our agent met Anna Vogel in Berlin yesterday. She insists on meeting Mr Bracken before agreeing to anything."

Churchill's lower jaw dropped. "What, in person?"

"Yes, sir."

Churchill slammed his hand down on the desk, sending the figurines and miniature airplane flying in all directions. "Who does she think we are?" he yelled. "Travel agents?"

Gubbins picked up the pieces and repositioned them on the squares of paper. "I know, sir, but I think we can handle it." He moved the female figurine from 'Berlin' to the 'German-Belgian border'. "If Anna Vogel can make her way to the clearing in the forest, the Heinkel can pick up both her and my stranded agent at the same time. She'll also be able to help my agent physically if he needs it."

"How far is the Eifel Forest from Berlin?"

"Four-hundred miles." Gubbins transferred the miniature airplane from 'England' to the 'German-Belgian forest'. "So the Heinkel flies empty to the Eifel Forest, picks up Anna and the stranded agent and brings them back to England." He moved the corresponding pieces to 'England' as he spoke. He then removed one of the two male figurines on 'England' and put it in his briefcase. "End of story for the stranded agent."

Churchill leaned forward. "So we now have Anna Vogel, Doctor McCrew and the Heinkel on 'England' and 'Doctor Frank Winter' on 'Berlin'."

"Correct. Anna Vogel then has her face-to-face meeting with Mr Bracken and if all goes well, the Heinkel flies her and Doctor McCrew to the Eifel Forest." He moved the corresponding pieces to the "German-Belgian border'.

"Why can't they land closer to Berlin?"

"We'd need to identify a new and suitably deserted place to land. The closer you get to Berlin, the fewer of those you're likely to find. We don't have enough time anyway. Assuming our pilot manages to land in that forest clearing and take off again, we're better off sticking with what he's familiar with. An additional problem with getting closer to Berlin is the Heinkel's range. The Heinkel we have is an older, less fuel-efficient model. Even with an additional fuel tank, Berlin's still a long way away."

They turned their attention back to the square sheet marked "German-Belgian border', which had the miniature airplane, a female figurine and a male figurine on it. "Once Anna and McCrew have been dropped off in the Eifel Forest," Gubbins said, moving the pieces accordingly, "they make their way together, probably by train, to Berlin. Meanwhile the Heinkel returns to England." He touched 'Berlin'. "So now we have McCrew, the persuader, Anna, his chaperone, and Winter, the German surgeon, in the same city. If all goes well, McCrew persuades Winter to travel with him to the Eifel Forest, where they rendezvous with the Heinkel and all fly to England so that Winter can operate on Mrs Churchill. What I've yet to work out is how to get Winter back to Germany or German-occupied territory after the operation. But I'm working on it."

Churchill grinned at Gubbins. "I'm impressed. Do we both need a stiff drink?"

"No, Prime Minister, we both need miracles. Note the plural."

Chapter 36

Monday 5 May 1941
Farnborough – Hampshire – England

"I don't remember asking you to sit down," James Firth said.

Roddy Danes stood back up and to attention. "Apologies, sir."

Leaning back in his chair, Firth flicked his pencil on to the desk. "Do you have anything to say before I send off my report? Did you manage to convince Farren of your daring creativity?"

"I stuck to objectives and technicalities, sir."

"And?"

"So did he."

Firth smiled. "I hope you realise that what Farren thinks doesn't matter. You're RAF first and foremost and that means the next direction your cock points in is my decision."

"Very well, sir."

The phone rang.

"Firth speaking." He listened. "Yes, he's here." He handed the phone to Danes.

"Danes speaking."

"Gubbins here. Don't use my name or call me 'sir', Can you speak freely?"

"No."

"Short answers then. How receptive would you be to another—" he cleared his throat "—slight change in plan?"

"No problem."

"Two flights instead of one. May 7th and 9th. Same destination. Different passenger arrangements. Imaginable? "

"Yes."

"Has your success rate with landings reached 80% yet?"

"No."

"Thank you, Danes. Goodbye."

"Goodbye."

Danes put the phone down.

"Who was that?" Firth asked.

"It's nothing, sir. Personal matter."

Firth turned sarcastic. "How serious must a personal matter be before someone phones my office to see if *you're* here?"

Danes stood there.

"Well, Danes, whoever it was and for whatever reason, you're suspended until I get an answer to my report on you and a copy of whatever Farren decides or recommends. You're also banned from Farnborough Airfield, including the RAE, with immediate effect. When you leave this office, you head straight for the exit gate without detouring by Hangar B or anywhere else. You do not pass by your office. You stay off the premises but in the area until I send for you again. Clear?"

"Yes, sir."

"Dismissed."

Danes turned and moved towards the door.

"One more thing, Danes."

Danes swung round. "Yes, sir?"

"Seems no one survived the crash of that German surveillance aircraft the other day. Did you know that?"

"I'd heard as much, sir."

"The day after the crash I had a chat with a local policeman at my local pub. He spared me none of the gory details. A local lady was found dead there as well. Walking her dog in the wrong place at the wrong time apparently. Poor dear."

"Sorry to hear that, sir."

Firth forced a frown. "Interestingly, the policeman said that none of the bodies had wallets on them. No papers, money, family photos, nothing."

Danes shrugged. "Perhaps getting rid of wallets and identification before a crash is German policy."

"Possibly. But do you think it's also German policy to take the time to strip off your uniform and throw it away as your aircraft plummets to the ground?

"I don't understand, sir."

"One of the German bodies was found stripped of its uniform. And I don't mean ripped off in the crash. No, someone took it away."

"My goodness."

"And then two days later at my birthday drink—thanks again for the beer, by the way—you turn up in a German airman's uniform. Quite fetching on you too, if I may say so. Isn't that an extraordinary coincidence?"

There was silence.

"That phone call didn't have anything to do with the police by any chance, did it, Danes?"

Danes slowly shook his head. "Goodbye, sir."

Chapter 37

Monday 5 May 1941
Bognor Regis – West Sussex – England

Sudner House had stood cold and unsold for five years in the countryside north west of Bognor Regis, a seaside resort on the south coast of England. That its last and second-last owners had committed suicide after discovering that their wives were having affairs was one thing. That both women had had their affairs with the same tradesman, an electrician, was quite another. This detail of local culture had discouraged potential buyers, especially married male ones, and estate agents alike ever since.

The place's generous dimensions, including twenty-five bedrooms and expanses of lawn ideally suited to sports, had attracted the Royal Navy's attention in early 1940. It had thus been requisitioned as a discreet place to care for high-ranking officers experiencing low-ranking mental disorders before becoming an all-purpose venue for navy-themed celebrations or training.

A single guard raised the safety barrier at the entrance to the grounds to let two buses cover the last three-hundred yards to the white and brown building. Craning their necks to get a better look at it, the crew of U-boat U693 discovered that their destination looked nothing like the prisoner-of-war camp they'd been expecting. The men filed out of the buses and up a flight of steps to Sudner House's main entrance, where a sailor in uniform directed them to a conference room in the east wing. The time was 11:15 am.

Seven rows of eight seats faced a screen with a large map of the United Kingdom on its left and a board covered by a rectangle of green cloth on its right. As the German submariners sat down, two sailors closed the room's curtains. Two projectors, one for films and the other for stills, stood side by side behind the rows of seats and not one of the Germans failed to notice the generous buffet laid out at the back of the room.

Two men strode into the room and stood before them. Their faces were expressionless. All chatting ceased.

"Meine Herren, good morning to you," the youngest of the two, a burly man in his late thirties, said in fluent German. "I'm Lieutenant Geoffrey Cernan of the Royal Navy and this is Mr. Brendan Bracken, who works for the British government. The objective of this meeting is to take you through three options regarding your next steps in the United Kingdom. As Mr. Bracken doesn't speak German, he'll stop every couple of sentences to let me translate. Should anything not be clear, please don't hesitate to interrupt. Do any of you speak fluent English?"

Eleven hands were raised.

"Fine. I'll be relying on you, gentlemen, to challenge me should I not translate Mr. Bracken's words faithfully. Thank you. The floor is yours, Mr. Bracken."

Flattening his red hair, Bracken was tempted to smile as he scanned the mostly pale faces in front of him but thought better of it. Most of his encounters with Germans up to that point had involved seasoned diplomats, politicians and businessmen, many of them sickeningly fluent in English and at least his equal in terms of education and world-weariness. This, he suddenly realised, was his first contact with ordinary German citizens, albeit exceptionally brave ones, and he wasn't sure how a smile from an enemy government employee might be interpreted.

"Good morning, gentlemen, and welcome to Sudner House, just outside a town called Bognor Regis. This place has been requisitioned by the Royal Navy and is reserved entirely for you. There are rooms, hot baths and fresh clothes for all of you here and I hope they'll contrast pleasantly with the kind of hospitality we've displayed over the last couple of days. As you've probably noticed, there is little security here. There are forty-eight of you and just a handful of us. So if you want to take the place over and use us as hostages, please carry on. Lieutenant Cernan said we'd be exploring three options for you this morning. Well, that was the first one."

No reaction.

"The second option is something you can observe in a short film we shot three weeks ago at a prisoner-of-war camp in Cumbria, in the north-west of England. We detain German and Italian officers there."

As he translated Bracken's words, Cernan pointed to Cumbria on the map of Great Britain. He then nodded to the two sailors, one of whom switched off the lights whilst the other switched on the film projector.

A table with four men sitting around it filled the screen. Three of the faces were visible. There was no sound.

"These men are German officers," Bracken said, "and they don't know they're being filmed. Does the man who's talking seem familiar?"

Several submariners whispered nervously to each other.

"Yes, that's Otto Kretschmer on the right," Bracken continued. "As you can see, your most deadly U-boat commander has been well looked after since his capture in—when was it, Lieutenant?"

"March of this year," Cernan said. He held up a slim folder. "May I ask who First Officer Hedner is?"

From the second row, Ernst Hedner raised a hand.

Cernan stepped forward to hand the folder to him. "Thank you, sir. That's the full four-page transcript of their conversation if you want to read it. We also have a recording of their voices, which is at your full disposal." He stepped back again to address the room. "Kretschmer is asking the other three, or rather ordering them, to help him set up a secret court martial to judge fellow officers. As prisoners court-martialling each other is forbidden by the Geneva Conventions, Kretschmer calls his little set-up a council of honour."

Several Germans frowned at each other.

Cernan approached the screen and gestured towards Kretschmer. "This man was feared for his extraordinary ability to sink enemy ships yet respected by friend and foe alike for helping survivors wherever possible. Now he's taking the law into his own hands to pass judgement on the behaviour of fellow German officers. What he wants to judge is whether captured officers displayed courage or cowardice during events leading up to their capture. The verdicts of the council of honour will determine how officers are treated by fellow prisoners at the camp. Guilty ones will be ignored if they're lucky, excluded otherwise. In other words, Kretschmer's council decides who, if anyone, talks to whom and when in the camp. This might sound petty or childish, but over time it can drive a man to suicide. In the long run Kretschmer fully expects Germany to defeat the UK and liberate all prisoners. When that happens, officers who didn't meet his council of honour's standards will be handed over for official court martial back in your country."

The film ended and the lights came on.

"That's Kretschmer doing what he's famous for," Hedner said. "Writing his own rules. He does it with his U-boat tactics as well."

Cernan translated this for Bracken before addressing the room again. "The question is, gentlemen, how will Kretschmer judge the behaviour of *your* officers? He'll ask tough questions about how much effort you put into scuttling your submarine before the Royal Navy captured you. He'll discover sooner or later that apart from your communication and coding equipment, which you managed to throw overboard, your submarine is intact and now safely moored in a British port. He'll ask how many men died or were injured during your final engagement. He'll wonder why, out of a complement of fifty, exactly one man, the captain, didn't make it whilst all the others got out safely? By the way, your captain's body was retrieved. It had a German bullet in it, not a British one. For the time being, we Brits have chosen to believe your explanation of what happened: that you prevented your captain from drowning you all. But what will Kretschmer's council of honour make of it?"

"Lieutenant, you've only mentioned officers so far," Hedner said. "What will happen to the rest of the men?"

Cernan cleared his throat. "You'll all be taken to London for tougher questioning than what you've experienced so far. Most of you will then be transferred to remote corners of the British Empire until the end of the war."

"Which brings us to the third option, gentlemen," Bracken said.

Cernan resumed his translating.

Bracken slowly scanned the submariners' faces as he spoke. "Before I explain what's on offer, I'd like us to take a look at the general situation. Your Luftwaffe has been bombing our cities for eight months now and is still doing so. In the Atlantic your U-boats have been sinking terrifying numbers of merchant ships filled with the food, raw materials and equipment we Brits need so desperately. The question before us is this one: what is likely to happen next? From our perspective, our only hope is for the United States to join the war. They've helped us with equipment so far, but it's mostly second-rate and far from enough. We need their troops and industrial power too, which is why our Prime Minister, Winston Churchill, is busy sleeping with as many American politicians as he can to speed up that process."

A few Germans laughed.

"Let's be realistic. If the Americans stay out, Germany will win the war. When the Americans jump in—and please note my use of the word 'when'—Germany will lose the war. For all its strength, efficiency, skills and ambition, the Third Reich is no match for the American economy."

A man in the third row raised a hand. "You're assuming we don't invade your country in the meantime, Herr Bracken. As soon as that happens, the Americans will no longer have a steppingstone into Europe."

"Correct," Bracken said. "But where is your invasion of this country? Where are the massed German troops and ships on the French and Belgian coasts just waiting to cross the English Channel? If they existed, they'd be visible. They're not. So where are they?"

Cernan signalled to the two sailors. The lights went off and the second projector came on. A series of stills flashed on to the screen.

"These are aerial photos of German trucks and tanks assembling at the Soviet border," Bracken said. "The build-up has been going on for months now. Your Führer and his generals have been trying to keep it quiet but you can't hide hundreds of thousands of soldiers for long."

A gaunt submariner in the front row spoke up. "How do we know those photos were taken on the Soviet border? Your reconnaissance aircraft don't have that range."

Bracken grinned. "Who said these are British photos? We all have our sources of intelligence, gentlemen. See the built-up area on this photograph? These two circular buildings with a pond between them are unique to a town called Suceava, near the border between Rumania and the Ukraine. Why are German tanks parked beside them?"

"That isn't Rumania, Herr Bracken," the same man said. "It's Cottbus in Germany. I grew up in a village near to it. Those two buildings are part of a college my brother went to."

"Could you tell me your name, please?" Bracken asked.

"Dermich."

Bracken signalled for the lights to be switched on. "Good try, Dermich, but you and I both know that photograph was not taken in Cottbus."

Dermich smiled. "Just checking, sir."

The room laughed.

"It's good to see you laughing, gentlemen. But I can assure you that the two million German men your Führer is preparing to send into the Soviet Union are not amused. Some of them may be smiling at the prospect of a few quick victories, but they'll stop as soon as food, supplies, spare parts, fuel and reasonable weather conditions run out."

Hedner raised a hand. "This is fascinating, Herr Bracken, but we're submariners. What's your point?"

"Your Führer will make my point better than I can."

Cernan uncovered the board to the right of the screen. Three blocks of German text in large lettering appeared. An English translation in smaller lettering was written below each. Cernan read the German text aloud.

...the life of many of our sons rests with the home country. Its sweat can save the blood of our soldiers. It is, therefore, the supreme duty of every German to do his best for our fighting front and to provide it with the arms which it requires...

...the German girl and the German woman can make yet a further contribution...

If the German soldier even now possesses the best arms in the world, then he will get this year and next year, even better ones.

"This is Adolf Hitler yesterday, speaking to the deputies of the Reichstag," Bracken said.

Cernan handed a second slim folder to Hedner. "This is a full transcript of the speech. It's been published all over Germany."

"Anyone notice anything?" Bracken asked.

The room remained silent.

Bracken put his hands in his pockets. "Saving the blood of our soldiers? Saving it from what? Why so defensive suddenly? German girls and women being asked to make a further contribution? Why is that necessary? What kind of contribution? What's changed? What's the problem? The German soldier getting arms this year *and next year*? Didn't the Führer proclaim a few months ago that the war would end this year, in 1941? Why does he suddenly think it'll last into 1942? What's come up? What's the worry? The answer to all those questions is his attack on the Soviet Union. Not that he ever mentioned it yesterday, of course."

The Germans looked at each other.

"I wouldn't bury the Third Reich just yet, Herr Bracken," Hedner said. "The spades you'd need to dig our graves are still on an American merchant ship in the middle of the Atlantic and I have it on good authority that a German torpedo is racing towards that ship right now."

The room laughed, including Bracken and Cernan.

"Allow me a moment of arrogant political philosophy," Bracken said. "Different leaders have different ways of staying in power. They can be as democratic, dictatorial, freedom-loving or murderous as they like in the short run, but they all depend on one thing in the long run: their ability to make ordinary people feel cared for. It is my privilege to work closely with the British leader, Winston Churchill. Does he show he cares for ordinary people? My answer might surprise you: not enough. He might care for them in the privacy of his mind and heart, but it certainly doesn't come out that way. What about Adolf Hitler? Does he show he cares for ordinary German men and women?"

Bracken waited. The submariners stared at him. The only sound in the room was Bracken's right index finger as it tapped the board displaying Hitler's quotes.

"Does he care for them in the privacy of his mind and heart then?"

He waited again. The finger kept tapping.

"Gentlemen, the third option I can offer you regarding your immediate future is unconventional. It's an opportunity for both our leaders, Churchill and Hitler, to show they truly care for ordinary people. I propose to send you and your U-boat, U693, back out into the Atlantic, but with a difference. Half your crew will be Kriegsmarine and the other half Royal Navy. Only volunteers, of course. The total crew will be smaller than the usual fifty because your submarine will be unarmed. All the space normally occupied by torpedoes and extra men will be filled with inflatable boats, provisions, medical essentials and blankets. U693 will prowl the Atlantic once more, looking not for opportunities to sink ships but to help survivors of ships that are sinking or have already sunk. Help will be given to survivors of any nationality: German, British, American, Canadian, whatever. U693's aim will be to keep survivors alive long enough for them to be picked up by other ships."

The room remained silent.

"That sounds like a propaganda exercise to me," Hedner said finally.

"A propaganda exercise is precisely what it is," Bracken said. "It's a symbol, a gesture. A single U-boat will be way too small and slow to make a significant physical difference. But its very existence and mission will make a huge psychological difference to ordinary men and women on both sides of the war. Our propaganda machine will make sure the whole world hears about U693, of course, including Germany. We'll make a noise so loud that Goebbels's propaganda machine won't be able to censor it."

Hedner shook his head. "You're dreaming, Herr Bracken. The Führer will order U693 sunk on sight."

"Will he? Really?" Bracken took a few steps closer to Hedner. "Then explain something to me: if your Führer cares so little about ordinary Germans and Brits working together to help ordinary Germans and Brits survive that he's prepared to sink them, what does he care about?"

A man in the third row suddenly stood up. "I'm in, Herr Bracken."

Hedner swung round to look at him, his expression hardening.

"So am I," said a man in the first row.

Hedner swung back to see who it was.

"And me," said another.

"Herr Bracken," said the man sitting on Hedner's left," how can you be so sure you'll find British volunteers to work with us?"

Bracken shrugged. "I'm not sure at all. I haven't asked anyone yet."

"Perhaps I can answer that," Cernan said. "I come from a navy family. I've already lost a brother and a cousin to U-boat torpedoes. So being in the same room as men who may have launched the actual torpedoes that killed them is difficult for me." He paused to scan the faces. "But if I were a submariner, I know I'd still volunteer for something like this. Not for the politicians who declare wars. Not for the generals who organise them. Not for the businessmen and criminals who profit from them. But for the ordinary people who fight them, who end up flailing in the water as their ship sinks, whom other ordinary people are missing and praying for and who want to get back to their ordinary lives."

The man who had stood up to say 'I'm in' was still on his feet. He now stiffened to attention and saluted Cernan. One by one, then en masse, the other Germans stood to attention too and saluted the Englishman. Hedner was last to do so. Biting his lower lip, Cernan saluted back.

"If you're wondering who the captain of this, er, mixed crew will be," Bracken said, "First Officer Hedner is an obvious choice. When U693 was about to be captured by us he faced a choice: either he helped a self-centred leader cover himself in undeserved glory or he showed four dozen fellow crewmen that he cared for them. The choice he made is the reason we were able to meet today. But gentlemen, please don't make any binding decision now." He gestured towards the buffet at the other end of the room. "Enjoy the food and drinks, sleep on it and let me know tomorrow. Thank you."

Cernan finished translating and stood close to Bracken as the Germans headed for the buffet. "I like the way that fellow tried to unhinge you about where the photograph was taken."

"He almost succeeded."

"I beg your pardon?"

Bracken shrugged. "I have no idea where that photograph was taken. I picked a random Rumanian border town out of an atlas this morning."

Cernan grinned in admiration. "Cheeky of you. But how long do you think the Soviet invasion story will hold?"

"What do you mean?"

"Sooner or later they'll discover the truth, won't they? What will you tell them then?"

"What truth, Lieutenant?"

"That you made it all up. Hitler and Stalin have a non-aggression pact, don't they?"

Bracken looked at him blankly. Cernan went pale.

Chapter 38

Monday 5 May 1941
Berlin – Germany

Anna Vogel wished she'd walked home from the Ministry of Propaganda instead of taking the tram. The elderly woman sitting beside her hadn't seen the inside of a bathroom for weeks, assuming she had access to one. As Anna turned her nose as far away from her as possible, she noticed the British agent at the other end of the tram. He promptly flicked his eyes towards the exit. At the next stop, at the eastern end of Kurfürstendamm, Anna got off first and began to walk in the direction of her home, on Fasanenstrasse.

"Fräulein?" the agent called from behind her.

She stopped and turned.

"You forgot your book on the tram," he said in German, kissing her on the cheek and handing her a copy of Karl May's "Der Ölprinz"[19]. "I see you're a Winnetou fan."

"Aren't we all?" She took the book. "Thank you."

"Even the Führer's a fan apparently."

They began to walk side by side.

"Take my arm, keep walking and give me an amorous smile from time to time," the agent said softly. "Transport to London has been organised. The aircraft will land in a forest clearing at nine in the morning the day after tomorrow. It will stay on the ground no more than two minutes, so be on

---

[19] " The oil prince"

time and stay hidden among the trees at the northern end of the clearing until the aircraft stops. You're one of two passengers the aircraft's picking up. The other is a British man who will spot your presence long before you spot his. If you don't forget to give him the password 'Winnetou', he won't forget to spare your life. He's physically diminished and might need your help. The landing spot is 600 kilometres from here, near the Belgian border. You'll find a map in the back cover of the book. Travel as light as possible—nothing more than a shoulder bag—and make sure you include walking shoes. I'm going to kiss you, so don't back away."

He stopped and kissed her on the lips. "I've just slipped a miniature compass into your handbag," he said as they resumed their walking. "Also in the back cover of the book is an envelope for Bracken. He's expecting it. Two more details. One, the aircraft will be German. Access is through a hatch underneath. Two, if the aircraft doesn't turn up or doesn't land or if it crashes, your top priority is your own life. Abandon the British guy and get away as quickly as possible in any direction except south, where there's a military camp. Questions?"

"Is this British man the one I'm supposed to be looking after in Berlin later on?"

"No, he's got nothing to do with you. But he's the reason the aircraft's being sent. He's being rescued and you're just piggybacking. Take it or leave it."

He kissed her on the lips again and walked away.

Chapter 39

Tuesday 6 May 1941
Berlin – Germany

Anna Vogel strode through glass doors into the office of Joseph Goebbels's private secretaries at the Reich Ministry of Public Enlightenment and Propaganda. She was a familiar sight to the three or four ladies working there at any given time, their desks arranged in a rectangle. But their half-smiles and relentless over-politeness had never made her feel welcome.

"Good morning," Anna said. "I need to see the minister immediately, please. It's urgent."

Without looking up, the eldest of the secretaries, Fraülein Krüger double-checked a list beside her typewriter, as if Anna's name had magically added itself to the minister's appointments in the last few seconds. "Sorry, but his next meeting's due to begin in—"

"Fraülein Krüger, either you go in there yourself and ask him for two minutes of his time or I will."

Krüger, whose first name Anna had never been able to discover, quietly decided she'd make this Vogel bitch pay one day for her insolence. In the meantime and due to the ambiguity of Anna's contributions to the Minister's activities, avoiding risks was a better idea.

"One moment." Leaving 'bitte' loudly absent, she walked over to the Minister's door, knocked and went in. The other two secretaries concentrated on their typing.

"He can't see you immediately," Krüger announced when she reappeared, a whiff of triumph in her tone. "If you'd care to—"

"No, I wouldn't care to," Anna said as she pushed past her into the Minister's office and closed the door.

"My goodness," Goebbels said from behind his desk. "That urgent? Are we invading earlier than planned?"

"Joseph, I'm sorry but my mother's not responding to my messages. I need to make sure she's all right. I'm not in the habit of asking for special favours but if you could—"

Goebbels gestured towards a chair. "Where is she?"

"In a small town called Düren, near Cologne."

"I thought your parents lived in the USA."

Anna remained standing. "They did but they divorced. My mother came back to Germany."

"Can't you ask a neighbour or the local police to check?"

Anna shook her head. "The war between Germany and Great Britain is nothing compared to the war between my mother and her neighbours, believe me. And if a policeman turned up at her door, she'd have a heart attack."

"Why is she at war with her neighbours?"

Anna looked away. "It doesn't matter."

"Yes it does. Tell me."

Anna took a deep breath. "My mother's house is one of four in an alleyway. The occupants of two of the other houses got together to denounce a Jewish family living in the fourth to the authorities. The Jews were close friends of my mother's; two parents and four children. They were taken away one night and never returned. The father was a doctor, the mother an accountant. One of the two families who denounced them had a son who'd just finished his medical studies and was looking for a place in the area to set up shop. The other family had a daughter who'd just finished her studies to be guess what—"

"An accountant."

"Close enough. A notary. She was also looking for a place in the area to set up shop. A quick call to the local authorities opened up two career opportunities. Hence the tense atmosphere in the alleyway."

Goebbels scratched his head. "I see."

"Joseph, I don't expect you to look kindly on my mother caring more for friendship than racial purity, but you asked for an explanation and I gave it to you. I just want to make sure my mother's safe and well."

"What do you need from me?" He stood up.

"A seat on an airplane to Cologne. I can make my way to Düren from there. I'll pay you back as quickly as possible."

"I won't hear of it. Come with me."

As he led the way out of the office, he came face to face with his next visitor, a female incarnation of the Third Reich's physical ideals. Anna recognised the blonde, blue-eyed woman in her thirties as Gertrud Scholtz-Klink, officially Nazi Germany's Reichsfrauenführerin[20].

"Good morning, Herr Reichsminister," she said with a friendly smile as the secretaries stood up behind their desks.

"Good morning, Frau Scholtz-Klink. Please go in and sit down. I'll be with you in a moment."

Scholtz-Klink and Anna smiled at each other with a silent nod of recognition. In March 1939, six months before war broke out, Anna had persuaded Scholtz-Klink, a mother of four[21], to accept an invitation to travel to England as a flesh-and-bones, peace-loving symbol of the Third Reich's enlightened treatment of women.

Goebbels spoke to Krüger. "Please check if a transport aircraft is flying for any reason, civilian or military, to Cologne today. I need Miss Vogel to represent me personally at a series of meetings there, the first of which is at 17:00 this afternoon. If nothing's available, Miss Vogel can use my aircraft. Make sure a car picks her up at Cologne airport."

"Yes, Herr Minister." Krüger flicked a sideways glance at Anna. "Will you need accommodation and a return flight, Fraülein?"

"I'll be staying with my mother, who lives in the area," Anna said. "As I'm not sure how long I'll be staying, I'll come back by train."

"Good luck, Fräulein Vogel," Goebbels said.

Many things could have happened to Anna's reputation in the secretarial office at that moment. She decided to make it soar and plummet simultaneously.

"Thank you, Joseph," she said. "I mean Herr Reichsminister."

---

[20] Reich Women's Leader.
[21] Scholtz-Klink had six children with her first husband, Eugen Klink. Two of them died.

Chapter 40

Tuesday 6 May 1941
Wanborough – Surrey – England

"Guten Morgen, Radke," Sylvia Rowe said as Neil McCrew sat down across the desk from her.

"Guten Morgen, Lieutenant."

"Let's stay in English for this session. You've had three full days of training so far. Three to go, including today. Shall we take a look at how you're doing?"

"Yes I'd appreciate that, Lieutenant."

"You're flying to Germany on the ninth, by the way. There have been a couple of changes and they both seem to be good news. First you'll be stepping off a plane in broad daylight as opposed to throwing yourself out of it by moonlight. Second the person who was supposed to pick you up and look after you in Berlin will be travelling with you all the way from here to Berlin by plane and train. She's due to arrive in England tomorrow for a couple of meetings before she meets you." Rowe took a piece of bright orange cloth out of a drawer to her right and threw it to him. "Blindfold. From now on you'll wear it at all times, including mealtimes, unless I say so. In Berlin you'll pretend to be a blind man."

"How about a pair of dark glasses and a white cane?"

"No." Rowe suddenly thrust her right fist towards McCrew's face. He backed away. "That's why. Any security check worth its salt would catch you out immediately. Blindfold, please."

"Now?"

"Yes." She waited for him to put it on. "So how do you think you're doing after three days?"

McCrew sat in silence.

"I'm waiting," Rowe said.

"I'm thinking."

"Make sure your thoughts include the elephant in the room."

"If there's an elephant in here, there's little chance of me seeing it now."

Rowe waited.

"I think my German basics are coming along nicely," he said. "Much better than expected at any rate."

"Agreed, but that's not the elephant."

"These surgeon's hands of mine now know how to kill or cripple a man in eight ways that no medical school teaches."

"Carry on."

McCrew shrugged. "I now know more street names in Berlin Mitte and Charlottenburg than in Central London."

"Do you beat around the bush like this with your patients as well?"

"You'd be surprised how many patients expect me to. What's the elephant, Lieutenant?"

Rowe sighed. "How many hours have you slept since you got here?"

"I'm a light sleeper."

"Cut the shit, Radke. I'm asking because you *look* like shit. If anything, the blindfold's an improvement. Why aren't you sleeping?"

McCrew shrugged. "How well would you sleep in my situation, Lieutenant?"

"Answer the question."

McCrew adjusted his blindfold.

"Terror," he murmured. "I was about to say fear but that doesn't come close. Trembling, inability to think, waking up in a sweat."

"Terrified of what? Anything specific?"

"I thought it was the parachuting at first but that's been removed from the equation. No, nothing specific. Just the enormity of what I'm about to do."

Rowe folded her arms. "What might have been can terrify us just as much as what will be. Is there a single meal you haven't thrown up since you've been here?"

"Oh, you noticed."

"We keep an eye on many things. Systematic visits to the loo during meals or just after are one of them. How do you feel right now?"

"I could throw up without much prompting."

"Do I have anything to do with it personally?"

"No. Ironically enough you're making my life hell but, er, reassuringly so. Predictably unpredictable if you see what I mean. It's difficult to explain."

Rowe took a deep breath. "I can give you pills to help you sleep and hold down your food if you like but as a doctor you know as well as I do that we'd only be playing around with symptoms. Sooner or later you'll fall apart and you don't want that to happen in Berlin. Before you go anywhere near Germany we have to allocate time to your terror. That's why you're going to describe your feelings, thoughts and physical states in minute detail. I want to know the exact shades of brown you're leaving in your underwear. I want to know which of your armpits sweats the most and smells the worst. I want to hear about the changing dimensions of your testicles. I want to know which words or thoughts accelerate or slow down your need to vomit. I want details of your darkest thoughts, including suicidal ones if any. I also want to know what gives you temporary respite from the terror. Masturbation, for example? A classic. But who or what do you fantasise about? Do you climax or stop short? When and where have you masturbated since you got here? Take the blindfold off."

McCrew did so and blinked.

Rowe handed him a notepad and pencil. "You've got two hours to write it all down. Don't try to be Shakespeare. Just Radke. I want excruciating details. Any idea why I'm asking you to do this?"

"Taking stock, I imagine."

"Taking control. Describing something—terror in your case—is the first step towards controlling it. Putting words on things. Labelling them." She paused. "For what it's worth, I've been where you are. I know what terror is. I discovered it quite unexpectedly one day. I was put in charge of what I thought was a routine mission and the preparation phase went well. Then, without warning, terror hit me. Up to that point I'd weathered all sorts of crises without losing my cool. I knew what it was like to be trapped with bursting lungs under ice on a frozen lake. I'd run through flames to get out of a burning building. I'd been shot at in several situations. I was fine. But this new mission threw me. Luckily a colleague noticed something was wrong and talked to me exactly as I'm talking to you. I ended up with a pencil and paper writing down all the things I was terrified of and exactly what feelings, thoughts and physical reactions they were triggering. Details, details, details. Dozens of them. Slowly I brought my terror under control. The fear remained, though. The fear never goes away. The moment it does and you begin to relax, you're in trouble."

McCrew watched her, cocking his head. "And how did the mission go?"

"It went well. Childbirth usually does."

Chapter 41

Tuesday 6 May 1941
London – England

Brendan Bracken caught up with Winston Churchill as he and a crowd of Members of Parliament streamed out of the House of Commons chamber for lunch.

"How's it going?" Bracken asked as they strode along a corridor.

Churchill grunted. "They want to pussyfoot around by claiming it's a debate on how I'm managing the war. I want to call it what it bloody well is: a vote on whether I'm the man to continue doing the job or not. I'm listening to you."

"I've just had word from Bognor Regis. The U-boat crew's confirmed they're up for it. They've even selected their men. I'm hoping for similar news from Cernan this afternoon about British volunteers."

"Do you really think they'll be able to get along?"

"A lot depends on First Officer Hedner and whether our boys accept his authority. Luckily he's fluent in English. We're giving them four weeks to shape up technically, linguistically and humanly. They'll all live, train and sleep on the U-boat from day one. Cernan expects them to start practice runs in 10 days or so.

"We should have a name for this thing. How about Operation Brandy? They'll be spending most of their time chucking the stuff at survivors, won't they?"

"It's about much more than that, Winston."

Churchill chuckled. "I know, Brendan, I know. Got a better suggestion?"

"Operation Brandy, it is. I'll tell Cernan. Incidentally we don't have a name for Clemmie's operation either."

"Yes, we do: simply The Operation. An operation can be both organisational and surgical."

"Fair enough. Have you persuaded Clemmie yet?"

Churchill suddenly stopped and looked up at Bracken. He seemed on the verge of tears. Members of Parliament swerved around them.

"You haven't told her?" Bracken asked.

"I have. She just won't hear of it."

"Well she'll have to change her mind soon. People are already risking their lives for her sake. Vogel's arriving tomorrow. She's another one who has to make up her mind."

They resumed their walking.

"Where are you meeting her? The Savoy again?"

"I was thinking of Chequers to make an impression on her."

"Forget it, Brendan. Engineering impressions is her profession, remember?"

"Still I'd like to give it a try. I could have McCrew brought there as well so they can meet and get to know each other."

"Go ahead," Churchill said distractedly.

They walked in silence.

"Question, Brendan."

"Yes?"

"What worries you the most in all this?"

"Why don't you ask me what I'm not worried about? It'll keep the conversation short."

"No, seriously."

"The thing I'm most worried about, Winston, is you. Whenever one of your bouts of depression comes along, you always tell me. Always. This time you haven't said a word. You're fighting depression right this very second—I can see it—and you haven't said a word. Not even to me, your friend. That's never happened before and that's what I'm worried about."

Chapter 42

Tuesday 6 May 1941
Cologne-Aachen – Germany

The Junkers Ju 52 began its descent towards Cologne Airport. If take-offs weren't a problem for Anna Vogel, landings worried her to the point of nausea—something about the undercarriage crumpling under the weight of the aircraft. For the first time since take-off in Berlin, she was thankful for the distraction of her neighbour's persistent attempts to seduce her.

Officially, Martin Wessel worked in the second of the Ministry of Public Enlightenment and Propaganda's seven divisions. Division Two was in charge of mass rallies, public health, race and youth. Unofficially he was one of three trusted thugs working across all seven divisions. Answering directly to Goebbels, he supplied muscular persuasion wherever the mental variety failed. Wessel enjoyed sharing a surname with Goebbels' handpicked martyr of the National Socialist cause, Horst Wessel, and carefully avoided pointing out that the two men were unrelated.

"I'm glad they're sending a car for both of us," Wessel said cheerfully. "We'll be able to carry on chatting."

Wessel and Anna were the only two passengers on the plane. Wessel had spent the last half of the flight explaining he was visiting Cologne to persuade its reluctant mayor to free up a hall for a political meeting starring Hermann Goering and Goebbels. The hall was due to host a sporting event for the Hitler Youth.

Anna hadn't pressed for details on Wessel's definition of the verb 'persuade' regarding the mayor. Nor had she supplied details of her own job at the Ministry of Propaganda or her reason for flying to Cologne. "It's as confidential as the persuasion methods you'll be using on the mayor if he doesn't comply," she'd remarked without a trace of irony. Mistake: Wessel had laughed and promptly found her even more desirable.

An invitation to dinner was now moments away.

"Why don't you just say you want sex?" she suddenly asked.

Wessel's eyes widened. "You said it, not me."

"You've done nothing but hint at sex since Berlin. I could complain about your behaviour straight to the Reichsminister."

The plane touched down.

"So could I, Fräulein. Your word against mine, of course. But I apologise if I gave you that impression. You'll see nothing but the gentleman in me from now on, I promise."

They disembarked and walked briskly to the terminal. It was quiet. A bored official checked their identity documents and lost all trace of boredom as soon as he saw who their employer was. He waved them through.

A black Mercedes Benz drove up as they arrived in the pick-up area. The driver, Ferdinand Opitz, a thin pale man in his sixties, beamed as he got out and opened the rear right passenger door.

"Guten Tag, Herr Wessel. Good to see you again."

"Guten Tag, Opitz. This is Miss Vogel." He turned to Anna. "Where's your meeting taking place? We'll drop you off first."

She gave an embarrassed smile. "Actually I'm here for two reasons. My first meeting's actually tomorrow but as my mother's ill, I thought I'd go and stay with her this evening."

"Where does she live?"

"Düren."

Wessel turned to the driver. "We're going to Düren first, Opitz."

"But it's seventy kilometres away," Anna protested. "I'll go by bus. Your work has top priority, Herr Wessel."

"Düren first. End of discussion."

As they drove through the countryside west of Cologne, Wessel prodded Anna with questions about where she and especially Goebbels thought the war was going. Why hadn't Germany beaten the British yet? When was the invasion of the United Kingdom going to happen? How long was the war going to last? Why was Hitler counting on women to work now? Anna politely pleaded ignorance.

"Yes but everyone knows you have breakfast regularly with the Minister, Fräulein Vogel. What else is there to talk about?"

Anna hesitated. "I don't talk at all most of the time."

"Ah yes, perhaps your mouth has other tasks to perform."

Anna swung round to face him. "That's not funny, Herr Wessel."

"I wasn't joking. Your special talents are the talk of the Ministry."

"My special talents are reserved for deserving individuals. The Minister isn't one of them."

"How can the Third Reich's Minister of Propaganda, your employer and mine, not be deserving?"

"The Minister has a wealth of special talents at his disposal. He doesn't need mine in that particular field and nor do I offer them."

"Am I a deserving individual?"

She looked out the window. "If you need to ask, you're not."

"Stop the car, Opitz," Wessel said loudly.

The car came to a halt just after a clump of trees. Open fields stretched in all directions.

"Fräulein Vogel and I are going to stretch our legs. Keep your eyes on the road ahead."

Wessel opened his door. Anna felt his enormous hand grab and pull her arm as he got out of the car. Holding on to her shoulder bag, she said nothing as he led her towards the trees. He chose a thick one about seven metres from the road, went round it and leaned back against it. Grabbing Anna's hair with one hand, he undid his flies with the other.

"I don't expect you to talk, don't worry. After me I want you to look after poor Opitz. He enjoys my leftovers."

He pushed Anna's head down to align it with his semi-erect penis. Crouching and no match for his strength, she put her bag on the ground and looked up at him.

"Is this the best you can do?" she sneered. "I open my mouth for erect penises, not dead fish. Yours smells like a dead fish, too."

He slapped her. She fell sideways. Bending down, he seized her by the hair again and pulled her up, his erection now almost full.

"So this is what violence does for you," Anna said as the fingers of her right hand closed around the base of his penis. She kissed it lightly down one side.

"Hurry up," he grunted.

"There's something you should know," she said as she multiplied the kisses, simultaneously reaching down to slip her left hand into her bag.

He thrust his hips towards her face but she backed away.

"Not so fast," she said playfully.

She rummaged blindly through clothing, toiletries, shoes and a travel alarm clock before finding the switchblade. She removed it discreetly from the bag and in a gesture practised dozens of times for situations like this one, turned it over so her thumb could safely press the blade's release button. Later she would blame nerves and fear for forgetting that all her practising had been done with her right hand. The blade thus flicked out not away from her hand but into it, its tip gashing her palm. As the knife slipped out of her hand and dropped to the ground she said, "I want you to know how grateful I am for the car."

"What?" he gasped.

"I said I'm grateful for the car." Her fingers prodded the ground. Her hand felt wet.

"You're welcome. It's only costing you a blowjob." He thrust again, but she managed to turn her head. Wessel's penis butted against her cheek.

Her fingers found the weapon. "This blowjob's costing *me* nothing, Herr Wessel, but it's costing *you* a car. And a little more besides."

Wessel's brain had no time to process her remark because she immediately took his entire penis in her mouth. He groaned with pleasure as she moved her head back and forth. Glancing up, she saw he was doing what many men did—recklessly in Wessel's case—in such situations: he was looking upwards. Mentally she rehearsed her next movements as his penis hardened even more, his orgasm building. Briefly letting go of him she switched the knife to her right hand and placed her left half way along his penis. The speed of her head movements increased.

Seconds from climaxing, Wessel became vaguely aware of her shifting the position of his penis inside her mouth. Three things then happened in quick succession which brought his pleasure to a halt. Anna slammed her jaws together, crushing his penis flat between her back teeth. A split-second later her right hand slashed downwards, the razor-sharp blade cutting deeply into the base of Wessel's penis. Another split-second later, jaws still clenched, Anna catapulted herself backwards from her crouching position. The remaining uncut penile muscle gave way with a dull ripping sound. Wessel looked down to see blood gushing from where his manhood had once jutted and Anna spitting out this same manhood to her right before landing on her back a couple of metres away.

Anna instinctively glanced towards the car, the rear of which she could just see through the trees. No movement.

A military truck rumbled by.

Wessel's legs crumpled beneath him. Eyes and mouth wide open in shock, he sat with his back to the tree and stared down at the wound. His arms were open in an involuntary gesture of helplessness.

Anna now felt pain in her left hand for the first time. Carefully retrieving her shoulder bag, she took out a handkerchief and bandaged her hand roughly, glancing every few seconds at Wessel or the car. As Wessel was making no effort to halt the bleeding or attract attention to himself, she estimated he'd faint and die in under five minutes. She stood up and checked her clothes. Three barely noticeably droplets of blood had landed on her navy blue blouse. Bending down she ripped a couple of leaves from a nearby bush to clean blood off the switchblade.

Wessel's eyes were closed, his face white.

"Thanks again for the car, Herr Wessel," she said casually as she set off back to the car. She pressed the switchblade against the underside of her shoulder bag to keep it out of sight.

Opitz was reading a newspaper as she approached his side of the vehicle from the rear. His left elbow was sticking out of the window.

"Herr Opitz, Herr Wessel asked me to give you my fullest attention. Would you like me to?"

His head turned towards her with a wide grin. "Of course, Fräulein."

Anna drove the steel tip of the switchblade through his right eye and the socket bone behind it. It then travelled a few more centimetres into his brain. She withdrew it and took a step back before his hands could grab her or anything. Opitz wailed as he touched his punctured eye and discovered vitreous humour on his fingers. The liquid began to trickle down his cheek. Anna checked the road in both directions before plunging the tip into his other eye. Opitz slapped both hands on his eyes, wailing even louder. Anna opened the driver's door and pulled firmly on his jacket. His body tumbled out of the car.

Grabbing one of his ankles and wincing at the pain in her left hand, she dragged his thin body around the car and towards the nearest trees. There was a dip in the ground just behind them. Kneeling, she slit the carotid arteries on the right side of Opitz's neck and stepped back as blood squirted powerfully from the wound. A minute later Anna returned to the car, checking over her shoulder that both men were out of sight.

Two military trucks were now heading towards her. Both were open at the back and transporting soldiers. As they approached, she got into the driver's seat, closed the door and started the engine. She pretended to be checking her face in the rear-view mirror as the trucks rolled by and several wolf whistles greeted her. Forcing a smile she turned and waved to the soldiers.

The trucks hadn't quite disappeared from view when her first tears came. They quickly became uncontrollable. Frantically wiping them away, she rummaged in her bag for the map the agent had hidden at the back of the Winnetou book. Now that she had a car, her plans over the next few hours needed adjustments. But the map remained a useless blur for several minutes. She was weeping too hard.

Chapter 43

Tuesday 6 May 1941
Farnborough – Hampshire – England

"One to go," Mike Paterson said as Roddy Danes held the twelfth smoke canister steady for him.

They'd been working inside the Heinkel He 111 for almost two hours, first installing a steel rack made by Paterson to raise the smoke canisters above the bomb slots and then hooking up the canisters to the control panel at the front of the aircraft.

"Who'll be with you in the front?" Paterson asked.

"The girl probably. If the guy's not in good shape he'd better stay in the back. Either way I hope I don't have to help him climb onboard."

Paterson finished fixing a tube to the canister. "Leaving the cockpit is out of the question, Roddy. You don't have enough time. Let the girl help him." He gave the last canister a tap. "You're all set."

They climbed down through the bomb hatch and crossed Hangar B to a sink next to Paterson's workbench. They washed their hands.

"I've got something for you," Paterson said.

He took a flat white box from a drawer and presented it to Danes.

Danes held it awkwardly. "In honour of what?"

"In honour of you getting back safely tomorrow. Open it."

The box contained a bright pink silk scarf.

Danes unfolded it and put it round his neck. "Mike, you really must get me something more showy next time. This is for funerals."

"As long as it's not your funeral. Will you wear it over Germany for me tomorrow?"

"It'll be the bravest thing I'll do. Thank you."

"It even suits you."

They kissed.

"I think it suits you too," said a familiar male voice.

They swung round. Standing beside the tail of the Heinkel, Churchill was smiling at them. Colin Gubbins and William Farren were on either side of him, struggling to regain their composure.

Churchill strode over to Danes and Paterson and shook hands with them. "Which one of you is Paterson?"

"I am, sir."

Churchill placed a hand on Paterson's arm. "People who know me can testify there's one thing I'm unable to resist: a display of deadly British ingenuity." He gestured towards the Heinkel. "Would you care to give an ageing Prime Minister a guided tour?"

Chapter 44

Tuesday 6 May 1941
Eifel Forest – Cologne-Aachen – Germany

Anna Vogel drove the Mercedes Benz round the northern edge of the Eifel Forest for twenty minutes before heading south-west. As the village of Hamich came into view she finally spotted what she was looking for: a track heading into the trees and just wide enough for the car. Two hundred metres into the forest she came to a small clearing with a wall of metre-long logs running along its left side. She manoeuvred around the logs, stopped the engine and got out to check the car was invisible from most directions. Satisfied, she surveyed the surroundings for signs of recent activity and found none. The time was 19:38.

From her current position, she knew the clearing was some three kilometres due east. After debating whether she had enough daylight left to walk there for a quick look and get back before nightfall, she decided not to bother. Searching the car instead, she found two bottles of mineral water in the boot and drank half of one of them in one go. The other, along with two cheese sandwiches found in Opitz's bag and a half-empty bottle of brandy from Wessel's briefcase, might come in useful the following morning.

Lying on the back seat of the Mercedes, she set her travel clock alarm for 5.30 and nursed her wounded hand. Determined to take her mind off the events of the day, she closed her eyes and began reviewing her options for London, assuming she got that far. A minute later she was asleep.

Chapter 45

Wednesday 7 May 1941
Munich – Upper Bavaria – Germany

Rudolf Hess became aware of birds chirping outside his home. Day was breaking over Munich and he'd been writing letters at his desk all night. After signing the ninth and last of them, he reread it whilst massaging his right arm.

Munich, May 7th 1941
Dear Adolf
If all has gone according to plan, this is the second of two letters you've received from me since May ___ , the day of my "disappearance". The first was brought to you at the Berghof by my adjutant the following day. My fate—alive, dead or missing—was most likely still unknown at the time you read it.
You're only reading this, the second letter, because two things have happened: the British have announced that I'm alive and that they've invited me to stay with them for a while, either as guest of honour or as prisoner of war. The trusted friend of mine who sent you this letter on my behalf was instructed to do so only if those two conditions were met.
If for any reason you didn't receive the first letter, here's a summary: in the firm belief that millions of lives can and should be spared rather wasted by prolonging this war, I have flown on my own initiative to the United Kingdom to offer peace terms to King George VI and his government. My intention is to make the offer via the Duke of Hamilton, a man I met at the Berlin Olympics in 1936. As the Duke lives in Scotland, I have aimed to land as close to his home as possible. The peace terms I'm offering are as follows: if Germany is left to act as it pleases in Continental Europe, the United Kingdom can preserve both its

independence and its empire. I am also requiring that Winston Churchill be removed from power.

The purpose of this second letter is more practical. I wish to ensure my family and I come to no harm because of my actions. Should my aforementioned trusted friend discover that someone close to me has been made to suffer personally, professionally or socially because of their association with me, he/she will send copies of this letter to three news organisations in Germany and six news organisations abroad.

I'd like to think your dignity and honour as Führer would prevent you from letting such a situation develop, but I have learnt to be prudent over the last four years. For whatever reason, you have gradually pushed me away from the inner circle of power. Although still officially third in line to succeed you, I know as well as you do that this is a sham. Although still willing and able to help build our success and future, I am now deprived of the means and influence to do so. The erosion of the trust and closeness that once bound us is one of the reasons for my flight to Scotland.

My growing prudence has led me to take precautions, therefore. My increasingly uncluttered schedule has given me time to tend to my favourite pastimes but also to do some research (luckily my name and title still open doors and mouths). I have thus spent four years gathering evidence on the more sensitive areas of the lives of nine of the Third Reich's most powerful officials, including you. This evidence includes documents, photographs, descriptions, tapes, names, dates, times, numbers and witness accounts. The originals are kept, as you can well imagine, in a safe place outside German-controlled territory.

Eight other National Socialist leaders are reading letters like this one at this very moment. None of them know who the other recipients are. Like you they're looking at detailed and undeniable proof of their moral, sexual or financial corruption, in some cases all three. Yes, this is blackmail and yes, this means that my own moral standing is as laughably low as that of any of the recipients. So be it.

In your case, Adolf, the evidence attached to this letter concerns the life and death of your half-niece, Geli Raubal, in 1931. What you didn't know at the time was how often and how openly Geli confided in me about your love affair with her. At first she tried to use me as a conduit to reach you and influence you but I always refused this role, choosing instead to just listen. It would be no exaggeration to claim she told me everything, including details I would have preferred not to know. Both to reassure her that I was taking her seriously and to convince myself that she was indeed talking about a friend I thought I knew, I took detailed notes. I did so with her permission. On three occasions she also agreed to let me record her voice talking about you.

What I concluded from the whole affair was that you played with her. She was vulnerable and no more mature than her age, which was two decades lower than yours. You manipulated her to keep her under control. You were also obsessively jealous, even using my wife to keep you informed of her activities in Munich.

Your relationship finally reached a point where she was so uncertain of your feelings, reactions and plans that she sent me two letters you'd written to her. She wanted my opinion as a man on the thinking and behaviour of another man. Tragically she committed suicide the day after I received them. When I called you to give you the tragic news, the two letters were in my pocket. You have no idea how angry I was. I was tempted to leave the letters beside Geli's body so the police would find them. I still have no idea why I didn't.

A photograph of one of the letters is attached. The sexual details you write about leave no doubt as to the nature of your relationship with her and the enormity of the lies you told the authorities investigating her death. Adolf, you destroyed her.

But did you murder her? I believe not. All the sordid rumours about your possible guilt were politically motivated and false. Were you guilty of anything then? Definitely. Attached is a photo you've never seen of Geli's naked body during her autopsy. It includes the bullet wound where she shot herself. There is no doubt she killed herself, but your shadow darkened her act and your gun facilitated it.

Although I've written these nine letters to protect my family from reprisals triggered by my actions, I realise their existence amounts to a call for ruthless cleansing at the very top of our state. Our preaching on racial purity and superiority stands in shameful contrast to the systematic corruption which defines us in practice. Before we accuse Jews and other minorities of being corrupt, we should look at ourselves. Our behaviour sets an example that the next generation of Germans cannot allow itself to follow. Refusing to do so would be to that generation's thousand-year credit.

Should the British respond positively to my peace proposals, there is a possibility you and I might meet again. May we find the courage to shake hands.

Yours,
Rudolf Hess.

Hess separated the two carbon copies from the letter and placed the three sheets on three separate piles. For the next hour he carefully sorted, folded and slipped letters and evidence into eighteen envelopes, nine thick ones for the news organisations and nine slimmer ones for the officials. He left the nine slimmer ones unsealed in order to add the date of his flight as soon as he picked it.

He rubbed his eyes. Doing so reminded him of the countless times he'd rubbed them in Landsberg prison seventeen years earlier, as Hitler dictated Mein Kampf to him for hours on end. Germany's future leader had been open to discussion and criticism back then. Doubt had been a source of an improvement, not an enemy. Their friendship had been a treasure, not a vulnerability. The only discussions Hitler now had were with himself, surrounded by listeners awed by his presence and achievements to date yet uneasy about his detachment from reality. The Führer had become passionately and dangerously self-centred, hearing only—and often receiving only—information which supported his rigid beliefs and claims uncritically.

Winston Churchill, Hess believed, was no different. But what about the King?

Chapter 46

Wednesday 7 May 1941
Eifel Forest – Cologne-Aachen – Germany

Anna Vogel reached the clearing shortly after seven, after a brisk eastwards hike through the forest. It was a cold and cloudy morning with rain, she felt, a likelihood. The clearing was deserted. Its northern end, where the aircraft was supposed to turn round to take off again, was several hundred yards to her left. She frowned.

"Awfully narrow, isn't it," a male voice said in English behind her. "Say the right word and I won't shoot."

"Winnetou."

"Thanks."

She turned round. Slightly shorter than her and much thinner, the owner of the voice was leaning against a tree and pointing a pistol roughly in her direction. His arm dropped to his side and he let himself slide to the ground. He looked exhausted.

"Victor Ramsay," he whispered as she knelt beside him. "Call me Vic."

She took the bottle of water out of her bag. "Anna Vogel. Drink this."

He took a sip. "They're sending us a Heinkel 111 apparently. It's not huge but it's not exactly small either. If the pilot so much as farts sideways he'll hit a tree. What's the time?"

She checked her watch. "Ninety minutes to go."

"Let's make our way to the northern end so I can rest a little."

"Shouldn't we check the whole length for obstacles?"

"I've already done that. It almost killed me. I still can't decide if the clearing's natural or man-made."

"Probably both. What happened to you?"

"Food poisoning of all things. The cold weather hasn't helped. How's my tan coming along?"

"White verging on whiter. You need a doctor." She handed him a sandwich, hoping he wouldn't ask questions about her hand.

"What happened to your hand?"

"I opened a switchblade with the wrong hand. I was distracted by a rapist's dick in my mouth."

She held his stare.

Chapter 47

Wednesday 7 May 1941
Over Belgium

Roddy Danes checked his watch—five minutes to go—and the Heinkel He 111's port engine. The black smoke was doing its job. He took a mental note to thank Paterson in style for coming up with such a reliable system.

But in what style to thank him?

Danes had come up with three options, all food based, by the time the underside of a German fighter, a Messerschmitt Me 109, appeared above him. This was an aircraft Danes knew little about for the RAE hadn't yet acquired one, a failing he deplored regularly.

As the Messerschmitt slowly positioned itself alongside the Heinkel's apparent engine problem, Danes checked in all directions for other aircraft. They were alone.

The German pilot waved to him, then held his hand open, cupping his right ear.

Danes made a cutting gesture across his throat.

The German turned his thumb up and down a few times.

Danes held his thumb up.

The German held his thumb up too, then pointed with his index finger at his own throat.

Danes watched him for a few seconds, then turned both palms up whilst shrugging.

The German pointed at his throat again, then at Danes.

Danes now understood. Loosening his jacket, he removed his pink scarf and held it up.

The German held up his thumb. He then fumbled around his neck and held up a scarf, too. It was red with yellow circles.

Danes held up his thumb.

The German smiled and saluted.

Danes blew him a kiss.

The German stopped smiling.

Danes blew him another kiss.

The Messerschmitt banked away and disappeared.

Chapter 48

Wednesday 7 May 1941
Eifel Forest – Cologne-Aachen – Germany

"How do we do this?" Anna Vogel asked.

They were sitting on the ground between two trees at the northern end of the clearing.

Ramsay had a coughing fit. "Before trying to land he'll probably do a low fly-by to check a few things, including whether we've turned up or not. So we'll make ourselves briefly visible before taking cover again. We won't move until he's facing the other way, ready to take off again. Access is through a hatch underneath." He winced. "Anna, I know your hand's hurting but I'll need your help to climb into the plane. Is that okay? The pilot won't want to leave the cockpit."

"Of course. By the way I—"

Ramsay raised a hand to silence her. A faint rumble of aircraft engines could now be heard.

Anna checked her watch and helped Ramsay to his feet. "If it's him, he's seven minutes early."

Peering up at the sky, they stepped ten yards out into the clearing and stood side by side.

"Looks like he's got engine trouble," Anna said a few seconds later, "Shit."

"No, don't worry."

"So the smoke's a good sign?"

"No, I've just understood something in the last message I got from London. It ended with 'Ignore smoke'. So whatever that is, it isn't engine trouble."

The Heinkel was losing altitude rapidly.

"The guy's got balls," Ramsay said, "From that height and angle, the clearing must look tighter than a coin slot."

"Would you have used a different metaphor in the presence of a man?"

"Yes."

"Then do so next time, please."

"Will do."

The Heinkel roared over them at a height of just over one hundred feet. Ramsay and Anna immediately turned to return to the trees.

"Guten Morgen."

An athletic man in running clothes was standing in their way. Panting and sweating, he looked expectantly from one to the other.

"Guten Morgen," Ramsay answered with a smile.

"Don't bother, I heard you talking," the man said in accented English. "Have we lost the war or has English suddenly become fashionable in this part of—?"

The bullet entering his chest put a stop to his questioning. Ramsay had shot him point-blank. The man crumpled to the ground, wheezing and coughing erratically.

Ramsay glanced up at the sky, where the Heinkel was circling back. "We've got to pull him out the way. I hope he wasn't standing behind us when the pilot flew over. He won't trust three passengers if he's been told to expect two."

In spite of her wounded hand, Anna did most of the pulling. The runner coughed up blood all the way. They left him to die behind a thick oak tree. Catching their breath, they returned to the edge of the clearing and peered back up at the sky. The Heinkel was losing altitude again.

"He's got to land this time," Ramsay said. "If anyone in the military camp gets curious, they'll be here in ten minutes."

"Treetops," Anna said.

"What?"

She pointed along the clearing. The highest branches of trees on both sides were swaying.

"Side wind," Ramsay said. "He won't like that one bit."

The Heinkel roared over them again.

"Shit," Ramsay said. "Did I see brandy in your bag? Now's the time."

Anna took out the bottle and to Ramsay's surprise drank a generous swig herself before handing it over. They both glanced back towards the runner, whose head and shoulders were visible behind the oak. He'd stopped moving.

"Did he not land because of the wind," Anna asked, "or because he couldn't see us anymore?"

Before Ramsay could answer, she put one of his arms over her shoulders and helped him out into the open.

"He's circling back again," Ramsay said. "Balls plus a hint of recklessness."

"Is that a complaint?"

"No. Wind's dropping, too."

They watched in silence as the Heinkel came in to land facing them. Its port engine was no longer smoking. The aircraft seemed to float forever, almost hesitant, about four yards above the grass before finally touching down. As it decelerated and taxied towards them, they took a few steps back to get out of its way. Anna felt Ramsay's body tremble as he struggled to stay upright.

Roddy Danes was now visible through the glazed nose, manoeuvring the aircraft into a turn and eyeing the tip of his starboard wing as it slowly swept full circle, only yards from the branches.

As soon as the aircraft stopped, Ramsay and Anna began to move towards the hatch. They would have reached it in seconds if the runner hadn't decided to alter their plans. Lumbering out of the trees behind them, he crashed into them and brought them both to the ground. That was when, lying full length on top of Anna, he died.

"Get him off me," Anna yelled, her voice no match for the din of the engines. "I can't breathe."

The runner's body had also trapped Ramsay's left arm. He struggled to pull it free, succeeded and staggered to his feet. Reaching down he pulled limply at the runner's right wrist but he was too weak to shift the body. He stood there blinking as reflexes and priorities hammered into him by months of training kicked in. *Two don't need to die if one can survive.* He lurched towards the aircraft, ducked under it and straightened up inside the hatch. All he could see was Roddy Danes's face pressing into his.

Danes was livid. "Why should I help you more than you helped her, you bastard? Here's the deal: if you can pull yourself up into the plane, you'll be a passenger. If not, you'll stay in Germany. Now excuse me."

Danes pushed Ramsay aside, ducked under the fuselage and rushed to heave the runner's body off Anna. He helped her to her feet as she gasped for air.

"London that way," he yelled, gesturing towards the hatch.

Whilst Anna moved towards the Heinkel, Danes dragged the body across the grass to hide it behind the trees. Then he ran back to the aircraft, climbed up through the hatch and grabbed Anna's arm. "I need you at the front to shut the hatch after take-off."

Anna nodded.

Ramsay had collapsed on his back at the rear of the hold. His nose was bleeding.

Danes glanced at Anna, who winked. Then he led the way between the two rows of smoke canisters and eased himself into the pilot's seat, on the port side. He pointed to a button on the right. "Sit there and keep your eye on me as we take off. When I give you a thumbs-up, press that button and check behind us that the hatch closes."

Engines thundering, the Heinkel accelerated along the clearing. Covering her ears, Anna watched a strange expression come over Danes's face as he stared ahead. He seemed at once focused and hypnotised.

As the Heinkel took off, she saw his eyes flick towards her to check she was still paying attention. Her left forefinger was on the button. Five seconds after take-off, Danes gave her a thumbs-up and she pressed.

The hatch flaps didn't move.

Instead the two rows of bombs stored under the smoke canisters were released. The aircraft bumped upwards as they dropped through the hatch. Realising what she'd done, Anna opened her mouth in shock as her eyes met Danes's.

The sound of explosions caught up with the Heinkel as the bombs hit the military camp south of the clearing.

Danes reached up and flicked a switch. The hatch flaps began to close. It was Danes's turn to wink at Anna.

1937

Two years before World War Two

Chapter 49

Friday 6 August 1937
New York – USA

Dinner turned out to be exquisite and relaxing, not least because David Cassell was no more interested in sleeping with Anna Vogel than she was inclined to remain polite if he nudged the conversation in that direction.

"We know your job interviews are in Europe," he said as she sipped her second glass of wine. "One in Berlin, one in London, in that order and both in November. After coffee with me at Dino's you sent telegrams to confirm both. You'll be attending the Berlin one out of half-serious curiosity and the London out of half-amused professional interest. Stop me if I'm wrong."

"Who's we?"

"I'll get to that. What I want to do now is explain why you should reverse the order of those interviews. Start with Bracken in London, find out what he wants, raise his expectations just a fraction and turn him down, frustrating him just enough to leave a mark, not a stain."

Anna scoffed. "What do you expect me to tell him?"

"You'll find something. Bring women into it. Tell him the Brits consider women useful *but* a pain in the ass whereas the Nazis consider women useful *because* they're a pain in the ass. That should shut him up. Either way Bracken isn't of much interest to us right now because his idol, Churchill, is in the wilderness and quite likely to stay there. Goebbels on the other hand is already in power and likely to stay there. The German offer is the one we want you to accept."

"Who's we?"

"You've become an important person, Anna." He let that sink in. "But important doesn't mean skilled. Don't get me wrong—I'm not talking about your academic and professional skills, which are in a class of their own. Bracken and Goebbels wouldn't both be courting you if that wasn't the case. The skills I'm referring to are the ones we need you to have."

Anna folded her arms. "David, there's no point in continuing if you don't tell me who you are."

"Berlin and London both want to control you so they can use you. We want you to control them so you can use them. If you like who we are and what we represent, we'll help you do just that. We'll train you. We'll show you how to keep them off balance, how to wrongfoot them, how never ever to fit into their plans, how always to force them to adapt to you, how never to be taken for granted."

"How to piss them off, you mean."

"On the contrary. We'll teach how to hide who you are and what you want in plain sight."

Anna scoffed. "And you, I presume, know who I am and what I really want better than I do."

Cassell smiled and raised his glass.

1941

Chapter 50

Wednesday 7 May 1941
Farnborough – Hampshire – England

Roddy Danes and Mike Paterson were waltzing a second lap around the Heinkel He 111, which was safely back in Hangar B at Farnborough Airfield.

"You should have seen her face when she realised she'd dropped bombs instead of shutting the hatch," Danes said.

Paterson laughed. "I'll reposition that button so you can release them yourself. How was the flight back?"

"I almost ran out of black smoke. One extra canister would keep things comfortable. Otherwise no problem. A fighter took a look at me on the way there and two others over the Belgian coast on the way back. A thumbs-up from me kept everyone happy."

"How was the landing strip or whatever you like to call it?"

Danes's features tensed. "Thank God we practised. A landing strip it definitely isn't."

"Gubbins called, by the way. He asked if you'd be, er, receptive to a slight change in plan."

The waltzing stopped.

"Another one?" Danes asked.

"He said to stand by for a third flight next Monday, Tuesday or Wednesday. Farren's approved it."

"Same destination?"

"Yes, you'd be picking up one or two passengers this time, depending on the outcome of a something in Berlin. Very vague. You should call him."

Paterson put his hands on Danes's shoulder. "I think he's pushing your luck a bit far."

"I won't insult your intelligence by saying 'third time lucky'."

"No, you'd insult my knowledge of probability theory."

Chapter 51

Wednesday 7 May 1941
Chequers – Buckinghamshire – England

Brendan Bracken and Anna Vogel strolled across the lawn towards the impeccably tended rose garden. There were each carrying a glass of champagne.

"What is this place?" Anna asked. "The security to get in was incredible."

"Chequers, the British Prime Minister's official country residence. Therefore it belongs to the government, not Churchill. He's got his own residence elsewhere."

"Ah yes, Chartwell. I've seen Goebbels study it on photographs. The war's forced Churchill to close it down, hasn't it."

Bracken didn't answer.

"Is he here?"

"No, sorry. He's been kind enough to let me use it for our meeting. We needed somewhere pleasant, safe and discreet to put you up for a couple of nights. I've also arranged for your Berlin protégé to be brought here for the night tomorrow. You'll be able to get to know each other before the big adventure."

She handed him an envelope. "From your agent in Berlin."

Bracken gave her his glass to hold, opened it and took out an official-looking German document. "Ah, yes. I'll send it on. Thank you."

"Don't pretend to understand German if you don't, Mr Bracken. It's a dispensation from military duties. The original owner it was stolen from is almost completely blind. I assume your forgers are going to adapt it to my protégé."

Bracken cocked an eyebrow as he replaced the document in the envelope and took his glass back. "So you opened an envelope addressed to me?"

She stopped and faced him. "What's this all really about, Mr Bracken? Your agent tried his best to look convincing and tried even harder to sound it but I don't think even he believed what he was saying."

"What he told you is correct. In exchange for you chaperoning our envoy to Berlin for a few days and then feeding us intelligence from within the Ministry of Propaganda for however long it takes, we can either pay you or guarantee you employment and immunity after the war. If you're expecting me to offer anything different, you've flown an awful long way and taken an awful lot of risks for nothing."

"Are the chaperoning and spying related in any way?"

"No. Once we'd come up with the idea of you chaperoning our envoy, the idea of you spying for us afterwards simply emerged. Given your closeness to Goebbels, it seemed obvious, almost natural. The only two things the chaperoning and spying have in common are their beneficiary—us—and their perpetrator—you."

"As you don't want to reveal your envoy's identity, can you at least tell me if he's meeting someone in the government or in the military?"

"Neither of those. His mission is to persuade his contact in Berlin to do something. That's all you need to know. What we expect of you is simple: to hide him at your place for a few days and to accompany him as often as necessary to within the vicinity of the contact. You won't know the contact's exact address." He took an envelope out of an inside pocket and handed it to her. "We've opened a Swiss account in your name. The balance is already generously positive and the details are in that envelope. Regardless of what happens from now on, the money is yours to keep. Should you decide to chaperone our envoy, the balance will triple as soon as the contact makes his decision, positive or negative. It will increase by a further 15% for every additional night our man needs to stay at your flat until we can get him back out of Berlin. Should you decide to continue working for us as an agent at the Ministry of Propaganda, we will no longer touch the Swiss bank account. We will however, and assuming we win the war, offer you ten years of full-time employment and research funding at one of our top universities. You will also be guaranteed fifty years of official amnesia regarding your association with Goebbels. You'll be a British state secret. It would be most helpful, by the way, if you didn't show up on too many photographs alongside Goebbels or start killing Jews or political opponents yourself."

Anna sipped her champagne as they resumed their stroll. "Goebbels is in an uncomfortable position right now. A key thing to understand with him is that he's addicted to his boss's attention, compliments and recognition. All the Third Reich leaders are the same to some extent, but Goebbels and the likes of Rudolf Hess are more addicted than most. Over the past few weeks, however, Goebbels has realised that Hitler's been keeping him in the dark or only partly informed about a few critical moves. If I said 'imminent Soviet invasion' to you, would it be a total surprise?"

Bracken said nothing. They left the rose garden and headed back to the house.

Anna scoffed. "I thought not. Well it's been on the cards since last year and Goebbels only heard about it in March this year. So the poor darling's feeling unloved and excluded. Add to that his belief that the invasion will fail and you end up with a minister of propaganda in deep despair."

Bracken adjusted his glasses. "You mean he's having doubts about Hitler?"

Anna nodded. "He's not the only one. And Hitler's speech to the Reichstag on Sunday didn't help matters."

"What are you trying to tell me?" Bracken asked

"If an immature attention addict like Goebbels can't get his fix of attention, compliments and recognition from his usual dealer, what's he likely to do?"

Bracken waited.

"Well?" she insisted.

"He'll have to get his fix of attention, compliments and recognition elsewhere."

"Precisely."

"But Hitler's the only dealer in that kind of thing. There's no one else in Germany to turn to."

"Precisely."

Bracken scoffed. "Precisely what?"

"There's no one else in Germany to turn to. You're right."

"I don't understand."

She turned sarcastic. "Doesn't Mr Churchill deal in drugs such as attention, compliments and recognition too, Mr Bracken? Or are his political ethics too elevated for that kind of thing? To answer your question, what I'm trying to tell you is that Churchill will never find a more desperate customer for attention, compliments and recognition outside this country than Goebbels. In fact, Churchill can do a lot more to weaken Goebbels and his Ministry from the outside than I ever could from the inside."

Bracken lit a cigarette, fingers trembling.

Anna handed the envelope back to him. "If I feed intelligence to you from Goebbels's Ministry, I'll do it in my own time for my own reasons and certainly not for money. Guaranteed employment after the war? I'm good at what I do, Mr Bracken. You and I both know I'll have no trouble finding work. As for my close professional association with a Nazi criminal, many people will want to hold me to account. Let them. But just as many others will see my kind of work experience as something to learn from, not to banish. Goebbels might be a murderous racist but knows a thing or two about stringing a message together. So what are we left with? Ah yes, my chaperoning of your little envoy to Berlin. Unless you tell me what it's about and why I should risk my life to help, sorry I'm not interested."

"Then why are you here?"

She took a deep breath. "When we first met four years ago, I told you your attitude towards women was naïve. Three days ago, your agent in Berlin used the words 'less naïve' to get my attention. Were those words just that, an attention grabber, or has something really changed for women around here since 1937?"

Bracken was ready for this. "The most obvious change is that we've recruited women massively for the war effort—something the Führer's only just getting round to doing, I see. They're doing a remarkable job. In many cases they've taken over."

"And what are you paying theme?"

Bracken's face sank. "Oh, for God's sake."

"What are you paying them, Mr Bracken? If they're doing such a remarkable job standing in for their men, they must be getting the same wages, right?"

"There's a war on. These are exceptional circumstances."

"Ah, I see," she snapped. "So you've had to lower their wages because of the war. Fine. But that can only mean that women are paid the same as men for the same work when there's no war on, right?"

Bracken scratched his head.

"Right, Mr Bracken?" she insisted. "Seems we're worrying about different things. You're worrying about one British man getting safely to a meeting in Berlin. I'm worrying about 25 million British women getting fair treatment. You talk about circumstances being exceptional. Well in one respect they're no more exceptional in this war than they were in the Great War in 1914-18. Women contributed enormously back then as well. Suddenly they had status. Suddenly they had respect even though they worked for a pittance. And what happened when the fighting ended? They were told to return quietly to their kitchens and laundry to make way for their returning husbands. What's the plan for the end of this war, Mr Bracken?"

He stared at her blankly.

"If Churchill and his party have their way, exactly the same thing will happen and you know it. You're assuming women will return quietly and gratefully to their pre-war status as pieces of furniture with voting rights. You've got nothing planned for them. No change. Or rather you do have a plan: containment. Don't worry chaps, there isn't a British woman whose ambition can't be demolished with a well-timed pregnancy. There isn't a woman whose political fire can't be extinguished with semen. That's how you men all think, isn't it?" She stood up. "Please find someone else to look after your envoy in Berlin."

"Fascinating," said a woman's voice behind her.

Anna swung round.

"I'm Clementine Churchill. You might have heard of my husband. You must be Miss Vogel from Berlin. Brendan's told me about you. Please don't storm off just yet."

They shook hands. Anna glanced nervously at Bracken.

"Miss Vogel, perhaps I can explain things differently. My husband needs that meeting in Berlin to take place because it's crucial to his future. That's what no one's telling you. If I knew why it's crucial to his future, I'd tell you. But I don't. I'm just a piece of furniture whose owner keeps things like that to himself, probably for fear they might trigger an ambition in me or light a fire. What I do know, however, is that he's calling on someone from the *outside* to ensure the meeting takes place because he doesn't want word to spread too quickly on the *inside* that he's vulnerable. May I tell you a story about him?"

"Of course."

"When the question of women's voting rights came up a quarter of a century ago, he was deeply against it. He thought it was a preposterous idea. But eventually he came round. He changed. How do you think that happened?"

Anna grinned. "Even a piece of furniture can be persuasive at times."

"Persuasive? My dear, I deprived him. Do I need to specify of what? Here's a clue: it wasn't food or alcohol. He ended up so desperate that he'd have given voting rights to horses and pigeons as well if I'd asked him to."

Anna laughed.

"My point is this, Miss Vogel: my husband's attitude to women has changed and it's changed for the better. But can he change the attitude of the powerful old fogeys around him? That's the question." She glanced at Bracken. "My husband Winston is the man this country needs to win the war. But he isn't the man this country needs to win the peace. At least not yet. To most ordinary people I talk to he represents this country's present and past, not its future. And when bombs stop falling from the sky at last, they'll remember that. My own belief is that he should retire from public life when it's all over. He's ageing fast and will run out of energy sooner or later. But I know him well. He'll want to stay in power and that's when he'll realise how much the British public, including women, has changed whilst the old fogeys around him haven't. My husband can't change them all, Miss Vogel, but he can get some of them to change just enough to tip the right balances at the right moment. That's why the meeting between our envoy and his contact in Berlin is important. If it doesn't happen or if it fails, my husband will succumb to his vulnerability and won't be able to tip any balances. So if you want to help 25 million women in this country, Miss Vogel, please do a little chaperoning in Berlin." She smiled. "Now, if you still want to storm off there's little we can do to hold you back. Do you mind if I steal Brendan from you for a moment? I need a quick word."

Anna raised a hand. "No, please stay here, Mrs Churchill. I'll go to my room and have a rest before dinner. It's been an honour meeting you."

"Likewise, my dear. Whatever you choose to do in Berlin, have a safe trip back."

They shook hands.

Bracken waited for Anna to disappear into the building before breathing a sigh of relief. "Thanks, Jenny. You did brilliantly."

Jenny Macleod grinned. "I can see why you asked me to do it. She's a tough wee lassie."

"She's impossible."

"Isn't that what an old fogey would say when a woman's right?"

Chapter 52

Thursday 8 May 1941
Munich – Upper Bavaria – Germany

Rudolf Hess hadn't had a good night's sleep for days. Everything he did, saw, thought about or even dreamt about circled him back to the controls and handling of the Messerschmitt 110 he'd be using for his flight to Scotland. All he needed now was the right weather.

He stared at the phone on his desk in Munich. It rang at exactly eleven.

"Hess."

"London. May 10th. Massive," a male voice said.

The line went dead. Hess checked through the weather forecasts collected by one of his secretaries and which covered his desk. May 10th seemed favourable enough for the trip but it was also two days away. Forecasts that far ahead were notoriously unreliable. He'd need to keep checking as the deadline approached.

It occurred to him that writing 'May 10th' as his flight date on his blackmail letters might tweak the weather in his favour. Deciding it would, he updated the contents of the envelopes and sealed them. He then took one last look at the names of the officials whose serenity, assuming they had any left, would soon be shattered: Hermann Goering[22], Heinrich Himmler[23], Joseph

---

[22] Supreme Commander of the Luftwaffe (German air force). German title: Reichsmarschall. Goering had several other titles and was took over from Rudolf Hess in 1939 as first in line to succeed Adolf Hitler.

[23] Supreme Commander of the Schutzstaffel (SS). German title: Reichsführer-SS.

Goebbels, Joachim von Ribbentrop[24], Wilhelm Frick[25], Wilhelm Keitel[26], Walther Funk[27], Martin Bormann[28], Adolf Hitler.

Again he tried to think of a compelling reason to remove any of them from the group.

Again he hesitated the longest about Hitler and Bormann. The Führer, he knew, would rely on the robustness of his personal popularity to resist any threat to it. Bormann, who was Hess's deputy but had made himself indispensable to Hitler over the years, would rely on a combination of relative obscurity, hard work behind the scenes and ruthlessness to do likewise. But neither could afford to ignore the quality of Hess's evidence and both would pause at least to wonder what else he might have in store.

Again Hess kept his selection of targets as it was.

---

[24] Minister of Foreign Affairs. German title: Reichsminister des Auswärtigen.
[25] Minister of the Interior. German title: Reichsminister des Innern.
[26] Chief of the Armed Forces High Command. German title: Chef des Oberkommandos der Wehrmacht.
[27] Minister for Economic Affairs. German title: Reichswirtschaftsminister. Funk also presided the Third Reich's central bank (Reichsbank).
[28] Chief of Staff at Hitler's headquarters and Rudolf Hess's deputy.

Chapter 53

Thursday 8 May 1941
Berlin – Germany

Joseph Goebbels's hand suddenly slapped the surface of the conference room table, startling the seven division heads and twelve other departmental representatives sitting around it.

"This is supposed to be a daily briefing where unpleasant decisions are made, not compliments exchanged," he yelled. "When you've quite finished trying to get into each other's beds, does anyone have a half-decent suggestion on how to handle this? It's been four days since the Führer told the people the war's far from finished and we're about to tell them their meat rations are being lowered by 100 grams. Doesn't anybody see the makings of a morale problem here? Has anyone even thought about it?"

Hans Fritzsche, head of German Press, raised a hand. "It depends if we want to contribute to people's discussions on such themes or distract them."

"Distract them? If your son were about to be put in harm's way for an extra year or if the plate in front of you were about to get emptier than it already is, what could possibly distract you, Herr Fritzsche?"

Fritzsche squirmed. "We could announce it as a temporary measure for the summer."

A young woman entered the room and whispered in Goebbels's ear.

"I'll be back in two minutes." He stood up. "When I return I expect to be exhilarated by your suggestions."

In a tiny neighbouring office, Goebbels picked up the phone.

"Good morning, Norbert. You've just saved nineteen of my employees from immediate hanging."

Gerscher laughed. "Good morning, Joseph. I don't know if this will put a smile back on your face but we've found out who the fourth person on Roosevelt's list is."

"Remind me. Are you talking about Winter?"

"No, he's fifth. I'm talking about McCrew. Turns out he's British, not American, but that he's a brain surgeon, too. One of our people in the States gate-crashed a medical students' party and met someone who recognised the name."

"So McCrew's a British brain surgeon working in the States?"

"No, he's based in London and this is where it gets interesting. He seems to have disappeared. He called in sick at the two hospitals where he works but he's clearly not in bed at home. We've been watching his house for two days now. His wife's still around, not him."

"What about Winter? Is he in England too?"

"We're checking that. No news yet."

Goebbels turned and stood with his forehead gently bumping the wall.

"Still there, Joseph?"

"Yes, thinking. Why would Roosevelt, an American, send the name of a British brain surgeon living in London to Churchill? Churchill could have found McCrew's name by himself."

Gerscher cleared his throat. "Maybe he asked Roosevelt for a list of the best brain surgeons and Roosevelt's medical advisers cast their net wider than the States."

"How scandalously open-minded of them."

"Joseph, what's your gut telling you about this? Is it important? Because if it is I can make arrangements for someone to find out where McCrew keeps his files and take a look at recent entries. We might be able to find out if his disappearance is linked to Churchill in some way or just a coincidence. How's the old man himself, by the way?"

Goebbels sighed. "He's in fine shape as far as we can tell, give or take his drinking. But even that isn't as excessive as we'd like to think. If anything it seems to help him more than it hinders him. I receive daily reports on his top people, the Royal Family and his own family and nothing seems out of place."

"Do you want us to break into McCrew's files or not? If you do, I'm going to need to inform people. Up until now I've been calling in favours and everyone's remained discreet. A break-in in London would be in a different league."

"Let's wait till we find out who Winter is."

"Shouldn't be long. If he's a surgeon he'll be visible. I've also put out feelers to Australia, New Zealand and South Africa."

Goebbels laughed. "Is there any part of the world that doesn't owe you favours, Norbert?"

"My sole concern is not to owe *you* any favours, Joseph."

Chapter 54

Thursday 8 May 1941
Chequers – Buckinghamshire – England

For the second time in less than an hour Anna Vogel felt a shortness of breath.

The first time had been in the hallway at Chequers, just after Bracken had introduced her to Neil McCrew, calling him Bruno Radke. McCrew had immediately pointed out with a tiny helpless shrug that Radke wasn't his real name and that he found all the secrecy tiresome and that the least he could do was to apologise for the trouble he'd be putting her through and Anna had blurted that not a cop in the entire Third Reich would believe he was German anyway and—

Shortness of breath.

She put it down to a sense of foreboding. One look at this man and she realised that lending him a couch to sleep on and accompanying him a couple of times from A to B in Berlin wouldn't just be nerve-jangling. His Englishness or at least his blatant non-Germanness, whatever that meant, would attract attention.

"You're wincing," McCrew said.

The Chequers staff had served them a meal that most Britons, rationing oblige, could now only dream of. They'd dined alone in the White Parlour, Bracken having excused himself at the last minute to, as he put it, 'save a couple of innocents from Churchill's mastery of the English language'.

"As your pain can't be due to the strawberries and cream, I'll make a wild guess that it's something to do with whatever's lurking under that bandage on your left hand."

Anna grinned. "Yes, I knocked a vase off a table in my room and stupidly decided to pick up the pieces. I probably destroyed a priceless piece of English history."

"May I?" It wasn't a question. He reached over the table, took her hand and gently undid the bandage.

She glanced towards the door. "Bruno, I can think of more appropriate places to have my blood and guts exposed."

"And I can think of less appropriate people to expose them to. I picked up a few medical basics in the army. Has this been disinfected?"

"A staff member drowned it in something, probably Churchill's whisky. Stung like hell."

She marvelled at McCrew's deftness and confidence as he closed the bandage again, securing it differently and swiftly.

"You're not far off needing stitches. I'll keep an eye on it and change the dressing tomorrow morning. I'll speak to the staff and stock up on bandages and disinfectant for our trip. I doubt we'll get much opportunity to look for a chemist in Germany." He paused, smiling. "I want to thank you, Anna."

A dog barked somewhere.

"What for?"

"For putting me at ease. My experience of dangerous overseas operations amounts to nil and I was terrified of embarrassing you, or even scaring you, with my patent lack of gung-ho courage. But somehow this meal has been a moment of relaxation." The tiny helpless shrug again. "So thank you."

"The only thing you've embarrassed me with so far is your lie about picking up a few medical basics in the army." Anna's voice had an edge to it. This man would be a problem. "I can tell you picked up much more than basics and I'm not sure it was in the army. But you're welcome."

His smile vanished. She felt a shortness of breath again.

"Suggestion," he said. "If you ignore my embarrassing lie about my medical skills, I'll ignore your embarrassing lie about a vase being the cause of your injury. What do you think?"

She nodded.

Chapter 55

Thursday 8 May 1941
Berlin – Germany

Tina Winter decided to leave her husband for good at some point between the third and fourth slap. A nail on his right hand had scraped her forehead and drawn blood during the third but hadn't stopped the violence, or even slowed it.

Frank Winter drank less than usual that evening and came home earlier, eager to settle an argument with her that had taken place entirely in his head and that he, apparently, had won anyway. He now wanted to punish her for starting the argument in the first place.

First slap.

"Go and fuck yourself," she responded. "Or better still, go back out and get really drunk. At least I'd have a fighting chance."

He swung at her again and missed. They were in their sitting-room and she manoeuvred to keep the couch between them. But he was nimbler than her and she quickly found herself trapped against the door.

Second slap.

She landed a punch in his stomach. He doubled up on the floor, retching. She watched him for few seconds before kicking him in the ribs. But instead of crippling him further, the pain gave him a surge of energy. Surging to his feet he trapped her against the door again. She began to raise her arms to protect her head but he was faster.

Third slap. Nail. Forehead. Blood.

She stood there panting, fingering her forehead, ignoring her husband.

Winter then made the mistake of assuming he'd won.

Fourth slap. Lighter. Casual. Almost an afterthought.

His testicles had always been a private joke between them. Earlier in their marriage, when they'd tried to have a child, Tina had taken to fondling them several times a day in the most unlikely public settings as 'gently urgent reminders'—her choice of words—of her expectations.

Her right knee now expressed different expectations—closer to conclusions—as it jerked upwards between his legs. Winter's body briefly hung as if weightless before slumping to the ground. He didn't make a sound.

Leaving him there, Tina checked her forehead in the hallway mirror. As she dabbed the blood away with a handkerchief she wondered if this time, at last, she'd be spared a confrontation with her worst enemy. An enemy she'd fought ever since running away from her family, friends and life in Cambridge to marry Frank and settle in Berlin: guilt.

Chapter 56

Thursday 8 May 1941
London – England

Lying in bed, Clementine Churchill gave up trying to blink her eyesight back into focus. The words of her book of Wordsworth poetry remained fuzzy. Snapping the book shut, she sighed in frustration.

"There's something you've got to help me with," her husband announced as he walked in. He was holding a thick notebook and a pencil.

"If you're going to bring up that ridiculous operation idea again, forget it," Clementine snapped.

Churchill sat on the edge of the bed and opened the notebook to a page covered in single words. "No, I'm finalising a little talk. I'm going to say a few words and I want you to give me the first rhyming word you can think of each time."

Clemmie closed her eyes and slowly shook her head. "Winston, really."

"Win." He prepared his pencil to write.

"I'm too tired."

"Win, Clemmie."

"Gin."

Churchill looked up from his notebook, pouted and crossed 'win' out in the notebook. "Defeat."

"Retreat."

He brightened up at this and scribbled her answer.

"Scare."

"Share."

Churchill nodded as he scribbled.

"Fear."

"Clear."

"Too easy."

"Near."

Churchill stared at her.

"You seem to be accusing me of something, "she said.

He stood up. "No, my dear, I'm thanking you."

Chapter 57

Friday 9 May 1941
Farnborough – Hampshire – England

The Heinkel He 111 stood in front of Hangar B. Roddy Danes, Mike Peterson, Anna Vogel and William Farren kept chatting on one side of it whilst Colin Gubbins and Brendan Bracken took Neil McCrew round to the other side.

Gubbins handed a set of documents to McCrew. "Two points. First I want you to study those carefully during the flight. Our forgers have officially declared you a German citizen. The pass on the top is crucial because it makes you officially blind and dispenses you of all military duties. Don't go anywhere without it. Second, you'll have at least three opportunities a day to send a message to us via our agent. He'll either contact you himself in his own way or time—in which case he'll mention strawberries to identify himself—or you can signal to him that you want to send a message by placing a white object in one of the street-facing windows of Miss Vogel's apartment. Do so any day just before eight am, one pm or six pm local time and then take a five-minute walk alone along Fasanenstrasse. Don't go out unless it's safe and don't approach him yourself. He'll approach you. It he doesn't approach you within five minutes, go back inside and wait for the next time slot. This isn't the most foolproof procedure we can think of, but it'll have to do. Remember: eight am, one pm or six pm German time. One more thing: no written messages, ever."

McCrew in turn gave a closed envelope to Bracken. "That's the person to contact in London as soon as you get confirmation from me that Winter has agreed to operate. He's a trusted colleague and he'll get the medical ball rolling at this end. My confirmation will include a preferred date and time for the operation, probably between May 14th and May 18th. I've already arranged for a hospital, an operating theatre and a supporting medical team to be on standby. The sooner they know exactly when and where it'll happen, the better. None of them have any idea who the patient is, of course."

They re-joined the others and formed a circle.

"I wish the three of you luck," Gubbins said to Danes, McCrew and Anna. "I've organised some strange things in my career but this one beats them all."

"Good luck from me as well," Bracken added. "I saw the Prime Minister last night and he asked me to let you know you're in his thoughts. He apologises for not being able to put the war on hold to increase your chances of success, but it's the thought that counts."

"If Mr Churchill can't put the war on hold," Danes said, "could you ask him to please cancel any wind at the German-Belgian border?"

They laughed.

Chapter 58

Friday 9 May 1941
Berlin – Germany

Frank Winter usually woke up with some form of hangover. This time he didn't but would have preferred a sore head and dry throat to the pain he felt in his genitals. He picked himself up off the sitting-floor and made his way carefully to the kitchen, where the first thing he noticed was the sheet of paper on the table.

Minutes later, coffee cup in hand, he sat down to read it. Although Tina's German was now excellent, she reverted English whenever she was angry, hurt, counting large sums or swearing.

"By the time you read this, Frank, I'll be on a train or perhaps in a car to somewhere, anywhere, where you're not. The outer boundary of our relationship was drawn by one of your nails on my forehead last night and you stepped over it.

Violence entered our marriage long ago. Forgiving you the first time and allowing the blows to become so regular that I got used to them was my life's biggest mistake. The second-biggest was allowing our professional activities to trap us both into the pantomime they've become. Luck has saved us from catastrophe so far but that luck has now, especially in your case, run out. Believe me, your balls aren't hurting you half as much as your future prospects are.

Although I say so myself, I wasn't just part of your future. Your future was me and I think that's why you began to hit me. Your dependence on me stretched far beyond what your dignity, manhood or identity could withstand. At first you used alcohol to try and forget it. Then you used violence to try and destroy it. Then you used both.

Now that the target of your alcohol and violence has walked out on you, I'd be curious to see how far you get. But frankly I no longer care."

Chapter 59

Friday 9 May 1941
Eifel Forest – Cologne-Aachen – Germany

"What's your landing trick, Roddy?" Anna Vogel asked over the Heinkel's intercom.

"What do you mean?"

"How do you avoid the trees?"

"I don't. If I tried to avoid them, I'd hit them. I do the opposite. I accept them. I include them. I work with them." He checked his watch. "Four minutes to go."

Mike Paterson had replaced the bombardier's seat to Danes's right with a makeshift bench which faced the pilot. Sitting side by side, Anna Vogel and Neil McCrew were both wearing leather head protection and intercom equipment. Their heads were turned towards the glazed nose of the aircraft.

"Did you hear me, Bruno?" Danes asked. "Four minutes to go."

McCrew didn't move.

"Anna, that's the Eifel Forest down there now," Danes continued. You'll soon be able to see the damage you did to the military camp on Wednesday. The landing area's just beyond. Bruno, I want you to look at me."

Still no reaction. Danes had asked Paterson to set up the bench sideways for precisely this kind of situation. The angle ensured passengers looked more at the pilot in front of them than at the scenery to their right whilst enabling the pilot to see their faces and spot symptoms of paralysing fear. Danes had seen this condition during training and knew its power to cripple an individual and by extension a team or a mission was devastating. He cursed himself for not having checked McCrew for five minutes or so.

"Bruno, look at me."

No reaction.

"Look at me right this fucking second, Bruno."

Swinging round to face McCrew, Anna nudged him repeatedly with her left elbow. His eyes stared into hers unseeingly. She slapped him on the right cheek. "Bruno? Snap out of it."

No reaction.

Danes was yelling now. "Bruno, you're going to look straight at me until we've landed. Don't look right, don't look left. Anna, hit him."

Anna elbowed McCrew as hard as she could, then grabbed his shoulders and shook him. "Bruno?"

"Hurt him, Anna. Insult him. Anything to get through. I've got to focus on the clearing."

McCrew's stare remained blank.

Anna slapped him again, shook him again.

Suddenly she kissed him, forcing her tongue into his mouth.

"Bloody hell," Danes said, glancing towards them, "is that your idea of hurting someone?"

After a few seconds McCrew blinked and backed away. "What are you doing?"

"Sorry about that," Anna said. "We'd lost you."

"Keep your eyes on me, Bruno," Danes said. "Don't look out the front."

McCrew turned to look at him.

"Say something."

"Yes, Roddy. I'm sorry."

Anna could now make out details of the military camp. Several tractors and bulldozers were visible.

As he eased the Heinkel down, Danes checked that black smoke was still coming from his port engine. He flew low over the entire length of the clearing, checking both the ground for any sign of obstacles and the treetops for any sign of wind. "Looking good. I'll circle back to land."

"Are you going to be okay?" Anna asked McCrew.

"As long as you don't kiss me again, I should be fine."

"Please shut up now," Danes said. "I need to concentrate."

They said nothing as he repositioned the Heinkel for landing. Anna watched him settle into the same deliberate hypnotic state she'd seen before take-off two days before. She turned towards the front and felt her stomach churn as the narrowness of the gap between the trees ahead hit her.

"Shit, we've got company," Danes said.

Two motorcycles had emerged from the trees half way along the clearing and were now crossing it.

"Where did they come from?" Anna asked.

The motorcycles came to a halt in the centre of the clearing as the Heinkel roared over them, pulling out of its descent.

"Listen, both of you," Danes said as the aircraft banked to port. "Option one: we land anyway. They're probably just curious because of the smoke and might want to help. That'll make them vulnerable to surprises for a few seconds. Option two: we cancel, head home and come back tomorrow, weather permitting."

"We're unarmed," Anna said. "What sorts of surprises were you thinking of?"

"I've learnt how to kill someone with my bare hands," McCrew said. "But I'd rather keep that knowledge theoretical."

Danes reached under his seat and produced a pistol. "This kind of surprise. It's a Walther P38, standard German issue. Do either of you know how to use one of these? I've got two if you want."

McCrew shook his head. Anna nodded, took the weapon, checked it was loaded, nodded again.

Danes raised his eyebrows at the casualness of her gestures. "Okay, down we go. Bruno, keep your eyes on me."

Nothing more was said as the Heinkel circled back to re-position itself for landing. This time Anna kept her eyes on Danes, who quickly settled back into his hypnotic state. In the distance the motorcyclists scrambled to clear their machines out of the way.

Anna waited for the wheels to touch the ground before talking to McCrew. "You stay in the aircraft whilst I get out and talk to them. Don't move until I come and fetch you."

"Hatch opening now," Roddy said calmly as the aircraft slowed.

Pistol in hand, Anna stood up and edged past McCrew to get to the hatch.

The aircraft slowed to taxiing speed as it reached the end of the clearing. Danes immediately set about turning it round as the motorcycles caught up with it, keeping out of its way. The riders were helmeted soldiers with machine-guns. They got off their bikes and stood watching as the Heinkel came to a halt.

Danes saluted to them. "They don't seem jumpy."

Saluting back, the soldiers stayed where they were. Anna emerged from under the hatch, straightened up and walked over to them. Her elbows were raised and both her hands were fumbling behind her head as if to remove her headgear. The motorcyclists were clearly surprised she was a woman.

"Guten Morgen, gentlemen, thank God you're here," Anna said with a smile. "Let me just remove this bloody thing so we can talk."

The soldiers smiled back until her hand appeared with the Walther and pointed it at them. "Put your machine-guns and pistols on the ground, put your hands on your heads and turn your backs on me so I can remove my slacks and change my underwear," she said.

They obeyed in silence.

Anna returned to the hatch and knelt so she could both see up into it and watch the soldiers. His headware already removed, McCrew was holding their bags and looking down at her.

Anna grinned at him. "Willkommen in Deutschland, Bruno. Kommst du mit?[29]"

She walked back towards the soldiers. They hadn't moved.

When McCrew caught up with her, she gestured towards weapons on the ground. "Take those and hide them behind a tree. Make a mental note of which tree in case you need them again."

McCrew dropped their bags on the ground, picked up the machine-guns and hurried towards the trees at the northern tip of the clearing. Hearing a sharp crack behind him, he stopped and looked back. The German to Anna's left was lying on the ground. She had shot him in the back of the head. As McCrew watched, the other soldier tried to run away. Anna calmly took aim and shot him in the head, too. She turned to look up at Danes in the Heinkel and gave him a thumbs-up.

"Put the bodies behind the trees," Anna ordered as soon as McCrew returned. "Then hide the motorcycles."

The Heinkel began to accelerate away.

She put the Walther in one of the bags McCrew had brought and moved to the side of the clearing. She sat down with her back to a tree to watch the aircraft take off. She'd killed four men in two days and knew this would catch up with her mentally in unpleasant ways soon. She only hoped it wouldn't be as nightmares.

Suddenly she wanted calm.

Suddenly she wanted safety.

Suddenly she wanted softness.

Suddenly she realised, as the Heinkel climbed and banked westwards and she turned her attention back to the clearing, that only one thing mattered to her: the welfare of the man struggling comically—he couldn't be described as muscular—to push the motorcycles out of sight. Her shortness of breath at

---

[29] "Welcome to Germany, Bruno. Coming with me?"

Chequers, she now understood, had had nothing to do with nervousness or foreboding about the mission and everything to do with the presence of this man, with the mere and unexpected fact of his existence. Her analytical brain had kept her awake all night at Chequers trying to find a reason for all this and had found none, which was a reason in itself.

McCrew picked up their bags and came to sit beside her, catching his breath and shaking his head. "Anna, you killed those men in cold blood. What sort of propaganda specialist does that with bullets instead of words?" He paused. "Who are you?"

She decided her left hand hurt much more than it actually did. "I'm a resourceful girl in need of a new bandage before any other curious Germans show up. We'll leave it at that, shall we, Doctor?"

Chapter 60

Friday 9 May 1941
Bognor Regis – West Sussex – England

U-boat U693 was moored in a secluded and heavily guarded pen near Bognor Regis, a seaside resort on the south coast of England. A camouflaged canopy rendered it invisible from the sky. The submarine's newly formed crew of thirty-four men—half German, half British—stood to attention in two rows on the deck. Their commander, First Officer Ernst Hedner, stood to attention on the quay, his eyes on a door at the far end of the pen.

The door opened and two men appeared. Hedner recognised both of them. The first was Geoffrey Cernan, the navy lieutenant who had translated for Brendan Bracken during their first briefing at Sudner House. The second, unexpectedly, was Winston Churchill.

"At ease, gentlemen," Churchill called as they strode along the quay.

"Prime Minister, this is First Officer Ernst Hedner," Cernan said as Hedner and Churchill shook hands.

"It feels a little strange to say this, sir," Hedner said stiffly, "but I'm honoured."

"Not as much as me, Erster Wachoffizier[30]. Would you permit me to address your men? Lieutenant Cernan here has offered to translate as we go along."

"Of course, sir."

Churchill turned to the U-boat and remained silent for a moment as he grinned at the crew members. "Gentlemen, I am famous for many things, some of which I can assure you I'd rather be forgotten for. One thing I am not famous for, however, is my humility. Never let it be said that Churchill died of a shortage of compliments paid to himself by himself.

"Yet I stand here before you today, a humble man. A man humbled by what you're about to undertake. A man humbled by his inability, as I look at your faces, to guess who is German and who is British. You all look exactly the same. But that, of course, is the point.

"What would Herr Hitler say if he were standing where I am right now? Would he make jokes about his fame? Would he speak of his own somewhat uncomfortable relationship with humility? Would he derive any satisfaction from living proof—and you are that proof, gentlemen—that what makes us the same can put to shame what makes us different?

"Given Herr Hitler's attachment to what he calls purity, I doubt that he would see such a mixed group as superior in any way. Well nor do I. For one thing, as my wife would hastily remind me, what group of human beings could ever be superior without a majority of female members? For another, and whether you like it or not, you are representatives of populations who, every night, drop bombs on each other's beautiful cities, on the homes of each other's innocent civilians, and on the heads of each other's terrified children. There's nothing superior in that.

"What I see in you, gentlemen, is a set of reasons—thirty-four of them to be exact—to believe that human beings from both sides of a blood-drenched conflict can come together as team members, as colleagues and, dare I say it, as friends to work towards a common goal. To move together from race to

---

[30] First Officer

embrace, from scare to share, from fear…" He paused and grinned. "… to beer.

"Your very existence will make the freezing vastness of the ocean a less lonely, less threatening, less murderous place to be.

"Your very existence will ensure that no victim of this terrible war can sink out there without one last tiny sparkle of hope. No one deserves to die without it. That tiny sparkle of hope is you. You will only save a tiny number of victims, of course, but you will save hope itself. Never forget that.

"Your existence will be a treasure nobody will want to hoard, a secret nobody will want to keep, a promise nobody will want to break.

"This vessel and the proud men aboard it are proof that our great countries have an even greater common enemy. It's an enemy we can only defeat in the air, on water, on land and within ourselves if we join forces. That enemy, gentlemen, is our ability to look the other way instead of helping each other. That enemy is our ability to turn a deaf ear to the giggles of each other's children instead of listening to them. That enemy is our ability to forget that we are but ordinary human beings, all of us."

Chapter 61

Friday 9 May 1941
Eifel Forest – Cologne-Aachen – Germany

Anna Vogel knew their hike through the Eifel Forest was almost over when she spotted an abandoned bicycle fifty metres to her right that she'd seen two days before. She would have preferred the man she only knew as Bruno Radke to walk beside her so that she could observe his non-verbal reactions to her comments and questions, but he'd stayed studiously a few paces behind her, saying little and showing less. She assumed he was mulling over what he'd seen her do to the two motorcyclists and didn't blame him. In his mind she was probably a cold-blooded murderer now, an assessment she'd have every difficulty dislodging.

But she also knew that trying to dislodge it was the wrong thing to do. If her work with Edward Bernays and Joseph Goebbels had taught her anything, it was reputations stood still whilst life moved on. The best she could hope for was to build a competing reputation for herself in his mind, one that would displace his thoughts of her as a killer, not dislodge them. The tricky part was that to be effective the competing reputation would need to be based on actions or behaviours, not words.

She kicked a stone out of the way.

But why bother to build up a competing reputation if he was going to disappear from her life in a few days' time anyway? Anna blinked a few times at the thought of this. Accustomed to ambiguity and reliant on it, she found herself confronting something she spent most of her professional life identifying and manipulating in others: certainty. No, she wouldn't let him disappear from her life in a few days' time, at least not until she'd fully understood the effect he was having on her. No, she wouldn't allow him to—

"Have you got children, Bruno?"

"Yes, I'm married."

"That wasn't my question."

"Yes it was."

She stopped and swung round to confront him. He walked past her without meeting her gaze.

"And no, I don't wear a ring," he said dryly.

"Most doctors don't."

"Most cold-blooded killers—or maybe 'assassins' would be a more accurate description—aren't as nosy as you."

She caught up with him. "Are you a father? Seriously?"

"Trying to soften your image, are you? Trying to show you care about family life and so on?"

She had no answer to that. They walked in silence.

"No, I don't have children," he said at last. "In fact I don't have much of a marriage either. If I did, I wouldn't be here."

She put a hand on Radke's arm to slow him down. "Moment of truth," she murmured.

"Let me guess. When you take a break from producing Nazi propaganda or killing people, you lead a happily married life and are currently expecting your fifth child by your third husband. You murdered the first two, of course."

"No, the moment of truth's behind those logs over there," she said.

As they rounded the logs, the Mercedes Benz came into view.

"Still there," she exclaimed.

McCrew's eyes widened. "Yours?"

"No, but I have the keys. Don't ask."

McCrew rolled his eyes. "That can only mean the owner died recently and violently. Am I wrong?"

She unlocked the passenger door for him. "Get in and shut up."

"Aren't we supposed to travel to Berlin by train?"

"We are, but the station in Aachen is about twenty kilometres from here. I've done enough walking for one day."

She got in beside him and started the engine.

McCrew studied her face. "Why the big smile?"

Chapter 62

Friday 9 May 1941
Surrey – England

Winston Churchill and Geoffrey Cernan sat in silence reading documents in the back of the Humber on their way back to London. Walter Thompson, Churchill's bodyguard, sat in the front with Reg Parker, his driver.

"May I ask you something, Prime Minister?" Cernan asked.

"Yes."

"What worries you the most about the U-boat mission?"

Churchill looked out of the window. "I worry that isolated farmers tilling fields in deepest Yorkshire or Prussia might not hear about it."

"But what if they hear about it and believe it's just propaganda?"

"In order to believe that, they'll first have to give the whole thing some thought. If they do that, we can be satisfied."

Cernan grinned. "I find that a little cynical."

"Welcome to politics, my dear man. By the way, what did you think of my remarks to the crew?"

Cernan stopped grinning.

Churchill turned to look at him. "Well?"

"Respectfully, sir, your speeches don't go down as well with fighting men as they do with civilians. And I suspect civilians will soon tire of them as well. To answer your question, today wasn't one of your finest performances. To me it sounded like sentimental drivel. You want to fill that U-boat with tonnes of compassion. But you know as well as I do that tonnes of compassion are no match for a few ounces of explosive."

Chapter 63

Friday 9 May 1941
Berlin – Germany

The bench Tina Winter was sitting on was less than five metres from the platform's edge. She didn't get up as the train, her train, pulled away. It was going to Frankfurt am Main, a city she'd picked for no other reason than she'd had a pen pal there as a teenager.

Carrying a small suitcase, she'd wandered around Berlin all day. Twice she'd ended up at the central station. Twice she'd bought a ticket. Twice she'd run out of energy, courage, despair or hate for her husband at the last moment. Twice she'd watched a train leave without her.

What was Frank doing now?

The question had drifted behind her into café after café. Had she injured him badly perhaps? Was he still lying where she'd left him? Had he banged his head on the floor? And why worry, damn it, about whether *he* was hurt when she had evidence etched into her forehead that she was the victim?

Between her two visits to the station, she had walked into a small hotel in Berlin Mitte and made a reservation. Within two seconds the owner, a red-haired woman in her sixties with a keen eye for younger women reduced to selling what she'd spent too many years of her own life selling, had examined Tina from head to toe and made key assumptions—marriage problems being the most accurate one—about what had brought this sad woman to the Hotel Schubert. Tina had signed in, booked two nights, paid in advance and resumed her wandering.

What was Frank doing now?

Chapter 64

Saturday 10 May 1941
Munich – Upper Bavaria – Germany

"Danke."

Rudolf Hess hung up and took a deep breath. All the pieces were now in place. He would fly to Scotland in a few hours' time. Not only had his personal astrologer, Ernst Schulte-Strathaus, recommended today, May 10th, as ideal for his flight to Scotland but the weather forecast was favourable and Hitler had just ordered a huge bombing raid against London. This was what the caller, a friend in the Luftwaffe, had confirmed. Hess's tiny personal peace offer to the British would thus share a page in the history books with a major impersonal war offensive, a juxtaposition that pleased him.

Standing by the window in his home office, he fingered a tube of Pervitin, a methamphetamine whose power to boost confidence and counter tiredness had been a crucial factor in the success of Germany's Blitz tactics in 1940. It was also one of the Third Reich's favourite recreational drugs. As Hess well knew, however, its appalling side-effects had led the Wehrmacht, Germany's armed forces, to stop distributing it widely and freely, forcing the countless addicts within its ranks to pester their families for supplies.

Hess rarely used Pervitin himself but knew it would help him stay alert during his flight. And if any side-effects popped up, he'd be including more than twenty other medicines in his luggage to mitigate them.

How to spend the remaining hours before take-off?

He decided to let his son Wolf, nicknamed Buz, decide on morning events as soon as he woke up—possibly a trip to the zoo. Hess would have preferred after that to have lunch with Ilse, his wife, instead of the Third Reich's principal ideologue, Alfred Rosenberg, but Ilse wasn't well and would probably stay in bed anyway.

Ilse, he imagined, was oblivious to his plans and the risk to life and limb he was about to take.

He was wrong. She had been observing his unusual behaviour, especially his renewed passion for flying, for months and suspected he was preparing something big, although she didn't know what.

Hess also imagined that his loyal adjutant, Karlheinz Pintsch, was unaware of his plans.

Wrong again. In the confusion of a previous failed attempt to fly to Scotland, Pintsch had discovered the specifics of Hess's intentions but had kept his discovery to himself. Pintsch was thus in a good position to guess why his boss had asked him to accompany him to Augsburg airfield that afternoon, some 80 kilometres away.

As the first sounds of Buz getting out of bed and moving around his bedroom echoed down to him from the first floor, Hess debated when to ask Pintsch to deliver the first of his two letters to Hitler. This would have to be done in person at the Berghof and Hess didn't doubt that Pintsch would be made to suffer for it. At best he'd be accused of complicity and be jailed, at worst of treason and be shot.

Hess decided to entrust the letter to Pintsch at the last second, in Augsburg.

Chapter 65

Saturday 10 May 1941
Berlin – Germany

Neil McCrew was asleep on the sofa in Anna's vast, magazine-strewn lounge, his face illuminated by rays of morning sunshine. Anna Vogel sat watching him from an armchair, sipping coffee in her nightgown and noting that he didn't snore.

The telephone rang. McCrew woke with a start and sat up. Stifling laughter, Anna placed a finger on her lips and answered.

"Guten Morgen, Anna."

"Guten Morgen, Joseph."

"So you're back. How are things with your mother?"

"Thanks for your concern. May we discuss it face to face? It's important."

Anna watched McCrew put his glasses on and step gingerly over magazines to look out the windows.

"Of course. I'm in Lanka for the weekend. If you have nothing planned tomorrow morning, would you mind if I sent a car for you at seven-thirty? I know it's early and it's Sunday morning and all that but I need your opinion on a few urgent topics. We'll discuss them after you tell me about your mother."

"My price is unlimited real coffee and black cherry jam for breakfast."

"Done."

After hanging up, Anna joined McCrew at the window. "By all means be curious but you should stand back at all times. Everyone spies on everyone else in Berlin these days."

"You're right, sorry." He peered into the distance. "Interesting to see that Berlin uses barrage balloons[31] as well. London's got more than five-hundred of them."

"Did you understand anything I said on the phone?"

He took her left hand and began to undo the bandage. "Only the caller's name. Was that the Joseph I'm thinking of? The undisputed master of Nazi propaganda himself?"

"Not undisputed. Yes, he's extraordinarily powerful but still within limits carefully set out by Hitler. For example, Goebbels writes a lot of press articles, but overall control of the press actually belongs to individuals like Otto Dietrich and Max Amann. Ideology is mostly out of Goebbels's hands, too. Alfred Rosenberg looks after that. Goebbels isn't in charge of censorship of party documents and books either."

"Divide and rule?"

She nodded. "Elevated to a fine art, in Hitler's case. Goebbels wants to see me tomorrow morning. Time for breakfast before you meet your mysterious contact?"

---

[31] To discourage enemy aircraft from flying low, cities such as London and Berlin floated huge balloons in the sky. These were held in position by tethering cables.

Chapter 66

Saturday 10 May 1941
Ditchley – Oxfordshire – England

Ditchley Park was a stately yet informal 29-bedroom home in the Oxfordshire countryside, some seventy miles west of London. Since November 1940 the Churchills had been borrowing it regularly at weekends from its Anglo-American owner and Conservative Member of Parliament, Ronald Tree. Less readily identifiable from the sky than Chequers, especially on moonlit nights, Ditchley was deemed to be a relatively safe weekend retreat for Churchill and his guests.

Clementine Churchill lay awake, having decided to treat herself to breakfast in bed. She was relieved not to have a headache but dreaded, as every morning, the dizziness or blurry vision due to her condition that she'd experience as soon as she stood up.

There was a knock on the door and a maid came in carrying a breakfast tray.

"Good morning, ma'am."

"Good morning."

After briefly putting the tray on a table in order to open the bedroom curtains, the maid placed it in front of Clementine, who then noticed she wasn't dressed as a maid. Their eyes met and Clementine's lower jaw went slack. In fact she wasn't a maid at all.

"Don't bother to say anything, dear." Jenny Macleod sat on the edge of the bed. "Believe me, this is as strange for me as it is for you. Like two mirrors facing each other for a chat, isn't it. That second cup on the tray is for me. I'll have tea as well, if you don't mind. I'm Jenny Macleod, I'm from Glasgow as you can hear, and your husband has recruited me to stand in for you at public events whilst you recover from your operation."

Clementine began to pour tea. "How brave of him to talk to me about it first," she said sarcastically.

"I'll get straight to the point, Clemmie. Do you mind if I call you Clemmie? Too late anyway. A little more milk for me, please. Listen, I'm a widow with three grandchildren and I'd much rather be looking after them whilst their parents go to work than sitting on the edge of your bed telling you what order to put your priorities in. But that's how it's turned out. Woman, you should be ashamed of yourself. Refusing expert medical care on principle because not everyone has access to it?" She took the cup Clementine was handing her. "That's lovely, thank you. It isn't expert medical care you're refusing, dear. It's a chance to spend more years with *your* grandchildren that you're throwing away. How dare you. There isn't a grandmother in this country who wouldn't let a Nazi operate on her so she can be with her grandchildren."

"Did my husband send you?"

"No, it was my idea. When he told me I might have to go home because you were refusing the operation, I lost my temper. I told him I hate having my time wasted. Then I told him there's no point trying to win a world war against Hitler if he can't win a local tiff with you." She grinned. "Oh, he didn't like that. He thinks the sun shines from his arse, doesn't he."

Clementine laughed.

Jenny stood up. "Well, the sun doesn't shine any brighter from his English arse than from my Scottish one, so I offered to come and give you a wee talking-to." She hesitated. "If you don't do this for yourself, Clemmie, do it for your grandchildren. They deserve a grandmother who can teach them a principle or two, not a grandmother who lets herself die because of one. Now you eat your breakfast. Cheerio, dear. Nice meeting you."

"Just a moment."

Jenny watched Clementine move the breakfast tray to one side.

"I have a favour to ask of you, Jenny. I'm afraid it's urgent."

"Yes, dear?"

"I need a hug."

Chapter 67

Saturday 10 May 1941
Berlin – Germany

As Neil McCrew walked along Schlüterstrasse with Anna Vogel holding his arm, he silently scolded himself for wondering how much choice local inhabitants were given about the red, white and black Nazi banners hanging down the façades of their buildings and blocking their view. The answer was obvious. Cloudy thinking on a cloudy morning.

A few metres before turning into Schillertrasse, he felt Anna squeeze his arm. Three soldiers in their early twenties, late teens perhaps, were strolling towards them, their body language at once arrogant and despondent, on the lookout for prey to dispel their boredom.

"Trouble," Anna muttered.

"Yep."

"Shall we cross the street?"

"Too late. They've already spotted us." Wearing sunglasses to hide his supposedly unseeing eyes, McCrew tapped the pavement with a white cane in his right hand and held a thin folder of documents in his left. To complete the effect, Sylvia Rowe of the SOE had taught him to tilt his head and hold his chin a fraction too high.

"Shutting my eyes," he murmured.

The shortest of the three soldiers positioned himself in McCrew's path and signalled to the others to remain silent. Two metres before the collision, Anna squeezed McCrew's arm to stop him.

"Please excuse us, gentlemen," she said, trying to divert McCrew around them.

The three soldiers moved sideways to block their way.

"War casualty, are we?" the shortest one said to McCrew. "A friend of mine tried to feign blindness to avoid active duty. He's in prison now and no longer my friend."

"How do we know you're not pretending?" the tallest one asked.

"Because he's got the right papers," Anna said calmly. "Want to see them?"

"Mutti Besuch[32]," McCrew said.

The shortest soldier brought his face closer to McCrew's. "What did you say?"

McCrew pulled his left arm away from Anna. "Mutti Besuch."

"Want to visit your mother, do you?"

The tallest soldier suddenly grabbed McCrew by the shirt and pretended to headbutt him, holding back his forehead just before actual impact. No reaction from McCrew.

The other pedestrians stepped wider and wider around them, nervously averting their eyes. Others crossed the street.

The shortest soldier laughed. "If his eyes are shut behind those glasses, you won't impress him."

"Yes, we'll take a look at his papers," the third soldier said to Anna.

She opened her handbag and handed a pass to him.

"Mutti Besuch," McCrew repeated more urgently.

"It's all right, Bruno," Anna said. "These gentlemen only want to help."

"Take off your glasses and we'll let you visit your mother," the tallest one said sarcastically.

"Mutti Besuch!" McCrew yelled.

He stepped off the pavement and into the path of an oncoming truck.

Anna screamed 'Bruno!' almost as loudly as the screech of the truck's brakes as the driver tried to avoid McCrew. He failed. The truck knocked McCrew backwards to the ground, sending his sunglasses white stick and documents in different directions as two other women screamed, one on each side of the street. Open-mouthed in shock, the three soldiers stared down at McCrew. Anna knelt beside him, yelling 'Bruno!' again. He lay still on his back with his eyes closed. As traffic came to a standstill in both directions, the truck driver jumped down from his vehicle

---

[32] "Mummy visit."

Anna murmured in English into McCrew's ear. "You'd better be pretending, you idiot."

"I am," he murmured back.

"Keep your eyes closed."

An elderly man stepped forward to help them both up. The truck driver picked up the white cane, sunglasses and documents and handed them to Anna.

"Is he all right?" he asked apologetically. "I'm, I couldn't—"

"Not your fault," Anna said. "He's fine. Thank you."

He returned to the truck. The traffic slowly resumed.

"Germany's pride indeed," the elderly man shouted at the three soldiers, who still hadn't moved. "Go back to your mothers and beg for a different upbringing."

They lowered their heads and turned to leave.

"Not so fast," Anna said as she guided McCrew back to the pavement. She held out the palm of her hand. "I'll have his pass back, please. As you can see, it specifically mentions blindness."

The crowd watched the third soldier hand back the pass and began to disperse.

Anna guided McCrew to a bench, where she brushed dust off his clothes, fitted his sunglasses and patted down his hair. "I can't believe you did that," she murmured in English.

"Nor can I."

"Scared the shit out of me. Still want to meet your contact?"

"I've got no other plans, assuming he's home."

"Schillerstrasse's just round the corner. If you still insist on not showing me where you're going, I'll wait for you in that café on the other side of the street."

"Which one? I see two of them."

"The Eden, but don't go in. When you've finished, come back to this bench and wait till I come out. Good luck."

McCrew got up and turned left into Schillerstrasse, tapping the pavement with his stick as he went. He crossed the street carefully, silently accepting the help of two young girls. Frank Winter's address, he knew from his training, was less than a hundred yards away. Before reaching it, he stepped into a doorway, removed his glasses, collapsed his cane and slipped them into the inside pockets of his jacket. Then he stood still for a full minute, looking back towards Schlüterstrasse to confirm that Anna wasn't watching him.

Everything about Winter's building, especially the perfectly silent hallway and staircase, suggested money, lots of it, trying to make itself discreet. Ignoring the lift, McCrew walked up the stairs to the third floor, took a deep breath and pressed the doorbell of the right-hand apartment. The door opened immediately.

Frank Winter stood there in blue silk pyjamas. "Guten Morgen."

"I haven't missed you either, Frank," McCrew murmured in English.

Winter pulled him inside the apartment and said nothing until the door was closed. "What the hell are you doing here?"

"The answer to that will cost you a cup of tea."

Smiling, McCrew held out his right hand. Winter shook it.

The apartment was full of cats, dozens of them, not one of them alive. Pictures of cats, engravings of cats, cat-shaped ornaments, coffee-table books about cats. McCrew realised he'd forgotten Tina's obsession with the bloody things. She'd been obsessed with them in Cambridge. Still was now.

Winter returned to the living room with coffee. They sat facing each other, Winter in a leather armchair, McCrew on the sofa.

"Sorry to barge in on you like this," McCrew said.

"No problem. Except of course that it is a problem unless you're in Berlin in some sort of official capacity."

"No, this is off the books."

"How would my government react if they knew you were here?"

"They'd get intrusive."

McCrew threw the file he'd brought with him over to Winter. "Female. Mid-fifties. British. Persistent headaches. Yes, we've tried aspirin."

Winter opened the file and skimmed through it in silence, briefly holding up two X-rays of Clementine's head to the light coming from the sitting-room windows. "Do I get three guesses at the patient's name or do I just assume she's royalty or the wife of some political bigwig?"

"Transport to and from London would be organised by us and a handsome sum of money for your troubles would find its way into a Swiss account conveniently opened in your name."

Winter closed the file and put it on the coffee table. "How much were *you* paid to come and ask me to do this, Neil?"

McCrew shook his head.

"I thought not. Money stopped being a motivation for either of us long ago, didn't it. Which makes me curious."

"About what?"

"About how you're going to try and convince me. You wouldn't have taken God knows how many risks to come knocking on my door on a cold Saturday morning if you hadn't given it some thought. Why don't you come for lunch tomorrow and convince me then? I'll have had a shower and got dressed by then. I'll also have taken a closer look at this woman's file. Would that be possible or are the Gestapo already chasing you?"

"Lunch would be fine. Thanks."

"I'll cook something to remind us both of Cambridge. Cheap and filling."

McCrew cleared his throat. "Speaking of Cambridge, how's Tina?"

"Tina's not cheap and filling, I can assure you."

They laughed.

Winter's expression turned sad. "I'm afraid Tina's not as well as she could be. We've had our differences recently."

"Meaning?"

"I lose my temper sometimes and Tina takes the brunt of it. The problem is that my means of expression aren't always as, er, literary or poetic as they should be. There must be some tiny part of you that can understand that."

McCrew balked at this, at once thankful for what Sylvia Rowe had taught him and suddenly convinced he'd never be able to persuade Winter. "Where is she, Frank?"

"No idea. She walked out the night before last. We had an argument. What about you? Any lessons to teach me about marital bliss?"

McCrew forced a half-smile. "None, I'm afraid."

"Then what's the real reason you're here, Neil?" Winter asked softly. "Are you running away from your wife or still in love with mine?"

Chapter 68

Saturday 10 May 1941
Berlin – Germany

Tina Winter lay on her bed at the Hotel Schubert watching a fly make its way in spurts across the ceiling.

She'd considered going for a long walk through Berlin, perhaps exploring an area or two she didn't know.

She'd considered returning to the station to buy a train ticket, her third, to somewhere, anywhere.

She'd considered suicide.

She'd considered doing some shopping. Not that wartime shopping was an interesting activity or that she did much peacetime shopping either but it was something to do.

What was Frank doing now?

She'd considered going to the zoo and had actually got up and dressed at the prospect, only to flop back on to the bed.

She'd considered suicide again.

Chapter 69

Saturday 10 May 1941
Berlin – Germany

Neil McCrew was relieved to find the bench on Schlüterstrasse unoccupied. He pretended to inspect it with a few taps of his white cane before sitting down. Customers, none of them Anna Vogel, were coming in and out of the Café Eden across the street.

A detail about Frank Winter was still troubling him. He'd noticed it early on in their brief conversation and had tried to ignore it, unsuccessfully. He made a mental note to check if it was still there at lunch the next day.

A man sat down on McCrew's left. "Guten Morgen," he said cheerfully.

McCrew didn't answer, now wanting Anna to appear across the street.

"Don't turn your head, Radke," the man said quietly in English as he untied his right shoelace. "Anna will have recognised me and won't show herself till I'm gone." He removed his shoe. "London's expecting a message from me tonight with Winter's decision." He turned the shoe upside down and shook it as if to remove a pebble.

McCrew said nothing.

The man took his time to put his shoe back on. "How were the strawberries at Chequers last night?"

"Winter's thinking it over."

"Next meeting?"

"Lunch tomorrow."

"His place?" The man finished tying his shoelace.

"Yes."

"Regards to Anna." Then man got up and walked away.

Chapter 70

Saturday 10 May 1941
Augsburg – Swabia – Germany

As he taxied out of the hangar at 17:35 and turned to head towards the Messerschmitt factory's own runway, Rudolf Hess felt a surge of confidence, all tiredness gone. He'd insisted on running the final checks on the Messerschmitt Bf 110 himself, paying close attention to the levels in the additional fuel tanks he'd asked the manufacturer to fit. Mechanical and weather-related problems had interrupted previous flight attempts since December 1940 and he didn't want a lack of diesel to hinder this one. He'd also checked the aircraft was unarmed.

He waved one last time to Pintsch, his adjutant, who was holding the envelope Hess had just given him with instructions not to open it for four hours. This attempt would be successful, Hess was certain of it. His only lingering doubts concerned the welcome he'd get from the locals and, hopefully, the Duke of Hamilton wherever he landed.

Germany, he knew, would suddenly have a new topic of conversation—himself—the following day. Adolf Hitler would suddenly pay attention to his second-in-line successor again, as he had back in the early days. Hess's surprise peace offer to the British would force the Third Reich, indeed the world, to take one step back from the abyss.

Chapter 71

Saturday 10 May 1941
Ditchley – Oxfordshire – England

Brendan Bracken caught the Prime Minister's eye across the noisy room and nodded towards the double-doors. Surrounded by his weekend guests at Ditchley Park, the Prime Minister had already consumed vast quantities of pre-dinner alcohol and was smoking a cigar. He excused himself and followed Bracken to an office at the rear of Ditchley's magnificent hallway.

"They're in Berlin," Bracken said. "McCrew saw Winter this morning."

Churchill's eyes lit up. "I didn't think McCrew had it in him. Splendid."

"No decision from Winter yet. McCrew's seeing him for lunch tomorrow."

"Good. I've got good news, too. Clemmie's agreed to the operation."

Bracken seemed sceptical. "What on Earth did you tell her?"

Churchill puffed on his cigar. "I didn't say anything. I simply arranged for her to take a long hard look in the mirror."

Chapter 72

Saturday 10 May 1941
Eaglesham – Scotland

Near Eaglesham, just south of Glasgow, the buildings of Floors Farm shook as Rudolf Hess's Messerschmitt flew low overhead. When it crashed a moment later, the only occupant of the farm who was still awake, a ploughman called David McLean, rushed out into the night. He was in time to see a moonlit parachute float down towards a nearby field.

Instinct told him the aircraft was probably German, so he looked around for something he could use as a weapon. Grabbing a pitchfork, he hurried across the field towards the parachute. Its owner was lying on his back and motionless.

"Are you German?" McLean asked, trying to make himself and his pitchfork sound threatening.

Hess smiled. "Yes, I am," he said in English. "I am Hauptmann Alfred Horn and I have an important message for the Duke of Hamilton. I'm afraid I've also hurt my foot."

McLean helped him up and they slowly made their way back to the farm.

"Can I make you some tea?" Mclean asked in the kitchen as other occupants of the farm, woken by the crash, joined them.

"No, I don't drink tea at this time of night," Hess said. "But I'd love a glass of water."

Chapter 73

Sunday 11 May 1941
Lanke – March Brandenburg – Germany

The Ministry car pulled into the driveway in front of Joseph Goebbels's house near Lanke and Anna Vogel got out.

Grinning broadly, Goebbels opened the front door himself. "Good to see you, Anna. I thought we might have breakfast in the garden but it's a little too cold. Come in."

"Thank you."

"Heard about last night?"

"What about it?"

"Biggest raid on London so far. Huge success. They even hit the Houses of Parliament."

They settled at a beautifully set table and Anna poured them both coffee.

"So how's your mother?" Goebbels asked impatiently.

Anna spoke calmly. "She died seven years ago in the USA."

Goebbels blinked.

"The excuse I gave you to go and see her was a lie, as was the story I told you about how her neighbours had conspired to get rid of a Jewish family. That happened to a childhood friend of hers, not to her."

If Goebbels was angry or upset, he didn't show it.

"I went to London, Joseph. I was flown there by the British government, specifically Brendan Bracken, and we both know who he works for. What I've never told you, and I had no reason to up until today, is that back in 1937 I received not one but two job offers: one from you and one from Bracken, who had also noticed my work with Edwards Bernays and the Democratic Party. I already had a preference for your offer but flew to London first out of curiosity. Turned out Bracken had little to offer. So I thanked him, came here and thought nothing more of his offer for four years. Then out of the blue last week, a man I'd never seen before approached me in a café. I assumed he was a British agent of some kind because he made it clear he'd been sent by Bracken. The Brits, he explained, wanted to recruit me for two purposes: short term they needed someone to look after a clandestine British visitor to Berlin and make sure he was able to rendezvous with a contact in Charlottenburg. Long term they wanted me to spy on you and the Ministry of Propaganda's activities."

Goebbels sat motionless. "And what was in it for you? Money?"

"A guarantee of employment after the war. Their assumption is that Germany will be defeated and that I will never find a job again because of my association with you."

Goebbels scoffed. "I'm almost flattered. But how naive of him."

"My instinct was that there was more, much more to it than that, which is why I insisted on meeting Bracken face to face. If he was blackmailing me about something else, I wanted him to do so openly. Well he wasn't blackmailing me. Turns out Bracken genuinely believes I'd do anything in exchange for a job after the war."

Goebbels sipped his coffee. "If ever we're defeated, my propaganda techniques will live on. They can be used by anyone to promote any idea or belief. Governments will fight to recruit you, Anna. You'll never be out of a job."

"I agree."

"You said he might blackmail you about something else. What was that about?"

"I'm Jewish."

Goebbels leaned back in his chair and closed his eyes. "Now she tells me. I didn't know Vogel was a Jewish name."

"Not many people do. It's Ashkenazi. Obviously, neither you nor I would benefit from The Times pointing out that Germany's Minister of Propaganda employs a Jew to produce anti-Jewish propaganda. But I don't think Bracken knows any more about my religion than you do." Anna cocked her head at him. "The fact that I'm Jewish doesn't change the quality of my work here, does it, Joseph? You aren't going to withdraw all the compliments you've made over the years, are you?"

Goebbels had gone pale. He crossed his legs. "Why, Anna? Why work for a man dedicated to ridding Europe or preferably the Earth of your own people? You've done nothing but help me hurt Jews."

"I work for you because you're the best at what you do. In terms of communication expertise, your only rival is Edward Bernays in the USA, but I've worked for him, too. My résumé is second to none. I've learnt a lot from both of you and sooner or later I'll use it for my own purposes. That's where we differ, Joseph. That's where Bernays and I differed, too. Purposes. We all have the same psychological bullets. It's what we shoot them at that matters. We all have the same techniques. It's how we apply them that makes a difference. Bernays sees human beings as machines who must be tricked by politicians and corporations into believing one thing: that happiness, status and success can be achieved by buying goods and services. Hitler sees human beings as machines who must be tricked into believing one thing: there are superior human beings and inferior ones. The superior ones can only maintain their superiority by getting rid of the inferior ones. Whether you believe in Bernays or Hitler, the result is the same: an awful lot of people get tricked, exploited, hurt or killed. My question is, how long will it take for people to understand what's going on? Communication techniques such as public relations, propaganda and marketing can disguise the trickery for a long time—you and Bernays have demonstrated that to me—but not for ever. My own belief is that people will continue to be exploited economically and continue to be hounded or killed for their religion, political beliefs, race or sexuality. Bernays won't be the last to disguise economic exploitation as freedom. Hitler won't be the last to murder Jews like me. The faces will change but the crimes will remain. In fact nothing will change until we sort out one fundamental problem: the role of women. As long as millions of men and some women feel free to see women as exploitable, inferior or disposable in some way, they'll feel free to see *any* group of human beings as exploitable, inferior or disposable. That's got to change and women like me will need some serious psychological weaponry to get our ideas across. I'm stealing that weaponry from you, Joseph. That's why I work for you."

Goebbels took a deep breath. "What answer did you give Bracken?"

"Regarding the spying activities I didn't commit to anything. I didn't totally shut down the idea either."

"And the clandestine British visitor to Berlin?"

Anna held his gaze. "That's happening. I accepted it as a sort of goodwill gesture. They flew both of us to the Eifel Forest the day before yesterday and we took a train from Aachen to here. He's hiding in my apartment."

Goebbels buried his face in his hands and shook his head. "You're insane, Anna. Who is he?"

"No idea. They've kept that information to themselves. I know him as Bruno Radke but that's not his real name. My job is to accompany him to his meetings in Charlottenburg and to hide him at my place in between. That's it.

I don't know who his contact is or why they're meeting. I don't even know the contact's exact address in Charlottenburg either."

"But why ask *you* to do that sort of thing?"

"My guess is that Bracken and Churchill don't want too many people in the British services to know that this little visit to Berlin is taking place."

Goebbels sat up straight. "If you're right, that makes this man's reason for being here both highly sensitive and highly personal to Bracken and Churchill. No hunches?"

Anna held up her left hand. "The man in question bandaged my hand at Chequers."

"Chequers? They invited you to Chequers?"

"I asked for Buckingham Palace or Chartwell but both were fully booked. So yes, Chequers. I even met Mrs Churchill there. Quite a lady. Imagine being the British Prime Minister and waking up every morning to face the combined firing power of your wife's sense of humour, her Scottish accent and the Third Reich. I'd have whisky for breakfast, too."

Goebbels laughed.

"Anyway this mysterious British visitor took an interest in my injury and claimed to have learnt a few first aid tricks in the army. I didn't believe him. In my opinion he's a doctor or has been trained as one. The way he spoke and his whole demeanour changed as he looked after my hand. A professional. Then I found something that probably confirms that. When we finally got to my place the day before yesterday, he was so exhausted from fear and strain that he fell asleep immediately. So I had a look through his things and found a medical file. It's the only object he took to the meeting with his contact in Charlottenburg yesterday. I tried to read it, of course, but it was too technical. The patient's name and personal details had been removed but it was clearly a woman because it talked about 'her' and 'she' all the time."

"So no idea what her problem is?"

"Seems to be something about her brain. The file also contains two X-rays of her head."

Goebbels slapped the tabletop and sprang to his feet to fetch a briefcase that was lying on his desk. He took out a single sheet of paper and handed it to Anna. "Those five names were in a message we intercepted a week ago between President Roosevelt and Winston Churchill. A friend of mine at the Abwehr has discovered that the first three are American surgeons. Brain surgeons. He concluded, obviously, that the other two were probably American brain surgeons as well, but that led nowhere. The fourth name, he eventually found out, belonged to a brain surgeon called Neil McCrew. Guess his nationality."

They looked at each other as Goebbels sat back down.

"That's right, British. My Abwehr friend still hasn't found the fifth name on the list but he's now looking for a brain surgeon called Frank Winter in Britain and its empire: Canada, Australia or South Africa and so on. He's making a mistake. Notice something interesting about the name Frank Winter?"

Anna shook her head.

"It's a perfectly British name. But it's also—"

Anna opened her mouth in shock. "—a perfectly German one. Have you got a Berlin directory here?"

"My desk. Bottom right-hand drawer."

Anna retrieved the directory and leafed through it. "There's a Doctor Frank Winter living on Schillerstrasse, Charlottenburg. Oh my God."

"Anna, you need to trick the man you're looking after into revealing his true name. But don't do so too quickly. You don't want to scare him off. Let's just assume he's McCrew for now. What we need to know is who the patient and why she's so important that Bracken and Churchill would send a British brain surgeon to meet a German one."

"A member of the Royal Family perhaps or the wife of an important official."

Goebbels walked over to the telephone and leafed through a card file. "I'll come back with you to Berlin. Do you mind if we stop by the Ministry for a few minutes? I want to show you something."

"Of course."

He picked up the telephone receiver.

Chapter 74

Sunday 11 May 1941
Berlin – Germany

Tina Winter lay on the bed of her hotel room, staring up at the ceiling.

She'd made her decision a little earlier at 3:20 in the morning, four hours earlier.

Dead marriage

Violent husband.

I'm hungry. Shouldn't be.

Make-believe life.

Nowhere to go.

Correction: I could go home to my parents in Cambridge.

And take over their jewellery shop.

And take over the watch repair business, her father's pride and joy.

He would love me to do that.

He'd told her all her life that her hands, like his, were made for precision work.

What's Frank doing now, the bastard?

Don't waste those hands, Tina, her father had said a million times. Wasting them would be a crime.

But how to get from Berlin to Cambridge in the middle of a war?

And even if I got there, I'm German now. The British authorities would be suspicious of her motives.

Her parents were dead anyway.

At 3:20 she'd decided to return once again to Berlin's central station.

But breakfast first.

Chapter 75

Sunday 11 May 1941
Berlin – Germany

"By the way," Goebbels said to Anna as two soldiers stood to attention at the entrance to the Ministry, "didn't you fly to Cologne with Martin Wessel last week?"

Anna felt a knot in her stomach. "Yes, I did. We chatted the whole way."

They walked along a deserted corridor.

"How did you get from the airport to the town centre?"

The knot tightened. "I took a bus."

"Did you see what Wessel did?"

"Yes, a car picked him up. He offered to give me a lift but I refused."

"May I ask why?" Goebbels asked. "The problem is that Wessel, the driver and the car have all disappeared. They were last seen by a couple of witnesses at the airport."

"To be perfectly honest, Joseph, Wessel wanted to sleep with me. Getting into the same car as him would have been like getting into bed. That's why I took a bus."

"Did he sound as if he expected trouble of any kind in Cologne?"

They took a lift to the second floor.

"Well he did mention, or rather brag about, his task in Cologne. Something about changing someone's mind about who would be able to book a hall."

Goebbels sighed. "Ah, yes."

"Well I wasn't going to let him change *my* mind about anything."

"I understand. May I suggest something, Anna?"

"Please do."

The lift stopped and they got out.

Goebbels gestured ahead. "Second door on the right. Avoid using the expression 'to be perfectly honest' in my presence from now on, would you? If you're being honest, you don't need to say so and I think you've amply demonstrated your ability to be less than honest with me."

She stopped and put a hand on his arm. "Will you accept an apology, Joseph? Or is this going to taint our entire working relationship from now on. I came clean this morning. I didn't need to say half the things I said and yet I did, regardless of the risk to me."

There was silence for a moment.

Goebbels suddenly smiled. "Apology accepted," he said in a low voice. "But there's one topic you came clean about that we obviously can't leave hanging in the air. It's a problem and we need a solution fast."

Anna was familiar with the second room on the right. It was a small cinema.

"Guten Morgen, Herr Reichsminister," said a tiny man standing on his tiptoes to fit a reel of film on to a projector.

"Guten Morgen, Herr Fangauf, and thanks for coming yourself on a Sunday morning."

Eberhard Fangauf was in charge of film newsreels at the Ministry. "No problem, no problem. It's a pleasure. I won't be a minute."

"What you're going to see is a very short clip and we can replay it as often as necessary," Goebbels said to Anna as they settled. "Your opinion is crucial and I want you to be absolutely sure of it."

The lights went out. The film clip was silent and lasted exactly fourteen seconds. It showed a woman standing on a stage and speaking to a crowd. It began with a close-up of her face as she read from a piece of paper and cut to a wider angle which included crowd members.

"That's the woman I met at Chequers," Anna said. "Clementine Churchill."

"Herr Fangauf, would you rewind it, please?" Goebbels called when the clip ended.

"Yes, Herr Reichsminister."

They watched the clip again.

"Where was this filmed?" Anna asked.

"An English town somewhere. I'm not sure which one and it doesn't matter for our purposes. She's consoling and encouraging inhabitants after one of Goering's bombing raids. Are you sure she's the woman you met?"

"Yes."

"Again Herr Fangauf, please," Goebbels said. "With sound this time."

Clementine's voice filled the room. "Your courage, determination and dedication in helping each other in these terrible times are an example to us all. I feel truly humbled by your suffering and sacrifices. My heartfelt good wishes to you. Thank you."

Anna sat staring at the screen.

"Lights, please, Herr Fangauf," Goebbels called as he turned to face Anna. "You described Mrs Churchill's accent as Scottish. My English might not be brilliant but it's good enough to recognise an upper-class English accent when I hear one."

Anna slowly shook her head. "The woman I met had a different voice, too. I don't understand."

"I've studied the people around Churchill, Anna. His wife lived briefly in Scotland as a child but has spent her entire life in England otherwise. My money's on the English accent, the one we've just heard, being the correct one."

"Then who did I meet at Chequers?"

Goebbels spoke slowly. "Clementine's younger sister, Nellie, and her brother are twins. Clementine doesn't have a twin sister herself. Nor do Clementine and Nellie look sufficiently alike to be able to switch roles. I think you met a stand-in and a very convincing one."

Anna took a deep breath. "Convincing enough to persuade me look after the man in my apartment right now."

"Now we would expect Churchill to use a stand-in for himself for security reasons, but his wife? Why would he do that? My guess is that he doesn't want anyone to know she's got a medical problem."

Anna scoffed. "Come on, Joseph, why would his wife's illness, even a serious one, be a state secret?"

Goebbels bit his lower lip. "The state secret isn't the illness, Anna. The state secret's the cure." He paused to organise his thoughts. "Assuming Mrs Churchill truly is the patient who needs brain surgery, why would Bracken and Churchill send a British brain surgeon to talk to a German one?"

"To ask for advice, perhaps. Winter might be an authority of some kind."

"If McCrew only needed advice, I'm sure he'd have found what he needed in the English-speaking world."

They looked at each other.

Anna's eyes widened. "This is about who performs the surgery itself."

"The list of names that Roosevelt sent to Churchill made clear that no Americans were available, presumably to do the operation. McCrew, the Brit in your apartment, clearly can't do the operation himself for some reason. That leaves Winter."

"So you think McCrew's here to persuade Winter to operate?"

Goebbels nodded slowly. "It's the only explanation I can think of. Obviously, Churchill doesn't want the British government or the British public to know that our unspeakably degenerate Third Reich can help him solve his problem."

Chapter 76

Sunday 11 May 1941
Berlin – Germany

Neil McCrew and Frank Winter left Winter's dining-room and went through to the sitting-room, where they flopped down in armchairs. On the coffee table between them were a bottle of cognac, two huge snifters and Clementine Churchill's medical file.

"I don't remember eating canard à l'orange at university," McCrew said. "I thought the meal was going to be cheap and filling."

"I couldn't find anything cheap, so I went for black-market extortionate."

"Thanks either way. It was delicious."

Winter poured the cognac and raised his snifter. "Cheers, Neil. Good to see you."

"Cheers."

Winter pushed the file across to McCrew. "The answer is no, I'm afraid. I can't do it. Sorry."

"Can't or won't?"

"Does it matter?"

"Actually I know the answer."

Winter sipped his cognac. "How do you mean?"

McCrew put his glass on the coffee table. "What's the trick, Frank? How have you been getting away with it?"

Winter frowned. "What are you talking about, Neil?"

"Hold up your glass."

"What?"

"Hold it up, Frank."

Winter slowly looked away, jaws clenched. "When did you notice?"

"Yesterday. I tend to notice details. I'd have mentioned it but I wanted to be sure. So I waited for confirmation today. If anything your hands are shaking more today than they did yesterday."

"Well, thanks for giving me a second chance."

"Is it the drinking? Are you an alcoholic?"

Winter nodded. "You know, my best friend once told me that admitting to a drink problem is a drink problem half solved. He died in a car accident on his way back from a rehab clinic."

McCrew raised his glass. "I'll drink to that."

Chapter 77

Sunday 11 May 1941
Berlin – Germany

Three was Tina Winter's lucky number.
She didn't know why.
It had always been that way.
Maybe because her older brother and sister had both died shortly after birth.
As child number three she'd come through.
Maybe because Frank had been her third boyfriend.
She had felt lucky to have him at the time. Proud.
Platform three stretched away before her.
Dozens of passengers were waiting.
Berlin's Lehrter Bahnhof[33] was busy, as always. She had always loved to come here, to lose herself in the bustle, noise and clouds of steam. The war had changed little of that so far, except for the considerably larger numbers of soldiers everywhere.
Where would the next train from platform three be going?
Did it matter?
She walked to the far end.
She looked down at the rails.

---

[33] **Lehrte Station**

Any incoming train, she calculated, would still be moving fast enough at this point to be useful.

Chapter 78

Sunday 11 May 1941
Berlin – Germany

Frank Winter took a deep breath as he poured more cognac. "Back in the twenties, after Cambridge, it only took a few years for my career to take off. There weren't many brain surgeons in Germany back then, so I was in high demand. My only real competition was myself but that didn't make me complacent. On the contrary I took professional risks, tried things that had never been tried before, experimented without permission, travelled a lot and was lucky, ridiculously lucky. There was only one black cloud in my life. I wanted us to have children but none came along. Tina didn't mind. I did. There was nothing wrong with us physically. It just never happened. And adoption was out of the question as far as I was concerned.

"That's when my drinking, which had never been moderate anyway, got out of control. To make matters worse, my hands began to tremble, which wasn't an advantage for a brain surgeon. Just to keep them steady I'd down a schnapps or two before operating on people. Then the alcohol and the strain began to affect my judgment. It was just a question of time before my luck ran out and I made a mistake.

"It happened in September 1933. I operated on the wife of a rich manufacturer and forgot a key step in a procedure. The woman ended up with brain damage and died. Her husband got suspicious and bribed one of my assistants for information on what had happened during the operation. He threatened to go public with the truth. What saved me was my membership of the National Socialist party. Hitler was in power by then and he'd kept a long list of rich Germans who'd refused to make contributions to his party's finances over the years. My rich manufacturer was one of them. I pulled a few strings and the manufacturer eventually backed off, even becoming a major contributor to the National Socialist cause himself.

"But this didn't solve my drinking problem and its consequences. By this time my career was in danger and my marriage a wreck. That's when Tina made a suggestion. If I promised to bring my drinking under control and clear my head, she would become my hands during operations. So we pretended to be taking a long holiday for three months so that I could train her. We worked day and night. Our secret and our success depended on two crucial factors: a steady stream of corpses for Tina to practise on and a team of medical assistants and nurses with a lot to lose if they denounced us. I never told Tina where I found the corpses, but she did notice that most of the male ones were circumcised.

"Ironically those three months did a lot of good to our marriage. They brought us closer. I was drinking less and was fun to have around again. It didn't last. As soon as our first real operations began, my surgical skills came in for a lot of recognition. I was in demand all over the place. My hands became famous. But my hands were actually Tina's hands. The whole thing was a lie that kept getting bigger and bigger. I also felt diminished. My role as a guide to Tina in surgery was crucial, of course, but I found it demeaning. So I started drinking again. I haven't stopped to this day. That's why Tina walked out the day before yesterday."

"What was the last straw?"

Winter gave this some thought. "One disagreement too many, I suppose. I woke up and she was gone. If she doesn't come back, the show's over. Dead career, dead marriage, dead everything."

"And she's fully aware of that, of course."

"Oh yes. Tina always knows exactly what she's doing." Winter poured himself more cognac. "Aren't you going to tell me who my—sorry, our—patient in London would have been? My drinking hasn't killed off my curiosity yet."

McCrew swirled the liquid at the bottom of his glass. "Churchill's wife. Clementine."

Winter whistled. "And why did you think I'd agree to operate on her?"

"I didn't, Frank. I'd insult your intelligence if I said this is about saving a war leader's wife. It's about saving the war leader."

"And you thought I might have enjoyed the twisted, almost depraved irony of it all."

"Something like that. Or at least some tiny part of you would have enjoyed it."

Winter smiled. "Let's say I'm a man of many tiny parts and not one of them can stand the sight, the sound or the thought of Churchill. By the way, you can drop the persuasion tactics. I've been trained in them, too. Didn't your trainer tell you that a persuasion tactic's like a bad driver? A bad driver survives until he meets another bad driver."

McCrew reversed the direction of his swirling. "Looks like Clementine Churchill's going to die then, doesn't it."

"Unless you take the risk of operating on her yourself. Why not trust your luck?"

McCrew shook his head. "I don't mix surgery and luck."

Winter leaned forward. "Bullshit, Neil. Every time you and I open a cranium, the first thing we find is a pair of dice. And we can't go any further without throwing them."

"Do you think Tina would approve of you letting Mrs Churchill die?"

"Find her and ask her yourself, Neil."

"I will. She's standing behind you."

As Winter swung round, he dropped his snifter. It disintegrated remarkably quietly on the floor.

Tina was standing in the sitting-room doorway, suitcase in hand. McCrew stood and crossed the room to her, avoiding the pieces of glass. He kissed her on both cheeks, then shrugged. "I wouldn't know where to start."

"Start by asking Frank to make me a cup of tea."

"On its way," Winter said. He left the room

McCrew squinted at the wound on Tina's forehead. "Frank said you'd had one disagreement too many. Was it only verbal?"

"No it's nothing."

They both knew she'd said it too quickly.

"Sit down," McCrew said as he glanced around the room. He spotted a notepad and pencil on a small table, walked over to them, scribbled something, ripped off the top sheet and folded it.

Tina sat stiffly on the sofa.

"Where have you been?" McCrew asked as he returned to his armchair.

"I wandered around. What was that about Mrs Churchill?"

"She's ill, fatally ill, and Frank's the only surgeon who can operate. At least that's what I thought before coming here to try to persuade him to help us. But he told me about your, er, surgical double-act. It's madness."

"It's survival, Neil. Speaking of which, London sounds as if it's in survival mode too?"

"Why?"

"The Luftwaffe bombed it to bits last night. One of the biggest raids ever apparently."

McCrew winced. "I want to be out of here before Churchill retaliates."

"Do you want tea as well, Neil?" Winter called from somewhere.

"No, thanks." McCrew handed the folded sheet of paper to Tina, who slipped it inside her blouse without reading it.

Winter returned with a single cup of tea and placed it in front of Tina.

McCrew crossed his legs and forced a smile. "I'm sure Frank would love to know why you've come back, Tina. I'm curious too, actually."

There was an awkward silence.

"I don't think that's any of your business, Neil," Winter said.

"It is now. Ten minutes ago you made it sound as if your wife had walked out forever. Now she's back. I think we both deserve an explanation, don't you?"

"It's all right, Neil, really," Tina said.

"No, it's not all right."

Winter spoke through clenched teeth. "It's time for you to go, Neil. It's been great seeing you again and I'm sorry I can't help you with your request. Tina and I need to talk alone."

McCrew stood up. "I've got a better idea. You clearly both need a break from each other and I'm going to help you organise it. You, Frank, are coming with me on an all-expenses-paid trip to London. We'll operate on Mrs Churchill's tumour together. You bring the knowledge, I'll bring the hands. Anglo-German teamwork as it should be. Meanwhile Tina can have a true rest right here in her own home. She's been wandering around Berlin for the last 48 hours and probably hasn't slept a wink."

"Get out, Neil!" Winter shouted. "I'm not coming to London. Churchill and his wife can get lost."

McCrew smiled. "If you don't help me, Frank, I'll inform the medical authorities in this country about your surgery scam and how long it's been going on. I'll also inform your friends at the local branch of the Nazi party. I'm sure they'd be fascinated."

Winter was on his feet now. "Oh yeah? And you know what'll happen? Nothing. Not a word will get out because that's the way things happen in Germany now. Revealing the truth about me would reveal even bigger truths about them, their shoddy standards and their rampant buddy-buddy corruption. It won't happen, Neil. So take your pressure tactics and return to where you came from."

McCrew shook his head. "You know as well as I do that reputation is everything in our line of business. The authorities might do nothing but rumours will start and very soon there won't be a patient in Germany who'll come near you." He paused. "I'm giving you one full day tomorrow to sort yourself out, sober up and postpone any surgery you've scheduled over the next seven days. That's how long you'll stay in London, assuming all goes well. Do you own a car?"

Winter stared at him defiantly.

"Yes, we do," Tina said.

"With enough petrol coupons to fill her up a couple of times?"

"Yes, doctors get a special allowance."

McCrew spoke dispassionately to Winter. "The two of us will be driving westwards on Tuesday or Wednesday. The exact timing and destination will depend on where the Brits can pick us up and fly us to London. Either way I'll be back here on Tuesday morning at eleven. We'll either leave immediately—so be ready—or I'll inform you when. Pack a pair of walking shoes. Oh, and don't try to send your SS or Gestapo friends to silence me. In the next hour, at least one person you don't know will be informed of your curious and highly personal definition of ethical brain surgery. If anything happens to me, that person will send your definition to an awful lot of people."

Winter looked drained. "If you denounce us, you realise you'd be hurting Tina as much as me."

McCrew put a hand on Winter's shoulder. "I don't think Tina can be hurt any more than she's being hurt already. Thanks for the meal, Frank."

Chapter 79

Sunday 11 May 1941
Berghof – Upper Bavaria – Germany

Two of Rudolf Hess's adjutants, Karlheinz Pintsch and Alfred Leitgen, stood nervously in the anteroom at the Berghof, Hitler's mountain retreat near Berchtesgaden.

"My only hope is that he's landed safely," Pintsch murmured.

"I'm worried about retribution against his family," Leitgen said. "We two are about to become targets as well."

The door opened and Albert Speer, Minister of Armaments and Munitions, strode in carrying a briefcase and a wad of sketches. The adjutants stiffened to attention as they exchanged "Heil Hitlers".

"Are you the queue to see the Führer?" Speer asked playfully

Pintsch cleared his throat. "Actually, Herr Reichsminister, our visit is a little unexpected. We have an urgent letter to deliver to the Führer from Reichsminister Hess. Would it bother you if we saw him before you?"

"Not at all." Speer sat down in an armchair. "From your demeanour I can tell your day is unlikely to end as comfortably as it began. Might as well get it over with."

A dark-haired soldier in his early thirties appeared in the doorway and spoke to Pintsch. "The Führer will see you now, Herr Sturmbannführer[34]."

"Thank you."

Adolf Hitler was eating noodles by himself at the end of a long table. As Pintsch entered the dining-room, the Führer wiped his mouth with a napkin. "Pintsch, how are you? Come and sit beside me and help yourself to apple juice."

"Guten Tag, mein Führer, und guten Appetit," Pintsch said.

Hitler waved his fork tentatively. "My apologies for welcoming you with my mouth full but Bormann had filled up the rest of my agenda with trivia such as wars, bomb raids and invasions. Can you imagine? I can't think where he finds them. So tell me, what's so urgent?"

"Thanks for finding time for us, mein Führer." Pintsch cleared his throat. "I have a letter for you from Reichsminister Hess. He insisted I deliver it to you personally."

"What dire warning has he read into the stars this time?" Hitler's face remained expressionless as he opened and read the letter. When he finished he looked up at the ceiling before closing his eyes, as if trying to control pain by thought alone. His right hand slammed the tabletop. One of his fingers clipped the edge of his plate, which spun away and crashed on the floor.

The sound Germany's leader then produced was heard by several officials and employees throughout the building. They variously described it as a yell, a cry or a scream. To Pintsch, who experienced its full force, and to Speer and Leitgen, who were in the next room, it sounded like an animal howl.

---

[34] **Major**

Chapter 80

Sunday 11 May 1941
Glasgow – Scotland

"And what do you expect me to do with your offer of peace terms, Minister?"

Douglas Douglas-Hamilton, 14th Duke of Hamilton, stifled a yawn. An RAF officer, he was in charge of aerial defence for an area straddling southern Scotland and northern England and had hardly slept for three nights. His conversation with Rudolf Hess could only be a prelude, the Duke realised, to a major political explosion on both sides of the English Channel, but it was also competing for his attention with his withering exhaustion.

"I chose to contact you because you and the King know each other, your Grace," Hess said. The man officially second in line to replace the Führer had been brought to St Mary's Barracks in Glasgow for medical treatment, especially for his sprained ankle. The German was sitting up in bed and listening intently, not having expected Scottish accents to be such a challenge to his English-language skills.

"Why not the government and Mr Churchill?"

"My offer depends specifically on Mr Churchill no longer being in power. We've offered to negotiate peace terms with him in the past and he has always either rejected them or avoided talking to us. Mr Churchill wants war and nothing else."

Douglas-Hamilton scribbled on his notepad. "You know, I'm still trying to remember meeting you at the Berlin Olympics in '36. Please don't take it personally but I can't."

Hess grinned. "I forgive you. Since the Führer came to power in 1933, being forgettable has been a legal obligation for everyone except him."

"I'm in no mood for jokes, Minister," Douglas-Hamilton said flatly, "unless the Luftwaffe's bombing raids on our cities, including London last night, count as humour in your book."

Hess folded his arms. "Well, avoiding that kind of tragedy and many more like it over the coming months is the reason I'm here, your Grace. Hundreds of thousands of lives can be saved. For that reason alone my peace offer must surely be of interest to the King."

"The King's in no position to decide such things, Minister. His influence is significant but his powers are at best limited. That's why I'll brief someone in the government, not Buckingham Palace, on the contents of our discussion. Churchill will be briefed sooner or later about what you've done but I have no idea, not even a gut feeling, how he might react. Your initiative might well make a much bigger bang in your country than in this one."

Hess shook his head. "I've taken extraordinary risks coming here, your Grace. As a fellow pilot you know that as well as I do. I think those risks underline the seriousness of my offer as well as my good faith."

"Quite," Douglas-Hamilton said calmly, "but I have yet to see something in your peace offer that makes it impossible to ignore."

"I beg your pardon?" Hess shouted. "Aren't millions of saved lives enough for you?"

"Minister, you're offering to let the United Kingdom keep its independence as well as its empire in exchange for Germany having a free hand in Europe. Have I understood you correctly?"

"Yes."

"Who's to say Germany won't attack us anyway in a couple of years' time? Hitler has a solid reputation for many things but not for his ability to keep promises. Then there's the question of how you define Europe. You've been very vague so far. Does Europe include the Soviet Union or not?"

"We signed a non-aggression pact with the Soviet Union in 1939, your Grace."

Douglas-Hamilton scoffed. "Minister, your country signed a no-aggression-just-yet pact with the Soviet Union and if Stalin thinks otherwise, he's an idiot. I repeat my question: does Europe include the Soviet Union in your geography books or not?" He waited for an answer and didn't get one. "If it doesn't, we'll need to correct the geography books we use around here at the first opportunity. If Europe does include the Soviet Union according to you, then please tell me what you mean by Germany keeping a free hand in Europe." He waited again; still no response from Hess. "To have any chance of success, Minister, your peace offer needs a few refinements. But that's just my humble opinion. If you're withholding those refinements for people higher up the power ladder than me, fair enough." He snapped his notebook shut. "Is there anything you'd like to add, Minister?"

"I'd like my family to be informed I'm safe, please. If you give me a sheet of paper, I'll write down the person to contact."

Douglas-Hamilton tore a sheet out of his notebook and handed it to the German.

"Given my position in the Third Reich and the purpose of my visit," Hess said as he wrote, "what is my status here?"

"You're a prisoner of war, Minister."

Chapter 81

Sunday 11 May 1941
Berlin – Germany

Neil McCrew snapped awake in the armchair and checked his watch: 5:57pm. On the other side of the coffee table Anna Vogel was asleep on the sofa. They had walked in silence back from Charlottenburg and McCrew had insisted on arrival that he needed a nap, not least because of his alcohol intake with Frank Winter over lunch. That was three hours ago.

McCrew tiptoed over to the window. He'd placed a plant in a white pot on the sill to signal his desire to send a message to England. Glancing down at the street, nothing seemed untoward. The pavements on both sides were deserted apart from a woman walking a dog in the distance to his left and a man a few metres behind her.

He debated whether to use his sunglasses and white stick again and decided against because they might attract too much attention from helpful strangers if he was alone. Leaving the door to the apartment ajar, he slipped out and trotted down the two flights of stairs to the street. Turning left he strode purposefully along the pavement, mentally counting off seconds. When he reached 150 he'd cross the street and turn back. No more than five minutes, Gubbins had said.

He found the risk, however brief, of walking undisguised in the Third Reich's capital curiously exciting. He'd return to Berlin one day, he decided. Something about what he'd seen so far, which wasn't much but which he wanted to see without red, white and black swastika drapes, appealed to him.

Approaching from the opposite direction, the man he'd seen from the window was still walking behind the woman with the dog, a poodle. As the woman was quite tall, McCrew could only see him intermittently. Was he the same man who'd talked to him on the bench whilst emptying his shoe? McCrew couldn't decide.

"Mein Gott!" the woman with the dog suddenly exclaimed as she drew level with him. She threw her arms around his neck and kissed him on both cheeks. "Bruno, wie geht es dir?"

The poodle yelped its disapproval. The man swerved to avoid them.

"Sehr gut," McCrew spluttered, struggling to recover his composure.

"Ich glaub's nicht!" The woman hugged him again, her voice suddenly dropping to a masculine mutter in his ear. "Give me your message in a low voice in English whilst I speak to you. I can lip-read. If I stop talking, just say 'Ja, alles in Ordnung'. Otherwise keep nodding slowly."

The agent broke the hug and launched into an excited high-pitched monologue in German, which McCrew guessed to be imaginary family news.

"Winter's agreed to do it," McCrew said, marvelling at the agent's make-up and femininity. "Please organise transport on the 14th, early in the morning. If that date holds, the operation should take place on the 16th. Also I want confirmation that my wife and mother are okay following the London bombing. That's all."

"Und dir?" the agent asked.

"Ja, alles in Ordnung."

The agent babbled something else in shrill German as he kissed McCrew on both cheeks again. "Auf Wiedersehen, Bruno, und bis bald." He turned to walk away.

"Auf Wiedersehen."

Dazed, McCrew walked briskly back to Anna's building and back up the stairs. The apartment door was still ajar and Anna still asleep. He quietly removed the white pot and plant from the window sill and went through to the kitchen to make tea.

When he returned to the sitting-room, Anna was stretching her arms and yawning.

"Looks like I needed a rest too," she said. "My goodness, a man making tea for me. Highlight of the war. Been awake for long?"

"Long enough to send a message to London." He nodded towards the window. "I met the agent just outside."

"Really? And how is the dear man?"

"In fine form."

She watched him and waited, grinning.

"What's so funny?" he said at last.

"You still haven't told me if your lunch was a success or not."

McCrew shrugged. "You know I can't say anything."

She sipped her tea. "Saying whether you succeeded or failed is no big giveaway. You're an appalling liar anyway."

"Am I? I'll have you know I've received body language training. I can pass myself off as an honest man or a liar at will."

"You scared the hell out of me when you threw yourself in front of that truck. Truth or lie? What's my body language telling you?"

He looked at her.

"It's the truth," she continued. "I've been thinking about it ever since and can't work out why. Is it because I admire you for having the guts to solve our problem with those soldiers that way? No. It's because I've realised I don't want anything to hurt you, ever. I care. Truth or lie?"

He blinked.

"In a few days you'll be gone from here and the thought of that makes me sick. Truth or lie? Since Bracken introduced us at Chequers, you've been on my mind every waking second. I can't think straight. I can't concentrate. I'm thirty-nine and this has never happened to me. Truth or lie?"

He tried to sip his tea but his hand was trembling. They both noticed.

"I can't be within twenty feet of you without wanting you to kiss me, to pay attention to me, to... to... desire me. Truth or lie, Bruno?"

He looked away.

"You lied to me about the person you met outside," she said quietly.

McCrew turned sarcastic. "Did I? How did my body language betray me on that one?"

"I saw you kissing and hugging that woman from the window. When I asked you how the dear *man* was, you didn't correct me. Who is she, Bruno? Why the lie? And I swear that if you tell me that woman was your agent in drag, I'll throw this teacup at you."

"Well as a matter of fact—"

He ducked as her teacup and saucer flew over his head and smashed against the wall behind him. "Anna, for God's sake."

She leapt up and stood over him, her face inches from his. "I spend all day every day surrounded by liars, Bruno. I live in a country that lies to the world and to itself every day, too. And I help them. I create lies, I design lies, I refine lies, I write lies, I publish lies. That's my job, that's my skill, that's what I'm good at and the last thing I expect is for a human being I care about to lie to me under my own roof. Who was that woman?"

He sat there stunned, scared, flattened. Then, as she stared at him, her expression gradually loosened. She looked less furious at him than bewildered at herself.

"I'm wrong," she whispered, backing away. "You told me the truth. That woman *was* the agent."

"What's going on, Anna?"

"I'm sorry." There were tears in her eyes as she returned to the sofa and hugged a cushion.

McCrew watched her for a moment, biting his lower lip. "If you really want to know, my lunch with mystery man was a success."

"Congratulations. So who's going to help whom?"

"I beg your pardon?"

"Did you come to Berlin to ask for his help or have you come to help him?"

McCrew hesitated. "He's helping me. There's something he can do to help me that I haven't learnt to do by myself yet."

"Listen to me and don't interrupt," she said calmly. "Your real name is Neil McCrew. You're a British brain surgeon with an important patient. Her name is Clementine Churchill, she's the Prime Minister's wife and her condition is a complex, life-threatening one. That's why you need help. You've tried the Americans but their three most capable brain surgeons are either unavailable or unwilling. The Americans did however suggest a German, Frank Winter, as a viable alternative. Hence your presence here. I was brought in to chaperone you but also to keep this whole thing as discreet and deniable as possible. The reason they picked me is that I met Brendan Bracken four years ago when he tried to recruit me to help boost Churchill's political career. Unluckily for him, Goebbels also wanted to recruit me. I made a choice. But that didn't stop Bracken remembering me when Mrs Churchill's medical problem popped up. Correct so far?"

McCrew nodded slowly.

"In case you're wondering, the list of five brain surgeons sent by Roosevelt to Churchill was intercepted by German intelligence, who decrypted it and forwarded to Goebbels for possible propaganda angles. When are you and Winter leaving?"

"If all goes well, we'll drive to the Eifel Forest the day after tomorrow and be picked up on Wednesday." Anxiety crept into McCrew's voice. "What do you think Goebbels will do?"

"If Churchill's telling his country that the Germans are nothing but a bunch of thugs and yet secretly calling on those same thugs to save his wife's life, he's a hypocrite and should be denounced as such. Hypocrisy is a legitimate target for propaganda. On the other hand, exploiting Mrs Churchill's illness for propaganda purposes is dangerous. It could easily backfire by making the propagandist—i.e. Goebbels himself—look cheap, desperate or even cowardly. Goebbels doesn't want that. So my guess is he'll do nothing. If he was going to stop you recruiting Winter, he'd already have done so."

McCrew arched his eyebrows. "What's that supposed to mean?"

"Goebbels knows you're here, Neil."

"What? How did he find out?"

"I told him this morning. There's just one thing he doesn't know for sure and he's relying on me to get an answer: why you came to Berlin to talk to Winter."

McCrew was pale. "Well you've got the answer now. Are you going to tell him that too?"

"Why shouldn't I? Again, the chances are he'll do nothing with the information. If four years working for Goebbels have taught me anything, it's that he's far more dangerous when he doesn't know something than when he does. He hates ambiguity. It drives him crazy. It's his greatest weakness as a communicator. In our line of business, ambiguity is a weapon. It's an ally and Goebbels knows that. But he doesn't have enough self-confidence to be comfortable with it. That's why he's an excellent propagandist, not an exceptional one."

McCrew stood up, gave one of his helpless shrugs and began to pace. "I still think you took a hell of a risk telling him about me."

"Did I? During the same conversation I told him I'm Jewish. How risky is that in this day and age?"

McCrew scoffed. "You're Jewish?"

"Yes."

"And you're working for—i.e. helping—that antisemitic monster?"

"I'm using Goebbels for my own purposes."

"I call it tightening the noose around your own neck."

"Then what do you call using the skills of a Nazi surgeon to save the British prime minister's wife?"

McCrew opened his mouth to respond but words failed him. He adjusted his glasses instead.

"I'm a pragmatist, Neil, and you're fast becoming one. Actually I'm not sure that's the kind of thing I'd like us to have in common."

"Just explain why you felt obliged to tell a man who condones the elimination of Jews that you're Jewish."

"I call it the Einstein effect. All pain is relative. If you want someone to ignore the pain they're in, remind them of something else in their life that's even more painful. It's a tactic Goebbels uses all the time in his propaganda. I simply used it against him. The fact that I'm Jewish is relatively more painful to him than your activities in Berlin."

Anna stood up too and moved closer to him. "If you're leaving Berlin the day after tomorrow, I have twenty-four hours left."

"To do what?"

"To look after you and make sure nothing hurts you." She kissed him lightly on the mouth. "Don't get any ideas, though. You're going to sleep on the sofa again tonight instead of in my arms." Another kiss, longer, deeper. "Truth or lie?"

Chapter 82

Sunday 11 May 1941
Ditchley – Oxfordshire – England

As dinner came to an end at Ditchley House, Brendan Bracken surveyed the thirty guests around the table and felt a twinge of guilt. Their good spirits and noisy chatting contrasted darkly with the devastation and deaths he imagined after last night's bombing raid on London, seventy miles away.

Out of habit he glanced at Clementine Churchill, who seemed fine this evening, and Winston Churchill, who was flicking his chin up and down at him. Bracken knew what question the chin was asking but didn't yet have an answer. Excusing himself he left the dining-room and put a phone call, his eighth that day, through to Colin Gubbins at the SOE.

"Winter has agreed to do it," the clipped voice announced. "The message came through three minutes ago. McCrew wants the operation to take place this coming Friday."

Bracken leaned back against the nearest wall. "My goodness. When are you picking them up?"

"Weather permitting, on Wednesday. Whilst I sort out Danes and his Heinkel, could you contact the medical team?"

"Of course. I'll also tell the Prime Minister. He's with me."

As Bracken crossed the entrance hall, a butler intercepted him.

"The Duke of Hamilton has arrived, sir. I've put him in the drawing room. Should I inform the Prime Minister or will you?"

"I'll tell him, thank you."

Bracken returned to the dining-room and approached Churchill. The guests were rising from the table.

"From the sublime to the bizarre," Bracken said quietly. "Our Nazi surgeon's operating on Friday and Hamilton's arrived."

Churchill beamed. "Splendid. Bring Hamilton in here, would you?" He turned towards the last guests filing out of the room. "Archibald, could you stay a minute, please? This might interest you."

Still wearing his pilot's jacket, Douglas-Hamilton strode in followed by Bracken.

"Douglas, how are you?" Churchill exclaimed. "Thanks for dropping by. You've come a long way."

"They diverted me from London."

"Do you know Archibald Sinclair, Secretary of State for Air?"

"How do you do, sir."

They all shook hands.

Churchill squinted at Douglas-Hamilton's face. "That deathly expression doesn't deserve a double scotch, my dear man." He looked around for a waiter but saw none. "Brendan, could you ask them to bring Douglas a triple, please?"

When Bracken returned, the three men listened to Douglas-Hamilton's account of Rudolf Hess's arrival.

Churchill made no effort to hide his scepticism. "Do you mean to tell me that the Deputy Führer of the Third Reich is in our hands? That he flew all the way from Germany to Scotland to see you personally, that he did so without telling anyone and that he's lying at this very moment in a hospital bed in Glasgow?"

"Yes," Douglas-Hamilton said. "I've compared the man to photos of Hess and it's got to be him, unless he has a twin brother."

Churchill turned to Bracken. "Have the Germans announced anything?"

Bracken shook his head. "If you were Adolf Hitler and Clement Attlee suddenly crash-landed in Bavaria with a peace proposal, would you rush to announce something?"

Churchill roared with laughter. The other two smiled politely.

"One detail troubles me," Douglas-Hamilton said. "It might be nothing but it made me uneasy. When he listed the terms of his peace proposal he said, and I quote, that hundreds of thousands of lives could be saved. Then, a moment later, he talked about millions of lives being saved."

"So?" Churchill asked. "Death tolls are notoriously difficult to predict."

"The problem is that when I first sat down with Hess he went to extraordinary lengths to describe his flight: distances, speeds, fuel consumption, times, altitudes, you name it. The information wasn't well organised but it was precise. He almost put me to sleep with his decimal points. This is a fussy man who doesn't play around with numbers. When he says hundreds of thousands, he means it. When he says millions, he means it as well."

"Might those numbers refer to different things?" Sinclair asked. "Hundreds of thousands of British lives and millions of European ones, perhaps?"

"He could also be correcting himself," Bracken said.

"That's what I think too," Douglas-Hamilton continued, "He corrected from hundreds of thousands to millions. Still vague perhaps but coming from a man like Hess, not random. Where is he getting millions of potential victims from? Who's he referring to?"

A waiter entered and placed a well-filled glass in front of him.

Churchill stood up. "Why don't you start by making sure your man truly is who he says he is. In the meantime, gentlemen, we have a film show here tonight. Hess or no Hess, I'm going to see the Marx Brothers."

Chapter 83

Monday 12 May 1941
Berlin – Germany

Neil McCrew kissed Anna Vogel's forehead as she slept in his arms.

She hadn't let go of him all night and had protested aggressively in her sleep at his two attempts, albeit feeble ones, to loosen her grip and get some sleep.

He fumbled for his glasses and squinted at the alarm clock.

7:45.

The agent would be in the street outside at eight.

Except that McCrew was now the one holding on to Anna and not wanting to let go.

He kissed her forehead again.

He didn't want this night with her to end because an agent in drag wanted to kiss him on the pavement outside.

He didn't want to forget how Anna had given herself to him and pulled him far inside her and held him there and locked her legs around him and whispered incessantly in his ear and burst into tears three, maybe four times as her feelings and desires and dreams and hopes exploded within her and because of him.

He didn't doubt she was telling the truth when she said she'd never felt this way about anyone and would he please do something to help her stop thinking about him, obsessing over him, wanting to be with him every second of every minute of every day and night and going crazy over the idea of him going away.

Another kiss.

She stirred, slept on.

He didn't want to forget how he'd felt—a tiny jolt but a lingering one—when she'd talked about the Einstein effect and how, in order to protect him, she'd made herself seem more threatening than him to Goebbels by revealing her religion. What kind of person would do that sort of thing?

He didn't want to admit to himself that that tiny lingering jolt could possibly change everything.

Another kiss.

This time she opened her eyes, kissed him on the lips. "What sort of woman's your wife?"

"Good morning to you, too. She's the sort who immediately saw the kind of person I was yet didn't run away. The sort who hoped I would change. The sort I'll soon be divorced from."

"Any married man would say that."

"My wife's the sort of woman to be pregnant with her lover's child."

Anna stifled a laugh. "Seriously?"

"You could at least pretend to be devastated."

She stifled another laugh. "Sorry."

"It's okay." He kissed her forehead. "As I see it, she's also the sort of woman who deserves to be happy with a man who truly loves her. I believe that. And I'm sure she will be."

Anna drew back to look into his eyes. "She doesn't sound like the love of your life."

"She isn't. She wasn't."

Anna waited.

And waited.

McCrew sighed. "The love of my life left me for another guy, okay? And if you really want to know, her name is Tina and she's married to Frank Winter, the man who's about to operate on Mrs Churchill. Tina's from Cambridge, the town where Winter and I both studied."

Anna's eyes widened. She pulled further back. "So the love of your life ran off with a rival surgeon and your wife's expecting her lover's child. What did you do to these women, Neil?"

McCrew gave this some thought. "I suppose they wanted my future and all I could give them was my past."

"Wow." She watched him get out of bed.

"I've got to see the agent," he said as he picked up his clothes. "I put the plant in the window last night."

Anna threw off the bedclothes. "I'll make breakfast. And no kissing or hugging someone who isn't me this time, okay?"

McCrew left the building at exactly eight o'clock and walked along the pavements of Fasanenstrasse for exactly five minutes, counting the seconds as he went. No sign of the agent.

As he stepped back into Anna's apartment, he inadvertently kicked a single folded sheet of paper that was on the floor just inside the door. He picked it up and read it:

14 i O   16 i O   M gesund Veilchen gestorben

He removed the pot and plant from the lounge window, then joined Anna in the kitchen. "I need your help. The agent's making wild assumptions about my German."

Anna read the words on the paper a few times. "The two letters after the numbers probably stand for *in Ordnung*, meaning *agreed* or *okay*.

"Those are the dates I asked for. The 14th is the flight and the 16th is the surgery."

"The other words are obviously a code of some kind. *M gesund* means *M healthy*. Do you know an M?"

"The German word for mother is Mutter, correct?"

"Yes."

"I asked for news of my mother after the bombing. It's probably her. What does the rest mean?"

Anna frowned. "A *Veilchen* is a kind of flower. No idea what it's called in English and I don't have a dictionary here. I can call the Ministry if you like."

McCrew frowned. "What does it look like?"

"It's a bluish purple colour. Not my favourite if ever you were thinking of—"

"Violet?"

Anna smiled triumphantly. "Yes, that's it."

"Violet's my wife's name."

Anna slapped a hand on her mouth.

McCrew stared at the floor. "Am I to assume *gestorben* means *killed*?"

"Dead," she whispered.

Chapter 84

Monday 12 May 1941
Ditchley – Oxfordshire – England

Winston Churchill quietly entered his wife's bedroom at Ditchley Park. Just enough morning sunshine was slipping through gaps between the curtains for him to see. He leaned over Clementine and kissed her cheek as she slept.

"Love you, Cat," he whispered.

She stirred. "I'm still trying to sleep, Pig."

He sat on the edge of the bed. "I'm off back to London. I need to see the bombing damage."

She sat up and switched on the bed lamp. "I'll come with you. Those poor people."

"No, you won't. You stay here in Ditchley and rest."

"Spit it out, Winston. You've got that tone in your voice. What's wrong?"

He took her hand. "An awful lot is wrong, but there's one piece of good news. McCrew's persuaded this Winter chap to come over. Your operation's on Friday. This is where you'll come to recover afterwards as well."

"Where's it taking place?"

"That's still unclear. The original plan was St. Thomas's but it's been badly hit by the bombing. In more ways than one we're in German hands here. A German surgeon will decide how to operate on your brain and German bomber pilots will decide where."

Chapter 85

Monday 12 May 1941
Berlin – Germany

"Thank you, everyone," Joseph Goebbels said. "Fräulein Vogel, don't go away. I need to see you for a couple of minutes."

The daily briefing for the Ministry of Propaganda's department heads broke up and Goebbels and Anna walked in silence back to the Reichsminister's office. They settled on either side of the small table where they regularly had breakfast.

"So?" Goebbels asked.

"The patient's Churchill's wife and McCrew's here because the Brits don't have the required surgical skills. They need Winter. Seems McCrew's found a way to persuade him to fly over there."

"How will that work?"

"The Brits will land an aircraft somewhere and pick them up."

"No idea where?"

"No, and McCrew doesn't know either yet. It could be the Eifel Forest again—that's where McCrew and I were dropped off—or just about anywhere. They use a captured Heinkel in broad daylight. The clever bit is that it's rigged to look as if it has engine trouble. The smoke actually attracts attention to it. But the plane's still flying. So any German pilot curious enough to take a closer look soon concludes the it will be able to land safely and loses interest. The radio's been shot up, of course."

Goebbels smiled admiringly. "So the Heinkel keeps on flying through all the checks until it reaches its destination."

"Exactly."

"Cheeky."

"All I know for now is that McCrew and Winter are setting off by car tomorrow at eleven to rendezvous with the aircraft on Wednesday. Winter's operating in England on Friday. I assume their agent here will give further details to McCrew later today."

"Good work, thank you." Goebbels paused for a moment, staring at the table. "Anna, I want you to go with them. You've got to leave the country."

"Because I'm Jewish?"

Goebbels nodded. "If you stay, someone will find out sooner or later and we'll both be in big trouble. Leaving with those two is a perfect opportunity."

"But how will you justify my sudden disappearance? Won't it attract precisely the attention you want to avoid?"

Goebbels folded his arms. "That's my problem. Didn't you once tell me you spoke French?"

"I studied it for many years. It's a bit rusty but I suppose I'm fluent more or less."

"I'll announce that I've sent you on an urgent confidential mission to Paris and that questions on the topic are not welcome. Our propaganda is such a mess there that no one will be surprised I'm putting you on it. You'll quickly be forgotten here, don't worry. No offense, of course."

"None taken. Will you be using Mrs Churchill's operation for propaganda purposes?"

Goebbels shrugged. "Possibly. But I can't use it until it has actually happened and I have proof. Otherwise no one will believe me. So in a way I want Winter and McCrew to succeed. In the meantime I want you to get out of Germany before you're…" He trailed off.

"Dealt with? Treated? Processed? What other delicate ways did we find to say murdered? Do you remember that discussion?"

He shook his head. "Don't."

"What other euphemisms did we come up with? Ah yes, relocated? Handled? Managed?"

"Stop it, please." He seemed anguished. "For what it's worth, you've been working for me for four years now and I've enjoyed every second of it. Seeing you go is the last thing I want, believe me. No, I'm not trying to help you, Anna. You're strong and creative enough not to need anybody's help."

"Then what?"

"I'm trying to thank you."

Chapter 86

Monday 12 May 1941
Berlin – Germany

When he thought he heard a knock, Neil McCrew was lying on Anna's sofa. He dismissed it and carried on thinking. How had Violet died? Where? At home? Alone? Trapped under rubble? Slashed by glass shards falling from a building after a bomb blast? Was she with her lover? Was he dead too?

Another knock. The doorbell, he knew, was highly visible, yet whoever it was had chosen to knock. He tiptoed through to the hall and squinted through the peephole. Tina Winter was standing nervously on the landing. He opened the door in such a way that he remained invisible as she stepped in.

"What are you doing here?" he asked.

"Well you did scribble this address for me yesterday, remember?"

He kissed her on both cheeks.

"Who owns this place?" she asked as they went through to the lounge and settled in armchairs. "Fasanenstrasse no less."

"The Ministry of Propaganda, as far as I know. The occupant of this place works there and is lending me her sofa. Long story."

Tina cocked her head. "*Her* sofa? Is she around?"

"No, she's at work. We'll be fine. How can I help you?"

"Why did you give me your address?"

"Victims of conjugal violence have a way of saying 'no it's nothing' too quickly when the physical evidence is scrutinised."

Tina looked away, tears welling.

McCrew got up and touched her shoulder as he walked by. "I'll make some tea."

"How long's it been going on?" he asked when he returned.

"Does it matter? Violence is violence. I pardoned him the first time, which was once too often. How's that for a cliché? I'm trapped, Neil. My skills have no value because they depend entirely on Frank. I operate without any medical qualifications whatsoever and if the authorities find out, which they will sooner or later, I'll end up in prison. Frank too, obviously. If I leave Frank, what can I do? I'm not a mother, I can't cook to save my life and I steer clear of churches. And even if I had qualifications I probably wouldn't be able to work anyway. Female doctors and lawyers have lost their jobs because Hitler believes they should produce kids rather than health or justice."

"What about the war effort? Hasn't Hitler just called on women to make a bigger contribution?" He smacked his own cheek. "Jesus, I can't believe I just said that."

Tina leaned back in her armchair. "It's all a joke, Neil. Everyone pretends here. Everyone lies to everyone else. The gap between what the regime says and what gets done just keeps getting bigger. Corruption's everywhere. I've got nowhere to go. I'm utterly dependent on a man who violently resents his utter dependence on me."

"How have things been since I left yesterday?"

"Fine, of course. An absolute darling. He's all over me with invitations to dinner and plans for holidays. I think I scared him by actually walking for a couple of nights, but it won't last."

"Will he be ready to leave tomorrow morning? The flight and operation are confirmed."

"Yes, he's ready. He packed his bag last night. I'm sure he loves the idea of making it work." Her eyes welled up again. "Neil, is there any way you can get me back to England? Could I come with you?"

McCrew stared at her in silence for a moment. "Frank's only motivation to help us with Mrs Churchill is that he believes he can travel back here after the operation and resume his surgical double-act with you. That motivation dies if you're not here in Berlin waiting for him."

"So you need me here as bait."

"No, Tina."

"Yes, Neil, as bait." Tears streaming down her face, she rose from her armchair. "The first thing to resume when he gets back here will be the violence against me and you know it."

"Tina, please."

"I'm desperate, Neil. Don't leave me here."

He stood up and took her in his arms. She sobbed there. As he hugged her, something caught his attention in the lounge doorway. Anna standing there, arms folded and her face a question mark directed at Tina's back.

McCrew coughed. "Tina, may I introduce you to my guardian angel in Berlin."

Tina let go of him and swung round just in time to come face to face with Anna, who had taken a few steps forward. With one finger applied to Tina's chest, Anna toppled her back into the armchair. She then placed her hands on the arms of the chair, leaned forward and brought her nose to within an inch of Tina's.

"Anna, this really isn't—" McCrew began.

Anna ignored him. "I know who you are," she said calmly to Tina. "I also know who you were in Neil's life before you pissed off with Frank Winter. What I witnessed a few seconds ago was the last time you ever lay so much as a fingernail on him. You had your chance way back in Cambridge days. These are Berlin days and he's mine now. Do I make myself clear?"

"Anna, please," McCrew said.

Anna kept her eyes on Tina. "Do I, Frau Winter?"

Tina managed to nod.

"And there's something else I witnessed for the last time from you a few seconds ago: it's that teary-eyed, oh-so-feminine, oh-so-vulnerable ploy of yours to get something from Neil. He owes you nothing, understood?"

Another nod.

"Because if I catch you so much as thinking of doing any of those things again, you'll not only have your husband's violence to contend with but mine, too. Would you like a practical demonstration of it?"

Tina shook her head.

"I thought not." Anna suddenly smiled, backed off and sat down on the sofa. "Now that the ground rules have been established, we need to find a solution for your physical safety. Two suggestions. The first concerns the hours between now and your husband's departure tomorrow. Is he likely to hurt you? If he is I can show you a couple of moves that'll make him regret it."

"No, it's unlikely," Tina said after a moment's thought. "He hasn't touched a drop of alcohol since yesterday."

Anna turned to McCrew. "Is there a plan to bring Tina's husband back to Germany after the surgery?"

McCrew shrugged. "I don't know the details yet, but yes."

"Second suggestion," Anna said slowly, building her idea as she went. "What if Tina were to hide somewhere close to her husband's landing spot? Once he's left the aircraft and moved away, she could make a dash for it and get *into* the aircraft just before it takes off again." She grinned. "What do you think?"

McCrew and Tina looked at each other and burst out laughing.

Tina went over to Anna, sat beside her and kissed her on the cheek. "It's a pleasure to meet you, Anna."

Chapter 87

Monday 12 May 1941
Farnborough – Hampshire – England

Colin Gubbins slowed his Morris Eight just short of the runway at Farnborough Airfield to let a Hurricane fighter land. Inside Hangar B he found Roddy Danes and Mike Paterson pouring over a technical drawing on a workbench.

"Good morning, gentlemen. It looks as if Radke's pulled off his mission and needs transport to get home.

"Good," Danes said.

"But something's worrying me." Gubbins took a large photograph out of his briefcase and placed it on top of the technical drawing. "This is your landing spot in the Eifel Forest, as photographed by one of our reconnaissance planes yesterday afternoon."

Danes and Paterson stared expectantly at it."

"What the problem?" Danes asked.

"You can still land there."

Danes and Paterson glanced at each other. "So?" Paterson asked.

Gubbins bristled. "Wouldn't you at least expect the Germans to put a pile of logs or something in the middle of it to stop anyone else landing?"

"I see what you mean," Danes said.

"My money says there's still a strong chance they'll do something like that before your next flight. So you'll need to take a close look at the entire clearing before you land. Those are the last photographs you'll see."

"And taking a close look means making a lot of noise, which will bring the Germans running," Paterson muttered.

"What if I used Nottuln again?" Danes asked

Gubbins folded his arms. "Nottuln?"

"It's a village with a disused airfield just north of it in Westphalia-North. I landed there the other day. It's fine. Tell Radke and his passenger to be there at dawn on Wednesday."

Chapter 88

Monday 12 May 1941
Berlin – Germany

Anna Vogel watched Neil McCrew place the white pot on the window sill. "You didn't ask me why I came home early."

He turned to face her, eyes ablaze. "Anna, you can't go around threatening people like that. You need to calm down."

"That's not what you said to me in bed last night."

"No, seriously. And you don't own me either. I can take care of myself."

She kissed him. "Can you? Why do you think the two most important women in your life so far either left you for another guy in Tina's case or got pregnant by another guy in your wife's case?"

"Drop the cheap psychology, please."

"Why, Neil? What did you do to them?"

"Believe it or not, I took care of them. That's what I did. I did exactly what most women accuse most men of not doing."

"Fair enough. But did you let them take care of you?"

McCrew thought about this.

"And what about the third most important woman in your life, your mother? How did caring work in that relationship?"

He rolled his eyes. "What's my mother got to with it?"

Anna kissed him again.

He turned away.

"Kiss me," she said.

He sat on the sofa, head down.

"What's the matter?" she asked. "I'm only asking questions."

He avoided her eyes. "Look, I've enjoyed every minute here with you, Anna. I've never been so terrified in my life but never felt more alive either." He looked up sheepishly. "The idea of not seeing you any more is beginning to eat away at me, too. It feels strange to say this but I've seen you kill two men in cold blood and yet I'm still going to miss you."

She laughed and sat beside him, taking his hands in hers. "Does that mean that given half a chance you'd take me with you to England?"

He shrugged.

Anna smiled. "Before I say anything else I think I'll get you some schnapps."

Chapter 89

Monday 12 May 1941
Berlin – Germany

Tina Winter shut the front door and bent down to remove her shoes. Barely had she straightened up again than her husband's hands grabbed her arms and flattened her against the wall.

"Where were you?" he hissed.

Smelling alcohol on his breath she switched instantly to assessment mode, ticking mental boxes or skipping them as she tried to work out how drunk he was. Skin colour? Time of day? Ability to speak? Clarity? Bloodshot eyes? Physical strength? Loudness? Strength of stench?

Still sober.

This was ominous.

"I went for a walk," she said casually.

"I'll give you a second chance, not a third. Where were you?"

She held his gaze. "If you've decided you know where I went, why don't you just tell me and I'll agree?"

"Where were you, Tina? You didn't go to see McCrew by any chance, did you?"

The first slap, she knew, was inevitable and less than thirty seconds away.

"Why would I do that? Let go of me, Frank."

"Catching up. Old times. Shoulder to cry on. Take your pick."

"No, *you* take *your* pick. I went for a walk."

"Which streets?"

Now she understood. He'd searched her clothes and found McCrew's scribbled address. Was this jealousy? Winter had displayed many weaknesses over the years but jealousy wasn't one of them. Or hadn't been until now. Should she just tell him the truth?

"Why don't you just beat me up and get it over with, Frank."

Tina couldn't believe she'd just said that but realised immediately it was the best thing to say. Now he'd be wondering what, if anything, she'd told McCrew about his violence and why she'd walked out for forty-eight hours. This would shine a different light on their teamwork in London.

Winter's grip loosened slightly.

That's when she understood what to do. The idea sprang fully formed into her mind, as did the words she needed to say.

"Yes, I walked to Fasanenstrasse and yes, that's where Neil's hiding and yes, I was hoping to see him and no, he wasn't there and yes, that pissed me off and no, I don't know what would have happened if I'd seen him, just him and me alone after all these years and both of us remembering how hot things once were between us. But more to the point, what would you have done to me if you'd been in his position? In what order would you have ripped my clothes off?"

Winter let his hands drop to his sides and looked away, as if giving up.

Tina pressed on. "I'll tell you what you'd have done if I'd come knocking at your door, all feminine and vulnerable. In fact you're about to do it now."

Three things surprised her then. The first was the power of Winter's punch. The second was the fact that he did in fact punch her; usually he slapped her several times, always starting with his right hand. Punches were rare. But when they did happen he aimed them at her stomach. This time, third, his punch went for her face and would have seriously injured her or even killed her had it landed. It didn't. She ducked just in time and listened for the snapping sounds of at least three bones breaking in his right hand as it slammed into the hallway wall behind her.

Chapter 90

Monday 12 May 1941
Berlin – Germany

Neil McCrew had fifty metres left to walk to Anna's building. The five minutes were almost up and the agent hadn't shown himself.

A black Volkswagen Kdf[35] pulled up beside him from behind. Its front passenger window was open.

"Entschuldigung[36]?" the driver called, leaning across.

Despite a fake beard and moustache, the agent's face was immediately familiar to McCrew, who stopped and bent forward to listen to him.

"Keep your head close to the window," the agent said quietly in English. "I'll talk first, you next. Drive tomorrow to a village called Nottuln in Westphalia-North, about five-hundred kilometres from here. There's a disused airfield just north of it. Get there before dusk so you can check the runway and remove any obstacles. You'll be picked up on Wednesday at 6.30 am by the same German aircraft that brought you. If the aircraft can't land or doesn't turn up, be there on Thursday at the same time. Friday will be the last attempt. If that doesn't work, you're on your own. Good luck to you. Your turn. I'll laugh and talk whilst lip-reading you."

The agent laughed briefly and said something McCrew guessed to be gratitude of some kind as it included 'Danke'.

---

[35] This is the official name of the car known as the "Käfer", meaning "beetle" in German.
[36] "Excuse me?"

"Three of us will be flying, not two," McCrew said. "The third's Anna Vogel. One-way ticket. She needs to leave Germany. That's all."

The car drove off. McCrew watched it for a few seconds before returning to Anna's apartment.

"Bedroom," she called as he took his shoes off in the hall.

He found her lying naked on the bed.

"Was that him in the car?" she asked.

"Yes. I've told them you're coming with me. We'll be taking off from a different place. Do you think Winter will have a good map of the country?"

She propped herself up on her elbows. "As a matter of fact I've got one. Do you realise this was supposed to be our last night together?"

"It isn't even evening yet."

"Isn't it? Well take your clothes off anyway."

He sat on the bed and stroked her hair. "I've got a question first. Why are you doing this? Why are you helping Churchill and Bracken?"

"Bracken offered to pay me but he already knew from our first meeting four years ago that I wasn't interested in money. So he offered to guarantee me a job and a clean sheet after the war, once Germany had been defeated. In return I was to do two things: chaperone you during your mysterious mission in Berlin and then work for Bracken as a spy at the Ministry of Propaganda. I wasn't interested in that either. The only thing I *was* interested in was an opportunity to work for a cause."

"A cause?"

"Women."

"Women?" He rolled his eyeballs.

"Don't you roll your eyeballs at me, Neil McCrew. This is serious."

McCrew raised his hands in mock surrender. "I know, I know."

"In the United Kingdom, Churchill and the ruling class he represents see women as a threat. They're a threat to be contained until motherhood drains them of all the time and energy they might otherwise use to demand a better deal in life. Well that's about to change and if Churchill and Bracken don't want to be thrown out by female voters after the war, they'll need help from a propaganda expert like me."

"So you agreed to chaperone me in exchange for a propaganda job promoting the cause of British women?"

"No. I was told that if anyone can help the cause of women in the United Kingdom, Churchill can. But he had a serious medical problem that needed to be sorted out first. If it wasn't sorted out, he'd be finished and women would lose a crucial supporter. What they didn't tell me was that the medical problem concerned his wife and not him but the end result was the same. If she died, he'd be finished. Then they told me that sorting out the medical problem depended heavily on you meeting someone here in Berlin. They asked if I could look help make that meeting happen and voilà." She held his gaze in silence. "My role was supposed to be a small and indirect contribution to a worthy cause. Afterwards my life in Berlin was supposed to go on as before. Then four days ago I met you."

"It looks as if Churchill and Bracken are going to get a lot more help on the female front than they bargained for."

Anna laughed. "That depends."

McCrew kissed her. "On what?"

"On how quickly motherhood drains all my time and energy away."

Chapter 91

Monday 12 May 1941
London – England

As Brendan Bracken entered Winston Churchill's study at 10 Downing Street, the Prime Minister was writing at his desk. A haze of cigar smoke filled the room.

"German radio has just announced Hess's disappearance," Bracken said as he sat down across from him. "That's the last doubt removed about our tourist's identity in Scotland."

"How are they playing it?"

"They don't know if he's alive or dead yet, so they're claiming he's been mentally ill for a while."

Churchill scoffed and put on a mock German accent. "Dear citizens of the Third Reich, I hereby declare insanity not to be grounds for exclusion from my government. I'd have to fire everybody otherwise, including myself as your deranged, beloved and thoroughly temporary Führer."

They laughed.

"I'll put a statement out tonight," Churchill said.

"Are you sure? What's the Cabinet saying?"

"Mixed bag. Some want to say nothing and keep the Germans guessing. Some want to publicise Hess's arrival as evidence that Hitler's losing control. Some want to put Hess on trial immediately as a war criminal. One or two even want to take a close look at what Hess is offering."

"What about you?"

"I rather like the idea of letting the Germans sweat a bit about what Hess might or might not be telling us. But rumours are already flying and not all of them to our advantage. I'll have to say something but no details about his peace offer just yet. Could you set up a meeting for eleven? I'll have a statement ready by then."

Bracken stood up. "Will do. Are they still questioning Hess?"

"Yes, Hamilton's being helped by a chap called Ivone Kirkpatrick from the Foreign Office, an expert on Germany. Hess is sticking to his tune: they get a free hand in Europe and have all their ex-colonies returned to them and we keep our independence and empire. Oh, and I lose my job."

Bracken opened the door to leave.

"Brendan?"

"Yes, Winston?"

"If you noticed a Cabinet member trying to cope with his insanity by signing up for flying lessons, you would inform me, wouldn't you?"

Chapter 92

Tuesday 13 May 1941
Berlin – Germany

Contrary to his usual practice of imposing his own views and decisions on the twenty or so participants in his daily Ministry conferences, Joseph Goebbels had encouraged an open discussion on Rudolf Hess's flight to Scotland. The previous evening's radio announcement of the deputy Führer's disappearance followed a few hours later by confirmation from the United Kingdom of his arrival on British soil had caused a sensation. Hitler in this case had directed communication on the matter himself, leaving Goebbels and his staff to hear the announcement at the same time as the nation.

"We need to stay calm and divert public attention away from Hess as much as possible, at least for the next couple of days," Goebbels said. "Key to the whole thing is what the British intend to do."

"But why is the Führer telling the public that Hess is insane?" asked Hans Fritzsche, head of German Press. "Everyone will wonder why he knowingly let a madman carry on in his top-level duties as usual."

"Maybe the Führer's been dropping hints about Hess all along by letting him do the yearly Christmas broadcast," said Karl Bömer, head of Foreign Press. "Perhaps he's been suggesting that our nation should no more believe in Hess than in Santa Claus."

The room laughed.

"The insanity claim isn't addressed to the German public," Goebbels said. "It's primarily for the British government's benefit. The Führer wants them to know that Hess flew to the United Kingdom on his own initiative, certainly not on the Führer's authority. Secondly, by claiming Hess is insane, he discredits anything he might reveal to the Brits." He paused to light a cigarette. "Anyway I'll find out more about what the Führer knows at the Berghof this afternoon. My personal opinion is that the main culprits behind this are Hess's wife and all those astrologers he consults. They're the ones putting strange ideas in his head."

There was a knock on the conference room door. The room fell silent as Kurt Frowein, one of Goebbels's closest personal assistants, came in and handed a large envelope to his boss.

Goebbels's name was handwritten on it and he immediately recognised Hess's elegant style. "Find out how this was delivered and by whom," he told Frowein.

"Yes, Herr Minister."

Goebbels rose from his chair. "We'll resume in thirty minutes. I have to see what this is about."

He hurried through the building to his office, slammed the door and ripped open the letter without bothering to sit down.

Munich, May 7th 1941
Dear Joseph
On May 10th, as you will no doubt be aware by now, I flew on my own initiative to Scotland to discuss possible peace terms with the Duke of Hamilton, whom I met at the Olympic Games in 1936 and who knows the King well. If you're reading this, two conditions have been met: the British have announced that I'm alive and that they've invited me to stay for a while in their country, either as a guest of honour or as a prisoner of war. The trusted friend who sent you this letter on my behalf was instructed to do so only if those two conditions were met.

The day after my flight, my adjutant gave Adolf a first letter from me with details of the peace terms I'm offering the British and advising him to describe me as insane if my initiative fails in any way. If he sees fit to share those details with you, he will.

Our Führer has now received a second letter from me. It's of a much more personal nature. Eight other high-ranking officials of our regime, including you, have received a similar one. I've written these letters to ensure my family and I come to no harm because of my actions. In the unlikely event that someone close to me should be made to suffer personally, socially or professionally over the coming months or years because of their association with me, my aforementioned trusted friend will send copies of this letter to three news organisations in Germany and six abroad.

Over the last four years I have patiently gathered evidence on the more sensitive areas of the lives of those nine officials. It includes documents, photographs, descriptions, tapes, names, dates, times, numbers and witness accounts. The originals are kept, as you can well imagine, in a safe place outside German-controlled territory.

The evidence provides detailed and undeniable proof of moral, sexual or financial corruption, in some cases all three. In your case, Joseph, the evidence demonstrates that one of your closest and most trusted advisers over the last four years, Anna Vogel, is Jewish. Two possibilities here: either you didn't run the compulsory background checks on this individual before recruiting her or you've been knowingly covering up the truth. Either way your behaviour has been grossly negligent at best, criminal at worst. Most worrying of all, it is highly likely that Vogel, given her religion and closeness to you, has systematically pushed you towards a softer approach regarding Jews, Jewish misdeeds and the international Jewish conspiracy. The evidence also includes photos of Anna and proof that she and her parents are Jewish.

Is this letter a form of blackmail? Of course it is. Does it show that my own moral standards are as laughably low as yours and everyone else's? Of course it does. I wish us all well nevertheless, Joseph.

Yours,
Rudolf Hess.

Goebbels rubbed his forehead with the tips of his fingers as he reread the letter. Then he reached for the telephone. "Put me through to Reichsmarschall Goering. Try the Berghof first. He's almost certainly with the Führer. Yes, it's urgent."

Goebbels and Hermann Goering, whose numerous responsibilities included supreme commandership of the Luftwaffe[37], had become close in 1938. Ordered by Hitler to end his affair with Czech actress Lida Baarova, a heartbroken Goebbels had been able to confide in Goering.

"Good morning, Herr Doktor Goebbels. Yes, I've received a letter from that idiot as well. And no, I won't tell you what it contains."

"Good morning, Herr Goering. Ah, what letter are you talking about?"

There was silence before Goering laughed. "You had me sweating there."

"Glad to hear it. More seriously, I think I can see a way to contain this, but I need your help."

"You've got my attention. Should any of the three photos I'm looking at land on the desk of a British or American newspaper editor, I want you to know it was a pleasure knowing you, Herr Doktor."

---

[37] German air force

Chapter 93

Tuesday 13 May 1941
Berghof – Upper Bavaria – Germany

The soldier walked briskly along the corridor towards the lounge. Adolf Hitler, he'd been told, was up earlier than usual and drinking tea alone before going for a stroll in the surrounding alpine countryside.

"Guten Morgen, mein Führer."

Sitting in an armchair, Hitler didn't look up from his newspaper. "What is it?"

The soldier held out a round silver tray to him. "A letter from Reichsminister Hess, mein Führer."

Hitler threw his newspaper on the floor. "Another one?" He grabbed the envelope—it was much thicker than the first—and ripped it open.

The soldier had also been told to expect an angry outburst and not to take personally any insults the Führer might scream at him. Duly forewarned he still needed a full hour to stop shaking after leaving the lounge.

Chapter 94

Tuesday 13 May 1941
London – England

Brendan Bracken caught up with Winston Churchill in a corridor on the first floor of 10 Downing Street. "News from Berlin, Winston," he said quietly. "McCrew's bringing Anna Vogel over with him. She won't be returning to Berlin this time."

"Oh? Pity. I was getting quite used to the idea of having a fly on Goebbels's wall. Does this affect Clemmie's operation?"

They turned into a stairway and descended side by side.

"No, I don't think so. Did you see that Hitler has named Hess's deputy, Martin Bormann, Head of the Nazi Party Chancellery?"

"No direct replacement for Hess, then."

"And Bormann has somehow managed to dissociate himself completely from Hess's actions."

Churchill grunted. "Or rather he's somehow managed to associate himself completely with Hitler's needs. We need to watch him." Churchill glanced at Bracken. "What's wrong, Brendan? There's something on your mind."

They reached the ground floor and moved to one side. Politicians and staff were hurrying in all directions.

"I've been thinking about Hess."

"Any news."

"Not yet. Kirkpatrick's still questioning him. He's supposed to be sending a fresh report by lunchtime." Bracken winced. "But something doesn't feel right."

"Understatement of the month, Brendan."

"If I were Hess I'd keep something up my sleeve and barter it for a meeting with someone high up. The King or even you."

Churchill turned sarcastic. "I hope it's not their imminent invasion of the Soviet Union. That's yesterday's news as far as we're concerned."

"No, that's too obvious. And the peace terms he's offering are too obvious as well. He knows damn well we won't accept them. There must be something else."

"Either that or Hess has truly lost it," Churchill said. "In which case Hitler's telling the truth."

They looked at each other. "No chance!" they shouted together.

Chapter 95

Tuesday 13 May 1941
Berlin – Germany

"Car's here!" Anna called from the lounge window sill.

McCrew appeared in the doorway with their bags. "What car?"

She pointed downwards. "Laid on by Goebbels himself to keep you off the pavements."

"Forgive me if I don't feel honoured."

Anna looked around. "I'm wondering whether I'll miss this place."

"Where are you going to leave the keys?"

"I'm taking them with me. They're the only souvenir I want of Berlin."

They locked up and walked down the two flights of stairs for the last time. A black Mercedes Benz was waiting for them outside the building, motor running. They said nothing during the short drive to Charlottenburg.

The hallway of Winter's building was deserted. Anna suddenly turned and pushed McCrew back against a wall. "I might not be able to kiss you for a while." She did so.

They took the lift up to the third floor and McCrew pressed the Winters' bell.

Tina opened the door. There was nothing welcoming about her. Her eyes expressionless, she stood stiffly to one side to let them in, then led them through to the lounge.

The first thing McCrew noticed was Frank Winter sitting in an armchair to the right, his right arm in a sling and right hand in plaster. The first thing Anna noticed was Joseph Goebbels in an armchair to the left, legs crossed and smoking. Two of his bodyguards were also in the room, one standing at each end of it.

"Now that we're all here," Goebbels said in English, "let's have a little chat, shall we?" He nodded to the bodyguards, who left the room and shut the door behind them.

McCrew and Anna sat on the sofa. Tina pulled up a chair.

Winter and Tina stared at McCrew, who turned to Anna. "What's going on here?"

Anna glanced nervously from Winter's sling to Tina's face before settling enquiringly on Goebbels. "I have no idea," she murmured.

Goebbels spoke cheerfully to McCrew. "You're probably less pleased to meet me than I am to meet you, Doctor, but I'm pleased all the same. I trust you know who I am?"

McCrew nodded.

"As you're aware, Miss Vogel was kind enough to keep me informed about your little plan to save Mrs Churchill's life. Until this morning I had nothing against it. In fact I supported it. But a couple of things have changed. By the way don't blame Anna for my presence here. She's as surprised to see me here as you are." He nodded towards Winter's sling. "The bad news is that Doctor Winter fell yesterday and broke his hand. Fortunately his wife had just returned from seeing a couple of friends and was able to take care of him immediately. As you can see, however, Mrs Churchill's operation can no longer take place in the way you anticipated. So my first question is, can the operation take place at all?"

McCrew squinted at Tina, then Winter, before answering. "Frank Winter's the man, Doctor Goebbels[38]. Everything depends on his skills. That's why I sneaked into your country to fetch him."

Goebbels raised his chin. "But you're a brain surgeon too, aren't you? Couldn't Doctor Winter stand beside you and give you instructions whilst you do the physical part?"

"To do that we'd need to be able to trust each other. But I've discovered since arriving here that the last thing Winter deserves is my trust. He doesn't deserve anyone's trust, for that matter."

Goebbels licked his lips. "Come, come, Doctor, couldn't the two of you make an effort for Mrs Churchill's sake? Doctor Winter, what do you think?"

---

[38] Joseph Goebbels's title was due to his degree in philology. It had nothing to do with medicine.

Winter smirked provocatively at McCrew. "I suppose I could manage it. I'd already accepted to operate on Mrs Churchill anyway. I'll just have to get used to my new hands."

"Excellent," Goebbels said. "Just out of curiosity, how did Doctor McCrew persuade you to operate? Hippocratic oath? Professional conscience? Gap in your schedule? What did he say?"

"I'm a doctor, Herr Reichsminister. Whatever McCrew says about my trustworthiness, I help people get better first and ask questions later."

Goebbels shook his head in mock admiration. "We have a genuine selfless hero amongst us, meine Damen und Herren. A man whose courage is so immeasurably great that he'll try to make me, the Minister of Propaganda, believe his bullshit. Try honesty, Winter. How did he persuade you?"

"I persuaded him Herr Reichsminister," Tina interjected.

All eyes turned towards her.

"Neil, my husband and I knew each other in Cambridge. I was Neil's fiancée at the time. But things got a little confused and I ended up marrying Frank instead and coming to live here. I know I broke Neil's heart at the time and I regret hurting him to this day. He didn't deserve it." She shrugged. "So when he came here at considerable personal risk to ask Frank for help, I felt we both owed him something after what happened all those years ago."

Winter smiled weakly at her. McCrew and Anna frowned suspiciously at each other.

"That's more like it," Goebbels exclaimed. "Please remind me to bring a handkerchief next time." He turned to McCrew. "So what's your decision, Doctor? Will you be Doctor Winter's hands during Mrs Churchill's operation or not?"

Everyone turned expectantly to McCrew, who was staring at the coffee table.

Tina broke the silence. "I will say this about you, Herr Reichsminister: you're not particularly good at detecting bullshit."

Goebbels's face lost all colour. "What did you say, Frau Winter?"

"You heard me. Everything I've just said is total bullshit. When I met Frank in Cambridge I dropped Neil like a ton of bricks. I didn't give it a second thought. Marrying Frank was the opportunity of a lifetime, or so I thought. To cut a long story short, when Neil turned up the day before yesterday to ask for Frank's help, I wasn't even here. I'd walked out on Frank and was drifting around Berlin, seriously contemplating suicide. You see, my husband, the famous Doctor Frank Winter, is an alcoholic. Worse than that, he's a violent alcoholic. This mark on my forehead is a reminder of it."

She glanced around the faces. Winter, McCrew and Goebbels were staring open-mouthed at her. Anna was staring in admiration.

Tina turned back to Goebbels. "As further evidence of your inability to detect bullshit, Herr Reichsminister, Frank didn't fall and injure himself yesterday. He threw a punch at me when I returned from a visit to see Anna and Neil. He missed and hit the wall in our hallway instead. Had I not ducked, I wouldn't be here to tell the tale."

"Is this true, Doctor Winter?" Goebbels asked.

Winter looked away.

Goebbels leaned towards him. "But you're in control here, aren't you. Whether you're a violent alcoholic or not, you're indispensable. Without your knowhow, everything stops. We need you and you know it. So here's what's going to happen, Winter. You're going to guide Doctor McCrew whilst he operates on Mrs Churchill. If you refuse to operate or if the operation fails in any way, I'll ask the two gentlemen waiting outside to perform their own special type of surgery on your fingernails. Then they'll turn their surgical attention to your testicles. And whilst they do all that they'll take special care to ensure that suicide, the thought of which is bound to enter your mind at some point, never becomes an option to you. They won't even allow you to faint." He turned to McCrew. "Have you made that decision yet?"

McCrew nodded.

"That's a bad idea, Herr Reichsminister," Tina interjected again.

Goebbels blinked as his tone turned steely. "Oh, is it? Am I due for yet another insult from you? You have one foot in deep trouble already, Frau Winter. The other's hovering dangerously close."

Tina swallowed her saliva. "The fact that Frank and Neil are both brain surgeons doesn't mean they can automatically work together. For example, Frank uses German vocabulary and Neil speaks English. They don't use each other's instruments or have the same habits either. All this can be harmonised, of course, but it takes time and time is what we don't have in Mrs Churchill's case."

"And you have an alternative, I suppose?" Goebbels asked quietly.

Tina turned to Winter. "Raise your left hand, Frank."

Winter didn't move.

Anna got up, crossed the room and slapped Winter on the cheek before grabbing his left hand and holding it up. It was trembling.

"His right hand was just as bad before he broke it," Tina went on. "Thanks, Anna."

"I don't understand," Goebbels said.

"Nor do I," Anna added as she sat down.

Tina spoke carefully to Goebbels. "Frank hasn't operated on anyone for several years. In fact the arrangement you were proposing for him and Neil to operate together in England was what they were going to do anyway."

"Then how come he's well known in Berlin as a practicing surgeon today?" Anna asked.

Tina forced a smile. "Yes, everyone talks about how wonderful Frank's hands are. But no one actually takes a close look at them." She raised her own hands and pretended to inspect them. "They're surprisingly feminine, don't you think?"

Anna and Goebbels stared at Tina in silence before Anna turned to McCrew. "Were you aware of this?"

He nodded.

"Well thanks for telling me," she said angrily.

"You're welcome."

"So, Herr Reichsminister," Tina said, "I'll be the one to operate on Mrs Churchill under Frank's guidance. All I ask in return is for you to let him and I continue with our unconventional surgical partnership after we get back from England." She gave Winter's right hand an affectionate glance. "I think he's learnt his lesson about violence now."

Anna and McCrew glared at her but she ignored them.

"Objections, Doctor?" Goebbels asked McCrew sceptically.

McCrew took a moment to answer. "I suppose not."

Goebbels took a deep breath and contorted his mouth. "Well I can't say I'm comfortable with such an arrangement but I suppose I'll have to be. For the next item on our little agenda, Doctor McCrew will need to take notes. Frau Winter, could you find a notepad and pencil, please?"

Whilst Tina did this, Goebbels reached down to a briefcase beside his armchair. He produced five different newspapers from it and handed them around.

"I don't know if you've heard the news but something surprising has just happened. Acting on his own initiative, Rudolf Hess flew to Scotland last Saturday to make some kind of personal peace offer to the British. As you can see from the headlines, the British have confirmed his arrival. He's now in their custody. We announced Hess's disappearance and obvious insanity to the German population last night."

They eyed the headlines of their respective newspapers for a few seconds.

"This situation can develop in several ways, but there's one scenario we don't want. For reasons I can't go into here, we want Churchill to keep Hess once they've interrogated him. Hess must stay in the United Kingdom indefinitely. In effect, therefore, we want Churchill to do us a favour by keeping one of Germany's deputy Führers away from Germany. Luckily it just so happens Churchill wants us to do him a favour, too. He wants us to operate on his wife to save her life. Now this might seem like a reasonable exchange but it isn't. What's to stop Churchill sending Hess back to Germany once the operation's finished?" He paused, as if expecting an answer. "Here's my solution. Mrs Churchill's operation will go ahead but it will take place here in Berlin, at the Winters' private clinic. The possible publication of photos of the British Prime Minister's wife arriving at one of Berlin's airports in May 1941 or of her receiving flowers from me at her bedside should ensure that Churchill stands by his side of the deal."

Turning to McCrew, he pointed towards the notepad. "I don't know how you communicate with London from here, but your next message will contain the information I'm about to give you. Everything has been organised in partnership with Hermann Goering, my colleague and Supreme Commander of the Luftwaffe, who doesn't know all the details but wants Hess to stay in England as much as I do. Please write this down." He slowed to dictation pace. "Mrs Churchill must be flown in a clearly marked British aircraft to Schiphol airport in the Netherlands on Thursday 15 May. The aircraft must land at exactly ten in the morning, German time. A few kilometres off the Dutch coast two German aircraft will join the British aircraft to escort it to Schiphol. The leader of the two German aircraft will identify himself as Fahrrad 2." Goebbels spelt it for McCrew. "The British pilot must identify himself as Fahrrad 1. When the British aircraft lands, it will be directed to a remote part of the airfield. Mrs Churchill will be transferred from the British aircraft to a German aircraft that will bring her here. You, Doctor McCrew, and Anna will be on the German aircraft to welcome Mrs Churchill and accompany her. Question: is Mrs Churchill mobile or not?"

"Depends on the day," McCrew said, "but be ready for a stretcher. I'll ask for her to be lightly sedated."

"Okay, I'll inform Goering." Goebbels resumed his dictation. "The German aircraft will be a flying ambulance and no doubt the British one will be, especially for the return flight after the operation. The operation itself will take place on Friday 16 April at a medical facility here—don't tell them the exact location—in Berlin. Assuming all goes well, we'll let Mrs Churchill rest in Berlin on Saturday 17 May before flying her back on the 18th. Question: how transportable will she be?"

McCrew cleared his throat. "That's the question you should have asked first, Doctor Goebbels. Moving her so soon, so far and by plane as well after an operation like that will be risky, to put it mildly."

"I agree," Winter interjected. "Ideally she shouldn't be moved until she's regained consciousness. Even if we use a lighter type of anaesthetic, I can't guarantee that'll happen in time for the flight."

"The flight back will take place on the 18th, regardless of Mrs Churchill's condition," Goebbels said quietly. "It's the only day Goering can arrange for the skies to be cleared and for an escort to be on hand without attracting too much attention. Regarding transport conditions, he and I give you full and immediate authority to order any changes you see fit to the German air ambulance. No expense is to be spared. You, Doctor McCrew, must give instructions to the British to adjust their aircraft, too. Questions?"

McCrew spoke first. "Churchill will not be happy about his wife having to travel to Berlin."

"He hasn't got a choice," Goebbels snapped.

"What if she dies here or is crippled for life?"

Goebbels spoke calmly. "She'll be transferred alive, crippled, dead, conscious or unconscious to the British aircraft on the 18th at ten in the morning at Schiphol. Doctor McCrew will accompany her the whole way. What Mr Churchill decides to do with her after that is his problem. Is that all? May I quickly double-check your notes, Doctor McCrew?"

McCrew handed him the notepad and pencil.

Goebbels read swiftly and scribbled something. "I'm adding the radio frequency the British pilot must use on the day." He stood up. "A few final details. From this moment onwards two cars from my Ministry are at your disposal twenty-four hours a day. One will be parked outside your building in Fasanenstrasse, Anna, and the other will be here. Use them at will. No questions will be asked. Doctor and Mrs Winter, I expect you to look after the medical aspects of all this and to get everything prepared. Doctor McCrew, I expect you to liaise back and forth with the British via your agent or however you do it." He turned to Anna. "I expect you to accompany Doctor McCrew at all times as you've been doing up till now and to help him in any way you or he sees fit. One exception: I want to see you in my office tomorrow morning. We have a problem to discuss."

Chapter 96

Tuesday 13 May 1941
London – England

King George VI and Winston Churchill walked side by side along a corridor on the first floor of Buckingham Palace.

The King ran a finger along a wooden panel and inspected it. "I suspect dust to be Germany's ultimate secret weapon. What do you think, Prime Minister?"

"Quite possibly, Your Majesty, although ultimately it will be no match for ours."

"Oh?"

"Ash."

As they entered a vast room called the Blue Drawing Room, the King gestured towards two armchairs and a small table comically isolated at the centre of it. A bottle of whisky, some water and two glasses had been placed on the table. "Shall we? Apologies for the lack of cosiness. Every other reception room seems to have workmen in it today."

They settled and the King poured for both of them. "Tell me about Hess."

"There's not much to tell at the moment, I'm afraid. He's still being questioned and still standing by his initial story."

"Do you really believe he did it by himself? Without Hitler's knowledge, I mean?"

"Some individuals around me believe there's a plot of some kind. Most don't, myself included. No, this was Hess's idea." He raised his glass. "To victory, Your Majesty."

"To victory, Prime Minister. I gather he was rather hoping to meet me. Would that be useful?"

"Not unless you want Goering, Himmler, Goebbels and a dozen assorted generals to pop over for a private chat as well."

They laughed.

"Seriously, Your Majesty, I can't see it being a good idea for now."

The King sipped his whisky. "What are you going to do with him?"

"That's being hotly debated. Some want him tried forthwith as a war criminal. Others think he should be sent back to Germany, where Hitler would almost certainly have him shot."

"What do you think?"

"Bracken, my private parliamentary secretary, thinks he's holding something back that he won't let go of until he's had afternoon tea with you or me or somebody from the Cabinet. I'm inclined to agree with him."

The King stroked his chin. "After tea, dear Lord. Do we really need to resort to torture?"''

"Heavens, no. We're already in breach of the Geneva Conventions with him as it is."

"Are we?

"He's had nothing but thick Scottish accents inflicted on him since he landed. The man's a wreck."

More laughter.

"The other dilemma is what to tell your subjects, Your Majesty. I'm in favour of coming clean and telling them what we know but that's a battle I'm unlikely to win. Most of the Cabinet think we should keep the Germans guessing."

The King narrowed his eyes. "As long as we don't mislead anybody, that's the main thing. I imagine this is putting you under ever more strain. How are you bearing up? Personally, I mean."

Churchill thought this over.

"Anything I can help you with?" the King asked.

"That's most considerate of you, Your Majesty. No, there's nothing you can help me with for now. But if all goes well I should be able to tell you exactly how I am on Friday evening. Can you wait till then?"

George VI smiled. "Of course."

"I only hope I can, too."

Chapter 97

Tuesday 13 May 1941
Berlin – Germany

McCrew checked his watch again. Anna was lying on her back on the sofa, her head resting on his thigh. She was holding a piece of paper angled so that he couldn't read it."

"Eight minutes to six," he said. "I'd better go down."

"No, let's run through it once more. You've only got it right twice so far. Your memory's appalling, Doctor McCrew. I really think you should write it all down."

McCrew sighed. "Nothing written. Gubbins was adamant. All right, one more time." He kissed her on the forehead, took a deep breath and closed his eyes. "Goebbels aware of surgery. Hess to be kept indefinitely in UK. Surgery in Berlin. Patient to be flown by British aircraft to Schiphol on May 15th, landing 10 am German time. Two German aircraft will escort British aircraft for final stretch to Schiphol. Radio identification for escort: Fahrrad 1. Radio identification for British aircraft: Fahrrad 2. McCrew to meet patient in Schiphol for flight to Berlin. Surgery May 16th. British aircraft to pick up returning patient alive or dead at Schiphol, May 18th, 10 am German time."

"You reversed the radio codes again. The British aircraft is one, the escort two."

McCrew stood up, went to the window and checked up and down the street, murmuring. "British one, escort two, British Fahrrad one, escort Fahrrad two. Does Fahrrad actually mean anything?"

"Bicycle."

"Bicycle? Is that supposed to be German humour? Tell me something: do you think Goebbels was acting on his own initiative this morning?

"Like Hess, you mean?"

"Do you think Hitler's aware that his propaganda minister is offering to swap surgery for Mrs Churchill in Germany for Hess's indefinite detention in the UK?"

"No idea. My instinct is that if Goebbels hasn't told Goering about Mrs Churchill, he hasn't told anyone. I'll try to find out tomorrow. Sit down, Neil."

"No, I've got to go."

"Sit down, Neil. There's something you forgot."

"What?"

"The radio frequency for the pilot."

McCrew stared blankly at her. "Shit, it's gone."

The doorbell sounded. Anna sat up, wide-eyed. McCrew put a finger to his lips, tiptoed through to the hall and carefully put his eye to the peephole. He could only see blackness.

Another knock. "Sofort aufmachen![39]" shouted a stern male voice.

Anna joined McCrew in the hallway. They exchanged a nervous glance. McCrew tried the peephole again. This time he could see the agent smiling and waving at him. He opened the door.

They said nothing until they were in the lounge.

"Sorry for breaking the routine and coming up here directly," the agent said, "but breaking the routine was the point. What happened? Couldn't find Nottuln on the map?"

---

[39] Open up immediately!"

Chapter 98

Tuesday 13 May 1941
London – England

Sitting at his desk in Berkeley Court, Colin Gubbins rubbed his eyes and shook his head in despair.
"Danes speaking."
"Gubbins."
Danes chuckled. "Would I be receptive etc., etc.?"
"If you said 'no', I'd understand."
"Do you often hear people say 'no' in your line of business, Brigadier?"
"Only when they're bureaucrats with a rule book to throw at me."
"What can I do for you?"
"Well you can forget the Heinkel and forget the smoke. You'll be flying a Bristol Bombay to German-occupied Holland. Ever flown one?"
Danes hesitated. "Er, yes I have. Am I expected to bomb something?"
"No, this one's been converted to an air ambulance. You're dropping off a patient at Schiphol the day after tomorrow. You'll even be escorted by two German fighters into Schiphol. That's how special the patient is."
Danes whistled.
"You'll be taking off early in the morning," Gubbins continued, "and flying back empty. Same again next Sunday to pick up the patient and bring her back along with at least one other passenger."
"So it's a woman, sir?"

"Yes."

"Where am I taking off from?"

"Kidlington. No prizes for guessing the patient's identity. Objections?"

"No, sir. Just curious as to why you chose me."

Gubbins cleared his throat. "We're still trying—and failing, if you ask me—to keep the number of people in the know to a minimum. Can a Bristol Bombay be flown by one person, by the way?"

"I suppose so but I'd prefer not to. Paterson's done some navigating before, so I'll take him along to be on the safe side."

"Fine. He'll also be able to help you with the stretcher at Schiphol if need be. Remember the man you dropped off with Anna Vogel the other day?"

"Radke, yes."

"Real name's McCrew. A brain surgeon. He's sent requirements for the inside of the Bombay. A few adjustments might be needed. Could Paterson handle them? He'll only have tomorrow."

"Of course."

"I'll have the Bombay flown to Farnborough in the next couple of hours. I'll call you again tomorrow with exact times and other details. Goodbye, Danes, and thanks."

"Goodbye, sir."

Gubbins put the phone down and reread the decrypted message from Berlin, debating whether to call Churchill and Bracken from his office or to tell them face to face in Downing Street. He chose the latter.

In the back of a chauffeured car a few minutes later, his sense of foreboding, which had faded on hearing that McCrew had met Winter and persuaded him to come, returned like a poorly managed hangover. His job was to give Churchill and Bracken his honest fact-based opinion on what to do or not do next but he knew what their answer would be.

What had gone wrong in Berlin? He guessed it was something to do with Anna Vogel, as she was the only link between McCrew and Goebbels. Deep down, though, Gubbins blamed Churchill for the mess and himself for not putting his foot down sooner and harder.

And how had Hess and his stupid peace initiative become involved? Why was Goebbels so desperate to keep him in the UK?

At Downing Street he was swiftly waived through security and accompanied to Churchill's study. On seeing his face the Prime Minister and Bracken dispensed with greetings and waited for him to sit down.

"Prime Minister," Gubbins began, "Goebbels has found out about your wife's operation. He's even met and talked to McCrew. He's offering to ensure the operation takes place but there are two catches. The first is that we must hold on to Hess indefinitely."

Churchill blinked and glanced at Bracken. "And the second?"

Gubbins shifted in his chair. "Your wife must be operated on in Berlin. All medical and transport arrangements have been organised on the German side." He handed a sheet of paper to the Prime Minister. "That's the latest message from our agent in Berlin."

Churchill read it and handed it to Bracken. "You're right, Brendan. Hess must be holding something back. Something that Goebbels prefers us to know than anyone in Germany."

Bracken read the message and looked up at Gubbins. "Dare I ask if we have a choice?"

"I'm sure I could come up with alternatives—kidnapping and torturing Winter, for example—but time is running out for Mrs Churchill."

"What about travel arrangements for Clemmie at this end if we do it?" Bracken asked.

"They're all set up. All I need is your go-ahead."

Churchill slammed his hands down on his desk. "Well I refuse to give it!" he yelled. "I won't let that degenerate assassin dictate his terms to me, do you understand? All he wants is to gather proof of Clemmie's stay in Berlin and blackmail me to kingdom come by threatening to publish it. Find an alternative, Gubbins, and find it bloody quick."

"I hope I'm not interrupting anything," said a female voice in the doorway.

Clementine Churchill walked in. Gubbins and Bracken stood up. There was an awkward silence.

"Clemmie, you were supposed to be resting in Ditchley," Churchill grunted.

She scoffed. "Whilst you decide my fate behind my back? Surely not. You were discussing my fate, weren't you? Half the building could hear you."

"Just my temper getting the better of me again." Churchill said as he glared at Gubbins. "And with good reason, I might add."

"May I join in for a minute?" she asked.

Bracken pulled up a chair for her between himself and Gubbins.

"What seems to be the problem?" she asked.

Gubbins and Churchill avoided her gaze.

"Your operation can't take place here, Clemmie," Bracken said. "Goebbels is involved now and he's blackmailing Winston into holding on to Rudolf Hess. In exchange, he'll make sure Frank Winter operates on you."

Clementine looked from one face to the next. Then she shrugged and smiled at Churchill. "Well I think it's a good idea."

"No dear, it isn't," Churchill snapped.

"Well I'm the patient, I'm your wife, I'm the only woman in this room and I think it's a good idea. There's something Goebbels has forgotten to take into account.

The three men waited.

"Winter's going to remove my brain tumour, not my vocal cords. Assuming I survive, I'll have a few things to tell Doctor Goebbels. By the time I've finished, he'll wish the operation had taken place in England." She stood up to leave. "Look on the bright side, gentlemen. After experiencing so many German bombing raids over this country, I'll be able to tell you what a British bombing raid over Berlin feels like."

Chapter 99

Wednesday 14 May 1941
London – England

A loud knock woke Brendan Bracken in his tiny room in the Cabinet War Rooms.

"You in there, Brendan?" Churchill's voice called.

"Come in."

Churchill entered with a cup of tea in one hand and an open envelope in the other. "Don't ever expect room service from me again, but I need you."

Fully dressed, Bracken sat up, put his glasses on and squinted at his watch as he took the cup. "Thank you. Two hours' sleep. Soon I'll be dubbing that a lazy lie-in."

Churchill pulled up a chair over and sat beside the bed. "Two favours to ask of you, one massive, one merely huge."

"I'm all ears."

"No, Brendan. The correct answer is 'yes unhesitatingly.'"

"Yes unhesitatingly, Winston."

Churchill's voice faltered, his eyes welling up. "Here I am, blubbing again. But I can't help imagining Clemmie sitting alone on that damn plane to Holland."

"She won't be alone, Winston."

Churchill placed his hand on Bracken's. "Would you do that for me, Brendan? I wanted to fly with her myself but she threatened never to talk to me again. She has a nasty habit of meaning such things."

"I'll accompany her, don't worry."

"Thank you. The second favour is to give this envelope to McCrew during the handover in Schiphol. It's not for him personally, though. I want him to give it to Goebbels should Clemmie not survive the operation or become crippled in some way. If Clemmie's okay he should destroy it, preferably without reading it although I suspect he won't be able to resist having a peek. I know I couldn't. Please read it."

Bracken removed a single page from the envelope and read aloud.

London, May 1941
Doctor Goebbels
If you're reading this, it can only mean that Doctor Winter's operation on my beloved wife has either killed her or damaged her brain irreparably. Although you didn't make things easier by insisting she be operated on in Germany rather than England, I wish nonetheless to acknowledge that you facilitated her operation and to thank you. War has its ironies and the fact that I entrusted the health and safety of the woman I love to a man I otherwise consider to be my enemy isn't the smallest of them.

We agreed to a successful operation on my wife's tumour in exchange for Rudolf Hess's infinite detention in England. As the operation has failed, I now consider myself unbound by any commitment regarding Mr Hess. What to do with him, then? Keep him here or send him back in a U-boat to you?

As I write this I remain convinced that he flew here with more to offer us than peace terms. Your insistent interest in his fate has only reinforced this belief. I have decided, therefore, to break down his resistance by subjecting him to a typically British form of torture: I'll invite him for Sunday afternoon tea (the alcoholic variety in my case, thus confirming the factual claims of your propaganda on the subject) and Red Cross biscuits (I'm told that one week of detention has already made Mr Hess an addict) on a peaceful country terrace. What Mr Hess reveals or not during that blood-drenched discussion will decide his fate.

Thanks again
Winston Churchill

Bracken slipped the letter back into the envelope. "What are Red Cross biscuits?"

Churchill scoffed. "Only a man sheltered from wartime rationing could ask that, Brendan. If you took an interest in what ordinary people nibble with their tea, you'd know what Red Cross biscuits are. Even the Führer's deputy knows."

Bracken hung his head in mock submission. "And whilst I wallow in my ignorance, you write to Joseph Goebbels to tell him he's a trustworthy individual who produces factual propaganda. Only a man desperate for his boss's approval and affection could fall for that."

Churchill grinned. "And what could you possibly know about such things, Brendan?"

Bracken turned serious. "One more thing, Winston. Before you torture Hess with tea and biscuits, do you mind if I borrow him? There's something I'd like to try to make him talk."

"Really? Tell me."

"No, Winston. The correct answer is 'yes unhesitatingly'."

Chapter 100

Wednesday 14 May 1941
Berlin – Germany

Anna Vogel winked at Fraülein Krüger as she strode past the rectangle of secretaries. She knocked on Goebbels's door and walked straight in. "Good morning, Joseph."

He was writing at his desk. "Sit down, Anna. I'll be with you in a second."

Regardless of what he was doing, Goebbels always looked up when she walked into his office. Today, she noted, and for the first time in four years, he hadn't.

He put his pen down. "Sorry for surprising you like that yesterday. I'd only just heard about Hess and needed to act quickly."

No coffee was offered.

"I understand. What's going on?"

"It isn't pretty. Hess genuinely seems to have lost it and Hitler's beside himself. I saw him at the Berghof yesterday afternoon. He and Ribbentrop are desperate to reassure anyone who'll listen, especially Mussolini, that this isn't some backhanded plot."

"Not that the Führer would ever lower his standards to doing such a thing."

Goebbels wasn't amused. "No fun and games, Anna."

"How does the Führer want to play it?"

"From as far away as possible. The more we talk about Hess, the more we'll seem rattled, which we are, of course. I believe the story will disappear from conversations within ten days if we ignore it and told the Führer as much. It's an embarrassment but only a temporary one. We'll get over it."

"Then why insist that Hess stay in the UK?"

Goebbels reached over the desk to hand her a sheet of paper. "This is a letter I received from Hess yesterday. Read the underlined part."

Anna read aloud. *"... the evidence demonstrates that one of your closest and most trusted advisers over the last four years, Anna Vogel, is Jewish. Two possibilities here: either you didn't run the compulsory background checks on this individual before recruiting her or you've been knowingly covering up the truth. Either way your behaviour has been grossly negligent at best, criminal at worst. Most worrying of all, it is highly likely that Vogel, given her religion and closeness to you, has systematically pushed you towards a softer approach regarding Jews, Jewish misdeeds and the international Jewish conspiracy. The evidence also includes photos of Anna and proof that she and her parents are Jewish...."*

They at anything but each other for a moment.

Goebbels lit a cigarette. "Should any harm come to him or his family, he's got someone who'll publish that far and wide. Interestingly and revealingly, he makes no attempt to protect his staff and friends."

Anna held up the letter by one of its corners. "Would I be correct in assuming Goering's received something like this, too?"

Goebbels hesitated before talking. "You would. Nine of us have. I don't know who the seven others are, but I'm assuming the Führer's amongst them. That's why Hess has to stay in the United Kingdom. It's the safest place for him to be. The British will question him but they're unlikely to harm him."

"I don't understand. Why couldn't Hess come back and simply be left alone?"

"Because the minute he sets foot in Germany, the Führer will have him shot, regardless of the consequences. The Führer's still popular enough to ride out any personal dirt being published and our political ideology doesn't include the concept of an election he might lose. But that's him. Things are different for the rest of us. If sensitive personal information gets out about us, and there's more than enough of that to go round, we're finished."

Anna spoke carefully. "In your case you could easily arrange for your problem with me to be solved before the scandal breaks. Are your henchmen about to burst in to take me to a concentration camp, Joseph?"

"That's up to you."

Anna froze. "I beg your pardon?"

Goebbels repositioned a large iron ashtray on his desk and flicked ash into it. "Yesterday morning two interesting things happened to me, both related to you. The first was that letter from Hess. The second was a phone call from a police inspector in Cologne. It seems two dead males have been found just off a country road west of the city. They've been identified as Martin Wessel and Ferdinand Opitz, two employees of my ministry. Both murdered. Opitz was stabbed through the eye and Wessel died of blood loss caused by a devastating injury to his genitals. Teeth marks were found on the wound. Around the time they died a military vehicle drove past the spot. One of the soldiers in the back told the police inspector he saw a black Mercedes Benz parked there with a woman answering your description at the wheel. He remembered her because she gave the soldiers a little wave. Was that you by any chance, Anna? Before you answer, let me add two more details. First, the murders took place near a village called Düren, which was where you originally said your mother lived. What a coincidence. Second, the vehicle was found three days later in Aachen, precisely the town where you said you and Doctor McCrew caught a train to Berlin after you landed. What a co—"

Anna raised a hand. "All right, Joseph, the police inspector's done a good job. Would you be interested in my version of what happened?"

Goebbels spoke softly. "I don't need to be, Anna. Several brave women reported Wessel's take on gentlemanly charm over the years. He always denied any wrongdoing, of course, and always won the ensuing her-word-against-his discussions." He paused. "The only reason he still had a job, and I'm embarrassed to say this, was his professionalism. He got the job done and got it done so well that the rest of us, myself included, got distracted from his darker sides. So whatever he and Opitz did to you, they deserved what you did to them."

"Is that what you're going to tell the police inspector?"

"I'll take care of him but that's not my principal concern right now." He paused again. "That's the second time in under a week that you've lied to me. So please forgive me for wondering how many other lies you've told me over the last four years."

"Joseph, I haven't—"

"Allow me to quote you: a ministry of propaganda cannot succeed if it lies to itself. Whatever we say to the outside world, we must be honest with each other."

"Joseph, please."

"Shut up. Until that police inspector called me yesterday, I was quite prepared to thank you for a job well done and to let you leave this country unhindered. Your lies have changed all that. So I've got a couple of options for you. Either I have you arrested right now and supply the SS with all the details they need to make your life hell, or you leave this country on the same aircraft as Mrs Churchill after her operation and you work for me from London. Got a preference?"

She stared at him.

"I thought so. Tell Bracken you've changed your mind about his job offer. Tell him you can't stomach National Socialism in general or me in particular anymore. Tell him what it's like to work for me: the petty details, the rants about Jews and Bolsheviks, the mistresses. Offer to make your communication expertise as indispensable to him and Churchill in the future as it's been to me since 1937. Gain their trust as you gained mine and keep feeding me information on everything they do."

"You're living in a dream, Joseph."

"Well you'd better join me in that dream, Anna. The alternative for you is living in a nightmare called Sachsenhausen or Ravensbrück[40]. And I'm not sure 'living' is the appropriate verb. Who's the expert in influence techniques around here? Use them on Bracken. Put stars in his eyes. I'll have one of our agents in London contact you about practical details. I expect your first report within a month."

Anna folded her arms. "Even if Bracken offers me a job, I won't be sitting in on any meetings or drinking sessions with Churchill. The usefulness of any information I might send you is likely to be low."

"I disagree. What you don't know yet is that Bracken's about to be appointed Minister of Information."

Anna's eyes widened.

"He probably doesn't know it himself yet. Yes, he's about to become my new opposite number. Mr British Propaganda himself. As his precious employee, you shouldn't find it too difficult to get invited to his top-level meetings."

Anna turned sarcastic. "And if you don't hear from me? Let me guess: photos of Wessel's and Opitz's injuries will suddenly begin to circulate in London with my name stamped on the back."

Goebbels scoffed. "Nothing so crude. But I have built up a collection of internal memos handwritten and signed by you and covering such topics as how this ministry might stigmatise Jews more effectively. I reread them regularly for inspiration. Now you wouldn't want that kind of thing to circulate in London, would you? Does anyone in England know you're Jewish, by the way?"

Anna shook her head.

"Frankly I still don't understand how you, a Jew, could have written such things. Some or your ideas are too perversely brilliant to be just a way of camouflaging your identity or hiding your religious beliefs in plain sight."

---

[40] Sachsenhausen and Ravensbrück were concentration camps 30km and 80km respectively from Berlin.

"I've never shown you brilliance, Joseph. The problem with brilliance is that it works so well as camouflage that sooner or later it arouses suspicion *precisely* because it isn't suspicious. What I've shown you instead, and I did so every single day I worked here, is professionalism. I get the job done and get it done so well that it distracts you from my darker sides."

"This conversation is over. Get out."

Anna leaned forward in her seat. "No, I won't. You know what, Joseph? I don't think you're interested in receiving intelligence from me on Bracken's activities at the Ministry of Information. I think you're much more interested in receiving proof on a regular basis that the last remaining person brave enough to tell you the truth hasn't cut you off. True, I lied to you about my whereabouts last week and true, I lied again about what happened with those two rapists, but you'd have lied in those situations, too. The only difference between us is that you'd have upheld your lies until the end of the Earth. You would never have backed down. At least I had the guts to relent and tell the truth. And why did I do that? Because I truly believe that an organisation that lies to itself must fail. The question is, do you believe it?"

Goebbels looked away. "Please leave, Anna."

"Joseph, you're about to mobilise this entire organisation, hundreds of people, in a campaign to persuade the world that we're about to invade the United Kingdom. How many of those hundreds of people—your own employees—are going to hear the truth: that we're actually going to invade the Soviet Union? How many will be told that the first target of the entire disinformation campaign is them, the very people who are running it? Three or four at most. All the others will be left to discover a few weeks from now that you, their boss, tricked them into believing their own lies and that you forced this organisation to break its own golden rule about not lying to itself. What will all those individuals, whose trust, loyalty and hard work you rely on, think of you then? Oh, they'll continue to leap to attention whenever you walk into the room, but their apparent respect for you will be a lie. They were your last allies, Joseph. Look around. You've said it yourself: the Führer's stopped keeping you informed of crucial strategic decisions. He prefers to lie to you. Your fellow National Socialist leaders spend more time stabbing each other in the back than doing what needs to be done to win this war. They prefer to lie to each other and to you. Even your marriage is only a marriage because the Führer won't let you and Magda get divorced. It's a lie, too." She stood up. "So tell me, Joseph, who apart from me can Germany's Minister of Propaganda still turn to to hear the truth?"

Goebbels held her gaze. "There is someone, Anna, and it's not you. You're right, my position has become a lonelier and lonelier place to be. No friends. No long-term allies. No undyingly loyal wife. But I still have one person I can rely on to tell me the truth. I see him every morning in the mirror, staring doggedly back at me. So don't worry: as long as I can refrain from lying to myself, I'll be fine. You should try a little humility, Anna. I'm not as indispensable to me personally as you might imagine. You're merely useful to me professionally. Which brings me back to Brendan Bracken. If I were you, I wouldn't make the mistake of underestimating him. He's one of the closest friends Churchill has ever had and, as far as our agents over there can ascertain, he influences the British Prime Minister in ways no man or woman could ever dream of influencing our German Führer. The reason I want you sitting in on Bracken's meetings at the Ministry of Information is that a lot of what gets discussed and decided there will find its way, or rather float its way on a steady stream of whisky and champagne, into Churchill's mind. And what finds its way into Churchill's mind is likely sooner or later to find its way into his decisions."

Anna turned to leave. "Goodbye, Joseph."

"Good luck in England," he called to her. "I'll look forward to hearing from you."

She kept moving towards the door.

"And I've got a good feeling about our little surgery deal for Mrs Churchill in exchange for her husband keeping that idiot Hess quiet."

Anna stopped at the door and spun round. "Why do you think it's going to work, Joseph?"

"Because we've done what you and I do best. We've used our intimate knowledge of influence techniques to manoeuvre the right people into the right places at the right times."

"Have we?" She took a few paces back towards him.

"Of course we have!"

"And I suppose you think you're a successful minister of propaganda for the same reason: influence techniques painstakingly studied and scientifically applied."

Goebbels shrugged. "What else? You've been watching me use them for four years. You've even taught me a few yourself."

Anna returned to her seat. "No, Joseph. People like us, people who know how influence works, always end up making the same mistake. You're making it right now. I saw Edward Bernays making it all the time back in the States. When we look back on situations we were involved in, we can't stop deluding ourselves that the words we deliberately chose, the gestures we deliberately made and the settings we deliberately tweaked had a huge, irresistible impact on our targets' behaviours."

Goebbels scoffed. "Didn't they? You know as well as I do that when—"

"Don't get me wrong: influence techniques do make a difference and some of your propaganda efforts are clear evidence of that. But only some of them. And that's because influence techniques offer no guarantees. They only increase the chances that people will do what we want them to. They only nudge the statistics. We're never as much in control of minds, feelings, behaviours and events as we think we are. The closest we come to acknowledging that fact is when we try to influence people and fail. We're quick to blame circumstances, coincidences or bad luck. Not that we use those words, of course; we rename them God's will, fate, destiny or providence. When we try to influence people and *succeed*, however, we take full responsibility. We convince ourselves that our influence techniques were implacable, that they dissolved all resistance before it could take shape. We ignore the fact that our success is as much due to circumstances, coincidences and luck as it is to our influencing expertise."

"I disagree with you. We're influence experts precisely because we manage circumstances, coincidences and luck as well."

Anna laughed. "Why do you think Bracken and Churchill asked me to chaperone Neil McCrew during his stay in Berlin? Oh, I'd love to claim they chose me because of my expert knowledge of influence techniques and my ability to manipulate people. Wrong! They needed someone they could trust more a less—they took a massive risk in my case—who could hide McCrew in her apartment for a few nights and who could speak German for him if anyone asked questions. Not an influencing skill in sight. How come you and I were able to work out that Mrs Churchill needed a brain operation and that Churchill wanted a German surgeon to do it? Oh, we'd both love to believe our influencing abilities made a difference. Wrong! What happened was that I noticed that McCrew had the manual skills of a doctor, you spotted a problem with Mrs Churchill's accent and we both worked out that the fifth name on Roosevelt's list wasn't an American surgeon or a British one, but a German one based here in Berlin. In other words we relied on a combination of circumstances, coincidences, luck and a sprinkling of common sense, not on our influencing expertise."

Goebbels sighed. "Have you made your point or are you getting to it?"

"My point is that the reflection that stares back at you every morning in the mirror is lying to you, too. You're not in control of circumstances, coincidences and luck. In fact the only thing you are, Joseph, is alone."

Chapter 101

Wednesday 14 May 1941
Berlin – Germany

Frank Winter walked across the tarmac at Berlin's Gatow airport, which was mostly reserved for government officials. Nothing about the Junkers Ju 52 ahead of him indicated it was an air ambulance rather than an ordinary transport plane.

Four men were chatting by the aircraft's open door as Winter approached. One of them, in his forties and mopping sweat from his brow, stepped forward with his right hand outstretched.

"Good morning, sir. I'm Doctor Ranzau, engineer." He withdrew his hand when he noticed Winter's sling.

"Good morning, I'm Doctor Winter. I'll inspect this aircraft exactly five hours from now. What I expect to find is a place to put a stretcher and secure it for a two-hour flight. The stretcher will have a patient on it who has just had an extremely sensitive operation. Frankly, gentlemen, I don't care how much this aircraft vibrates as it takes off, flies through the air and lands. What I do care about is the extent to the patient experiences those vibrations personally. My instruction to you engineers and mechanics or whatever you are is simple: the patient will experience no vibrations at all. See you later."

"But Doctor Winter—" Ranzau began.

Winter had already turned his back on them and set off towards the terminal.

Chapter 102

Wednesday 14 May 1941
Drymen – Scotland

Buchanan Castle, near the village of Drymen in Scotland, had been converted into a hospital at the beginning of the war. Rudolf Hess had been transferred there from St Mary's Barracks in Glasgow after treatment for his ankle injury.

Douglas Douglas-Hamilton and Ivone Kirkpatrick exchanged a weary look as they waited for Hess to return from the toilet. A day room had been cleared of other patients so that they could talk.

"This is day four," Douglas-Hamilton said. "We'll get nothing more out of him. He's just repeating himself and getting a little more creative with each repetition."

Kirkpatrick ran a finger along his moustache. "God knows what Hitler saw in him. Bracken called me last night by the way. They're seriously discussing sending him back."

Douglas-Hamilton sat up on his chair. "Really?"

Kirkpatrick shrugged. "It's dicey. Hitler will almost certainly have him executed as a warning to his other henchmen. And some journalists here are bound to point out that Churchill knowingly sent a deluded but brave pacifist to his death."

"If Hess could murder every Jew alive, he'd do so in an instant. Not my idea of a pacifist. When will they decide?"

"Soon, if they haven't decided already. Here he is."

Hess limped in and sat down. "As I was saying, the Americans clearly want to take over your empire and will do so at the first opportunity. But is anyone paying attention here? No."

Douglas-Hamilton and Kirkpatrick rolled their eyes simultaneously.

Chapter 103

Wednesday 14 May 1941
Berlin – Germany

As Tina Winter opened the front door to the apartment, she briefly closed her eyes, building up her courage, hoping she wouldn't find what she dreaded.
"Hello?"
"Kitchen," her husband called.
Leaving her bag and shoes in the hall, she walked through to the kitchen and found him standing by the table. Some thirty bottles of wine and spirits were lined up on it.
Raising his sling, he shrugged. "This is as far as I got. I need your help to open them."
"Why?"
"Just do it, please."
Tina removed a cork from a half-full bottle of cognac, the contents of which he promptly poured down the sink behind him. They did likewise in silence for every bottle on the table. The kitchen soon reeked of alcohol.
"This won't solve my problem," he said when they finished, "but I hope it shows I at least acknowledge it."
Tina said nothing as she opened the kitchen window.
"Is the clinic ready?" he asked.
"Yes. Erich, Detlef and Ulrike will be there for the surgery. Frida, Ingrid and Jasmin will work shifts for the nursing."
"Did you tell them who the patient is?"

"No, but I'll have to tell the nursing crew after the operation, once we're sure it's gone well. Sooner or later Mrs Churchill's bound to say something and it won't be in German. The nursing crew all speak reasonable English. How was Gatow?"

"It's done. It took them four hours to prepare the aircraft as I wanted. I had a team of engineers and mechanics to myself." He hesitated. "May I kiss you?"

She looked away and remained still as he kissed her lightly on the cheek.

"I'm sorry," he said softly.

She faced him, chin raised defiantly. "Apologies won't solve your problem either."

Chapter 104

Thursday 15 May 1941
Kidlington – Oxfordshire – England

Clementine Churchill didn't stir in her sleep—she had been lightly sedated—as two ambulancemen finished securing her stretcher on the starboard side of the Bristol Bombay's cabin.

The only other passenger, an ashen-faced Brendan Bracken, sat on the port-side bench, level with her head. His right hand rested on her arm.

The ambulancemen left the aircraft as Mike Paterson emerged from the cockpit. He checked the stretcher's fastenings, then shut and secured the passenger door at the rear.

When he returned to the cockpit Roddy Danes was positioning the Bristol Bombay for take-off. Paterson buckled himself into the co-pilot's seat and put on his headphones.

"All set back there?" Danes asked over the intercom.

Paterson grinned. "Bracken's praying without moving his lips. Mrs Churchill's fast asleep."

Danes pushed the throttle and the aircraft began to accelerate.

"No husband or family to see her off?" Paterson asked. "I'm disappointed."

Instead of answering, Danes thrust his chin towards the runway ahead. Paterson followed his gaze. Standing in a black suit to one side, Winston Churchill cut an isolated figure in the grassy vastness of the airfield. As the aircraft accelerated towards him, he removed his homburg hat, balanced it on the tip of his walking stick and held it aloft.

Danes and Paterson saluted him as they roared past and took off. The draft sent the hat spinning away.

Chapter 105

Thursday 15 May 1941
Over Germany

Anna Vogel watched Neil McCrew pull, push and weigh down on a similar stretcher-supporting structure on the Junkers Ju 52. He hadn't said a word since take-off from Berlin. What McCrew couldn't know was that the German and British engineers had coincidentally refitted the two aircraft for Clementine's journey in similar fashion. Both teams had removed the bench running along the starboard side of the cabin to make room for a stretcher-supporting structure. And both teams had incorporated additional side springs and suspension refinements in the structures to absorb bumps and lurches of any kind. In both aircraft the port-side bench had been left so that other passengers could sit in a row facing the patient's right flank.

"German engineering, Neil," Anna said. "Why does the world trust it and not you?"

"Oh, I trust it all right. I'm actually taking mental photographs of it for future reference. Look at the suspension on this thing. Beautiful." He opened a wooden cupboard at head height above the structure and removed two bottles from it. "What are these?"

Anna squinted at the labels. "Disinfectant."

"Perfect. I'll give this thing a thorough clean before we fly her back."

"You mean that's what you'll do to work off your nervousness."

He flopped down beside her. "We need to talk."

She kissed him on the cheek, waiting.

"You really don't need to come back to Berlin. Clementine's plane will be flying back empty to England. You could be on it."

She took his hand, squeezed it. "It's out of the question. I'm here to help you and I will. I'll go to England when you do."

"But I can handle Mrs Churchill by myself," he pleaded. "What if Goebbels changes his mind and has you arrested?"

"Trust me, he won't." She took his face in her hands. "My place is with you, so get used to it. Or else tell me right now to fuck off out of your life and I will."

Up until that moment he would have described Anna as fearless. Now he could see in her eyes that she wasn't. She was dreading his answer, terrified of it. So he found himself deciding he never wanted to see fear of that kind, of any kind, in her eyes again. He put an arm around her and pulled her close. "Before you fuck off out of your previous life and into mine, would you do something for me?"

She blinked as tears welled up. "What?"

"At least wait until we land." He kissed her forehead.

Chapter 106

Thursday 15 May 1941
Over The Netherlands

"Here's the welcoming committee," Paterson said.

Two Messerschmitt Me 109s appeared from behind at the Bristol Bombay's wingtips. The Dutch coast was now visible ahead. Paterson switched radio frequencies.

"Fahrrad two to British aircraft," a crackling voice said in heavily accented English. "Please identify yourselves, gentlemen."

"Fahrrad one to Fahrrad two," Danes answered. "Good morning to you, too. Are your Messerschmitts going to be able to keep up with us?"

"That screeching sound in the background is our brakes. It shouldn't disturb us."

"Ha ha."

Danes and Paterson waved to the Germans on their respective sides of the aircraft. The pilot who was talking was on Danes's side.

"You'll land from the south at Schiphol," the German said calmly. "At the end of the runway, turn left on to the grass and stop as close as possible to the aircraft from Berlin. It will be a Junkers Ju 52. If it hasn't arrived yet, we'll circle above Schiphol until it does. My colleague on your starboard side will land first, then you, then me. We've been told to stay well away from you and the aircraft from Berlin whilst you do your business. Clear so far, Fahrrad One?"

"Clear."

"Once we've finished on the ground, all four aircraft will take off in a north-south direction. The Junkers will take off first, my colleague second, you third and me fourth. We'll escort you back out to where we first picked you up. Still clear, Fahrrad One?"

"Clear."

"Questions, Fahrrad One?"

"Yes, Fahrrad Two. Is there somewhere at the end of the runway to get a cup of coffee?"

Chapter 107

Thursday 15 May 1941
Over The Netherlands

McCrew adjusted his glasses as he felt the Junkers Ju 52 begin its descent. "My father was killed at Gallipoli in 1917," he was explaining to Anna, "and I've spent most of my life blaming Churchill for the senseless decisions that sent him to his death. But I've realised that things aren't as black and white as that. I thought that helping Churchill with his wife's operation might be a way, my way, to give him the benefit of the doubt."

"Doesn't sound like an enthusiastic benefit to me," Anna said.

"It isn't. One thing has changed, though: my opinion of Churchill himself. I now know him a little better. Up close I can confirm he's the calculating politician that all the other calculating politicians accuse him of being. But he's also full of doubt and not many people see that."

"Well you have that at least in common with him."

McCrew grinned. "I wish I had more, believe me. But I've realised you can't understand Churchill if you don't consider his wife. He treats her like shit but her kind of shit is special. It's got teeth. It bites back. And he respects that. He needs it. She keeps his feet on the ground. Take her away and he'll lose any surviving trace of humility."

"I thought it was Brendan Bracken's job to keep him humble. Or Beaverbrook's."

"True but they both have a terrible, debilitating problem." He smiled wistfully. "They're not women."

Chapter 108

Thursday 15 May 1941
Schiphol – The Netherlands

As the Bristol Bombay and two Messerschmitts crossed the Dutch coastline, Paterson eased himself out of the co-pilot's seat and went through to the cabin. Bracken was reading a document. Clementine was still asleep.

"Landing in a few minutes," Paterson said. "Will you be able to help me move the stretcher? If not, Roddy can."

"Yes, of course. I'll need a minute to speak to McCrew, too."

Paterson returned to the cockpit. Glancing right he saw that the Me 109 on his side of the aircraft had disappeared.

"Looks as if the plane from Berlin has already arrived," the German pilot said. "My colleague's going in to land now. Let's circle once and then it's your turn."

As Danes banked to circle above Schiphol he looked down and spotted the Junkers Ju 52 manoeuvring just off the end of the runway. The emptiness of the area around it contrasted with the large number of aircraft and vehicles scattered elsewhere around the airport. He watched the first Me 109 land.

"Fahrrad One, you're cleared to land," the remaining German said.

Just over a minute later Danes landed the Bristol Bombay smoothly.

"Been to Holland before?" Danes asked Paterson.

"First time on the Continent, actually."

Danes taxied to the end of the runway, turned left and stopped beside the Ju 52. The two aircraft were now at a standstill facing in opposite directions so that their passenger doors faced each other. Both kept their engines running.

Paterson opened the Bombay passenger door and unfolded a short flight of steps as McCrew did likewise on the Ju 52. Followed by Anna, McCrew stepped down to the grass and jogged over to the Bombay. Glancing left and right he could see they were protected by a wide circle of back-turned, heavily armed soldiers positioned two by two every fifteen metres.

McCrew and Paterson shook hands.

"Need help?" McCrew asked.

"I think we're okay." Paterson handed him a travel bag. "Hers."

He disappeared briefly back into the cabin. When he reappeared a moment later, he and Bracken were holding Clementine's stretcher. With McCrew ensuring they didn't bump into anything on either side, they manoeuvred out the door and down the steps.

Anna walked beside the stretcher as they crossed the grass to the Junkers Ju 52. Clementine opened her eyes.

"Welcome to the Netherlands, Mrs Churchill," Anna shouted over the din of the engines.

Clementine gave her a sleepy smile and a nod before closing her eyes again.

Danes caught up with them and took over from Bracken to load the stretcher into the German aircraft.

Hands now free, Bracken turned to McCrew and gave him an envelope. "That's a collection of specially crafted insults from Churchill to Goebbels should something goes wrong with the operation. If all goes well don't give it to him, of course. Just destroy it, understood?"

"Okay."

They shook hands. "Good luck and see you on Sunday," Bracken said.

Chapter 109

Thursday 15 May 1941
Bognor Regis – West Sussex – England

The thirty-four crew members of U693 stopped chatting and stood up as Ernst Hedner strode into Sudner House's reception hall and positioned himself in front of them.

"Please sit down, gentlemen." Hedner took his time to peer at their faces before speaking. "Some signs are unmistakable. The first is that I am speaking in English and feel no need to translate my words into German. We have a common spoken language, gentlemen, and nothing useful could be done without it. That said, we haven't changed a single written sign or label on our U-boat either. Everything's in German and will stay that way. We therefore have a common written language, too. Second, you received no instructions on where to sit in this hall today. You simply sat down as a mixed group, Brits and Germans together in no particular order. I wouldn't call us a smoothly operational crew yet—we still have work to do on that area—but I would certainly call what I see in front of me right now a team. We can all be proud of that. We met for the first time exactly eight days ago. Up until that moment we were sworn enemies. Our duty was to shoot at and sink each other at the first opportunity. Then, as the days went by, something happened, something that sends shivers down my spine every time I think of it. Each of you decided with no special encouragement from me to work hard, fucking hard as our British friends put it so poetically." He paused as the room laughed. "From the word go, your enthusiasm to help each other, to learn from each other, to sweat together, to make this crazy idea look like a project worth trying knew no limits. Gentlemen, you have achieved in one week what I thought, optimistically, would only be possible in three." Hedner held up a single sheet of typed paper. "So much so that I have just received orders for our first mission. They're setting us a little test to see how we perform." He smiled as the crew members looked excitedly at each other. "Let's impress them."

Chapter 110

Thursday 15 May 1941
Over Germany

Ten minutes after take-off Anna Vogel saw Clementine Churchill open her eyes again. "It's good to see you again, Mrs Churchill."

"It's good to see you again too, dear."

Anna instantly felt a knot in her stomach but let nothing show. The patient on the stretcher in front of her had a Scottish accent, not an English one. Anna glanced at McCrew, who was frowning.

"What's going on here?" Anna asked the patient.

"You didn't imagine for a second that Churchill would let his wife fly to Berlin, did you?"

Anna glanced at McCrew again. "Frankly we did."

The patient chuckled. "An American brain surgeon is flying from New York to London as we speak. My mission in Berlin is a completely different one."

"What mission?" McCrew asked. "And which American brain surgeon?"

"Brigadier Collins believes Goebbels won't be able to resist the opportunity to visit me, if only to have a chummy photograph taken of us for blackmailing purposes. When that happens I'll be close enough to him to ensure he doesn't survive the experience."

"Assassination?" Anna whispered.

"At the SOE they prefer to call it opportunism, dear. They put a wee pistol in my bag. Who in a Berlin clinic would dream of searching the British Prime Minister's wife?"

Anna shook her head in disbelief. "But how—?" She interrupted herself when she saw the patient stifle a laugh.

"I'm sorry, Anna, I just couldn't resist it." Clementine had switched her accent back to English. "I know you met Mrs Macleod at Chequers and it just so happens I can do a convincing Scottish accent. You should have seen your face."

Embarrassed, Anna and McCrew rolled their eyes.

"Allow me to shake your hand, Miss Vogel" Clementine said, "and to thank you for helping us organise all this."

They shook hands.

"So you're really Mrs Churchill?" Anna asked sceptically. "I don't know who to believe now."

"Yes, it's her," McCrew said. "This isn't the first time she's caught me out."

Clementine smiled. "If I could be any other body right now, I would be. Yes, I'm Clementine Churchill and I've got a brain tumour to prove it. You can also check my bag for wee pistols. You won't find any."

Chapter 111

Thursday 15 May 1941
Kidlington – Oxfordshire – England

The staff at Kidlington Airfield's tiny terminal pretended to ignore Brendan Bracken as he waited to be put through to Downing Street. Churchill, he calculated, would be back there by now. He'd considered having the room emptied for the call but had decided this would attract even more attention and speculation. Although Churchill was a familiar figure at the airfield, something about that morning's events had felt strange. They hadn't seen who had boarded the Bristol Bombay but they'd all stood at the terminal's large windows to peer at the Prime Minister's silhouette in the distance, raising his hat as the aircraft took off.

"Churchill speaking."

"Brendan here. It went smoothly. She slept all the way."

"Did you see McCrew?"

"Yes. I gave him the envelope."

"Let's hope it will never be needed. Brendan, I want to thank you for doing that. It might not have felt risky but it was."

"Thank me on Sunday, when it's all over." Bracken paused, holding up his free hand to inspect it. It was still trembling. " Can I ask you something?"

"By all means."

"If I'd been married, would you have asked me to do you that favour?"

Chapter 112

Thursday 15 May 1941
Berlin – Germany

McCrew and Anna turned round to peer out of the Ju 52's windows. The aircraft was taxiing towards an ambulance parked well away from Gatow's terminal. It was still a cloudy morning in Berlin and the ground was wet.

"Doesn't look as if Goebbels has alerted the press," McCrew said.

"There's more than enough room for a photographer in the back of that ambulance."

"He won't send anyone," Clementine said.

They turned to look at her.

"If that monster has any decency left in him, the thought will have crossed his mind that the situation could be reversed. I could be Magda Goebbels, mother of his six children, arriving for an operation in London. Would he want my arrival to be immortalised by a photographer?"

There was silence as the engines stopped.

Anna winced. "Yes he would, Mrs Churchill."

Chapter 113

Friday 16 May 1941
London – England

"I don't care how you solve the problem, but I'm hungry," Rudolf Hess announced.

The two armed men sitting opposite him didn't look away from the countryside racing by outside the window. The train carriage had been emptied for Hess, with two other guards posted at either end of it.

The man to Hess's left, a Scot with a red beard, sighed impatiently. "I offered you a sandwich an hour ago, Mr Führer Substitute, and you turned it down because you think we want to drug you. I took that rather personally, I must say, but not so personally that I threw the sandwich away." He turned to face Hess. "So this is my second and final offer: do you want the sandwich or not? Bear in mind that we've got at least four hours to go."

Hess folded his arms. "I should report you to your superior for such rudeness."

"Consider it done. This is my superior right here beside me. He hasn't said much so far but when he speaks up his rudeness will impress you much more than mine. Sandwich or not?"

Hess rolled his eyes and held out a hand.

From a bag on the floor the Scot produced a sandwich and watched as the German bit deeply into it. "Do our drugs at least taste good?"

"Fine, thank you. Are you going to tell me who I'm meeting at the Tower of London or should I just repeat the question every two minutes till we get there or you go mad?"

The two armed men pretended to pay no attention to Hess as the drug took effect. Two minutes later the German was fast asleep and snoring loudly, his sandwich unfinished on his thigh.

"Powerful stuff," the Scot said. "That should keep him quiet till London."

"We're not going to London," his superior said.

Chapter 114

Friday 16 May 1941
Berlin – Germany

"Mrs Churchill?" Tina Winter stood over Clementine's bed and touched her arm.

Clementine opened her eyes and blinked at the early morning light coming through a window. "Am I where I'm not dreaming I am?"

Tina smiled and sat on the edge of the bed. "You are. Nothing's changed since last night. You're still in a clinic in Berlin—one of the more comfortable ones, I might add, and in one of the quietest neighbourhoods. In fact the only thing that could disturb the peace and quiet is British bombs. You do remember me, don't you?"

"Yes, Nurse, I'm sorry. It's the nerves, I suppose."

"I quite understand. We'll be giving something to sedate you before the operation. But we need to talk first and I need you to be fully alert."

"You speak wonderful English, Nurse, if I may say so."

Tina smiled. "I grew up in Cambridge. It helps. Then I married a German and came here."

"Now there's a potent mix. What can life possibly be like for an Englishwoman in this place?"

"I've got used to it. I'm German now and have spent embarrassing amounts of money on language and accent coaching." She lowered her voice. "What I'll never get used to, though, is the politics. It's horrifying."

Clementine tapped Tina's arm playfully. "So there's still a hint of British rebelliousness left in you, is there?" Her features suddenly froze as she touched her skull in several places; it was bald. "I've just remembered they did this to me last night. What do I look like?"

Tina winked. "I wouldn't leave you alone with my husband, if that's what you mean."

The door opened and Frank Winter walked in. "Good morning, ladies."

"Speak of the devil," Anna continued. "This is my husband, Doctor Frank Winter. And I'm not a nurse, by the way. I'm Doctor Tina Winter."

Winter sat on the opposite edge of the bed. "My apologies for not shaking your hand but I have a good excuse as you can see." He raised his plastered hand.

"Ah, the famous Doctor Winter," Clementine exclaimed, squinting at his sling. "You must be good at what you do because even our American friends speak highly of you. Pleased to meet you. Tell me, is 'doctor' a title they also give to magicians in Herr Hitler's Germany? Or are German surgeons so brilliant that they only need one hand to operate?"

Both Winters smiled.

"That's what we wanted to talk to you about, "Tina said. "We could have kept quiet about it but we prefer to come clean. You see, hand injury or not, my husband hasn't been able to operate for a quite a few years now anyway. His hands are no longer as steady as they should be. His brain, however, is fully functional. So instead of giving up his profession, he trained me to be his hands. We work as a team. He thinks, I act."

Clementine looked suspiciously from one to the other.

"An illegal team, needless to say," Winter added. "If word got out, we'd go to prison—well I would at least—for a very long time. But we've been careful and we've been lucky. We've also had staff who've stood by us and supported us over the years. None of this would have been possible without them."

"My goodness," Clementine murmured.

"Obviously we realise this must sound alarming to a patient we're about to operate on," Tina said. "That's why you're the first patient we've ever told the truth to."

"Should I feel privileged?" Clementine looked down at her hands. "Is Doctor McCrew aware of this? What about my husband?"

"Doctor McCrew is aware of everything," Tina said. "We informed him as soon as he got here. He isn't comfortable with the situation, of course, but he agrees that this is the best we can do given time constraints. Frank and I know each other perfectly. We've done countless operations together. But Doctor McCrew insisted you be given an opportunity to inform your husband if you want to."

"You mean my husband has no idea?"

The Winters shook their heads.

"Well that's a relief," Clementine said. "At last a decision I can make without him interfering."

"What this all boils down to, Mrs Churchill," Tina said, "is that if you don't want us to go through with this, you can stop everything right now."

"Do I have a choice?"

"Yes," Winter said. "To be brutally frank and as McCrew has already told you, this operation is dangerous. Your brain's already under attack from cancer. Now it's going to be under attack from us as well. We believe we can succeed, but the odds that the conversation we're having right now will be your last remain high. If you decide not to go through with the operation, we'll put you back on an aircraft and send you back to England, where you'll be guaranteed a little more time for conversations with your husband and family before things get difficult. It might not sound like much of a choice but it is a choice all the same. We insist on that. And that choice is yours."

Clementine stared at him. "If I were your wife in this bed, Doctor Winter, would you do such a dangerous thing to her? Would you let her be attacked, as you say?"

"I, er—" Winter fell silent.

"Of course he would," Tina said casually. "Wouldn't you, Frank?"

The Winters waited in silence as Clementine closed her eyes and lay still.

"My husband's found a body double for me," she said at last, eyes still closed. "A Scottish woman called Jenny Macleod. In the unlikely event that I survive, she's supposed to replace me at public events during my recovery." She opened her eyes. "I've actually met this woman. We had a chat and found her most pleasant but I started to worry. I began to wonder what my husband would do if I died and he had this mirror image of me around him. Would he fancy her as much as he still fancies me, even though I say so myself?" She winked at them. "What would happen? Probably nothing, I thought at first. Then I realised that apart from our appearance, Mrs Macleod and I have something else in common. She would stand up to that arrogant self-centred man as much as I do and as well as I do. She'd make herself as indispensable to him as I am and you know what? He'd find her irresistible. Well I'm afraid I'm not keen on that idea. So let's give this operation a try, shall we?"

Chapter 115

Friday 16 May 1941
Berlin – Germany

"You're one hell of a cook, Doctor McCrew," Anna said with her mouth full. "Best lunch I've ever eaten in this apartment."

McCrew put his knife and fork down on the kitchen table. "I'd love to agree with you but I can't bring myself to eat anything. Sorry."

"Having conscience issues with those two poking around Mrs C's brain?"

"No, I'm just wondering how I would break bad news to her husband if I had to." He checked his watch. "Ten past one. We've missed the agent."

"You didn't have anything to tell him."

McCrew poured himself some water. "News or no news, I'll speak to the agent at six anyway. Churchill will be going up the walls by then."

The doorbell rang.

"I'll go," Anna said.

She wiped her mouth and hurried through to the hall. Seeing Frank Winter through the peephole, she let him in and led him through to the lounge. McCrew joined them.

"As far as I can tell, it went well," Winter said quietly. "Tina surpassed herself."

"Is Mrs Churchill awake?" McCrew asked.

"Not yet. And we won't push her either. All other vital signs are good though."

"How optimistic are you?" Anna asked.

Winter shrugged. "No more no less than before the operation. Neil knows what I mean."

"Where's Tina now?" McCrew asked.

Winter grinned. "Fast asleep on a spare bed at the clinic. She's exhausted. I'm going home to sleep myself."

"Thanks for dropping by, Frank," McCrew said.

Winter nodded, averting his eyes. "It's the least I could do."

Chapter 116

Friday 16 May 1941
Berlin – Germany

Staring across his office at the Ministry of Public Enlightenment and Propaganda, Joseph Goebbels drummed his desk with one hand as the other fiddled with a cigarette, his third in twenty minutes. He picked up the phone receiver.

"Put me through to Norbert Gerscher at the Abwehr. It's urgent."

"Gerscher," said his childhood friend's voice after a couple of minutes. "Glad you called, Joseph. Roosevelt's just sent Churchill a new list of five names. The first three are zookeepers. What do you think the other two do?"

"Ha ha."

"How's this Hess thing progressing?"

"How's it dying, you mean. Quickly, my friend, as these things always do if you pay lavishly silent attention to them. Norbert, I need a small favour."

"Tell me."

"I'd rather not talk about it on the phone."

Gerscher laughed. "Who else is likely to be listening apart from my own team next door?"

Chapter 117

Friday 16 May 1941
London – England

The clock in Winston Churchill's study at 10 Downing Street chimed eleven-thirty pm. It was an unusually early hour for the Prime Minister to be leaning back and fast asleep in his chair. His right hand loosely held an unfinished glass of whisky on his lap and an unlit cigar dangled from his lips.

Brendan Bracken teased the glass and cigar away from him, placed them on the desk and walked over to the door. Glancing back at the man whose skills, ideas and well-being he had devoted his life to, he wondered how much more his friend could take.

If Clemmie didn't pull through, Bracken was more convinced than ever that Churchill would fall apart. God knows what would happen then.

If she did pull through, Churchill would barely have time to catch his breath, let alone light a cigar, before colossal challenges took centre stage again.

Challenges such as, for instance, overcoming the USA's ominous reluctance to send troops to Europe. As Bracken could observe week after week, Churchill was running out of ways to entertain and cajole visiting American diplomats so that they in turn would cajole fellow officials back home into intervening.

Challenges such as dealing with the consequences, as the USA dragged its feet, of the German navy's devastating attacks on trans-Atlantic supply lines. Like Churchill, Bracken could only shake his head in despair at the harrowing numbers of merchant ships being sunk by Hitler's U-boats.

Challenges such as working out whether Hitler would really be stupid enough to open a second front in the east—one with the Soviet Union in addition to the existing one with the United Kingdom—or whether some brilliantly impenetrable strategy lay behind it. And if so, what did Rudolf Hess know about it?

Challenges such as Churchill's own longer-term prospects. How to fight and win the war in such a way that the British voting population would give Churchill, his ideals and his party a chance to win the peace as well? How were wartime hardships affecting the British population's expectations?

Bracken peered at the sleeping figure behind the desk. How much more pressure could the attention, energy, will and unhealthy lifestyle of a sixty-six-year-old man withstand?

He turned off the light and closed the door as quietly as he could as he left.

Chapter 118

Saturday 17 May 1941

Rudolf Hess woke up but kept still with his eyes closed, running a mental check on his situation.

First, apart from a slight headache, he wasn't in any pain.

Second, this couldn't be the Tower of London because the surface supporting his back was soft and sagging, perhaps a hammock. He could also feel thin vertical surfaces of netting or canvas on either side of his body, holding it in place. Yes, definitely a hammock.

Third, he could hear engines of some kind thudding in the background.

Fourth, the air reeked of a combination of fuel or lubricant of some kind, stale air, humidity and body fluids.

Fifth, he wasn't alone. Ten, fifteen, maybe twenty voices, none of them female, were chatting around him.

And sixth, they were speaking German.

He opened his eyes and struggled to sit up. The space around him was cramped, with a metal ceiling and metal walls covered in piping and gauges. Silence fell as eighteen male faces, all in their early twenties, looked up or across at Hess from various interrupted conversations, card games or partly eaten plates of food.

"Should I say good morning, good afternoon or good evening?" Hess asked in German, trying to sound unimpressed. "Or is there some other kind of greeting customary on a U-boat?"

A blond crew member stood up and handed him a metal cup of water. Only then did Hess realise how thirsty and hungry he was.

Chapter 119

Saturday 17 May 1941
Berlin – Germany

Jules Verne was Nurse Jasmin Clemens's favourite author but she was unable to concentrate on chapter seventeen of *Twenty-thousand leagues under the sea*. Her attention kept drifting back to the woman sleeping on the clinic bed beside her chair. She dreaded having to respond in English to the British Prime Minister's wife if she woke up. Her grammar was shaky and her vocabulary even more so and the last thing she wanted—God forbid—was for their poor quality to shape Mrs Churchill's first impression of her.

For her own safety and to prevent any sudden movement, Clementine was strapped on her back to the bed. Her bandaged head was held firmly in place by a metal and rubber structure.

Clementine's mouth opened slightly. Eyes closed, she whispered something. Jasmin stood up and leaned in to listen. Clementine whispered again. Assuming she was saying something, Jasmin couldn't make it out. Or was Jasmin simply unable to understand?

The whispering stopped. Jasmin waited a couple of minutes, debating whether to call the Winters or not. She decided not to. Instead she noted the time, four-fifteen, and the words 'jumbled whispering' on a chart at the foot of the bed before resuming her reading.

Chapter 120

Saturday 17 May 1941

"Eins W.O.[41], our guest is awake," said a crew member behind Ernst Hedner.

Hedner looked round from the periscope. All activity in the submarine's control room ceased. "Herr Hess. Welcome aboard. I'm Erster Wachoffizier Hedner."

Hess raised his chin a couple of millimetres. "I have a title, Erster Wachoffizier. I expect you to use it."

"You had a title, Herr Hess. The Führer stripped it from you three days ago. What I'm welcoming you to are the lower rungs of German existence, naval existence in our case, although I suspect you'll discover even lower rungs as soon as we return you to the Fatherland. Until then, you'll be Herr Hess as far as the forty-eight men on this boat are concerned. Would you like me to show you around? Ever been on a type VII U-boat, Herr Hess?"

"No I haven't and I have no intention of staying anyway. Where are we, Hedner? And how did I get here?"

Hedner nodded in the direction Hess had just come from. "Coffee won't change your questions or my answers. So let's have some through there, shall we?"

---

[41] Erster Wachoffizier = Eins W.O. (pronounced "Eye-ns Veh Oh"; three syllables) = First Officer

Hedner led Hess to a tiny area reserved for officers. They settled on either side of a fold-away table, where a crew member placed two cups of ersatz coffee and biscuits.

"Would you like something more substantial to eat, Herr Hess?" the crew member asked.

"Yes please, as long as it's not meat."

"There's some omelette left from our last meal. Will that do?"

"Perfect."

The crew member left.

Hedner folded his arms. "In answer to your first question, we're currently a few metres beneath the surface of the Atlantic Ocean. The reason we've dived is that we've been warned there are British destroyers in the area. We don't want to engage with them."

"Isn't that your job?"

"Our job, yes, but not our orders in this case. Our target is an American merchant convoy farther north. Several boats are heading there as we speak."

Hess sipped his coffee. "Don't you think you should take me back to Germany first?"

"There's no reason to rush."

Hess scoffed. "I doubt anyone in Germany would share that opinion, Erster Wachoffizier."

Hedner grinned. "In answer to your second question—how did you get here—what's the last thing you remember?"

"I was being taken by train from Scotland to London. The Tower of London, they told me. They gave me a sandwich at one point and I can't remember anything else. They've been drugging me anyway since I arrived. They must have doubled the dose."

"Tripled, most likely. We found you floating in a dinghy west of Cornwall. You were sleeping like a princess. The British clearly left you where a German ship might find you, but it was still a long shot. Frankly it doesn't look as if they cared what happened to you. You're lucky. The sea's been remarkably calm these last few days."

"What's the date?"

"May 17th."

Hess scratched his head as he calculated. "I took the train on the sixteenth. So I've been sleeping for 24 hours or so. The bastards."

"We'd have woken you sooner, but we couldn't find a crew member drunk enough, homosexual enough or National Socialist enough to kiss you. Given the predicament we found you in, may I assume that what you were trying to do in the United Kingdom failed?"

Hess folded his arms. "Respectfully it's none of your business."

"Respectfully I disagree. You are or were third in line to replace the Führer. So your mission was the business of every single man and woman in Germany. What you did is public knowledge anyway."

"Is it?"

"The government's describing it as a personal initiative taken by a lunatic. You, that is. So most Germans are now wondering what kind of leadership team would maintain a lunatic in its ranks for so long."

"Still it's none of your business."

"In which case I wish you a not too unpleasant trip with us. Please accept my advance apologies for the permanent humidity and any discomfort caused by withering boredom interrupted by depth charge attacks. The bad news is that your chances of survival in a U-boat are 25%. The good news is that those chances are higher than they were on that dinghy."

"Haven't you received orders to turn back and hand me over?"

Hedner munched a biscuit. "Herr Hess, we have a mission to carry out and you're going to participate in it whether you like it or not. Your spot of tourism in Great Britain didn't interrupt the war."

"Is that what Berlin told you to do? Is this their way of punishing me?"

"No, their way of punishing you will probably be a firing squad."

Hess froze as he realised something. "You haven't told them you've found me, have you."

Hedner smiled. "Oh, I intend to. But I love a good story and I'm looking forward to hearing one from a member of the Führer's immediate entourage. Irresistible."

Hess shook his head. "You've got balls, Hedner, I'll grant you that. But when your superiors find out you withheld information about my presence on this U-boat, I'm confident there will be consequences."

"That's my problem, not yours. The Third Reich's priority, and therefore my priority, is to cripple Churchill and his people by sinking the merchant ships that feed them, not to coddle a man whose career and life are over anyway. Whether you die in two days or two weeks makes no difference. My original mission orders stand, therefore. But that shouldn't be an obstacle to us getting to know each other."

Hess glared at him. "How did a man like you ever become a U-boat captain?"

"First Officer, actually. Respectfully, it's none of your business."

"All right, all right," Hess said, raising his hands in surrender. "I'll tell you what happened."

"Good. Shall I go first? I'm in charge of this boat because our captain committed suicide. The Kriegsmarine hasn't yet decided whether to promote me or appoint a new captain."

"Why did he do that?"

"I presented him with all the available options. There weren't many. I didn't think he'd have the guts to kill himself, though. Courage wasn't his forte." He paused. "The Brits haven't given you many options either, have they. They left you floating exactly where they knew we'd find you. Which raises questions about how they got that information, of course."

"Not necessarily. They could have dropped me off and sent an open message with my bearings to all ships in the area."

"They didn't."

"What about a direct message from the Royal Navy to the Kriegsmarine? It's not unheard of."

"If they'd done that, we'd have received a direct order from the Kriegsmarine to pick up a man overboard. We didn't. My course was radioed to me *after* we left our French harbour. Standard practice. No mention of drifting deputy Führers along the way."

"And your course was encrypted, I imagine."

"If my years of experience in the Kriegsmarine have taught me anything, it's that the Atlantic is too big for coincidences. The Brits knew exactly where we were going."

Hess shrugged. "So you're suggesting they've broken our coding system."

"I'm suggesting that if the Brits haven't broken our coding system, Germany might as well surrender immediately. Nobody can beat an enemy that lucky. Herr Hess, let's assume for argument's sake that the British read transcripts of our messages every day over tea and biscuits. Right now they'll be expecting a message from me to my bosses confirming that we found the ex-deputy Führer floating in a dinghy. But they won't find that message because I haven't sent it. So they'll send out a couple of aircraft to make doubly sure you aren't still floating around out there and when they don't find you, they'll conclude that a German ship has almost certainly picked you up and that the ship in question has a good reason not to mention you in a message. What could that good reason be? If I were a Brit, I'd assume one of three possible scenarios. Scenario one: we Germans have an alternative message transmission system that they haven't detected yet and that I made use of to talk about you. Scenario two: we Germans have found a way to include additional coded messages *within* our coded messages. In other words, we can encrypt the same text twice, with different hidden messages at each level of encryption."

Hess frowned. "Is that feasible?"

"If something's imaginable in encryption, it's feasible. Intelligence services who assume otherwise are doomed. I trained for a few months at B-Dienst, our naval intelligence service, and we routinely discussed ideas like that. The Brits do likewise, I'm sure."

"What's the third scenario?"

Hedner smiled. "That there's a deranged captain or first officer out there who, for his own personal reasons, is holding back information on the recovery at sea of the deputy Führer. A deranged authority acting on his own initiative, therefore, and without telling his boss. Sound familiar?"

Resentment crept into Hess's voice. "You've had your fun, Hedner. As much as I'd enjoy shitting myself during British depth charge attacks, I think you should turn this boat around and hand me over to the authorities."

"Sorry to disappoint you, Herr Hess. We are both opportunists. My opportunity is to hear directly from you why you flew to the United Kingdom on your own initiative and why the Führer and his entourage can't think of a more believable explanation for your behaviour than 'Hess is a lunatic'. At the very least, your initiative suggests serious disagreements between the men running the Third Reich about what this war is all about and what the hell to do next. Now if those disagreements were just words yelled across conference rooms in Berlin or the Bavarian Alps, little guys like me wouldn't give a shit about them. But that's not the case. Those disagreements stop U-boats like this one from being built in sufficient numbers to make a difference. The British could be starving and surrendering as we speak if only the Hitlers, Goerings and Raeders[42] of this world could agree on priorities. The days, weeks and months those leaders spend disagreeing with each other cause three out of four men like the ones on this boat to die. Three out of four. You're currently one of the four, by the way. So I'm listening, Herr Hess. Tell me why you flew to the UK. Give me one good reason to believe any of the bullshit I hear from my bosses all the way up to the Führer. More to the point, give me one good reason to tell my men to fight on."

A bald crew member with fresh oil marks on his face appeared briefly. "It's repaired, Eins W.O."

"Thank you."

Another crew member reappeared with an omelette, which he placed with a fork in front of Hess.

"Thank you," Hess said as the crew member withdrew.

"Guten Appetit, Herr Hess," Hedner said as he got up. "Please excuse me for a minute. Nature calls."

When Hedner returned, Hess was looking up at a hanging photograph of Rear Admiral Karl Dönitz, Supreme Commander of Germany's U-boats.

---

[42] Erich Raeder was Supreme Commander of the Kriegsmarine (German navy)

"You have a problem with authority, don't you," Hess said.

"If I do, then Dönitz is the exception. You won't find a German submariner anywhere who doesn't respect him. The man without the balls to stand up to the Führer is Dönitz's boss."

"Raeder," Hess muttered.

"Yes."

Hess finished his omelette and pushed the plate to one side. "I've just realised something, Erster Wachoffizier. The true reason you haven't reported my presence on this boat has nothing to do with the Brits, does it. Your problem is us Germans. You're wondering what order the Führer might give regarding this boat if he found out I was on it."

Hedner clapped softly in mock admiration. "You clearly place as much trust in authority as I do. Herr Hess, you know Adolf Hitler better than any man alive. You were in prison together, for God's sake. Would he hesitate to order us sunk?"

Hess gave this some thought. "No, he wouldn't."

Reaching into a wooden locker above his head, Hedner produced a bottle of schnapps and two small glasses. He filled them to the brim.

"To the things we share," Hedner said, raising his glass. "Opportunism and mistrust of authority."

"Indeed."

Neither of them emptied their glass in one. Both sipped.

Hess took a deep breath. "I flew to the United Kingdom because I believed I could convince the Brits to negotiate peace terms with us. In a nutshell, if they let us keep continental Europe, we would let them keep their island and empire. Not my idea, by the way. It's the Führer's."

"Then why didn't Hitler fly to the United Kingdom and offer those terms himself?"

"It took him too long to give up but he no longer believes in a negotiated peace with Churchill. Churchill never wanted it anyway. The situation required a little creativity."

"What made you think that you, personally, could break the deadlock?"

"A combination of surprise and my status as number three in the Third Reich. I was wrong."

"Did you talk to Churchill?"

"No, and I didn't want to. My money was on the Duke of Hamilton, who could then give me access to the King. I met Hamilton but got no further. I was handed over to interrogators and treated as an ordinary prisoner of war."

Hedner emptied his glass. "What didn't you tell them, Herr Hess?" His tone was suddenly aggressive.

"What do you mean?"

"A good negotiator never reveals all. He always holds something back. What's your trump card?"

They stared at each other.

"We're about to invade the Soviet Union," Hess began. "Operation called Barbarossa. Two to three million men. Despite our obvious troop movements on the Soviet border, Hitler's denying it and I've been denying it so far, too. But I hinted to the Brits that something isn't quite what it seems. I suggested that millions of lives might be saved if we signed a peace treaty now. And millions of potential victims being saved is exactly what I meant. That's a colossal number. But what does it refer to? British victims? No. Even after eight months of relentless bombing, the Luftwaffe hasn't killed more than forty- or fifty-thousand civilians in British cities. Soviet victims, then? Possibly, but the number still sounds too big. So it must refer to something covering the entire continent, including the Soviet Union and including huge numbers of civilians. This is what I wanted the British to think and worry about. My plan was to hold back full details until I could have a private chat with the King or even with Churchill and when they put me on a train to London, I thought I'd succeeded. But it wasn't to be. I ended up enjoying your underwater hospitality instead."

"What do you mean by full details?"

"Respectfully, Erster Wachoffizier, they're a private matter between the King or Churchill and me." Hess stood up. "I think it's time for you and me to stop this little charade, don't you? You have all the information you need for your report."

"I'll be the judge of what I report to my bosses."

Hess placed his hands flat on the table, his face inching closer to Hedner's. "No, Hedner, I mean the report you'll submit to British intelligence, who in turn report to Churchill. German U-boat captains are remarkably brave men, but none would have the guts to ask the questions you asked me. Are you really a U-boat captain? Are you really German? Your little show down here has been most enjoyable but there are loopholes in your script. I noticed them immediately.

"Loophole one: you said yourself that this U-boat's mission to attack an American convoy has just begun. Where are your reserves of fresh food to feed your men? At the start of a U-boat mission and due to a lack of storage space, fresh food typically hangs from every available hook, bolt or pipe. No sign of fresh food hanging around here. In fact your boat looks as if it's returning from a mission, not heading out on one.

"Loophole two: a type VII U-boat is built with two kinds of engine on board—a diesel one for surface travel and an electric one for underwater mobility. When we sat down at this table, you told me we were travelling a few metres under the surface to avoid a British ship. But correct me if I'm wrong, the engine sound I've been hearing since I opened my eyes in that hammock through there is a diesel one. We're not underwater, Erster Wachoffizier, we're on the surface.

"Loophole three: you went to the toilet during our conversation and headed towards the rear of the boat to do so. True, U-boat Type VIIs have two toilets but only one is used, the one towards the front of the ship from where we're sitting. The other toilet, the one closest to the galley, is used to stock food.

"Loophole four: given that we're travelling on the surface and judging by the lack of swell, I'd say we haven't moved a centimetre in any direction since the start of our conversation. In fact this submarine's so still I'll bet it's moored in a port somewhere, certainly not in the middle of the Atlantic. The question is, which port? Or should I say, which *British* port? Southampton? Plymouth? Do you mind if I climb up the conning tower and take a look?"

Hedner grinned and poured more schnapps. He raised his glass. "To loopholes."

Hess ignored his glass. "Who are you, Hedner?"

"Come with me."

Hedner led Hess through to the control room, climbed up the conning tower and opened the hatch. The air outside was warm but reeked of diesel fumes. The two men stood on the bridge and looked up at the canopy camouflaging the submarine.

"You're in Bognor Regis on the south coast of England," Hedner said. "The Royal Navy captured this boat two weeks ago. Yes, I really am its first officer and yes, our captain really did commit suicide just before we surrendered. The British gave me and my crew a choice between a prisoner-of-war camp and a crazy joint mission with them to help stranded sailors and passengers of all nations."

"Seriously?" Hess asked.

Hedner nodded. "Half the crew members on the boat are German, the other half British. We've been training, eating, shitting, puking, cleaning, and working together twenty-four hours a day for a week now. Fooling you was our first in-the-flesh test."

Hess smiled. "Well you certainly look the part. And if I hadn't visited a few U-boats in my career, I'd have believed we were underwater at sea. Are you going to write a report on our conversation?"

"The Brits hope I will but it will be my decision. A lot depends on whether I think you're a traitor or a genuine peace maker. A lot also depends on what those so-called full details are on those so-called millions of victims. But put it this way: if you think those full details can put an end to this war any sooner, I'm prepared to tell the Brits you deserve a few minutes of Churchill's time. I'm pretty sure they'll listen to me."

"I'd appreciate it."

"Consider it done." Hedner gestured towards the end of the quay. "You'll find a car and three or four well-armed soldiers waiting for you through that yellow door over there. They'll take you to the Tower of London, as promised. This was only a detour."

They shook hands.

"One more thing, Hedner," Hess said. "Do you see me as a traitor?"

"I see us both as traitors, Herr Hess. By disobeying orders and taking personal initiatives, we've both betrayed the Third Reich in our respective ways. But you've taken your betrayal one stage further. As my youngest sister would say, you're 'very not nice'. Your betrayal began when you co-wrote Mein Kampf and helped create all that anti-Semite claptrap. It continued as you gave all those hate-filled speeches in halls full of idiots who ended up voting for you. It continued when you personally got as much Jewish, gypsy, homosexual, handicapped and communist blood on your hands as all the other National Socialist leaders. Don't get me wrong—I've got blood on my hands, too. But when I sink a merchant ship with one of my torpedoes, I do what I can to help the survivors. Oh, it's not much. I throw blankets and food to them in their lifeboats, that sort of thing. But you and your sort wouldn't do that, would you. You wouldn't do it because helping survivors would mean having to check first that there are no Jews or undesirable minorities among them. It wouldn't do to save the wrong kind of innocent victim by mistake now, would it, Herr Hess. As I see it, there are two facts that no high-risk flight to Scotland or face-to-face meeting between you and Churchill can change: the first is that you've betrayed the human race and the second is that because of traitors to the human race like you, I'll never see my sister again. I loved her dearly. She lit up any room she walked into. But she had Down's Syndrome and was murdered by you and your people during a hospital visit last November. A victim of the Third Reich's so-called T4 euthanasia programme. Are you going to share the *full details* of that little venture with Churchill as well? Very not nice."

Chapter 121

Saturday 17 May 1941
Berlin – Germany

Frank and Tina Winter stood on either side of Clementine Churchill's bed. She was still asleep. Tina looked questioningly at her husband, who nodded.

"Mrs Churchill?" Tina said quietly.

She gently squeezed Clementine's right arm.

"Mrs Churchill?" A little louder.

Winter sat beside her.

"Mrs Churchill?"

Clementine stirred. A few seconds later she opened her eyes.

Tina smiled at her. "Mrs Churchill?"

Clementine's eyes struggled to focus on her.

"How are you feeling?" Tina asked.

"Guten Tag," Clementine said.

"Guten Morgen actually. It's ten o'clock. But Guten Tag will do."

Clementine smiled weakly. "Thank you. I practised saying it for hours. When's the operation due?"

"The operation's over," Winter said.

Clementine tried to turn her head to look at him but the metal and rubber structure holding her head prevented any movement. "Ouch. Yes, I can confirm that."

"The pain you feel is where we removed part of your skull to operate. Don't worry, we put it back again afterwards. Is the pain bearable?"

"I wouldn't swap it for childbirth if that's what you mean."

Winter squeezed her hand. "We can give you something to make you more comfortable. In the meantime, if someone asks you a tough question that you need to think about, please scratch something other than your head."

"I have unscratched body parts to spare, don't worry. Does all this banter mean I'll be flying back tomorrow as planned?"

"That depends on the tests we put you through this afternoon," Tina said. "The final decision will be Frank's and no one else's. Not even Goebbels's, whatever he says."

Clementine closed her eyes. "Whatever happens, I want to thank you both for what you've done. The fact that I can still string a sentence together shows you must have done something right. I have a big favour to ask of you."

"Of course," Winter said.

"My husband desperately wanted to accompany me on the first leg of my trip here. Regardless of the risk to his safety, he wanted to say goodbye to me at Schiphol in Holland rather in England. Given half a chance, I'm sure he'd have come all the way here, too. That's the way he is: a little reckless at times. Anyway I ordered him to stay in England and he obeyed me. For my trip back, however, I know he'll insist on meeting me at Schiphol and no one will dare oppose him. As I can't do anything about it I thought it would be an opportunity to introduce you both to him so he can thank you personally. My operation was as much for his benefit as for mine. Would you consider doing that? It would mean a lot to me."

The Winters glanced at each other.

"We'd be glad to," Tina said.

"Thank you."

Tina took Clementine's hand in hers. "But there's something you said that I disagree with. Your husband wasn't reckless to want to accompany you. He was just showing you that he loves you."

"I'm starting to believe I deserve it. Now tell me, my dear, how does *your* husband show *you* that he loves you?"

Chapter 122

Saturday 17 May 1941
Berlin – Germany

Neil McCrew and Anna Vogel shared an umbrella as they walked along Fasanenstrasse in the rain.

"One hundred and fifty," McCrew said quietly. "Let's cross and head back."

"One hundred and fifty what?"

"Seconds. Meaning that half the five minutes are up and it's time to turn back."

They crossed the street.

"I'd like a kiss in the rain, please," Anna said as they reached the opposite pavement.

"Not likely. You've probably scared the agent off just by being with me in the street, let alone kissing me."

Anna giggled. She was about to grab his face to kiss him when a black Volkswagen Kdf stopped beside them. The driver leaned over and wound down the passenger window.

"Need shelter from the rain?" the agent asked in German.

They got in, Anna in the back.

"What are you playing at?" the agent yelled at McCrew as soon as the car accelerated. "I had to drive past three times to be sure that was Anna with you. I couldn't see her face for the umbrella."

"Apologies," McCrew muttered.

They turned into Kurfürstendamm.

"I've tried to keep these meetings as easy for you as possible. I make the rules and I alone can change them, not you."

"Blame me," Anna said. "I've got this thing about being kissed in the rain. Sorry."

"The patient will be flown to Schiphol tomorrow as planned," McCrew said.

"How many passengers?"

"Three: the patient, Anna and myself."

They took a right turn.

"So it's a success," the agent said, checking his rear-view mirror again.

"The patient's conscious but they're still running tests. So there's still a chance we'll need to postpone. If so you'll see the pot in the window at six this evening. Otherwise this is our last meeting."

The agent stopped the car. "I'll drop you here. Fasanenstrasse's the next on the right. Good luck to you."

He shook hands with McCrew.

"And to you," McCrew said. "Thanks for your help."

Anna leaned forward between them. "I've got a thing about being kissed in cars too, especially on the left cheek."

The agent laughed and kissed her before checking the mirror again.

Anna remained in position. Her tone suddenly changed from playful to serious. "The car following you has been in front of you the whole time. See it? Keep smiling and turn your head sideways when you speak. The passenger's looking at you through binoculars and might be able to lip-read."

The agent forced a smile and glanced through the windshield. A car had pulled in forty metres ahead.

"They're using a three-car technique," Anna said as she grinned and kissed the agent on the cheek. "They all stay ahead of you as much as possible. At every junction the car you're closest to makes an educated guess as to which way you're going to turn." She turned to kiss McCrew. "If he gets it wrong, the second-closest car takes over and so on. You don't notice any of this, of course, because you're too busy watching the cars behind you. You're a bit old school, I'm afraid."

"How do you know all this?" the agent asked.

"Shut up and listen. Your Berlin days over. Now go to wherever you send your messages from, tell London we need that aircraft tomorrow and then get out of Germany. You've been left alone up till now because Goebbels needs you to help us. Tomorrow that all ends and you'll be dispensable. Good luck. Let's go, Neil."

Chapter 123

Saturday 17 May 1941
Berlin – Germany

Clementine Churchill was drifting off to sleep when she heard a soft knock on the bedroom door.

"Herein?[43]" she ventured.

The door opened and Joseph Goebbels walked in carrying a bunch of flowers. Someone closed the door behind him.

"Good afternoon, Mrs Churchill," he said quietly in English. "I'm Doctor Joseph Goebbels. I took the liberty of coming to see for myself how you are."

He held the flowers up so she could see them.

"Thank you, Doctor Goebbels. They're lovely. Could I ask you to put them on the table over there, please? The nurse will take care of them."

Goebbels did as asked and moved towards a chair on Clementine's left. "May I?"

"Of course."

He hesitated, then took the chair round the bed to sit on her right.

"Forgive me, Doctor, but I can't move my head and it's a bit of a strain to see you. Could I ask you to stay standing?"

"Of course." He stood up again.

"Thank you. Frankly, I'm surprised you haven't turned up with a photographer."

---

[43] "Come in."

"Why would I do that?"

"The existence of a photograph of you and me in this clinic in Berlin could put a lot of useful pressure on my husband. Useful to you, of course."

Goebbels stiffened. "I disagree, Mrs Churchill. For one thing, I wouldn't dream of it. For another, such a photograph would do more damage to me than to your husband. Assuming history remembers me at all, why would I want to go down as the man who tried to blackmail the British prime minister using his wife's medical condition? No, the only photograph I'd tolerate of our meeting here would be one proving that no cameras were present. Alas, such a photograph is by definition impossible."

"Then why insist on flying me here for the operation?"

"Three reasons. The first is that I wanted him to feel in his bones how important it is that he keep Rudolf Hess in the United Kingdom. The second is that in order for your husband to feel that I had to make him *worry* about being blackmailed with photos of you and me. In reality, of course, your stay here will leave no trace. I will have no means of proving your operation took place in Germany and no means, therefore, of blackmailing your husband into keeping Hess. But I'm confident he'll make the right decision. He doesn't know what other aces I have up my sleeve."

"Ever the manipulator, I see."

"Creating illusions is what I do for a living, Mrs Churchill. "So do all politicians, including your eloquent husband."

"And the third reason?"

"I'm interested in power and I wanted to meet the most powerful individual in your country. As the Prime Minister's wife, that individual is you."

"Well I hope you're impressed. Tell me, what's the problem with Rudolf Hess?"

"A man in his position knows many things, some of them highly sensitive. My assumption is that sooner or later he'll be tempted to use them to protect himself. When that happens I'd rather he shared them with your husband than with the German population. It's quite ironic, really."

"And what do you think my husband would do with that information?"

Goebbels folded his arms. "Please forgive me if I don't answer that question."

"But you have an answer?"

"Yes, I do. In fact it's a certainty."

Clementine smiled. "You do realise my husband might get a little piqued that you see the German population as a bigger threat to your career than him."

Goebbels chuckled as he shook his head. "Your lucidity must give your husband nightmares."

"Let's focus on *your* lucidity for a moment, shall we, Doctor? Where's this war going?"

Goebbels gave this some thought. "It's not going anywhere comfortable. Which is why, I suppose, we're all grabbing any opportunity for comfort we can find. Has your stay with us been comfortable, Mrs Churchill?"

"It has, thank you. But tell me, Doctor, how many opportunities for comfort are still available to the Jews of this country?"

Goebbels held her gaze. "None. Do you really wish to discuss that topic?"

"One detail: you have six children yourself. How can you inflict so much pain on Jewish children?"

"British bombs inflict pain and death on children in our cities, Mrs Churchill. They make no difference between Aryan children and Jewish ones."

"That's not an answer to the question."

"Well it's my answer. Whatever the circumstances, reasons or responsibilities, the United Kingdom will also go down in history as a country prepared to bomb children. Any other questions?"

Clementine looked away.

"If not," Goebbels said lightly, "then I'll leave you to rest. It will of course be an honour for me to accompany you to Schiphol tomorrow. My presence should ensure that everything goes even more smoothly."

Clementine's eyes widened.

He shook her hand. "Goodbye, Mrs Churchill. See you on the plane tomorrow."

Goebbels closed Clementine's door behind him and entered the room next door without knocking. A camera had been set up on a tripod against the left-hand wall, its lens aligned with a hole giving into Clementine's room. The man peering into the lens looked up as Goebbels entered.

Standing next to him, Norbert Gerscher grinned at the Reichsminister. "This is Erich Schönmann, a photographer I once told you about. He keeps himself out of trouble by always letting me be the highest bidder for his most sensitive work."

"Did you take the photographs I asked for, Herr Schönmann?" Goebbels didn't bother to hide his contempt.

"Yes, Herr Reichsminister."

Chapter 124

Saturday 17 May 1941
Chartwell – Kent – England

The government car roared along the narrow country lanes of Kent towards Chartwell, Churchill's mothballed country home. Sitting terrified in the back, Brendan Bracken had reasoned this was the only place Churchill could be. He had spent most of the morning and all the afternoon searching high and low for the Prime Minister. No one had seen him leave Downing Street or arrive at Chequers or Ditchley. Bracken had also called several clubs and restaurants as well as staff, colleagues and members of his so-called secret circle—in vain.

He breathed a sigh of relief when he saw Churchill's car parked under a tree outside the estate. Reg Parker, his driver, was leaning against it, reading a newspaper. Bracken's car went straight to the gate.

"Good morning, Mr Bracken," said one of the two guards on duty.

"Grounds or house?"

"Grounds probably, sir. He said he had a gate to paint somewhere."

"A gate? Oh, for God's sake."

The guards let Bracken's car through. Clutching a large envelope, he waited till the car came to a halt outside the house's main entrance, got out and dashed round the building towards the annexes, gardens and lakes. Unsure which of these to explore first—a gate? What gate?—he glanced in all directions and was about to yell the Prime Minister's name when he spotted him walking up the grassy slope from the two lakes. Wearing one of his oversized single-piece siren suits, Churchill was carrying two large cans of paint, both empty with a thick brush sticking out of each. Walter Thompson, his bodyguard, was a few feet behind him, gingerly carrying two further cans and trying to avoid getting stained.

"Ah, Brendan," Churchill shouted. "Just in time for refreshments. Do you mind doing the honours on the terrace? Everything's prepared. No staff, I'm afraid."

Bracken stood where he was, blocking Churchill's way. "What are you doing, Winston? I've been worried sick."

"Painting a gate down there. Nothing quite like it to take one's mind off things."

Bracken squinted at Churchill's face. "Looks like the gate's been painting you, too."

Churchill put one of his cans down and tried to wipe a drop of red paint off his right cheek. It promptly became a smear, which stretched back towards his ear. "Do I now look like the clown your tone of voice suggests I am?"

Bracken didn't bother to hide his anger. "Whilst you were unreachable, Hitler called at 2.30 pm to surrender unconditionally. He said Germany can't possibly defeat a country whose Prime Minister has enough time to paint gates."

Churchill usually responded with a grin or a groan to Bracken's wit. This time he just stood there sheepishly. "Go on, Brendan, I'm ready. How is she?"

"Well enough to hold a conversation."

The tip of Churchill's chin began to tremble. Before his inevitable tears appeared, he dropped the other can. As it clattered to the ground and to Bracken's astonishment, Churchill stepped forward and hugged him. Thompson looked on, no less astonished.

"When is she coming back?" Churchill asked, not letting go.

"Assuming she remains stable, tomorrow. It's Winter's decision."

They let go of each other. Churchill produced a handkerchief from an inside pocket and dabbed his tears. "I want to greet her in Schiphol. A little surprise."

"That decision's mine, Winston, and it's no. I refuse to let Britain's Prime Minister gallivant around behind enemy lines. They'll arrest you in an instant. Now let's sit down. There's something else we need to discuss."

They walked up to Chartwell's terrace and sat down.

Bracken served a watered-down whisky to both of them before removing three sheets of typed-up paper from his large envelope and handing them to Churchill. "Our U-boat captain's had a chat with Hess. That's his report."

Churchill waved it away. "Give me the gist, please. I'm too tired to read anything."

"Hess has confirmed they're about to invade the Soviet Union. They're calling it Operation Barbarossa. It'll start a month from now."

Churchill sighed. "Well, Stalin can't pretend we didn't warn him. It'll be a bloodbath."

"He insisted again that millions of lives can still be saved if we sign a peace agreement now."

"No, I can't see Hitler pulling out this late in his little game. We'd hear his generals sniggering from here."

"But why's Hess talking about millions of potential victims again? It's unthinkable."

Churchill shook his head. "If he's right, that number must include civilians on a massive scale as well. Didn't Hedner challenge him on that?"

Bracken turned over one of the sheets of the report. "He did but Hess will only provide full details to the King or you. He concludes by recommending that you meet him."

Churchill sipped his whisky as Bracken returned the sheets to the envelope.

"I'd like you to have two cases of wine sent to Hedner and his men to thank them," Churchill said. "They've been most helpful. It looks as if I'll have to invite Hess for afternoon tea."

Bracken frowned. "I thought that was only supposed to happen if Clemmie's surgery failed."

"Yes and I was going to bring him right here. Well I'll do it anyway. With two to three million Germans about to go on the rampage at the other end of Europe, I can't afford to miss out on information that might be useful."

"Meeting you will be a huge personal victory for Hess."

"If he ever brags about it, I'll deny it happened. I'm only going to listen to him. He can still shove his peace offer up his arse."

"Good luck with that, Winston."

Churchill scoffed. "What do you mean, good luck? You'll be here with me to help do the shoving. You didn't have anything else planned tomorrow, did you?"

Chapter 125

Sunday 18 May 1941
Berlin – Germany

Clouds hung over Berlin's Gatow airport as Joseph Goebbels's car sped across the tarmac towards the Junkers Ju 52. As it approached, an ambulance accelerated away.

"Guten Morgen," he announced cheerfully as he climbed into the cabin.

Conversations stopped as four people began to rise from the bench on the left. Clementine's stretcher had already been secured to its supporting structure on the right. Her head was held steady by a metal and rubber device similar to the one back in her clinic room and which was attached to the stretcher. Two drip bottles dangled from vertical metal rods on either side of her, one feeding into each arm.

Goebbels switched to English. "Please stay seated." He approached Clementine and smiled down at her, fingertips touching her right arm. "Good morning, Mrs Churchill. How are you today?"

"As well as can be. I've come to realise how much I shake my head around when I speak and feel a little constrained."

Anna Vogel and Neil McCrew, who was holding a writing pad and a pen, slid away from each other so that Goebbels could sit between them. Frank and Tina Winter sat at the ends, Tina beside Anna towards the door and Winter beside McCrew towards the front.

"May I ask you something, Doctor Goebbels?" Clementine asked.

"Of course."

"I've dictated a thank you note to Doctor McCrew for the medical staff who looked after me. Nurse Clemens, Nurse Oesten, Nurse Hagenau, wonderful people. Doctor Winter will pass the note on to them but I was wondering if you might organise something more formal, omitting me of course, to acknowledge the importance of their work. You can send me the bill after the war. I'll pay you back with interest, of course."

"Consider it done," Goebbels said. "What if I wrote an article praising the work of medical staff in general and published it, coincidentally, alongside photographs of the individuals who nursed you?"

Clementine's eyes glistened. "That would be splendid, thank you."

Goebbels glanced at the faces on both sides of him. "Of all the places to be in the Third Reich this morning, there can't be a more interesting one than this. I see no enemies here. Just a group of people with a common purpose: to ensure that a wife is safely reunited with a husband who, I suspect, has never felt lonelier and more in love with her in his entire life. There are many things I wish I could deprive your husband of, Mrs Churchill, but you and alcohol are not among them."

A car screeched to a halt beside the aircraft.

"Please excuse me." Goebbels stood up again and returned to the door, which was still open.

He watched two burly men in civilian clothes pull a woman out of one of the rear doors and frog-march her to the aircraft, where she hesitated before climbing the steps. Goebbels stood aside to let her in. Smoothing down her blue dress, she looked around self-consciously, waiting for instructions. Anna, McCrew and the Winters stared open-mouthed at her.

"Danke, die Herren[44]," Goebbels called to the two men as he pulled up the steps and secured the aircraft door. Turning, he gestured for the new arrival to sit beside Tina. "An unexpected additional traveller to London," he said mockingly as he edged back to his place between Anna and McCrew. "For those of you who haven't met him, this is one of British intelligence's local representatives in Berlin, although intelligence in his case is perhaps not the most appropriate word. He was caught this morning trying to board a train to the Swiss border dressed like that."

The aircraft began to taxi.

Goebbels shook his head in contempt at the agent. "You're lucky my people got to you before the Gestapo, my friend. You're also lucky I don't want your mission to save Mrs Churchill's life to end on a sour note with your

---

[44] Thank you, gentlemen. »

arrest. That's why I'm offering you a faster trip back to England. Unless you insist on Switzerland, Mr Stepney? That is your name, isn't it? John Stepney?"

Surprised and embarrassed, Stepney looked away and took a deep breath. "England's fine, Herr Reichsminister." He hesitated. "Thank you."

Goebbels turned his attention to the Winters, glancing suspiciously from one to the other. "I must admit I wasn't expecting to see you two here. May I ask—?"

"If you're talking about the Winters, I invited them, Doctor Goebbels," Clementine interrupted. "I hope you don't mind. It's just that I know my husband will be sending a representative to Schiphol with a token of his and my gratitude for the work they've done. I have a soft spot for symbols, you see, and I'd like their German hands to receive our token of gratitude from British ones. Too bad it'll be on a windswept Dutch airfield."

"You might have noticed I have a soft spot for symbols too, so I understand," Goebbels said. "Is your husband aware of Mrs Winter's contribution?"

"No, I don't think so. So I'm praying he isn't sending cigars and cufflinks."

They all laughed, apart from Stepney, as the Junkers Ju 52 accelerated for take-off.

Goebbels turned to look at Anna. "I hope you don't mind me telling everyone here that I'm pleased to have one more opportunity to see you, Anna. Ladies and gentlemen, Anna and I have exchanged harsh words over the last few days, words whose significance and relevance neither of us will ever forget. But they can't be allowed to tarnish the work, skills, creativity, dedication and courage that Anna has displayed as a member of my staff over the last four years. I want you all to bear witness to my gratitude to her for a job well done. I knew a thing or two about how to influence people before I met her, but she has taught me a lot more. But she made me realise something else: if she's representative of what the next generation of women wants and is capable of, we men had better watch out. I wish you luck, Anna."

Anna stared straight ahead. "Thank you."

"As to you, Doctor McCrew," Goebbels continued, "it took extraordinary courage to come to Berlin as you did. You were fully aware that your chances of success were close to zero but you came anyway. Now whilst I can appreciate that a chance to help Mrs Churchill was a chance to jump at, I'm also a man interested in people's motivations. Something's missing here. If you had so little to gain personally by coming here, were you running away perhaps from something in England?"

McCrew folded his arms. Goebbels crossed his legs, waiting.

"You're right, Joseph," Anna interjected without looking at him. "He was running away from something in England. But he was running even faster *towards* something in Germany. Something that could help him move on." She turned and held Goebbels's gaze. "He just didn't know it yet."

"You've got me curious now."

"He was running towards me." She smiled. "I didn't know it yet either. And I forgot to get out of the way."

Goebbels frowned briefly, then smiled as he understood. "By the way, Mrs Churchill, my wife Magda sends you her best wishes for your recovery. Don't worry, she won't tell anyone else about your little visit, least of all the Führer."

"Give her my regards too, Doctor," Clementine said flatly. "Tell me, are you as difficult a husband for her as Winston is for me?"

Goebbels looked at Frank Winter and held his gaze as he answered Clementine. "How would you define a difficult husband? Alcoholic and violent?"

"The fact that you have to ask the question is as clear an answer as you'll ever give. Yes, you're a difficult husband. Now tell me something else. What is your real reason for being on this plane?"

Goebbels shrugged. "Common courtesy."

"Come, come, Doctor. I put it to you that you're hoping to bump into my husband at Schiphol."

Goebbels laughed. "I think the British government's hands are full enough with Rudolf Hess, Mrs Churchill. You don't need me taking personal initiatives of that sort as well." He turned serious. "Your husband won't be there to meet you in Schiphol. He might be desperate to see you again but he still has enough common sense to stay out of German-occupied territory." He looked at the Winters and winked. "Looks like you'll have to wait till the end of the war to shake his hand. Assuming we're all still alive."

"How can you be so sure?" Clementine said. "I know my husband. Taking risks like that is second nature to him."

Goebbels made a show of scratching his head. "I'll try to put this as diplomatically as I can. Let's just say that for all its unquestionable successes, British intelligence has a habit of underestimating German intelligence." He nodded towards Stepney. "The presence of one of your Berlin agents on this aircraft is just one example of that. So I apologise for not having a more cynical explanation for my presence here, Mrs Churchill. I simply have a soft spot for good manners."

Chapter 126

Sunday 18 May 1941
Bognor Regis – West Sussex – England

Lieutenant Geoffrey Cernan walked half the length of the quay again and placed a second case of Beaujolais red wine on top of the first. The camouflaged submarine pen was deserted and eerily quiet, betraying nothing of the presence of three dozen submariners inside the grey mass of U-boat U693.

A short gangway linked the quay to the deck of the submarine. Cernan picked up a short metal bar off the ground, crossed the gangway and climbed the conning tower. Bending down he struck the hatch four times.

A minute later the hatch opened and a crew member's bearded face appeared. He smiled warmly as he recognised Cernan. "Guten Morgen, Lieutenant Cernan."

"Guten Morgen. Could you ask First Officer Hedner to step outside for a moment, please?"

Another minute later Hedner climbed out of the hatch and shook hands with Cernan. He spoke in German. "This is a surprise. How can I help you?"

Cernan nodded towards the cases on the quay. "From Churchill himself. Apparently you and your men did something he's grateful for. Could you give me a hand to bring them on board?"

They crossed to the quay, where Hedner nodded in appreciation at the markings on the cases. "Can I ask you something in confidence, Lieutenant Cernan?"

"Of course."

"Why do I get the feeling you're less than enthusiastic about all this?"

"Because that's what I am, First Officer. I've told the Prime Minister as much as well."

"Would you care to explain?"

Cernan shook his head. "No, it would only sour the wine."

"I won't let it. Speak your mind. Please."

Cernan took a moment to collect his thoughts. "Before the war I was a speechwriter for the brass of a large producer of business machines. What I discovered is that when a leader wants his public to ignore an unpleasant truth, he can do one of several things. He can either present a competing truth that's doubly or triply more pleasant than the unpleasantness of the first one. Or he can present a competing truth that's even more unpleasant than the first one. Or he can let the air fill up with several truths, most of which are false or contradictory, of course, but *all* of which are believable if the public doesn't look too closely. This is key. Also key is the fact the leader often creates some of these different truths himself."

Hedner frowned. "Why would he do that?"

Cernan grinned. "To undermine the very idea of truth. Once all the different truths are out there, the public gets confused. It doesn't know which truth to believe. It might dig a bit but not for long; it's too lazy for that. The truth is hard work and it's just been made harder. So what does the public do? It either gives up on truth completely or it looks for something simpler. That's when the leader steps in as a saviour to sort out the chaos—which he triggered himself, remember—and to impose one truth, his truth, and by brute force if necessary."

Hedner stared in Cernan in disbelief. "So what's your point?"

Cernan was in full swing. "One unpleasant truth for Churchill is that we can't win the war against Germany without active American involvement—I mean troops on the ground. Another unpleasant truth is that the Americans are showing no sign of wanting to help defend their future export markets. Another unpleasant truth is that German bombs are falling on our heads every night. The British public is aware of these unpleasant truths and expects a solution. So what can their leader Winston Churchill tell them? So far, a truth he's filled the air with is that you Germans are a horde of vicious, rapacious, ruthless, racist killers. All of you. But he said that when he still believed he could get the Americans to join the fight on our side. Now he's not so sure. Now it looks as if he might have to negotiate peace terms after all with Herr Hitler in order to prevent a massacre. But wait a minute. How can you possibly negotiate with people you have yourself described as vicious, rapacious, ruthless, racist killers? What would that look like to the British public?"

Cernan gestured towards the U-boat.

"So Churchill decides, discreetly, to let a different truth fill the air, a truth where ordinary, decent U-boat sailors—yes, such Germans do exist after all—work together with ordinary, decent British sailors to save victims of all nationalities. Suddenly there are two different truths about the Germans out there: vicious killers and saintly saviours. Which truth should the public believe? What's true? What's false? What's real? What's fake? Help me! Meanwhile opposition politicians make the problem even worse by filling the air with their own truths. At that point, with perfect timing, Churchill steps in and says, 'Stop! The only truth that matters is this one: you need food, clothes and heating coal for your children and yourself, do you not? If so, our only solution is to negotiate with the Germans, some of whom are quite decent chaps, actually.'"

Cernan handed a box of wine to Hedner and picked up the second one himself. "You and your men are not on a mission to help survivors of sinkings, First Officer. You're on a mission to make Germans seem less like the killers Churchill's been describing so far and more like human beings he can justify negotiating peace terms with. That's why I might seem less than enthusiastic about what you're doing."

"I see," Hedner said. He was about to cross the gangway when he turned round. "And you've told Churchill all that?"

Cernan gave an embarrassed grin. "Well maybe not the last bit."

"You didn't look like the suicidal type to me."

They laughed and crossed the gangway.

Chapter 127

Sunday 18 May 1941
Over The Netherlands

"Fahrrad Two to British pilots, how badly have you missed us?"

The same two Messerschmitt Me 109s appeared on either side of the Bristol Bombay and held steady.

"Fahrrad One to Fahrrad Two," Danes said. "Your tight little backsides have been starring in our dreams. Good morning."

Danes and the pilot on his side waved to each other.

"Do you need a reminder of our little routine at Schiphol?" the German asked.

"I think we remember," Paterson said. "Where the hell did you learn to speak English like that?"

"Oh, dear. Do I detect a pissed-off quality in your tone of voice, Mr Co-Pilot?"

"You do," Danes said, "and you're detecting it in mine, too. You must have lived in England."

"Two words for you, dear British pilots: German education."

Danes switched to German. "Piss off. English education has its merits as well."

After a stunned silence the German pilots laughed. "Approaching Schiphol now," one of them said. "Stand by."

Chapter 128

Sunday 18 May 1941
Schiphol – The Netherlands

As the Junkers Ju 52 began its descent towards Schiphol, its seven passengers were silent. Clementine had fallen asleep.

Goebbels turned to Anna, speaking quietly. "I don't want to disturb Mrs Churchill to say goodbye. Would you do that for me?"

"Yes, I will."

They shook hands awkwardly.

Goebbels turned to McCrew. "Goodbye, Doctor. I'm pleased the Third Reich's medical system could be of, er, unorthodox service to you."

"It was. Goodbye, Doctor Goebbels."

They shook hands.

Goebbels then reached across Anna's and Tina's legs to shake hands with the British agent. "Promise me you'll buy a different-coloured dress for future missions to Berlin, Mr Stepney."

"Fashion will have changed many times by the time I come back, sir."

Three minutes later the aircraft landed. The bump was gentle but it still woke Clementine.

"We're in Schiphol, Mrs Churchill," McCrew said gently. "Ready to get up and sprint across the grass to the other aircraft?"

"Ready when you are."

The aircraft came to a standstill just off the end of the runway, in the same position as three days before.

McCrew caught Stepney's eye. "Can you help me with the stretcher?"

Stepney nodded. They all stood up and edged their way to the rear of the cabin, where there was more space.

McCrew took Tina Winter in his arms and hugged her. "Sorry this isn't answering all your hopes," he said in her ear, "but Frank now knows you can call Goebbels if there's any more trouble." He stood back. "And you will, won't you? Thanks for everything. I still can't believe your hands did all that." He turned to Winter and shook his left hand. "Thanks for guiding Tina's hands, Frank. Please take care of her."

Winter nodded. "And you take care of Mrs Churchill. She's not out of danger yet."

Anna hugged Tina and Stepney and made a show of ignoring Winter.

Goebbels stood over Clementine and shook hands with her. "Would you believe that Germany's Minister of Propaganda is at a loss for words, Mrs Churchill?"

"Try sticking to goodbye then."

"I will. Goodbye, Mrs Churchill. Since meeting you I've realised I'm an even more difficult husband than I thought. I promise to work on it."

"You do that. Goodbye, Doctor Goebbels."

"They're here," McCrew called, looking through a window. Glancing sideways he saw that a wide ring of pairs of back-turned soldiers had been arranged again around the two aircraft

The Bristol Bombay came to a halt beside the Junkers Ju 52. As before they were facing in opposite directions. This time, both aircraft switched off their engines.

Goebbels released the door clamp and pulled it open. Anna unfolded the steps.

Some forty metres away the Bombay's door opened at the same time. Brendan Bracken stepped down on to the grass and stood to one side, peering expectantly towards the Junkers. Paterson stepped out next and began walking towards the Junkers.

Recognising Bracken from photographs, Goebbels stood in the doorway and waved to him before stepping down on to the grass as well. Bracken hesitated, unsure the Minister of Propaganda was signalling to him, then did likewise.

Inside the Junkers, McCrew and Stepney released the stretcher from its supporting structure whilst the Winters said goodbye to Clementine. Tina wiped away a tear.

Nodding to Goebbels, Paterson reached up to place a steadying hand on either side of McCrew's chest as he backed down the steps holding one end of the stretcher. Then he walked beside Clemmie as McCrew and Stepney carried her slowly across the grass to the British aircraft. "Good morning, ma'am. I'm Mike Paterson, the navigator."

"Good morning, Mr Paterson. Is this your second trip for my benefit?"

"Yes, ma'am. You were a little sleepy last time."

She reached up and touched his arm. "Thanks for doing this."

From the door of the Junkers, Anna watched them move away.

Paterson turned to look at Stepney. "Good morning, er—"

"The name's John Stepney. Don't ask. Good morning."

Bracken met them half way between the aircrafts and walked back alongside the stretcher. "Welcome back, Clemmie. It's a relief to see you."

"Thanks for coming, Brendan."

McCrew glanced back at the Junkers, looking for Anna. She had disappeared inside the cabin.

As they reached the Bombay, Danes appeared in the doorway, his attention immediately drawn to Stepney.

"The name's John Stepney," Paterson said with a broad smile. "Don't ask."

Goebbels's voice interrupted them from across the grass. "Mr Bracken?"

Bracken swung round.

"Time for a few words?"

Bracken hesitated a second too long to appear relaxed at the prospect. "Why not?"

The two men walked awkwardly towards each other. Neither smiled as they shook hands.

"This is unexpected," Bracken said.

"How could the Third Reich's current Minister of Propaganda miss an opportunity to meet the United Kingdom's future Minister of Information? Congratulations."

Bracken's eyes opened wide. "This is even more unexpected."

"Reliable information sometimes travels as fast as the other kind. Mr Churchill did ring me to ask if I approved of your nomination. I said I didn't, which was all the encouragement he needed to nominate you anyway." He winked.

Bracken rolled his eyes. "After the war, Herr Reichsminister, I'll want to know how that information reached you."

"I'm still trying to find out myself."

Bracken held Goebbels's gaze but could see behind the Minister that Anna was standing in the doorway of the Junkers. She was gesturing for him—for them, perhaps?—to move away from the aircraft.

"Shall we walk a little?" Bracken asked. "I've been sitting all morning."

"Of course."

From the cockpit of the Bombay, Roddy Danes watched them walk past the tail of the Ju 52 and heading casually towards the protective ring of soldiers. Goebbels offered Bracken a cigarette, which he accepted. Guessing that Anna wanted him to keep Goebbels distracted, Bracken wracked his brain for a suitable topic.

Goebbels came to the rescue. "I won't ask you to give my regards to Mr Churchill, but please tell him that for the briefest of moments I was tempted to."

"What I'll tell him is that even though you forced our hand to send Mrs Churchill to Berlin, you took the trouble to accompany her back to Schiphol. He'll appreciate that. He'll also be thankful to whoever cleared flight paths and organised an escort for our aircraft."

"That would be Goering himself. And whilst we're on the topic of my dear colleagues, how are you enjoying Rudolf Hess's presence among you?"

Bracken looked at Goebbels as he searched for an answer. As he did so his peripheral vision caught two silhouettes dashing across the grass towards the Bristol Bombay. "He's driving our interrogators crazy. They can't stop the man talking. Hess has told us about the Führer's plans to invade Mars, so don't even think of trying to hide that one from us. What about you? How are you enjoying Rudolf Hess's absence from among you?"

Goebbels looked up at the sky. "Let's say that his absence is helpful."

"Any chance of knowing why?"

Goebbels stopped and faced Bracken. "It's personal, Mr Bracken. Just as Mrs Churchill's operation was personal to your Prime Minister. Can you understand that?"

Bracken took a deep breath. "I can but please humour me with one detail: was Hess's flight to Scotland a surprise to the Führer or not?"

"May I say something in confidence?"

"Of course not."

"The Führer might be a formidable showman, Mr Bracken, but he's only an average actor. When he was informed of Hess's disappearance his pain was genuine. The man's heartbroken and probably realising quite a few simple yet important things too late. I'd love to tell you Hess's flight was some clever plot of Hitler's to mislead you, but it wasn't. Hess is an idealist of the purest variety. And I'm afraid there's less and less room left in Germany for people like him."

"Less room or less Lebensraum?"

Goebbels grinned. "Touché. It's all the more ironic as Hess did more than any of us to plant the Lebensraum idea in the Führer's mind."

"What about you, Doctor Goebbels? Aren't you an idealist of the purest sort yourself? Or has the war made you realise a few simple yet important things as well."

The Bristol Bombay's engines spluttered to life. Goebbels was deep in thought.

"Mrs Churchill needs to get back to a hospital," Bracken said, "For what it's worth, it's been interesting to meet you."

Goebbels seemed flattered. "My thoughts exactly. I hope Mrs Churchill recovers fully and comfortably but also terribly slowly. The longer her husband is unable to fully focus on the war, the better for us."

They shook hands

"Oh, one more thing," Goebbels said. "Would you like to thank Doctor Winter on Mr Churchill's behalf? He's over there in the aircraft. I'm sure he'd appreciate it. His wife played a significant role in the operation, too."

Bracken's features hardened. "I don't know about the Third Reich but when an invitation is forced upon us in England, we feel no obligation to turn up with wine and flowers. Goodbye, Doctor Goebbels."

They returned to their respective aircraft. Goebbels stayed on the grass next to the Junkers Ju 52 and watched the Bristol Bombay taxi back on to the runway, pause and roar away. He waited till the British aircraft became a speck in the sky before boarding the Junkers.

"Well that was strange," he said as he pulled up the steps and closed the door.

Neither Frank nor Tina Winter responded.

Surprised, Goebbels turned and froze. Tina had disappeared. Her husband was now sitting with his eyes closed on the structure where the stretcher had been. His left hand had been raised and stabbed through its palm with a flick knife to pin it to the wooden cupboard where McCrew had found bottles of disinfectant. Sandwiched between the hand and the cupboard was an envelope, also pinned by the knife.

Goebbels approached slowly. "Winter?"

Winter opened his eyes.

"What happened?" Goebbels asked.

"Anna Vogel," Winter whispered, wincing.

Goebbels inspected the knife, the hand and the envelope from several angles. Blood was trickling down Winter's arm.

"Shall I remove this?" Goebbels asked casually, without looking at Winter.

The aircraft began to move. Goebbels steadied himself.

"Yes, please," Winter muttered. "With this sling on my other arm I'm hardly likely to do it myself."

Goebbels pulled out the knife, catching the envelope as it fell. "What's this?"

"Mrs Churchill's note to my staff," Winter said, inspecting his hand. "McCrew left it on your seat but Anna was clearly worried you might miss it."

Goebbels sat down opposite Winter, opened the envelope and removed two sheets of paper from it.

Winter groaned. "Excuse me, Herr Reichsminister, could I ask you to help me disinfect my hand and put a bandage on it?"

Goebbels began to read. "First things first, Doctor."

Chapter 129

Sunday 18 May 1941
Bognor Regis – West Sussex – England

First Officer Ernst Hedner broke a golden rule of U-boat housekeeping that morning. But he reasoned it was an acceptable thing to do given that he and his crew weren't on active duty at sea yet and that the boat would be well lit at all times, making injury unlikely. No high-speed drills had been planned that day either. It was Sunday.

He therefore separated the two cases of wine and positioned them where no one could miss them, one on the floor in the control room and the other next to the toilet. As the crew stepped over the cases time and time again, Hedner knew expectations would build about the liquid aspects of their evening meal.

Forty-five minutes after Cernan's departure, the time bombs concealed in the cases—four of the twelve bottles in each had been removed to make room for them—exploded simultaneously. The blasts and fireballs they caused met little resistance as they travelled the full length of the U-boat in an instant.

A discreet Royal Navy enquiry would later estimate that thirty-three of the thirty-four German and British crew members had died instantly or in under a minute. The thirty-fourth, who had been refitting a torpedo storage area to accommodate inflatable dinghies and blankets, had probably survived a few minutes longer.

Chapter 130

Sunday 18 May 1941
Over the North Sea

The Bristol Bombay crossed the English coastline a little south of Aldeburgh, Suffolk. In the cockpit Roddy Danes and Mike Paterson winked at each other.

In the passenger cabin behind them Clementine spoke up. "Does it say something for our country, I wonder, that nobody made a desperate dash from the British aircraft to the German one back there?"

The other five passengers laughed. Bracken sat in the middle, between Anna and Tina to his left and McCrew and Stepney to his right.

"I'm curious," Clementine continued. "When did the idea of bringing Tina along pop up?"

"I had it as I sat looking at her husband in the plane," Anna said. "Miracle worker in a hospital, violent brute anywhere else. Goebbels is aware of that. I wonder what they're talking about right now."

"Oh, my goodness."

"Anna, what are your own plans in England?" Bracken asked. "If you want us to organise onward travel to the States for you, just say the word. We're indebted to you."

Anna sat up. "You can settle your debt to me in three ways, Mr Bracken, none of them negotiable. First, I want your government to issue two new British passports, one for Tina and one for me. But that doesn't mean we're giving up our German nationality. One day, I hope, we'll dare to be proud of it again."

"Agreed."

Anna held Bracken's gaze. "I know I'd become British anyway as soon as Neil marries me but I have to survive the transition period."

McCrew shrugged helplessly.

"Second, as you're about to take over the Ministry of Information, I want you to give me a job there. I don't think I need to describe my qualifications to you, but I want you to describe my future job to me."

Bracken stiffened. "Is there anyone on this planet who hasn't heard about my new job?"

Anna was enjoying herself. "Well?"

"I was thinking you might be interested in a division called Home Intelligence," Bracken managed at last, "It probes the British public for its opinion on anything and everything at any given time. When I take over, I'd like it to focus a lot more on how the British public sees its prospects and expectations after the war. That would be your job."

"Hear, hear," Clementine said.

Anna shook Bracken's hand. "Done. Third, I expect to be able to recruit at least one assistant of my own choosing. Is there a problem with that?"

"I don't see why not. But there is a vetting process to be followed."

"Yes or no, Mr Bracken?"

Bracken sighed and closed his eyes. "Are you like this all the time, Miss Vogel?"

"It's just a question, boss."

"Yes."

Anna placed her other hand on Tina's thigh. "In that case the vetting process is over. Let me introduce you to my new assistant. Her name's Tina Winter and she'd rather make her own way in the world than depend on her parents or a violent alcoholic husband. In fact she's exactly the sort of free-thinking, assertive modern woman the UK needs many more of. Fluent in German too should the war go the wrong way."

Chapter 131

Sunday 18 May 1941
Over Germany

Joseph Goebbels finished reading the two pages from the envelope as the Junkers Ju 52 flew over Göttingen on its way to Berlin. He looked up.

Staring blankly at the ceiling, Winter was holding up his bleeding hand at head level, as if to ask something. Sweat glistened on his chin.

Goebbels folded the pages and returned them to the envelope. "Frau Churchill says some very nice things about your staff." He paused. "Their professional future's looking a little brighter than yours, isn't it."

Wincing, Winter struggled to sit up straight. "Herr Reichsminister, my wound really should be disinfected."

"Your entire existence depended on your wife. Your redemption, too. Now she's gone. Any deeply philosophical thoughts to share on the matter?"

"She'll regret it. No job, no qualifications, no parents. Probably no friends left either. They'll have all moved on since Cambridge days. Tina thinks England's still the same old predictable country she grew up in. She's wrong."

Goebbels slowly shook his head. "You think she's going to come back, don't you."

Winter grunted and looked away.

Goebbels lit a cigarette. "Tell me, Doctor Winter, how do you imagine our arrival at Gatow? Do you think we're going to shake hands, or whatever's left of them in your case, and return to our respective lives?"

Winter shrugged. "Why wouldn't we? My life might be a little more challenging than before but I'll find a way."

"You're finished, Winter. Your medical tricks have been exposed, your career is over, you have no other career to switch to and you have no other source of revenue. You could turn to the National Socialist party for last-resort support, of course, but it isn't exactly famous for its benevolent attitude towards cripples, is it. So what is a desperate man like yourself likely to do? Why not put your very last trump card to good use? Why not make one last bid for survival by revealing to Himmler or even the Führer himself what you know about Mrs Churchill's operation here and my involvement in it?"

Winter shook his head, his voice trembling. "I wouldn't dream of it."

"Desperation's a whore, Doctor Winter, and you're desperate."

"I can assure you that—"

"Shut up. I'm the one who's going to make promises around here. Two of them actually. The first is that as soon as we land in Berlin, I'll have you arrested not only for gross medical malpractice but for violent conduct towards your wife. Given my position in the government, there is little doubt I'll be listened to. My second promise is to be open over the next hour or so to any alternative suggestion from you as to how we might conclude this affair in a more efficient, less uncomfortable way."

Winter's eyes narrowed as he considered this. Gradually his features relaxed. "I can only think of one alternative suggestion."

"Same here."

Winter hesitated. "Is it available right now?"

"If you want it."

"Thank you." Winter looked down at his useless hands. "But I may require a little assistance."

"Of course." Goebbels placed his cigarette in an ashtray, stood up and made his way to the aircraft door at the rear. As he opened it and stood back, a cold draft filled the cabin. Winter staggered towards the door, paused and turned to look at the Minister. Goebbels held his gaze dispassionately. He waited to be alone in the cabin before closing the door and returning to finish his cigarette.

Chapter 132

Sunday 18 May 1941
Kidlington – Oxfordshire – England

An ambulance and three cars were parked just off Kidlington Airfield's runway. Roddy Danes halted the Bristol Bombay so as to block any line of sight between the terminal and the four vehicles. Mike Paterson left the cockpit and hurried through the passenger cabin to open the door. Winston Churchill, Colin Gubbins and three ambulancemen looked up at him. Paterson grinned at the Prime Minister.

Everyone watched in silence as the ambulancemen carefully manoeuvred Clementine's stretcher, including head-clamp and drip bags, out of the aircraft. They paused at the foot of the steps to let Churchill, tears in full flow, lean over his sleeping wife's face and kiss her forehead. They moved away towards the ambulance.

Dabbing his tears with a handkerchief, Churchill extended his right hand to McCrew as the surgeon stepped out of the aircraft carrying Clementine's bag. "Thank you, McCrew. Words fail me and you should consider that a sign of utmost respect in my case."

"I do, Prime Minister. If you'll forgive me, I'll go with Clementine to Ditchley. She's stable but we have to watch out. I'll stay on hand a couple of days."

"Of course, of course. Stay with her as long as you like. I'll join you there this evening. Bracken and I have a sensitive matter to attend to this afternoon."

The other passengers filed out of the Bombay, forming a row at the foot of the steps. Colin Gubbins joined them.

McCrew was about to head off towards the ambulance when Churchill caught his arm and pulled him to one side, lowering his voice. "Has all this been useful to you too somehow?"

McCrew didn't seem to understand.

"If your father were here, McCrew, he'd be proud. He'd be asking me to lend him a handkerchief, I'm sure."

McCrew bit his lower lip. "If you don't mind, Prime Minister, I'd prefer us to let my father rest in peace where he is. That's something I've never been able to let him do. Then today, somewhere in the sky between Berlin and The Netherlands, I suddenly realised I could let him go. And should."

Churchill blinked a few times. "I'm glad for you."

McCrew gave Churchill a small nod and began to walk away. After a few yards he froze, suddenly remembering something. Rushing back to the other passengers, he kissed Anna on the cheek and shrugged apologetically.

"Death penalty cancelled," Anna called as he ran towards the ambulance.

They all laughed.

Bracken stepped forward. "Winston, this is Anna Vogel, Doctor McCrew's chaperone in Berlin."

"And much else besides, I see." Churchill shook her hand. "Miss Vogel, I have it on good authority that a suite at the Savoy for a few days would put you in a good mood."

"It would, Prime Minister. Thank you."

"Good choice. I often have lunch there myself. One of those three cars over there is waiting to take you there."

"And this is Tina Winter, Frank Winter's wife," Bracken continued. "It's a long story but your wife owes as much to Mrs Winter's surgical skills as to her husband's. On the spur of the moment in Schiphol, Mrs Winter also decided that her future lay on this side of the English Channel."

Churchill and Tina shook hands. "Whatever you did for my wife's benefit, thank you, Mrs Winter. Something tells me I shouldn't ask why your husband isn't with you, so I'll ask instead if you have somewhere to stay in England."

"Yes she does, Prime Minister," Anna interrupted. "If it's all the same to you, Tina can share my suite at the Savoy until we find accommodation."

Churchill grinned at Bracken. "I suggest you find a telephone and inform the Savoy they have an extra guest."

"And this is John Stepney of the SOE, Prime Minister," Bracken said. "His decision to travel with us was also spur of the moment."

"Stepney?" Gubbins blurted, stepping back to get a better look at Stepney's female clothes. "My dear man, I didn't recognise you."

"I'll take that as a compliment, sir. Goebbels doesn't have your taste. Could you please give me a lift back to London?"

"Of course."

Churchill shook the agent's hand. "Thanks for your help, Stepney. The brigadier will brief me on what happened."

Danes and Paterson stepped out of the aircraft and shook hands with Churchill.

"Thank you, gentlemen," the Prime Minister said. "You're the only ones who don't need to hurry home to loved ones, aren't you."

They glanced self-consciously at each other.

"I think we'd better get back to Farnborough, sir," Paterson said. "We've got a bunch of trainee pilots coming to see our collection of captured enemy aircraft tomorrow and we haven't prepared anything for them yet."

Churchill laughed. "Well give a thank you kiss to the Heinkel 111 from me. It did a good job. And if you find time you go near the RAE bar, I've already told them that anything you two drink there over the next month is on me. So treat your thirst as I treat mine, gentlemen. Obediently."

Chapter 133

Sunday 18 May 1941
London – England

Rudolf Hess found his cell at the Tower of London surprisingly comfortable. He had said as much to the impossibly muscular, impeccably polite guard who had brought him lunch on a tray. He was lying on his bed reading 'Three men in a boat' when the cell door opened and the same guard walked in.

"A car's waiting for you in the courtyard, Mr Hess."

Hess didn't look up. "Why?"

"I'm not at liberty to say, sir."

"Then I'll stay here. I've had enough of all this secrecy. This also happens to be one of my favourite books."

The guard cleared his throat. "If you'd prefer me to pick you up physically and throw you in the back of the vehicle, I'd be quite happy to arrange that. With all due respect, sir, it's up to you."

Hess closed his book.

Chapter 134

Sunday 18 May 1941
Southern England

Churchill's car swerved yet again to avoid a tractor. Reg Parker, the Prime Minister's driver, was following instructions to 'blur the difference' between the vehicle and a 'Spitfire in hot pursuit' to cover the distance between Oxfordshire and Chartwell, north-west Kent, in record time. Buoyed by Clementine's safe return, Churchill was indifferent to the speed and risk. The white faces of Walter Thompson, his bodyguard, and Brendan Bracken suggested otherwise, especially as the journey was due to last at least two hours.

"Did you get through to the Savoy?" Churchill asked.

Bracken swallowed nervously. "Yes. I also put a quick call through to Colville in Downing Street. There's been, er..." He trailed off.

"Yes?"

"There's been a problem in Bognor Regis. An explosion."

Churchill's good mood vanished. "The U-boat?"

Bracken was sweating. "According to Colville, Lieutenant Cernan was let into the U-boat pen this morning to deliver two cases of wine. What happened inside the pen wasn't witnessed but Cernan came out again after fifteen minutes. About forty-five minutes after that, the guards outside the pen heard an explosion—possibly two in quick succession—and discovered black smoke belching from the conning tower hatch."

"Did anyone get out?"

Bracken shook his head. "The entire crew was inside. That was part of their training. The hatch was probably already open for ventilation purposes when the bombs went off. No blast would be powerful enough to punch through it."

Churchill twisted to face him. "Bombs?"

Bracken took a deep breath. "The guards immediately reported Cernan's presence prior to the explosions and a search was organised. He still hasn't been found. But the police broke into his flat and found a note on the kitchen table. Colville dictated it to me." Bracken took a crumpled piece of paper out of his jacket's inside pockets. "Auf Wiedersehen, Herr Churchill. Auf Wiedersehen, Herr Bracken. You turned noble German fighters into prisoners. Then you turned them into traitors. Then you tried to turn them into propaganda tools of the international Jewish conspiracy. But I managed just in time to turn them back into what destiny had designated them to be: fallen martyrs of the Thousand-Year Reich. But enough of my sentimental drivel. Enjoy the war. Geoff Cernan. Heil Hitler."

Churchill stared out of the window. "They won't find him. He's already left the country. Cernan and I sat in this very car a few days ago. He described my remarks to the U-boat crew as sentimental drivel as well. I thought that was rather brave of him. He even referred to the project's vulnerability to explosions. I almost offered him a job on the spot. I need people like him around me. People who speak their minds. People like Clemmie. People like Beaverbrook, Pug or the Prof. People like you, Brendan. But then again, based on what's happened to those poor men, honesty, openness and facts—all those lofty ideals we hammer into children and boast of in our electoral campaigns—are just alternative ways to hide evil intentions in plain sight."

Chapter 135

Sunday 18 May 1941
London – England

At the reception desk of the Savoy Hotel, neither Anna Vogel nor Tina Winter failed to notice the hint of suspicion and condescension in the eyes of the effeminate man who greeted them. The receptionist in turn hadn't failed to notice they only had one small battered suitcase between them.

"Good morning, how can I help you?" The virility of his voice contrasted with his mannerisms.

"Anna Vogel. A suite's been booked for us."

The receptionist blinked sceptically as he checked a list for their reservation, then blinked twice as fast when he saw who had made it. He stood noticeably straighter.

"Of course, Mrs Vogel. Welcome to the Savoy."

"Were you told there'd be two of us?"

"Indeed. Welcome to you too, Mrs Winter."

"We'll be needing clothes, champagne and a bath in that order," Anna announced. "We didn't have time to pack."

"Of course. I'll have our Mrs Collins pop up to your suite in ten minutes. I'm sure she'll be able to answer most of your expectations directly and to point you in the right direction otherwise."

As he handed them a key, a man tripped up behind Anna and crashed to the floor. The papers he was carrying flew in all directions.

Anna and Tina knelt to help him up. "Are you all right, sir?" Anna asked.

"Yes, fine."

Anna thought she detected an American twang in his voice.

Several customers and staff members helped to gather up his papers.

"Thanks everyone," the man called. "I'm so clumsy."

American, definitely.

The man flashed a smile at Anna. Simultaneously she felt something small, flat and square being pressed into her hand. She closed her hand immediately.

The man disappeared into the crowd in the lobby.

Anna put her other hand on her forehead.

"Are you okay?" Tina asked her. "You're a little pale."

What the hell is David Cassell doing here? Anna wondered as she picked up the suitcase. "I'm fine," she said. "Let's go and test Mrs Collins's resourcefulness." And how the hell did he know I'd be at the Savoy?

1937

Two years before World War Two

Chapter 136

Friday 6 August 1937
New York - USA

As Anna Vogel hadn't responded to his raised glass, David Cassell turned his attention to the waiter, who was serving their desserts.

Anna gazed out across Manhattan, aware she had little or no control left over the conversation or situation. If there was an ideal moment to get up and leave, this was it. One problem, though: he knew where she lived and would, inevitably, turn up at her door with that casual smile of his, put further pressure on her and smile again.

Except that he wasn't putting pressure on her, at least not in any definable sense. Just hinting. Just suggesting. Just holding back enough information to pique her curiosity.

"Tell me what you know about the Haganah," he suddenly said.

"Who's we, David? Why won't you tell me?"

"Indulge me."

She made a show of sighing in terminal despair. "I'm not a practicing Jew, David, so I—"

"Indulge me."

Anna took a moment to gather her thoughts. "What I know about the Haganah is probably what any self-respecting Jew knows, i.e. not much and much of it rumour based. As far as I know, the Haganah's some kind of unofficial military organisation based in Palestine, which is currently run by the British[45]. They're a bunch of fighters doing whatever they can, or whatever the British turn a blind eye to, to defend Jews brave enough to live in that area."

"Defend them from what?"

"Arab hostility, I suppose. Are you a member of the Haganah yourself?"

"Yes, but covertly. Let's say I represent interests of theirs outside Palestine."

"And David Cassell isn't your real name."

"Of course not. The Haganah wants you to accept the German job offer, Anna, not the British one. No prizes for guessing why."

"If I do that, it's just a question of time before Goebbels finds out I'm Jewish. The Nazis vet everyone and everything."

"I disagree. Goebbels is so impressed by the fact you've worked for Edward Bernays and so desperate to pick your brains that either he already knows your Jewish and doesn't care or he's getting careless."

Anna shook her head. "What you want me to do is steal or conceal information. I'm about bringing information out into the open."

Cassell shook his head, too. "What we want you to do is something you know is right, Anna. It's also something your father would be proud of."

Anna squinted at him. "What's my father got to do with it? He didn't give a shit about his religion and never told anyone he was a Jew. The closest he ever got to God was to thank him one day for having a name not many people associate with Jewishness. When I was a child he consistently steered me clear of synagogues, Torahs, Talmuds, any of that stuff. So did my mother."

Cassell smiled smugly. "Anna, your father was one of the Haganah's most active and valuable members outside Palestine. He helped our organisation in general, and me in particular, in ways you can't begin to imagine. Some of those ways weren't exactly soft and gentle, I'll grant you that. But our organisation was and still is at war, and wars tend not to be soft and gentle, especially when they're about our survival. Your father's key skill was fundraising. He excelled at it."

"And you can prove this, I imagine?"

"I'll prove it right now. One day when you were fifteen, just after the Great War, you helped a neighbour sort some vegetables in his workshop. This neighbour had a nervous tic. He always seemed to be winking at you

---

[45] In 1922 the League of Nations mandated the United Kingdom to administer an area known as « Mandatory Palestine ». This would become, after years of mutual suspicion, territorial disputes and violence between British, Jewish and Arab interests, the independent state of Israel in 1948.

with his right eye. Well that day he suddenly grabbed you and forced you to perform oral sex on him. Unluckily for him your father came home early from work that day and popped into the neighbour's workshop to say hello. They'd been close friends up to that point. You were still on your knees in flagrante. Your father told you to leave the workshop, picked up a knife and stabbed the neighbour to death. But you hadn't left. You'd hidden in a corner to watch the situation play out. Suddenly, as your father looked around for something to wrap the body in, it moved. The neighbour was still alive. And coincidentally he looked in your direction and winked again. So you went over to him, picked up the knife where your father had dropped it and stabbed him in that winking eye. This time he died. Your father managed to get rid of the body without attracting attention in the neighbourhood and the police investigation never got anywhere. You and your father never talked about it again. Nor have you ever told anyone else about it, have you?"

Anna slowly shook her head.

"Your father informed just one other person: me. He reasoned that a father wouldn't tell anyone that kind of story about his daughter unless he trusted that person entirely. He also reasoned that one day you might need my help or I might need yours and that you'd require proof that you could trust me."

Anna took a sip of water. "Did my mother know he was in the Haganah?"

"She suspected he was closer to his religion than he let on. More militant, too. But she preferred to believe his frequent absences were caused by a time-consuming mistress." He gave a half-smile. "She found that idea less scary."

"So what do you want from me?"

"We believe Germany's going to cause another war in Europe and we want to know what fate Hitler has in store for our people. The more information we have, the better and the sooner we can help them. Goebbels is a member of Hitler's inner circle and we want you to work your way into Goebbels's inner circle. We'll supply communication equipment and training, of course."

"And if I refuse?" Anna asked calmly.

"You can't refuse," Cassell answered even more calmly.

"Oh yes I can, David. Your battle is the fate of Jews. My battle is much bigger and much more ambitious: the fate of women. I can't fight both."

"Then choose to fight for your own people. Fight to continue the work your father started."

"Sorry, David, I've made my choice. Besides I wouldn't describe the fate of some women in our religion as flourishing. I'm going to accept the British job offer."

"Then I've made my choice, too." He steepled his fingers. "If you don't accept Goebbels's job offer, I'll make sure both offers get cancelled."

Anna scoffed. "I'm surprised my father trusted a man who'd resort to those kinds of tactics."

"Your father *taught* me those tactics, Anna. He was a great man and as much a father to me as he was to you. But with all due respect, your father is also a dead Jew now. His work is now ours. He died of natural causes but thousands of Jews are dying of unnatural causes in Germany. And we consider it our duty to do whatever it takes, including putting pressure on people like you, to stop hundreds *more* of our people, possibly *thousands*, possibly *tens* of thousands, dying of unnatural causes, too. So who's your next boss going to be, Anna? Goebbels, Bracken or the owner of that charming café on Sixth Avenue?"

1941

Chapter 137

Sunday 18 May 1941
Chartwell – Kent – England

At four p.m. exactly, the guards at Chartwell's main gates waved a car through. It slowly covered the last few yards to the house's main entrance, where Churchill and Bracken stood waiting. They watched as one of the two passengers in the back seat removed handcuffs and a blindfold from the other.

Churchill stepped forward and opened the passenger door closest to him. "Good afternoon and welcome to Chartwell, Herr Hess."

Blinking in amazement, the German got out of the vehicle and shook the Prime Minister's extended hand.

"And this is my parliamentary secretary, Mr Bracken."

Hess shook Bracken's hand, too. "I've heard or seen your name a few times, Mr Bracken."

"Not on a list of targets, I hope."

"Well, not at the top of it."

"I need an immediate decision from you," Churchill said. "Afternoon tea now or shall we stretch our legs first?"

Hess looked up at the house. "The Tower of London is comfortable enough but it isn't a sports club. So I'd love to stretch my legs, if it's all right with you."

"Follow me."

They made their way in silence around the house and stopped to take in the east-facing view over Chartwell's twin lakes.

Hess was impressed. "Congratulations on your taste, Mr Churchill. This is magnificent."

"But sadly unusable for now because of the Luftwaffe. It's also not as breath-taking as the Führer's Berghof, but it's enough for myself and my family." Churchill stopped and faced Hess. "Let's skip the small talk, shall we? I've read all the transcripts of your conversations with Hamilton and Kirkpatrick in Scotland. I've also received a report on your conversation with Hedner on the U-boat."

Hess grinned. "Ah, the U-boat was a clever trick. Whose idea was it? I almost fell for it but not quite."

"This is your big chance, Hess. I know you'd rather I were out of office or dead and buried but I'm all you've got. What was your real reason for flying here? And please try to tell me something I don't already know."

Hess took a deep breath. "All right. My reason for flying here was and still is a peace offering. What I haven't mentioned to your interrogators or to anyone here so far is an additional reason to take my offer into consideration. Our invasion of the Soviet Union—Operation Barbarossa—will begin in a few weeks away. Most of our people are confident it will be a huge success at first but almost no one believes, apart from the Führer, that it will be over by the end of August."

"How rude of them," Churchill mused. "I agree with Hitler. I mean, apart from launching the attack too late, overstretching supply lines, fighting on two fronts, believing tactics used on France can work just as well in the Soviet Union and underestimating the Soviet Union's fighting spirit and equipment, what could possibly go wrong?"

"Our victory is assured, of course," Hess continued, "but it won't happen until next year or possibly 1943. By that time the number of Jews under our control will have increased from four to six or seven million."

There was silence.

Bracken broke it first. "Didn't you have some weird plan to exile them all to Madagascar? What happened to that idea?"

"The Führer dropped it last year at about the same time your country forgot to surrender to us."

They began to walk down the slope towards the lakes.

"So what's the plan for all these people?" Churchill asked.

"There is no plan. In practical terms, if the war lasts into next year, everyone will have a winter to endure. A Russian winter. Right now we Germans don't have a plan to supply appropriate winter clothing to all our own soldiers. That's two to three million men. There will only be enough clothing, assuming it gets through to those who need it, for a much smaller number. So we're hardly likely to feed, clothe and shelter millions of Jews, let alone millions of captured soldiers, when temperatures drops below minus twenty degrees and stay there."

"In other words," Bracken said, "you fully expect millions of people to either starve or freeze to death."

"Assuming they haven't been executed beforehand," Churchill added sourly.

Hess looked down at the grass. "If you agree to negotiate peace terms with us right now, those millions of lives can be saved. The rest is the same: you keep your islands and empire and we keep continental Europe."

"Just out of interest, does continental Europe include the Soviet Union or not?" Bracken asked. "You told Kirkpatrick that it didn't."

Hess coughed awkwardly. "We'll obviously need to have new talks with Stalin."

Churchill scoffed. "Talks? I can imagine what they'd be like. Comrade Stalin, whilst we have our quiet dispassionate chat about our future relations, please ignore the 3 million German soldiers, 300,000 tanks and 600,000 horses massed along your border."

"If for any reason the Soviet Union fell under our control," Hess said carefully, "what would we do with six or seven million European Jews? The answer is up to the pragmatist in you, Mr Churchill. Your vast British Empire is certainly big enough to absorb them all. If Jewish lives and well-being are so important to you, why not welcome them? All we need to agree on is how to transport such vast numbers of people from our occupied territories to yours."

"Otherwise they all die?" Bracken asked.

"The Third Reich's position on Jews and other undesirable minorities is crystal clear," Hess said calmly. "As far as we're concerned, their fate is sealed. We want to get rid of them. All I'm doing here is point out that you still have an opportunity, if you want it, to change the fate of all those people. It's no exaggeration to say their fate is now your decision and your responsibility."

"No, Hess, that's too easy," Churchill said. "Their fate is not our decision and responsibility. We're not the ones killing Jews or letting them starve or freeze to death in the first place. You are. That's your decision and your responsibility. Is that why you flew here? To warn us that if we don't stop Hitler killing off millions of Jews, we'll be the murderers? Is that the best you can do? Let me tell you what I think: when you flew over here, you genuinely thought the King would welcome you with open arms and that we as a nation would jump at any chance to accept your peace terms. But surprise, all you got was confirmation that we lost interest in peace deals with terrorists like you a long time ago. We chose to fight you. So you began to panic. It suddenly looked as if we would just put you in a prison cell and throw away the key or even send you back to Hitler with your tail between your legs. So you began to poke around your brain for something more compelling to shove under our noses. You decided to shift the discussion away from what we all might *gain* by signing a peace treaty to what millions of Jews and members of other minorities might *lose* if we didn't. And as a bonus, if I turned you down you could present me as a heartless shit and yourself as a heroic peace-maker who only wanted to save millions of lives. Make no mistake, Hess, the heartless shit is you. And in case you're wondering, you won't ever be able to prove you met me face to face."

Hess smiled smugly. "As my excellent colleague Joseph Goebbels keeps on reminding me, there comes in point in reputation management where the accuser no longer has to prove that something happened. It's up to the accused—you in this case—to prove it didn't." He paused to enjoy his own words. "How will history judge you, Prime Minister? If a man is warned about millions of avoidable deaths and does nothing, he becomes an accomplice, does he not?"

They stopped half way down the slope as Churchill turned to face Hess. "If a man is warned about a clique of murderers and does nothing to defeat them and ensure they never come to power again, he becomes an accomplice."

An aircraft suddenly flew low over the estate, a hundred yards to the left of the three men. They all ducked instinctively, although technically too late.

"No markings," Bracken said, peering up at the aircraft. "What's he playing at?"

"That's a Stuka," Hess said. "It's one of ours. And it's armed."

They watched as the German dive-bomber climbed and banked to circle above them. The shape of the single bomb attached below its fuselage was unmistakable.

"We have to assume he's seen us," Bracken said. "We need to take cover."

Bracken and Hess simultaneously grabbed one of Churchill's arms each and turned him round to rush up the slope.

"I disagree," Churchill protested, digging his feet in and struggling to loosen their grip.

"Bracken's right, Mr Churchill," Hess said. "We've got to move."

Churchill managed to yank his arms free. He promptly grabbed Bracken's right shirtsleeve and Hess's left one to stop them going anywhere. Now it was their turn to try and yank themselves free.

The Stuka completed its circle above them and suddenly rolled to face downwards and dive in their direction.

Hess tried desperately to free himself but Churchill held tight.

"Hold steady, gentlemen," Churchill shouted. "He won't bomb us."

"What are you doing, Winston?" Bracken shouted.

The Stuka's signature wailing siren now audible. Churchill stared up at the aircraft, mesmerised by the four tonnes of metal hurtling towards him at a speed approaching 350 miles an hour. Ripping his arm free, Hess tried to run away but tripped and fell.

Still gripping Bracken's shirtsleeve, Churchill lowered his voice. "Call Farnborough and tell them that if Danes ever pulls another stunt like this around here, I'll shut him and his unit down."

Bracken shut his eyes and ducked as the Stuka roared overhead.

Churchill stayed upright, smiling and swivelling round to watch the aircraft pull out of its dive. "You see, Brendan, it might not look like it but even I have neighbours to consider. And mine complain about noise at the drop of a hat, believe me."

The sound of the Stuka's engines faded.

Hess had rolled himself into a ball on the ground, arms over his head. He picked himself up and straightened his clothes.

"Was that another of your tricks to make me talk, Mr Churchill? First a U-boat, now a Stuka?"

Churchill winked at Bracken. "Make that phone call, please."

Bracken set off back up the slope towards Chartwell's main building.

Churchill turned to Hess. "Ready for afternoon tea now?"

Chapter 138

Sunday 18 May 1941
Farnborough – Hampshire – England

In full RAF pilot's gear, Roddy Danes walked past Farnborough Airfield's largest canteen. He stopped after a few yards and turned back. He needed a cup of tea before the training session began.

"Roddy!" a female voice called breathlessly from the other end of the corridor. "Call for you," she said, beckoning him to join her. "Someone called Bracken. Urgent."

"Where can I talk to him?"

She led him to an office and gestured towards a phone, which was ringing.

"Danes speaking."

"Danes?" Bracken sounded surprised. "You're already back?"

"Back from what, sir?"

There was silence.

"Are you there, Mr Bracken?"

Bracken spoke slowly. "It this is a joke, it has to stop."

"What joke, sir?"

"Listen to me. A Stuka has just nosedived straight at the Prime Minister and myself here at Chartwell. Was that you or not?"

"What?"

"Just answer me, Danes."

Danes's voice was trembling. "No, it wasn't me. I'm due to test-fly a Stuka in thirty minutes. We've got trainee pilots coming tomorrow and—"

The line went dead.

Chapter 139

Sunday 18 May 1941
Chartwell – Kent – England

Winston Churchill's study was the only room at Chartwell that hadn't been mothballed because of the war. On the rare occasions he visited his country home he used a separate little house called Orchard Cottage.

Sitting on the edge of the Prime Minister's desk in the study, Bracken waited to be put through to Neil McCrew at Ditchley. He reached for a pen but left it where it was because his shaking hand would prevent him from using it.

"McCrew here."

"Bracken. Everything all right with Clemmie?"

"Yes, fine. The driver avoided bumps and potholes as best he could, so progress was slow. She's in her room sleeping now."

"Good," Bracken said, struggling to sound casual. "Something else: remember that envelope I gave you from the Prime Minister for Goebbels?"

"Yes, I gave it to him."

Bracken closed his eyes to let this sink in. "But I told you only to give it to him if the operation failed."

"I know."

"For God's sake, McCrew, what the hell are you—?"

"It's simple, Mr Bracken. As I see it, at least four people—Anna Vogel, John Stepney, Roddy Danes and myself—risked their lives to make that surgery on Mrs Churchill possible. The only person risking a lot but not his life was Winston Churchill himself. Well it came to my attention that the same thing happened twenty-six years ago, in April 1915: tens of thousands of men, including my father, were risking their lives at Gallipoli whilst Churchill remained in London, risking life and limb in an armchair with a cigar in one hand and a whisky in the other. My father and thousands of other lost their lives and never returned. Churchill lost his job but returned to see his wife and children. That struck me as unfair. So I decided to give Churchill's message to Goebbels *regardless* of the outcome of the operation. It was my way of making him take a risk as well. I left the message on his plane back to Berlin. I attached it to a thank you note from Mrs Churchill to the staff of her clinic."

Bracken rolled his eyes. "Did you read the message?"

McCrew sounded shocked. "Of course not. It was private, wasn't it?"

"You're an idiot, McCrew. A bloody idiot."

"Why, what's happened?"

Bracken struggled to control himself, his voice a hiss. "I can confirm you made Churchill take a risk. A bigger risk than all four of you took together."

"Well I'm not displeased to hear it," McCrew said casually. "Unless you want to give me details, will that be all, Mr Bracken? I need to get back to Mrs Churchill."

"Yes, go ahead."

Bracken hung up and let himself collapse in Churchill's chair. Seconds later he sat up straight again. He had several valuable skills but one invaluable gift: an excellent memory. Reaching for a pen and notepad he forced his mind back to Churchill's message to Goebbels. He scribbled one particular passage as it returned to him. *'I'm convinced he flew here with more to offer than peace terms. Your insistent interest in his fate has only strengthened this belief. I will break him, therefore, with typically British torture: I'll invite him for Sunday afternoon tea (alcohol in my case, in line with your factual propaganda) and Red Cross biscuits (Hess is addicted) on a peaceful country terrace. That blood-drenched discussion will decide his fate."*

Today was indeed Sunday, Bracken thought, and the Stuka had indeed appeared shortly after four pm, a widely used time for afternoon tea. Goebbels could also have deduced that the quiet country terrace was a reference to Chartwell. But how had the pilot identified Churchill's estate with its camouflaged lakes amongst all the other homes in the area?

Chapter 140

Sunday 18 May 1941
London – England

Tina Winter let her body slip under the generous thickness of bubbles and immediately felt her muscles begin to relax in the hot water. To her left Anna Vogel appeared in the bathroom doorway, holding two glasses of champagne.

"Refuel, ma'am?"

"God, yes. Pull up a chair."

"No, I'll stand. I've got to pop down to reception to sort out a few details."

"I insist. Sit down for a second."

Anna repositioned the bathroom stool and sat beside the bath. Their glasses clinked.

"To a new start?" Anna asked.

"To full disclosure. I'd prefer."

Eyes narrowing, Anna hesitated a fraction of a second too long. "To full disclosure."

Their glasses clinked again.

Tina sat up in the bath. "Anna, you stabbed Frank's hand on that aircraft as if you'd been doing it all your life. I've worked in hospitals long enough to recognise professionalism when I see it. Your gestures were self-confident, precise and practised. So please drop the pretence that you're just a communication specialist. If we're going to be working together, I need to know who my boss really is."

Anna sipped her champagne. "I was a Jew working close to one of the Third Reich's most powerful officials. The reason I know how to defend myself is that I was in permanent danger of being found out. So I paid someone to teach me a few tricks. Simple, really."

"Why would a Jew work for one of Germany's most rabid anti-Semites?"

"My interest was first and foremost professional. I'd already worked for the world's top communication specialist, Edward Bernays, and I thought it would be good career move to check out his closest rival as well : Joseph Goebbels. Both were cynical monsters in their respective ways but also charming and brilliant. I knew I could learn a lot from them in order to further my own cause: the cause of women. My second interest in working for Goebbels was political. I was horrified, of course, by his attitude towards Jews and other minorities but I was even more horrified by his attitude towards *all* German people. He, a highly educated man, genuinely wanted to strip one of the world's finest cultures of all its refinements and produce a nation of unthinking, homogenous, fighting conquerors in the case of men, of baby factories in the case of women. So what could I, a woman acting alone, do to damage his enormous organisation? Two things. The first was to do everything I could to widen the gap between the claims of Nazi propaganda on the one hand and the reality the German people could see around them on the other. In theory those two things should be consistent with each other and that's exactly what I told everyone all the time. Consistency, consistency, consistency. But in practice I worked to drive them apart. I couldn't do this in any obvious way, of course, but the choice of a single word or colour or pattern or symbol on a poster or in a film can make a difference. It adds a tiny extra millimetre to that gap between your propaganda and their reality. So I worked on that gap for four years, tiny millimetre by tiny millimetre.

"The second thing I did was to get as close as possible to Goebbels himself, to build his trust. It took a while, again millimetre by millimetre, even though he was the one who recruited me and knew my skills could be useful to him. Once I got that trust I moved to the next stage: staying close to him in order to isolate him. I did this, for example, by challenging him constantly so he got the impression *everyone* was challenging him. Not so. Most other people, including those with useful things to say, kept their mouths shut. I also organised training workshops where I encouraged him to talk to and especially listen to new recruits. This gave him the impression he was a good listener. But these were insignificant, toothless young employees. He didn't listen to the employees that mattered. His daily policy meetings with department heads were Goebbels monologues, not productive conversations. He was listening to himself. And the more Goebbels listened to his own voice, which was the only part of his body he was proud of, the more he believed himself to be fully in touch with the wants, needs, hopes and fears of the German people. Fully connected to them. Fully in control. It didn't help that I spent four years spreading rumours around the Ministry that challenging Goebbels on anything was the fastest way to get the sack."

Tina held out her glass for Anna to fill it. "So what happened? Did big Joseph find out that little Anna was a Jew?"

"No, that came later and I told him myself. What happened was that I met Doctor Neil McCrew, your ex-fiancé."

They stared at each other for a moment.

"This only happened a few days ago and we might hate each other by next week. But for the first time in my life I realised I couldn't imagine my life without someone else in it. Neil's life's in Britain, so now I work for the British government. Simple, really."

Tina scoffed. "Come on, Anna, this isn't a propaganda campaign. Keep the simplicity bit for the idiots, one of whom I am not."

Anna sighed. "Before I met Neil, none of the messages I helped produce at the Ministry about fighting heroically for the Fatherland, building a thousand-year Reich and dying an Aryan martyr, if need be, affected me personally. And it wasn't because I was secretly a Jew. I've never felt personally affected by my Jewish roots anyway. I was just doing my job whilst discreetly trying to widen that gap I talked about. I had never wondered what life was actually like for the men out there doing the fighting and feeling the fear, the cold, the damp, the stink, the explosions, the injuries, the screams, the deaths. As nobody in my life was actually experiencing those things, I didn't feel a connection to what they might be going through. I didn't look for a connection either. I was busy. Then, when Neil appeared, I discovered what it felt like to possibly lose someone or to worry he might get hurt. I discovered what it felt like to care for a man, to want him to be safe, to miss him the second he was out of my sight and not breathing the same air as me. I discovered that the idea of Neil being in pain somewhere or unhappy or cold or ill without me around to look after him could make me physically sick." She grinned self-consciously. "All this was new to me."

"I experienced the same thing but not with Neil. With Frank."

"And something else was new. With Neil on my mind day and night, my work at the Ministry took on a whole new meaning. I could feel myself the gap—no, the abyss—between the smooth messages about fighting for the Fatherland and the rough fear that a loved one might never return home. I wasn't seeing tens of millions of Germans as propaganda targets anymore. I felt like a target myself." She paused. "When that happens to you in my line of business, you're probably not doing your job as professionally as you can."

"Or else you're doing it too well."

Chapter 141

Sunday 18 May 1941
Chartwell – Kent – England

Bracken paced back and forth in Churchill's study, reading and re-reading his scribbles.

"I'm convinced he flew here with more to offer than peace terms. Your insistent interest in his fate has only strengthened this belief. I will break him, therefore, with typically British torture: I'll invite him for Sunday afternoon tea (alcohol in my case, in line with your factual propaganda) and Red Cross biscuits (Hess is addicted) on a peaceful country terrace. That blood-drenched discussion will decide his fate."

The first time he'd read the message something had struck him as odd but he hadn't been able to pinpoint it. Now he had the same feeling again. Having read hundreds of documents written by Churchill, Bracken was accustomed to his style. Something here didn't fit. 'Insistent interest', perhaps? Rather clumsy for Churchill but not entirely incongruous either. What about 'blood-drenched discussion'? Not the subtlest use of irony but Churchill clearly wasn't trying to be subtle. He actually wanted Goebbels, or so Bracken assumed, to imagine Hess covered in splashes of red whilst sipping tea—

Bracken froze.

Hess covered in splashes of red.

Splashes of red.

Bracken tore out of the study, along the corridor and through the front door. He rounded the house, passing under the terrace where he knew Churchill and Hess would now be sitting. He then slowed to a brisk walking pace to go down the grassy slope again towards the lakes. This time he retraced in reverse the path Churchill had followed yesterday on his way back from—how had he called it?—ah yes, painting a gate.

"Painting a gate, my arse," Bracken muttered.

There had been a fleck of paint on Churchill's face. A splash of red.

Bracken stopped to scan the two lakes. Nothing unusual apart from the camouflaging. Only the southernmost tip of the larger one was still hidden from view by trees and the lay of the land. Bracken took a few more steps to see it all.

As the lake had almost entirely been drained, its outer perimeter was a wide, sloping expanse of earth and brushwood. Lying flat on it was a circular board that Bracken guessed to be made of wood or cardboard. Five yards in diameter, the board was a bright beige colour. A large red cross was painted on it.

Bracken wanted to kick himself. No wonder he had never heard of Red Cross biscuits. Churchill had invented them to distract from his true intention: to create a landmark identifying Chartwell from the sky. It was all a well-informed Stuka pilot needed.

Bracken sat on the grass, staring at the Prime Minister's handiwork and shaking his head.

"McCrew gave my message to Goebbels, didn't he," Churchill's voice suddenly said behind him. "How naïve of me to assume he wouldn't do such a thing."

Bracken leapt to his feet, yelling. "How dare you, Winston! That wasn't a message to Goebbels. It was a set of instructions telling him exactly where and when a German dive-bomber could find you if Clemmie's operation failed. You wanted to... to..."

Churchill looked down.

Bracken's eyes were welling up. "You're my boss, Winston. You're my guiding light. You're my companion. Above all you're the closest friend I've ever had. In case you hadn't noticed, I'd do anything for you. But what am I to you? If Clemmie had died, wouldn't I have been someone to turn to for help and support? A shoulder to cry on, perhaps. Someone to pour you a fifth whisky and gently hold you back from a sixth? Evidently not. Turns out you didn't see me as a supplier of solutions, or maybe just attention. You wanted to give that role to Joseph Goebbels."

Churchill took Bracken in his arms and hugged him. "I'm sorry, Brendan. That was unforgivable of me."

They stood like that for a moment.

Churchill spoke first. "There's a problem, though. Goebbels knew I'd be here with Hess this afternoon. Yet even though that Stuka pilot had us in his sights, he didn't release the bomb."

They let go of each other.

"Maybe it jammed," Bracken tried.

"No, he'd have circled back to try again."

Bracken scratched his head. "So the Stuka was just a message? Goebbels telling you he *could* have had you killed but deliberately chose not to?"

"It's not about me, Brendan. It's about Hess. Goebbels is telling us not only that he wants Hess to stay here indefinitely, but also that we must keep him alive. He wants us to protect him, presumably from SS commandos."

Bracken shrugged. "Why is Hess so important?"

Churchill grinned. "Let's get back up there and ask him, shall we? He'll have finished his tea and my whisky by now."

He turned to walk back up the slope but stopped when he realised Bracken wasn't following him.

"You coming, Brendan?"

Bracken had his hands on his hips. He kicked away a stone. "Winston, that was the first time I've ever heard you apologise."

Chapter 142

Sunday 18 May 1941
Farnborough – Hampshire – England

As Roddy Danes walked across the runway towards Hangar B, its giant left-hand door slid open, pushed by Paterson. The RAE's captured Stuka dive-bomber slowly appeared. Paterson secured the door and positioned himself with his hands on his hips in front of the aircraft's single propeller.

"You took your bloody time," he shouted to Danes, who was still fifty yards away.

"Took a shower," Danes shouted back. "Alone?"

"Depends what you're threatening me with."

"Just a kiss."

"I'm not alone actually. Five people heard that."

"Ha-ha."

Paterson took a step sideways to peer past Danes. "A police car has just stopped at the gate."

Danes looked over his shoulder as he walked. The main airfield gate was two-hundred yards away. A sentry was talking to the driver.

"I don't like the look of that," Paterson said.

"Nor do I. There's something I should tell you." Danes looked over his shoulder again. The sentry and the driver were still talking. "After the Ju 88 crashed in the forest the other day, you asked me if someone saw me taking the cash, pistols and clothing off the victims."

Paterson glared at him. "Don't tell me you lied to me, Roddy. Who saw you?"

"A lady with one dog and too many questions. She asked me to give her one good reason not to report me."

"And?"

Danes stopped in front of Paterson without looking round. "What's the police car doing now?"

"Heading this way. And?"

"I gave her a reason." Danes kissed him on the cheek. "Or rather I hit her with it. But I forgot to wipe my fingerprints off it."

The police car had covered a third of the distance.

Paterson took a step back. "You killed her?"

"There's something I'd like you to do," Danes said.

Paterson was shaking his head, pleading. "I can't believe it, Roddy."

"I know. I just need a small favour."

Paterson was shouting now. "You bastard!"

"One last dance?"

Danes grabbed Paterson and led him in a waltz in front of the Stuka.

The police car stopped beside them and two uniformed officers got out. They paused to take in the sight of the dancing couple.

"Which one of you is Mike Paterson?" the tallest officer asked.

Danes and Paterson looked suspiciously at each other.

"I am," Paterson said, holding Danes's gaze.

"If you'd care to come with us, sir, we've got a few questions regarding some metal canisters. Someone answering your description was seen stealing a whole bunch of them from a factory in Aldershot two weeks ago. Hunt and Sons. Sound familiar?"

Chapter 143

Sunday 18 May 1941
Chartwell – Kent – England

"I'm surprised you didn't make a run for it," Winston Churchill said to Hess as he and Bracken joined him on Chartwell's terrace.

A full afternoon tea was laid out for them. Hess was eating a piece of cake. Bracken poured himself some tea as Churchill took a sip of whisky.

"It would have been rude of me to run away without saying goodbye," Hess said.

Churchill winked at him. "So you said goodbye to Hitler before you ran away from him, did you?"

Hess acknowledged his defeat with a smirk.

Bracken cleared his throat. "The Stuka could have killed all three of us but deliberately didn't. So I made a couple of phone calls to find out why. There's a 90% chance it was sent by Joseph Goebbels, probably with Goering's help. He wanted to tell us something."

Hess seemed surprised. "By Goebbels?"

"I put it to you that not only does he want us to keep you indefinitely in the United Kingdom, but he also wants us to keep you fit and healthy. Why else would he throw away a unique opportunity to kill the British Prime Minister?"

"Or to put it another way," Churchill said, "what would happen to Goebbels, Goering and God knows who else in that Nazi leadership team of yours if you died?"

Hess's eyes went blank. He remained silent.

Churchill turned to Bracken. "Looks like we might have to send Herr Hess back to apologise to the Führer after all."

Bracken made a show of wincing.

"I took a few precautions," Hess said, "in case things didn't work out, either here or in Germany. As soon you announced I was alive and in the United Kingdom, I had arranged for Goebbels, Goering and seven others to receive a letter from me. Each letter contained evidence of corruption or misdeeds of some kind and a warning. If my family or I were harmed, copies of the letters would be sent to news organisations around the world."

"Blackmail," Bracken said.

"Yes."

"Who are the seven others?" Churchill asked.

"Himmler, von Ribbentrop, Frick, Keitel, Funk, Bormann and Hitler."

Churchill and Bracken glanced at each other.

"That's why Goebbels and Goering want me to stay alive. Their reputation and careers, indeed their lives, depend on my health."

"Hang on a second," Churchill said. "Goebbels and Goering can't stop you telling us what's in those letters. And if you tell us, they can't stop us informing the world ourselves."

"True," Hess said, "unless…"

"Unless?"

Hess's deep-set eyes suddenly turned inquisitive and playful. "Unless they also have sensitive information about you two that they could publish. Does any such information exist, gentlemen? Corruption? Sex? Dubious practices? Whatever you do, do not underestimate our intelligence services."

Churchill and Bracken glanced at each other again, both doing their utmost to appear unmoved.

"Should you reveal the contents of those blackmail letters to us," Bracken said, "what would you expect in return?"

"A new identity and a comfortable place for my family and I to hide in your empire somewhere."

Churchill took his time to light a cigar. "Herr Hess, you can take that idea and shove it up your anus. Once this war is over, you and your Nazi accomplices will be captured, tried and in most cases executed for crimes of the worst kind against humanity. You're tragically right about one thing, though: millions of people will probably die in the interval. But I will not be blackmailed or pressured in any way into thinking of myself and my country as responsible for the deaths of those people. Again, you are the murderers. You are the criminals. There is one thing however that can I be pressured into doing, and that's ensuring that the sons, daughters, grandsons and granddaughters of those millions of dead people can live where they want to live, can do what they want to do, can say what they want to say and can believe in the gods they want to believe in without any retribution from miserable cowards like you. If you want to blackmail me into doing that, be my guest."

"Mr Churchill, I think you—" Hess began.

"Shut up, Hess. I haven't finished yet. You said you've gathered compromising evidence regarding your Nazi friends."

"Yes, I have."

"Keep it. It's of no interest to us. You see, I've been watching Hitler and his cohort of yes-men for a while now and I've reached a conclusion. Do you know what our best hope of winning this war is? Forget about destroying the Third Reich's leaders by publishing proof of their incompetence, corruption or perversions. Our best hope is to leave those incompetent, corrupt and depraved monsters exactly where they are, especially Hitler, and let them lose the war for us. The last thing we want is for them to be thrown out and replaced by competent, able-minded Nazis who can keep their trousers on. Earlier on you tried to speak to the pragmatist in me. Well he's just given you an answer."

Chapter 144

Sunday 18 May 1941
London – England

The note David Cassell had pressed into Anna Vogel's hand in the lobby of The Savoy supplied a room number. The door to this room now opened before she could knock. Cassell put a finger to his lips and led through to the bathroom. Both bath taps were running. He gestured towards a chair for Anna and himself sat on the rim of the bath. "

"You've got ten minutes before my room-mate sends out a search party," Anna said reproachfully. "This was supposed to be an evening of celebrations, David, not a Haganah ambush."

Cassell smiled. "It's good to see you, Anna. Four years of messages from you without ever hearing your voice is a long time. You did an incredible job in Berlin. Thank you."

Anna cocked her head. "Really? How many Jewish lives has my work spared?"

"Your job wasn't to rescue Jews. Your job was to rescue the truth about what's going or what's intended and to feed it to us. Which you did."

"Glad you're grateful, David, but it's over. I'm in England now and I'm staying. Please find someone else to spy on Goebbels."

Cassell folded his arms, studying the ceiling. "Three days ago the Haganah created a special fighting sub-unit. I'm part of it. In Palestine the British tolerate our existence more or less, but mutual trust levels hover somewhere between low and non-existent. Officially our aim is to defend Jews living in Palestine against harassment from Arab locals. Nothing new there. But increasingly our job will be to protect those same Jews from Nazi Germany as well, for Herr Hitler, as you're no doubt aware, also has ambitions in the Middle East and North Africa."

Anna sighed. "Why are you even bothering to tell me this?"

"The British occupying our land believe that by tolerating our organisation they can control us. Yeah, sure. What they don't know is that we're extending our operations outside the Middle East and North Africa. The closer we are to our enemies here in Europe, the better we can keep an eye on them and act where necessary. But to do that effectively we need reliable information. Lots of it and constantly."

Anna shook her head. "I'm not returning to Berlin, David. I've given four years of my life to the Haganah and risked my life at every turn. I'm done."

Cassell raised a hand to cut her off. "Anna, the single most important skill I taught you was how to listen. What did I just say?"

Anna thought for a moment. "You said 'enemies here in Europe', in the plural."

"That's better. And who are our enemies—plural—in Europe?"

Anna waited.

"Clue," he added playfully. "They're not paying much attention to the Haganah right now because they're too busy fighting each other."

Anna frowned. "Germany and the United Kingdom?"

Cassell clapped slowly. "Both are enemies of the Jews, but in different ways. The Nazis are our current enemy. They want to shut us down worldwide. Their aim is elimination. The Brits are our *potential* enemy. They don't want to eliminate us, but they don't want us to be a problem either. So as soon as the war ends, they'll want to shut us up in Palestine or even shut us out. Their aim is neutralisation." He paused. "If we Jews want to both survive in the short run and have somewhere to call home in the long run, our only option is to fight Germany *and* the United Kingdom. Did you and Goebbels part on friendly terms?"

Anna gazed at the running taps.

Cassell left the bathroom briefly and returned with two glasses of champagne. "We have reasons to celebrate here, too."

He raised his glass but Anna was already emptying hers.

"Goebbels has a hold on me," she said, putting her glass down on the floor. "I had an unfortunate and somewhat terminal incident with two of his employees a few days ago. And he can prove it. So if he wants to destroy me here, all he needs to do is spread a few rumours and photographs of the evidence."

"Let me guess. He's offered to shut up about the incident if you spy on Bracken for him, right?"

Anna gave a single nod.

"Then do it," Cassell said, putting his glass down on the end of the bath. "Work for both of them. Play them off each other. Make the Germans and the Brits both believe you're loyal to them and them alone. In reality and as always you'll be loyal only to us, the Haganah. We'll help you every step of the way, of course."

Anna shook her head. "No, I'm done, David. I won't let anyone blackmail me, least of all Goebbels. If he wants to spread rumours about me, so be it. I have other plans now."

"Other plans involving Doctor Neil McCrew by any chance?"

It took Anna a split-second to have Cassell's throat in a choke hold in her left-hand and his genitals in a tight grip in her right. "If you so much as look up McCrew's phone number in the directory, you're dead, do you hear me?"

In turn it took Cassell a split-second to break both her holds and expertly twist her body round, arching it over the edge of the bath. Pinning her right arm high up her back with one hand, he pushed her head under the running cold water with the other and kept it there. His spoke casually. "It's not about hundreds of our people being murdered anymore, Anna. Nor is it about thousands, tens of thousands or hundreds of thousands of them. We'll soon be up in the millions of innocent victims, both short term and long term. On that scale, whether your new boyfriend has an unfortunate accident or not makes no difference to the body count. Nor does it make a difference to me. But it does make a difference to you. So if you want Doctor McCrew to stay in good health, you'd better get back to work, lady."

He released her and picked up his glass again, waiting for her to straighten up and face him.

To his surprise she picked up her glass as well and stood there, dripping and blinking. She raised her glass. "In that case I'd like to propose a toast, although not to McCrew's health, nor to mine, nor even to yours, Martin. That is your real first name, isn't it?"

Cassell's eyes narrowed.

"Martin Aronson, correct?" Anna continued playfully. "Now how could I possibly have found out such a thing? I'll let you worry about that. In the meantime I'd like to propose a toast to your wife Martha, who's waiting for your return in that charming white house of yours, the one with the green front door in Massachusetts. You wouldn't want her to have—how did you call it?—an unfortunate accident, would you? When's the baby due, by the way? Is it next month or the one after?" She raised her glass. "So get back to your wife and take special care of her, Mister. Meanwhile I'll decide who I work for and why. Cheers."

Epilogue

On Monday 19 May 1941 **two German parachutists** were arrested near Luton Hoo, some fifty miles north-west of London. They turned out to be SS soldiers in plain clothes. Markings on a map in their possession suggested their target was Rudolf Hess. After questioning they were hanged.

Clementine Churchill supported her husband loyally—many would say heroically—until his death in 1965. Like him she fought a running battle with depression, a vulnerability exacerbated as much by her own tendency towards hypochondria as by the strain Winston's duties, needs, whims, requirements and disregard for domestic practicalities put her under. But she stood up to her husband as well, stubbornly supplying advice, criticism and warnings where others failed to do so or didn't dare. She died of a heart attack in 1977.

To the world's astonishment, British voters threw **Winston Churchill** and his Conservative Party out of power in August 1945, just as the Second World War was ending. Whilst British voters generally acknowledged Churchill's ability as a wartime leader, a majority of them refused to take a chance on his ability as a peacetime one. After years of restrictions and uncertainty, they had developed expectations of more personal comfort, predictability and social justice in their lives. Churchill eventually returned to power in 1951 but health issues quickly diminished him, eventually forcing his resignation four years later. He died in 1965.

Adolf Hitler launched Operation Barbarossa, his long-planned invasion of the Soviet Union, on 22 June 1941, expecting victory before winter. By the time the Soviets finally forced his tanks and troops to retreat, three years had passed, including three Russian-style winters, and millions of soldiers and civilians had died, including two million Soviet prisoners of starvation. Hitler committed suicide in Berlin in 1945.

Rudolf Hess was detained in the United Kingdom until the end of the war. At the post-war Nuremburg Trials he was sentenced to life imprisonment for crimes against peace and for conspiracy to commit crimes, but not for war crimes or crimes against humanity. He committed suicide in Spandau, a German prison, in 1987.

Ilse Hess, wife of Rudolf Hess. Following Hess's unexpected flight to Scotland in May 1941, his ambitious and ruthless deputy, Martin Bormann, sought to make life financially difficult for his wife Ilse. But Hitler, possibly encouraged by his mistress, Eva Braun, soon put a stop to this.

Brendan Bracken became the United Kingdom's Minister of Information on 20 July 1941. A conservative, he kept the position until the end of the war, constantly supporting research into the British population's expectations whilst carefully avoiding political favouritism. In 1942, for example, his Ministry gave wide publicity to the Beveridge Report, a landmark and well received set of recommendations for social and economic reform in the United Kingdom. Churchill's less than enthusiastic support for the report probably contributed to his party's electoral trouncing in 1945. Bracken died in 1958.

Joseph Goebbels stayed on as Nazi Germany's Minister of Propaganda until shortly before the end of the war. He committed suicide in May 1945.

Colin Gubbins of the Special Operations Executive (SOE) masterminded several daring sabotage operations behind enemy lines throughout the war. He took supreme charge of the unit in 1943. In 1944 he oversaw the planning stages of a plot codenamed Operation Foxley to assassinate Hitler at the Berghof. But the plot was never approved, not least because opponents feared that a more competent strategist than Hitler might take his place.

The Holocaust. In May 1941, although Nazi Germany's treatment of Jews, political opponents and other minorities was appalling and often murderous, it hadn't yet morphed into systematic annihilation in death camps. Speculation that "millions" would die for multiple reasons if the war continued wasn't outlandish at the time, but few could have guessed, let alone believed, that the Nazis would turn murder into an industry. Formal Nazi decisions to build death camps using gas chambers were taken between late 1941 and early 1942, and implemented in 1942.

Author's notes and acknowledgements

Spoiler alert. Although *Influencers* is fiction, some readers may be interested in exploring topics raised in the story. This chapter is for them.

- Clementine Churchill, Winston's wife, had health issues during World War Two, most notably strain and depression, but thankfully never developed a life-threatening brain tumour. For more on this remarkable woman, I can recommend Sonia Purnell's *Clementine: the life of Mrs Winston Churchill* and John Colville's *The fringes of Power*.

- Rudolf Hess, Hitler's deputy, never met Winston Churchill. Nor is he known to have taken measures ahead of his trip to protect his family or himself against possible, indeed likely, Nazi retribution. The most useful discussions of his flight to Scotland are to be found in the biographies or personal diaries of other Nazi figures, especially Hitler.

- Brendan Bracken, who became the United Kingdom's Minister of Information on 20 July 1941, never met or communicated with Nazi Germany's Minister of Propaganda, Joseph Goebbels. For more on this highly influential yet almost totally forgotten man, I can recommend Charles Lysaght's *Brendan Bracken*, Ian McLaine's *Ministry of Morale* and Michael Balfour's *Propaganda in war: 1939-1945*.

- No one interested in 21st-century communication and influence techniques, whether political, commercial or social, can ignore the legacies of two controversial men: Edward Bernays, who operated mainly in the USA, and Nazi Germany's Joseph Goebbels. The communication methods they pioneered or refined are still with us today, their power and reach amplified by software and digital networking. It should be noted however that whilst Goebbels is known to have taken an interest in Bernays, who was born to an American Jewish family and was Sigmund Freud's nephew, Bernays is *not* known to have supported Nazi beliefs or practices in any way. Indeed Bernays turned down at least one opportunity to work for Nazi Germany. For more on Bernays, whose name is regrettably unfamiliar to most people today, I can recommend Stuart Ewen's *PR! A social history of spin*, Bernays's own books and Adam Curtis's BBC documentary series *The century of the self*, which is viewable on YouTube. For more on Joseph Goebbels's thinking and techniques, I can recommend Willi Boelcke's *The secret conferences of Dr Goebbels: 1939-1943*, Ernest Bramsted's *Goebbels and National Socialist Propaganda: 1925-1945*, Michael Balfour's *Propaganda in war: 1939-1945*, Goebbels's own diaries, Peter Longerich's superb biography and Randall Bytwerk's remarkable online archive on Nazi propaganda (//research.calvin.edu/german-propaganda-archive/).

- Readers interested in influence techniques in general should start with Robert Cialdini's *Influence* and *Pre-suasion*, Daniel Kahneman's *Thinking, fast and slow*, Thomas Levine's *Duped*, Will Storr's *The power of storytelling*, Daniel Pink's *To sell is human* and my own *Your influencing instincts*. The darker sides of influence are explored in Shoshana Zuboff's forensic *The age of surveillance capitalism* and Kai Strittmatter's harrowing *We have been harmonized*.

I'm indebted to several people for their suggestions, comments, eye for detail, expertise or personal recollections of World War Two. They include Susanne Demierre, Sylvie Roth and Christophe Pellier in Switzerland; Annabelle Lancaster, Reg Lancaster, Don Smith, Rosemary Smith and David Taylor in England; Nadia Cuper in the USA; Malcolm Campbell in Scotland; and the astonishingly helpful www.quora.com community around the world (English- and French-speaking platforms). To their credit, my wife, Michèle, and two daughters, Roxane and Carol, endured my silences, moodiness, swearing and absences in Switzerland as *Influencers* took shape. Thanks to you all.

If you enjoyed *Influencers*, you may be interested to know that Anna Vogel, Joseph Goebbels, Winston Churchill and several other characters will return in *Influencers II*, which I expect to publish in 2022.

The author

Influence techniques and research in that field have been Ray Lancaster's passion for four decades. He has tested research findings in all sorts of professional and non-professional contexts over the years.

Retired since 2018 as a training programme director at Nestlé's international training centre in Switzerland, Ray remains active as an independent trainer in personal communication, which includes influence techniques, and languages.

Influencers draws on Ray's passion for influence techniques and his lifelong interest in the Second World War. Combining these topics into a thriller has been one of the most enthralling challenges of his life.

Ray is British. Born in Scotland, he grew up in England and France in the 1960s and 70s. Apart from a year in Germany, he has been living and working in Switzerland since 1978. He is married, with two daughters.

Online, Ray contributes regularly to the English- and French-speaking platforms of quora.com.

Printed in Great Britain
by Amazon